# THE MISSION

Yassen sat quietly until a quarter past six. At exactly the moment that the second hand passed over the twelve on his watch, he pressed the button to place a bid, then entered his User ID—false, of course—and password. Finally, he entered a bid of $2,418.12. The figures were based on the day's date and the exact time. He pressed Enter and a window opened that had nothing to do with eBay or with Roman coins. Nobody else could have seen it. It would have been impossible to discover where it had originated. The message had been bounced around a dozen countries, traveling through an anonymity network, before it had reached him. This is known as "onion routing" because of its many layers. It had also passed through an encrypted tunnel, a secure shell that ensured that only Yassen could read what had been written. If someone had managed to arrive at the same screen by accident, they would have seen only nonsense, and within three seconds a virus would have entered their computer and obliterated the motherboard. The computer, however, had been authorized to receive the message, and Yassen saw three words.

KILL ALEX RIDER

They were exactly

## ALEX RIDER MISSIONS:

*Stormbreaker*
*Point Blank*
*Skeleton Key*
*Eagle Strike*
*Scorpia*
*Ark Angel*
*Snakehead*
*Crocodile Tears*
*Scorpia Rising*
*Russian Roulette*

## ALSO BY ANTHONY HOROWITZ

### THE DIAMOND BROTHERS MYSTERIES

*Public Enemy Number Two*
*The Falcon's Malteser*
*Three of Diamonds*
*South by Southeast*
*The Greek Who Stole Christmas*

*The Complete Horowitz Horror*
*Bloody Horowitz*
*The Devil and His Boy*
*Granny*
*Groosham Grange*
*Return to Groosham Grange: The Unholy Grail*
*The Switch*

# RUSSIAN ROULETTE

# ANTHONY HOROWITZ

PUFFIN BOOKS

FOR J, N, AND C BUT NOT L.
FULL CIRCLE.

PUFFIN BOOKS
An imprint of Penguin Random House LLC
375 Hudson Street
New York, New York 10014

First published in the United States of America by Philomel Books,
an imprint of Penguin Young Readers Group, 2013
Published by Puffin Books, an imprint of Penguin Young Readers Group, 2014

THE LIBRARY OF CONGRESS HAS CATALOGED THE PHILOMEL BOOKS EDITION AS FOLLOWS:
Horowitz, Anthony, 1955–
Russian roulette / Anthony Horowitz.
pages cm.—(Alex Rider ; 10)
Summary: Presented with an unexpected assignment, Alex Rider's greatest nemesis,
Yassen Gregorovich, recalls his life and the path that led him to become an assassin
while his onetime friend, Alex's uncle, became a spy.
ISBN 978-0-399-25441-3 (hardcover)
[1. Assassins—Fiction. 2. Adventure and adventurers—Fiction. 3. Orphans—Fiction.
4. Russia (Federation)—History—1991–   —Fiction.] I. Title.
PZ7.H7875Rus 2013
[Fic]—dc23
2013015810

Puffin Books ISBN 978-0-14-751231-4

Edited by Michael Green. Design by Semadar Megged.

Printed in the United States of America

10 9 8 7 6 5 4 3 2

# CONTENTS

# RUSSIAN ROULETTE

# PROLOGUE

## BEFORE THE KILL

HE HAD CHOSEN THE hotel room very carefully.

As he crossed the reception area toward the elevators, he was aware of everyone in the area around him. Two receptionists, one on the phone. A Japanese guest checking in—from his accent, obviously from Miyazaka in the south. A concierge printing a map for a couple of tourists. A security man, Eastern European, bored, standing by the door. He saw everything. If the lights had suddenly gone out, or if he had closed his eyes, he would have been able to continue forward at exactly the same pace.

Nobody noticed him. It was actually a skill, something he had learned, the art of not being seen. Even the outfit he wore—expensive jeans, a gray cashmere jersey, and a loose coat—had been chosen because it made no statement at all. The clothes were well-known brands but he had cut out the labels. In the unlikely event that he was stopped by the police, it would be very difficult for them to know where they had been bought.

He was twenty-eight years old. He had fair hair, cut short, and ice-cold eyes with just the faintest trace of blue. He was not large or well built, but there was a sort of sleekness about him. He moved like an athlete—perhaps a sprinter approaching the starting blocks—but there was a sense of danger about him, a feeling that you should leave well alone. He carried three credit cards and a driver's license, issued in Swansea, all with the name Matthew Reddy. A police check would have established that he was a personal trainer, that he worked in a London gym and lived in Brixton. None of this was true. His real name was Yassen Gregorovich. He had been a professional assassin for almost half his life.

The hotel was in King's Cross, an area of London with no attractive shops and few decent restaurants, a place where nobody really stays any longer than they have to. It was called The Traveller and it was part of a chain; comfortable but not too expensive. It was the sort of place that had no regular clients. Most of the guests were passing through on business and it would be their companies who paid the bill. They drank in the bar. They ate the "full English breakfast" in the brightly lit Beefeater restaurant. But they were too busy to socialize and it was unlikely they would return. Yassen preferred it that way. He could have stayed in central London, in the Ritz or the Dorchester, but he knew that the receptionists there were trained to remember the faces of the people who passed through the revolving doors. Such personal attention was the last thing he wanted.

A security camera watched him as he approached the elevators. He was aware of it blinking over his left shoulder. The camera was annoying but inevitable. London has more of these devices than any city in Europe, and the police and secret service have access to all of them. Yassen made sure he didn't look up. If you look at a camera, that is when it sees you. He reached the elevators but ignored them, slipping through a fire door that led to the stairs. He would never think of confining himself in a small space, a metal box with doors that he couldn't open, surrounded by strangers. That would be madness. He would have walked fifteen stories if it had been necessary—and when he reached the top, he wouldn't even have been out of breath. Yassen kept himself in superb condition, spending two hours in the gym every day when that luxury was available to him, working out on his own when it wasn't.

In fact, he was on the second floor. He had thoroughly checked the hotel on the Internet before he made his reservation, and number 217 was one of just four rooms that exactly met his demands. It was on the second floor, too high up to be reached from the street but low enough for him to jump out the window if he had to—after shooting out the glass. It was not overlooked. There were other buildings around, but any form of surveillance would be difficult. When Yassen went to bed, he never closed the curtains. He liked to see out, to watch for any movement in the street. Every city has a natural rhythm, and anything that breaks it—a man lingering on a corner or a car passing the same way twice—might warn him that it was time to leave at once. And he never slept for more than four hours, not even in the most comfortable bed.

A DO NOT DISTURB sign hung in front of him as he

turned the corner and approached the door. Had it been obeyed? Yassen reached into his pants pocket and took out a small silver device, about the same size and shape as a pen. He pressed one end, covering the handle with a thin spray of diazafluoren—a simple chemical re-agent. Quickly, he spun the pen around and pressed the other end, activating a fluorescent light. There were no fingerprints. If anyone had gone into the room since he had left, they had wiped the handle clean. He put the pen away, then knelt down and checked the bottom of the door. Earlier in the day, he had placed a single hair across the crack. It was one of the oldest warning signals in the book, but that didn't stop it from being effective. The hair was still in place. Yassen straightened up and went in using his electronic pass key.

It took him less than a minute to ascertain that everything was exactly as he had left it. His briefcase was 4.6 centimeters from the edge of the desk. His suitcase was positioned at a 95-degree angle from the wall. There were no fingerprints on either of the locks. He removed the digital tape recorder that had been clipped magnetically to the side of his service fridge and glanced at the dial. Nothing had been recorded. Nobody had been in. Many people would have found all these precautions annoying and time consuming, but for Yassen they were as much a part of his daily routine as tying his shoelaces or brushing his teeth.

It was twelve minutes past six when he sat down at the desk and opened his computer, an ordinary laptop.

His password had seventeen digits and he changed it every month. He took off his watch and laid it on the surface beside him. Then he went into eBay, left-clicked on Collectibles, and scrolled through Coins. He soon found what he was looking for: a gold coin showing the head of the emperor Caligula with the date 11 AD. There had been no bids for this particular coin because, as any collector would know, it did not in fact exist. In 11 AD, the mad Roman emperor Caligula had not even been born. The entire website was a fake and looked it. The name of the coin dealer—Mintomatic—had been specially chosen to put off any casual purchaser. Mintomatic was supposedly based in Shanghai and did not have Top-Rated Seller status. All the coins it advertised were either fake or valueless.

Yassen sat quietly until a quarter past six. At exactly the moment that the second hand passed over the twelve on his watch, he pressed the button to place a bid, then entered his User ID—false, of course—and password. Finally, he entered a bid of $2,418.12. The figures were based on the day's date and the exact time. He pressed Enter and a window opened that had nothing to do with eBay or with Roman coins. Nobody else could have seen it. It would have been impossible to discover where it had originated. The message had been bounced around a dozen countries, traveling through an anonymity network, before it had reached him. This is known as "onion routing" because of its many layers. It had also passed through an encrypted tunnel, a secure shell that ensured that only Yassen could read what had been written. If someone had managed to arrive at the same screen by accident, they would have seen only nonsense, and within three seconds a virus would have entered their computer and obliterated the motherboard. The computer, however, had been authorized to receive the message, and Yassen saw three words.

KILL ALEX RIDER

They were exactly what he had expected.

Yassen had known all along that his employers would insist on punishing the agent who had been involved in the disaster that the Stormbreaker operation had become. He even wondered if he himself might not be made to retire . . . permanently, of course. It was simple common sense. If people failed, they were eliminated. There were no second chances. Yassen was lucky in that he had been employed as a subcontractor. He didn't have over-all responsibility for what had happened, and so he could hardly be blamed when things went wrong. On the other hand, they would have to make an example of Alex Rider. It didn't matter that he was just fourteen years old. Tomorrow he would have to die.

Yassen looked at the screen for a few seconds more, then closed the computer. He had never killed a child before, but that particular thought did not trouble him.

Alex Rider had made his own choices. He should have been at school, but instead, for whatever reason, he had allowed the Special Operations division of MI6 to recruit him. From schoolboy to spy. It was certainly unusual—but the truth was, he had been remarkably successful. Beginner's luck, perhaps, but he had brought an end to an operation that had been several years in the planning. He was responsible for the deaths of two operatives. He had annoyed some extremely powerful people. He very much deserved the death that was coming his way.

And yet . . .

Yassen sat where he was with the computer in front of him. Nothing had changed in his expression, but there was, perhaps, something flickering deep in his eyes. Outside, the sun was beginning to set, the evening sky turning a hard, unforgiving gray. The streets were full of commuters hurrying home. They weren't just on the other side of a hotel window. They were in another world. Yassen knew that he would never be one of them. Briefly, he closed his eyes. He was thinking about what had happened. About Stormbreaker. How had it gone so wrong?

From Yassen's point of view, it had been a fairly routine assignment. A Lebanese businessman by the name of Herod Sayle had wanted to buy two hundred liters of a deadly smallpox virus called R5, and he had approached the one organization that might be able to supply it in such huge quantities. That organization was Scorpia. The letters of the name stood for *sabotage, corruption, intel-*

*ligence,* and *assassination,* which were its main activities. R5 was a Chinese product, manufactured illegally in a facility near Guiyang, and by chance, one of the members of the executive board of Scorpia was Chinese. Dr. Three had extensive contacts in East Asia and had used his influence to organize the purchase. It had been Yassen's job to oversee delivery to the UK.

Six weeks ago, he had flown to Hong Kong a few days ahead of the R5, which had been transported in a private plane, a turboprop Xian MA60, from Guiyang. The plan was to load it into a container ship to Rotterdam—disguised as part of a shipment of Luck of the Dragon Chinese beer. Special barrels had been constructed at a warehouse in Kowloon with reinforced plastic containers holding the R5 suspended inside the liquid. There are more than five thousand container ships at sea at any one time, and around seventeen million deliveries are made every year. There isn't a customs service in the world that can keep its eye on every cargo, and Yassen was confident that the journey would be trouble-free. He'd been given a false passport and papers that identified him as Erik Olsen, a merchant seaman from Copenhagen, and he would travel with the R5 until it reached its destination.

But as is so often the way, things had not gone as planned. A few days before the barrels were due to leave, Yassen had become aware that the warehouse was under surveillance. He had been lucky. A cigarette being lit behind a window in a building that should have been empty told him all he needed to know. Slipping through Kowloon under cover of darkness, he had identified a team of three agents of the AIVD—the Algemene Inlichtingen en Veiligheidsdienst, the Dutch Secret Service. There must have been a tip-off. The agents did not know what they were looking for, but they were aware that something was on its way to their country, and Yassen had been forced to kill all three of them with a silenced Beretta 92, a pistol he particularly favored because of its accuracy and reliability. Clearly, the R5 could not leave in a container ship after all. A fallback plan had to be found.

As it happened, there was a Chinese Han Class nuclear submarine in Hong Kong going through final repairs before leaving for exercises in the Northern Atlantic. Yassen met the captain in a private club overlooking the harbor and offered him a bribe of two million dollars to carry the R5 with him when he left. He had informed Scorpia of this decision, and they knew that it would dig into their operational profit, but there were at least some advantages. Moving the R5 from Rotterdam to the UK would have been difficult and dangerous. Herod Sayle was based in Cornwall with direct access to the coast, so the new approach would make for a much more secure delivery.

Two weeks later, on a crisp, cloudless night in April, the submarine surfaced off the Cornish coast. Yassen, still using the identity of Erik Olsen, had traveled with it. He had quite enjoyed the experience of cruising silently through the depths of the ocean, sealed in a metal tube.

The Chinese crew had been ordered not to speak to him on any account, and that suited him too. It was only when he climbed onto dry land that he once again took command, overseeing the transfer of the virus and other supplies that Herod Sayle had ordered. The work had to be done swiftly. The captain of the submarine had insisted that he would wait no more than thirty minutes. He might have two million dollars in a Swiss bank account, but he had no wish to provoke an international incident . . . which would certainly have been followed by his own court-martial and execution.

Thirty guards had helped carry the various boxes to the waiting trucks, scrambling along the shoreline in the light of a perfect half-moon, the submarine looking somehow fantastic and out of place, half submerged in the slate gray water of the English Channel. And almost from the start Yassen had known something was wrong. He was being watched. He was sure of it. Some might call it a sort of animal instinct, but for Yassen it was simpler than that. He had been active in the field for nine years. During that time, he had been in danger almost constantly. It had been necessary to fine-tune all his senses simply to survive. And although he hadn't seen or heard anything, a silent voice was screaming at him that there was someone hiding about twenty meters away, behind a cluster of boulders on the edge of the beach.

He had been on the point of investigating when one of Sayle's men, standing on the wooden jetty, had dropped one of the boxes. The sound of metal hitting wood shattered the calm of the night and Yassen spun on his heel, everything else forgotten. There was limited space on the submarine, and so the R5 had been transferred from the beer barrels to less protective aluminium boxes. Yassen knew that if the glass vial inside had been shattered, if the rubber seal had been compromised, everyone on the beach would be dead before the sun had risen.

He sprinted forward, crouching down to inspect the damage. There was a slight dent in one side of the box. But the seal had held.

The guard looked at him with a sickly smile. He was quite a lot older than Yassen, probably an ex-convict recruited from a local prison. And he was scared. He tried to make light of it. "I won't do that again!" he said.

"No," Yassen replied. "You won't." The Beretta was already in his hand. He shot the man in the chest, propelling him backward into the darkness and the sea below. It had been necessary to set an example. There would be no further clumsiness that night.

Sitting in the hotel with the computer in front of him, Yassen remembered the moment. He was almost certain now that it had been Alex Rider behind the boulder, and if it hadn't been for the accident, he would have been discovered there and then. Alex had infiltrated Sayle Enterprises, pretending to be the winner of a magazine contest. Somehow he had slipped out of his room, evading the guards and the searchlights, and had joined the convoy making

its way down to the beach. There could be no other explanation. Later on, Alex had followed Herod Sayle to London. He had already been responsible for the deaths of
two of Sayle's associates—Nadia Vole and the disfigured
servant, Mr. Grin—despite little training and no experience. This was his first mission. Even so, he had single-
handedly smashed the Stormbreaker operation. Sayle had
been lucky to escape a few steps ahead of the police.

## KILL ALEX RIDER

It was what he deserved. Alex had interfered with a
Scorpia assignment and he would have cost the organization at least five million dollars . . . the final payment
owed by Herod Sayle. Worse than that, he would have
damaged their international reputation. The lesson had to
be learned.

There was a knock at the door. Yassen had ordered
room service. It wasn't just easier to eat inside the hotel,
it was safer. Why make himself a target when he didn't
need to?

"Leave it outside," he called out. He spoke English
with no trace of a Russian accent. He spoke French, German, and Arabic equally well.

The room was almost dark now. Yassen's dinner sat
on a tray in the corridor, rapidly getting cold. But still he
did not move away from the desk and the computer in
front of him. He would kill Alex Rider tomorrow morn-

ing. There was no question of his disobeying orders. It didn't matter that the two of them were linked, that they were connected in a way Alex couldn't possibly know.

John Rider. Alex's father.

The two of them together. Hunter and Cossack.

He couldn't help himself. He reached into his pocket and took out a car key, the sort that had two remote control buttons to lock and unlock the doors. But this key did not belong to any car. Yassen pressed the unlock button twice and the lock button three times, and a concealed memory stick sprang out onto the palm of his hand. He glanced at it briefly. He knew that it was madness to carry it. He had been tempted to destroy it many times. But every man has his weakness, and this was his. He opened the computer again and plugged it in.

The file required another password. He keyed it in. And there it was on the screen in front of him, not in English letters but in Cyrillic, the Russian alphabet.

His personal diary. The story of his life.

He sat back and began to read.

# ДОМА

"YASHA! WE'VE RUN OUT of water. Go to the well!"

I can still hear my mother calling to me and it is strange to think of myself as a fourteen-year-old boy, a single child, growing up in a village nine hundred sixty-five kilometers from Moscow. I can see myself, stick thin, with long, fair hair and blue eyes that always look a little startled. Everyone tells me that I am small for my age and they urge me to eat more protein . . . as if I can ever get my hands on anything that resembles fresh meat or fish. I have not yet spent many hundreds of hours working out and my muscles are undeveloped. I am sprawled out in the living room, watching the only television we have in the house. It's a huge, ugly box with a picture that often wavers and trembles, and there are hardly any channels to choose from. To make things worse, the electricity supply is unreliable and you can be fairly sure that the moment you get interested in a film or a news program, the image will suddenly flicker and die and you'll be left alone, sitting in the dark. But whenever I can, I tune into a documentary, which I devour. It is my only window onto the outside world.

Already there is so much to explain.

I am describing Russia—about ten years before the

end of the twentieth century. It is not so long ago and yet it is already somewhere that no longer exists. The changes that began in the main cities became a tsunami that engulfed the entire country, and yet they took their time reaching the village where I lived. There was no running water in any of the houses and so, three times a day, I had to make my way down to the well with a wooden harness over my shoulders and two metal buckets dragging down my arms. I sound like a peasant, and a lot of the time I must have looked like one, dressed in a baggy shirt with no collar and a waistcoat. As a matter of fact, I had one pair of American jeans that had been sent to me as a present from a relative in Moscow, and I can still remember everyone staring at me when I put them on. Jeans! They were like something from a distant planet. And my name was Yasha, not Yassen. Quite by accident, it got changed.

If I am going to explain what happened to me and what I became, then I must begin here, in Estrov. Nobody speaks of it anymore. It is not on the map. According to the Russian authorities, it never existed. But I remember it well, a village of about eighty wooden houses surrounded by farmland with a church, a shop, a police station, a bathhouse, and a river, bright blue in the summer but freezing all the year round. A single road ran through the middle of it, but it was hardly needed as there were very few cars. Our neighbor, Mr. Vladimov, had a tractor that often rumbled past, billowing oily black smoke, but I was more used to being woken up by the sound of horses' hooves. The village was wedged in between a thick forest in the north and hills to the south and west, so the view never really changed. Sometimes I would see planes flying overhead and I thought of the people inside them, traveling to the other side of the world. If I was working in the garden, I would stand still and watch them—the wings blinking, the sunlight glinting on their metal skin—until they had gone out of sight, leaving only the echo of their engines behind. They reminded me who and what I was. Estrov was my world and I certainly didn't need an airplane to get from one side to the other.

My own home, where I lived with my parents, was small and simple, quite similar in style to the sort of building that might be found beside a French or Swiss ski slope. It was quite close to the church, set back from the main road, with similar houses on either side. Flowers and brambles grew right beside the walls and were slowly creeping toward the roof. There were just four rooms. My parents slept upstairs. I had a room at the back, but I had to share it whenever anyone came to stay. My grandmother, who lived with us, had the room next to mine, but she preferred to sleep in a sort of hole in the wall, above the stove, in the kitchen. She was a very small, dark brown woman, and when I was young, I used to think that she had actually been cooked by the flames.

There was no railway station in Estrov. It was not considered important enough. Nor was there a bus service or anything like that. I went to school in a slightly larger village that liked to think of itself as a town, three kilometers away down a track that was dusty and full of potholes in the summer, thick with mud or covered in snow during the winter. The town was called Rosna. I walked there every day, no matter what the weather, and I was beaten if I was late. My school was a big, square brick building on three floors. All the classrooms were the same size. There were about six hundred children in all, boys and girls. Some of them traveled in by train, pouring out onto the platform with eyes that were still half closed with sleep. Rosna did have a railway station and they were very proud of it, decking it with flowers on public holidays. But actually it was a mean, run-down little place, and nine out of ten trains didn't even bother to stop there.

We students were all very smart. The girls wore black dresses with green aprons and had their hair tied back with ribbons. The boys looked like little soldiers with gray uniforms and red scarves tied round our necks, and if we did well with our studies, we were given badges with slogans—"For Active Work," "School Leader," that sort of thing. I don't really remember much of what I learned at school. Who does? History was important . . . the history of Russia, of course. We were always learning poems by heart and had to recite them, standing to attention beside our desks. There was math and science. Most of the teachers were women, but our headmaster was a man named Lavrov and he had a furious temper. He was short but he had huge shoulders and long arms, and I would often see him pick up a boy by the throat and pin him against the wall.

"You're not doing well, Leo Tretyakov!" he would boom. "I'm sick of the sight of you. Buck up your ideas or get out of here!"

Even the teachers were terrified of him. But actually, he was a good man at heart. In Russia, we were brought up to respect our teachers and it never occurred to me that his titanic rages were anything unusual.

I was very happy at school and I did well. We had a star system—every two weeks the teachers gave us a grade—and I was always a five-star student, what we called a *pyatiorka*. My best subjects were physics and math, and these were very important to the Russian authorities. Nobody ever let you forget that we were the country that had sent the first man—Yuri Gagarin—into space. There was actually a photograph of him in the front entrance, and you were supposed to salute him as you came in. I was also good at sports and I remember how the girls in my class used to come along and cheer me when I scored a goal. I wasn't all that interested in girls at this time, which is to say I was happy to chat to them, but I didn't particularly want to hang out with them after school. My best friend was the Leo that I just mentioned, and the two of us were inseparable.

Leo Tretyakov was short and dumpy with sticky-out ears, freckles, and ginger hair. He used to joke that he was the ugliest boy in the district, and I found it hard to disagree. He was also far from bright. He was a two-star student, a dismal *dvoyka,* and he was always getting into trouble with the teachers. In the end they actually gave up punishing him because it didn't seem to make any difference, and he just sat there quietly daydreaming at the back of the class. But at the same time he was the star of our NVP—military training—classes, which were compulsory throughout the school. Leo could strip down an AK7 automatic machine gun in twelve seconds and reassemble it in fifteen. He was a great shot. And twice a year there were military games when we had to compete with other schools, using a map and a compass to find our way through the woods. Leo was always in charge. And we always won.

I liked Leo because he was afraid of nothing and he always made me laugh. We did everything together. We would eat our sandwiches in the yard, washed down with a gulp of vodka he had stolen from home and brought to school in one of his mother's old perfume bottles. We smoked cigarettes in the woodland close to the main building, coughing horribly because the tobacco was so rough. Our school toilets had no compartments, and we often sat next to each other, doing what we had to do, which may sound disgusting, but that was the way it was. You were meant to bring your own toilet paper too, but Leo always forgot and I would watch him guiltily tearing pages out of his exercise books. He was always losing his homework that way. But with Leo's homework—and he'd have been the first to admit it—that was probably all it was worth.

The best time we had together was in the summer

when we would go for endless bicycle rides, rattling along the country roads, shooting down hills and pedaling backward furiously, which was the only way to stop. Everyone had exactly the same model of bicycle and they were all death traps with no suspension, no lights, and no brakes. We had nowhere to go, but in a way that was the fun of it. We used our imagination to create a world of wolves and vampires, ghosts and Cossack warriors—and we chased each other right through the middle of them. When we finally got back to the village, we would swim in the river even though there were parasites in the water that could make you sick, and we always went to the bathhouse together, thrashing each other with birch leaves in the steam room, which was meant to be good for your skin.

Leo's parents worked in the same factory as mine, although my father, who had once studied at Moscow University, was the more senior of the two. The factory employed about two hundred people who were collected by buses from Estrov, Rosna, and lots of other places. I have to say, the place was a source of constant puzzlement to me. Why was it tucked away in the middle of nowhere? Why had I never seen it? There was a barbed wire fence surrounding it and armed militia standing at the gate, and that didn't make sense either. All it produced was pesticides and other chemicals used by farmers. But when I asked my parents about it, they always changed the subject. Leo's father was the transportation manager, in charge of the buses. My father was a research chemist. My mother worked in the main office doing paperwork. That was about as much as I knew.

At the end of a summer afternoon, Leo and I would often sit close to the river and we would talk about our future. The truth was that just about everyone wanted to leave Estrov. There was nothing to do and half the people who lived there were perpetually drunk. I'm not making it up. During the winter months, they weren't allowed to open the village shop before ten o'clock in the morning or people would rush in as soon as it was light to buy their vodka, and during the months of December and January it wasn't unusual to see some of the local farmers flat on their back, half covered with snow and probably half dead too after downing a whole bottle. We were all being left behind in a fast-changing world. Why my parents had ever chosen to come here was another mystery.

Leo didn't care if he ended up working in the factory like everyone else, but I had other ambitions. For reasons that I couldn't explain, I'd always thought that I was different from everyone else. Maybe it was the fact that my father had once been a professor in a big university and that he had himself experienced life outside the village. But when I was watching those planes disappear into the distance, I always thought they were trying to tell me something. I could be on one of them. There was a whole life outside Estrov that I might one day explore.

Although I had never told anyone else except Leo, I dreamed of becoming a helicopter pilot—maybe in the army, but if not, in air-sea rescue. I had seen a program about it on television and for some reason it had caught hold of my imagination. I devoured everything I could about helicopters. I borrowed books from the school library. I cut out articles in magazines. By the time I was thirteen, I knew the name of almost every moving part of a helicopter. I knew how it used all the different forces and controls working in opposition to each other to fly. The only thing I had never done was actually sit in one.

"Do you think you'll ever leave?" Leo asked me one evening, the two of us sprawled out in the long grass, sharing a cigarette. "Go and live in a city with your own apartment and a car?"

"How am I supposed to do that?"

"You're clever. You can go to Moscow. Learn how to become a pilot."

I shook my head. Leo was my best friend. Whatever I might secretly think, I would never talk about the two of us being apart. "I don't think my parents would let me. Anyway, why would I want to leave? This is my home."

"Estrov is a dump."

"No, it's not." I looked at the river, the fast-flowing water chasing over the rocks, the surrounding woodland, the muddy track that led through the center of the village. In the distance, I could see the steeple of St. Nicholas. The village had no priest. The church was closed. But its shadow stretched out almost to our front door and I had always thought of it as part of my childhood. Maybe Leo was right. There wasn't very much to the place, but even so, it was my home. "I'm happy here," I said, and at that moment I believed it. "It's not such a bad place."

I remember saying those words. I can still smell the smoke coming from a bonfire somewhere on the other side of the village. I can hear the water rippling. I see Leo, twirling a piece of grass between his fingers. Our bicycles are lying one on top of the other. There are a few puffs of cloud in the sky, floating lazily past. A fish suddenly breaks the surface of the river and I see its scales glimmer silver in the sunlight. It is a warm afternoon at the start of September. And in twenty-four hours everything will have changed. Estrov will no longer exist.

When I got home, my mother was already making dinner. Food was a constant subject of conversation in our village because there was so little of it and everyone grew their own. We were lucky. As well as a vegetable patch, we had a dozen chickens that were all good layers, so (unless the neighbors crept in and stole them) we always had plenty of eggs. She was making a stew with potatoes, turnips, and canned tomatoes that had turned up the week before in the shop and had sold out instantly. It was exactly the same meal as we'd had the night before. She would serve it with slabs of black bread and, of course, small tumblers of vodka. I had been drinking vodka since I was nine years old.

My mother was a slender woman with bright blue eyes and hair that must have once been as blond as mine but was already gray, even though she was only in her thirties. She wore it tied back so that I could see the curve of her neck. She was always pleased to see me and she always took my side. There was that time, for example, when Leo and I were almost arrested for letting off bombs outside the police station. We had got up at first light and dug holes in the ground, which we'd filled up with the gunpowder stripped from about five hundred matches. Then we'd snuck behind the wall of the churchyard and watched. It was two hours before the first police car drove over our booby trap and set it off. There was a bang. The front tire was shredded and the car lost control and drove through a bush. The two of us nearly died laughing, but I wasn't so amused when I got home and found Yelchin, the police chief, in my front room. He asked me where I'd been, and when I said I'd been running an errand for my mother, she took my side, even though she knew I was lying. Later on she scolded me, but I know that she was secretly amused.

In our household, my mother and my grandmother did most of the talking. My father was a very thoughtful man who looked exactly like the scientist that he was, with graying hair, a serious sort of face, and glasses. He lived in Estrov but his heart was still in Moscow. He kept all his old books around him, and when letters came from the city, he would disappear to read them and at dinner he would be kilometers away. Why did I never ask more questions about him? I ask myself that now, but I suppose nobody ever does. When you are young, you accept your parents for what they are and you believe the stories they tell you.

Conversation at dinner was often difficult because my parents didn't like to discuss their work at the factory and there was only so much I could tell them about my day at school. As for my grandmother, she had somehow got stuck in the past, twenty years ago, and much of what she said didn't connect with reality at all. But that night was different. Apparently there had been a fire at the factory . . . nothing serious. But my father was worried and for once he spoke his mind.

"It's these new investors," he said. "All they think about is money. They want to increase production and to hell with safety measures. Today it was just the generator plant. But suppose it had been one of the laboratories?"

"You should talk to them," my mother said.

"They won't listen to me. They're pulling the strings from Moscow and they've got no idea." He threw back his vodka and swallowed it in one gulp. "That's the new Russia for you, Eva. We all get wiped out and as long as they get their check, they don't give a damn."

This all struck me as very strange. How could the production of fertilizers and pesticides be so dangerous?

My mother seemed to agree. "You worry too much," she said.

"We should never have gone along with this. We should never have been part of it." My father refilled his glass. He didn't drink as much as a lot of the people in the village, but like them, he used vodka to draw down the shutters between him and the rest of the world. "The sooner we get out of here, the better. We've been here long enough."

"The swans are back," my grandmother said. "They're so beautiful at this time of the year."

There were no swans in the village. As far as I knew, there never had been.

"Are we really going to leave?" I asked. "Can we go and live in Moscow?"

My mother reached out and put her hand on mine. "Maybe one day, Yasha. And you can go to university, just like your father. But you have to work hard . . ."

The next day was a Sunday and I had no school. On the other hand, the factory never closed and both my parents had drawn the weekend shift, working until four and leaving me to clean the house and take my grandmother her lunch. Leo looked in after breakfast, but we both had a ton of homework, so we agreed to meet down at the river at six and perhaps kick a ball around with some other boys. Just before midday I was lying on my bed, trying to plow my way through a chapter of *Crime and Punishment,* which was this huge Russian masterpiece we were all supposed to read. As Leo had said to me, none of us knew what our crime was, but reading the book was certainly a punishment. The story had begun with a murder, but since then nothing had happened and there were about six hundred pages to go.

Anyway, I was lying there with my head close to the window, allowing the sun to slant in on the pages. The time now was five minutes past twelve. I was wearing my watch, a Pobeda with black numerals on a white face and fifteen jewels, which had been made just after the Second World War and had once belonged to my grandfather. And that was when I heard the explosion. Actually, I wasn't even sure it was an explosion. It sounded more like a paper bag being crumpled somewhere out of sight. I climbed off the bed and went and looked out the open window. There was absolutely nothing to see. I returned to the book. How could I have so quickly forgotten my parents' conversation of the night before?

I read another thirty pages. I suppose another half an hour must have passed. And then I heard another sound—soft and far away but unmistakable all the same. It was gunfire, the sound of an automatic weapon being emptied. That was impossible. People went hunting in the woods sometimes, but not with machine guns, and there had never been any army exercises in the area. I looked out the window a second time and saw smoke rising into the air on the other side of the hills to the south of Estrov. That was when I knew that none of this was my imagination. Something had happened. The smoke was coming from the factory.

I leaped off the bed, dropping the book, and ran down

the stairs and out of the house. The village was completely
deserted. Our chickens were strutting around on the front
lawn of our house, pecking at the grass. There was a dog
barking somewhere. Everything was ridiculously normal.
But then I heard footsteps and looked up. Mr. Vladimov,
our neighbor, was running down from his front door, wiping his hands on a cloth.

"Mr. Vladimov!" I called out to him. "What's happened?"

"I don't know," he wheezed back. He had probably been working on his tractor. He was covered in oil.
"They've all gone to see. I'm going with them."

"What do you mean . . . all of them?"

"The whole village! There's been some sort of accident!"

Before I could ask any more, he had disappeared
down the muddy track.

He had no sooner gone than the alarm went off. It
was extraordinary, deafening, like nothing I had ever
heard before. It couldn't have been more urgent if war
had broken out. And as the noise of it resounded in my
head, I realized that it had to be coming from the factory,
more than a kilometer and a half away! How could it be
so loud? Even the fire alarm at school had been nothing
like this. It was a high-pitched siren that seemed to spread
out from a single point until it was everywhere—behind
the forest, over the hills, in the sky—and yet at the same
time it was right next to me, in front of my house. I knew
now that there had been another accident. I had heard it,

of course, the explosion. But that had been half an hour ago. Why had they been so slow raising the alarm?

The siren stopped. And in the sudden silence, the countryside, the village where I had spent my entire life, seemed to have become photographs of themselves and it was as if I was on the outside looking in. There was nobody around me. The dog had stopped barking. Even the chickens had scattered.

I heard the sound of an engine. A car came hurtling toward me, bumping over the track. The first thing I registered was that it was a black Lada. Then I took in the bullet holes all over the bodywork and the fact that the front windshield was shattered. But it was only when it stopped that I saw the shocking truth.

My father was in the front seat. My mother was behind the wheel.

## КРОКОДИЛЫ

I DIDN'T EVEN KNOW MY mother could drive. We hardly ever saw any cars in Estrov because nobody could afford to buy one, and anyway, there wasn't anywhere to go. The black Lada probably belonged to one of the senior managers.

Not that I was thinking about these things just then. The front door opened and my mother got out. Straightaway, I saw the fear in her eyes. She raised a hand in my direction, urging me to stay where I was, then ran around to the other side and helped my father out. He was wearing a loose white coat that flapped around his normal clothes, and I saw—with a sense of horror that was like a pool of black water sucking me in—that he had been hurt. The fabric was covered with his blood. His left arm hung limp. He was clutching his chest with his right hand. His face looked thin and pale and his eyes were empty, clouded by pain. My mother had her arm around him, helping him to walk. She at least had not been hurt, but she still looked like someone who had escaped from a war zone. There were streaks running down her face. Her hair was wild. No boy should ever see his parents in this way. It is not natural. Everything I had always believed and taken for granted was instantly smashed.

The two of them reached me. My father had no more strength and sank to the ground, resting his back against our garden fence. And all the time I had said nothing. There were a million questions I wanted to ask, but the words simply would not reach my lips. Time seemed to have fragmented. The first explosion, the smoke and the gunfire, going downstairs, seeing the car . . . they were like four separate incidents that could have taken place years apart. I needed them to explain it for me. Somehow, perhaps, they could make it all make sense.

"Yasha!" My father was the first to speak and it didn't sound like him at all. The pain was distorting his voice.

"What's happened? What is it? Who hurt you? You've been shot!" Once I had begun to speak I could barely stop, but I was making little sense.

My father reached out and grabbed hold of my arm. "I am so glad you're here. I was afraid you'd be out of the house. But you have to listen to us very carefully, Yasha. We have very little time."

"Yasha, my dear boy . . ." It was my mother who had spoken and suddenly there were tears coursing down her cheeks. It didn't matter what had happened at the factory. It was seeing me that had made her cry.

"I will try to explain to you," my father said. "But you can't argue with me. Do you understand that? You have to leave the village immediately."

"What? I'm not leaving! I'm not going anywhere."

"You have no choice. If you stay here, they will kill

you." His grip on me tightened. "They're already on their way. Do you understand me? They'll be here in a few minutes . . ."

"Who? Why?"

My father was too weak, in too much pain to say anything more, so my mother took over.

"We never told you about the factory," she said. "We weren't allowed to. But it wasn't just that. We didn't want you to know. We were ashamed." She wiped her eyes, pulling herself together. "We were making chemicals and pesticides for farmers, like we always said. But we were also making other things. For the military."

"Weapons," my father said. "Chemical weapons. Do you understand what I mean?" I said nothing, so he went on. "We had no choice, Yasha. Your mother and I got into trouble with the authorities a long time ago, when we were in Moscow, and we were sent out here. That was before you were born. It was all my fault. They stopped us from teaching. They threatened us. We had to earn a living and there was no other way."

The words were like a stampede of horses, galloping through my head. I wanted them to stop, to slow down. Surely all that mattered was to get help for my father. The nearest hospital was kilometers away, but there was a doctor in Rosna. It seemed to me that my father was getting weaker and that the blood was spreading.

But still they went on. "This morning there was an accident in the main laboratory," my mother explained.

"And something was released into the air. We had already warned them it might happen. You heard us talking about it only last night. But they wouldn't listen. Making a profit was all that mattered to them. Well, it's over now. The whole village has been contaminated. We have been contaminated. We brought it with us in that car. Not that it would have made any difference. It's in the air. It's everywhere."

"What is? What are you talking about?"

"A form of anthrax." My mother spat out the words. "It's a sort of bacterium, but it's been modified so that it's very contagious and acts very quickly. It could wipe out an army! And maybe we deserve this. We were responsible. We helped to make it . . ."

"Do it!" my father said. "Do it now!" With his free hand, he fumbled in his pocket and took out a metal box, about fifteen centimeters long. It was the sort of thing that might contain a pen.

My mother took it. Her eyes were still fixed on me. "As soon as we knew what had happened, our first thoughts were for you," she said. "Nobody was allowed to leave the factory. That was the first protocol. They had to keep us there, to contain us. But your father and I had already made plans . . . just in case. We stole a car and we smashed through the perimeter fence. We had to reach you."

"The siren?"

"That was nothing to do with the accident. They set it off afterward. They saw we were trying to escape." She drew a breath. "They sounded the alarm and the guards fired machine guns at us. Your father was hit. We were so frightened we wouldn't be able to find you, that you wouldn't be at the house . . ."

"Thank God you're here!" my father said. He was still holding on to me. He was breathing with difficulty.

My mother opened the box. I didn't know what would be inside or why it was so important, but when I looked down, I saw that it contained the last thing I had expected. There was some black velvet padding and, in the middle of that, a hypodermic syringe.

"For every weapon there has to be a defense," my mother went on. "We made a poison, but we were also working on an antidote. This is it, Yasha. There was only a tiny amount of it, but we stole it and we brought it to you. It will protect you."

"No. I don't want it! You have it!"

"There isn't enough for us. This is all we have." My father's hand had tightened on my arm, pinning me down. He was using the very last of his strength. "Do it, Eva," he insisted.

My mother was holding the syringe up to the light, tapping it with her finger, examining the glass vial. She pressed the plunger with her thumb so that a bead of liquid appeared at the end of the needle. I began to struggle. I couldn't believe that she was about to inject me.

My father wouldn't let me move. As weak as he was, he kept me still while my mother closed in on me. It must be every child's nightmare to be attacked by his own parents, and at that moment I forgot that everything they were doing was for my own good. They were saving me, not killing me, but that wasn't how it seemed to me. I can still see my mother's face, the cold determination as she brought the needle plunging down. She didn't even bother to roll up my shirtsleeve. The point went through the material and into my arm. It hurt. I think I actually felt the liquid, the antidote, coursing into my bloodstream. She pulled out the needle and dropped the empty hypodermic onto the ground. I looked down and saw more blood, my own, forming a circle on my sleeve.

My father let go of me. My mother closed her eyes for a moment. When she opened them again, she was smiling. "Yasha, my dearest," she said. "We don't mind what happens to us. Can you understand that? Right now, you're all we care about. You're all that matters."

The three of us stood there for a moment. We were like actors in a play who had run out of lines. We were breathless, shocked by the violence of what had taken place. It was like being in some sort of waking dream. We were surrounded by silence. Smoke was still rising slowly above the hills. And the village was still completely empty. There was nobody in sight.

It was my father who began again. "You have to go into the house," he said. "You need to take some clothes with you and any food you can find. Look in the kitchen cupboard and put it all in your backpack. Get a flashlight and a compass. But most important of all, there is a metal box in the kitchen. You know where it is . . . beside the fire. Bring it out to me." I hesitated, so he went on, putting all his authority into his voice. "If you are not out of the village in five minutes, Yasha, you will die with us. Even with the antidote. The government will not allow anyone to tell what has happened here. They will hunt you down and they will kill you. If you want to live, you must do as we say."

Did I want to live? Right then, I wasn't even so sure. But I knew that I couldn't let my parents down, not after everything they had done to reach me. Not daring to speak, my mother silently implored me. I could feel my throat burning—I reeled away and staggered into the house. My father was still sitting on the ground with his legs stretched out in front of him. Looking back, I saw my mother go over and kneel beside him.

Almost tripping over myself, I ran across the garden and through the front door. I went straight up to my bedroom and, in a daze, pulled out the uniform I had worn on camping trips with the Young Pioneers—which was a sort of scouting organization that existed throughout Russia. I had been given a dark green anorak, waterproof pants, and leather boots, which were still covered in dried mud. I wasn't sure whether to carry them or to wear them, but in the end I pulled them on over my ordinary clothes. I also took my backpack, a flashlight, and a compass from under the bed. I looked around me, at the pictures on the wall—a football club, various helicopters, a photograph of the world taken from outer space. The book that I had been reading was on the floor. My school clothes were folded on a chair. I could not accept that I was leaving all this behind, that I would never see any of it again.

I went downstairs. Every house in the village had its own special hiding place, and ours was in the wall beside the stove. There were two loose bricks and I pulled them out to reveal a hollow opening with a tin box inside. I grabbed it and took it with me. As I straightened up, I noticed my grandmother, still standing at the sink, peeling potatoes, with her apron tied tightly around her waist.

She beamed at me. "I can't remember when there's been a better harvest," she said. She had absolutely no idea what was going on.

I went over to a cupboard and shoved some cans, tea, sugar, a box of matches, and two bars of chocolate into my backpack. I filled a glass with water I had taken from the well. Finally, I kissed my grandmother quickly on the side of the head and hurried out, leaving her to her work.

The sky had darkened while I was in the house. How could that have happened? It had only been a few minutes, surely. But now it looked as though it was going to rain, perhaps one of those violent downpours we often had during the months leading up to winter. My father was sitting where I had left him and seemed to be asleep. His hand was clutched across the wound in his chest. I wanted to carry the tin box over to him, but my mother moved around and stood in my way. I held out the glass of water.

"I got this. For Father."

"That's good of you, Yasha. But he doesn't need it."

"But . . ."

"No, Yasha. Try to understand."

It took a few moments for the significance of what she was saying to sink in, and at once a trapdoor opened and I plunged through it, into a world of pain.

My mother took the box and lifted the lid. Inside there was a roll of banknotes, a hundred rubles, more money than I had ever seen. My parents must have been saving it from their salaries, planning for the day when they returned to Moscow. But that wasn't going to happen, not now. She gave it all to me along with my internal passport, a document that everyone in Russia was required to own, even if you didn't travel. Finally she took out a small black velvet bag and handed it to me too.

"That is everything, Yasha," she said. "You have to go."

"Mother . . . ," I began. I felt huge tears swell up in my eyes, and the burning in my throat was worse than ever.

"You heard what your father said. Now, listen very carefully. You have to go to Moscow. I know it's a long way away and you've never traveled on your own, but you can make it. You can take the train. Not from Rosna. They'll be checking everyone at the station. Go to Kirsk. You can reach it through the forest. That's the safest way. Find the new highway and follow it. Do it for your father. Do you understand?"

I nodded miserably.

"You remember Kirsk. You've been there a few times. There's a station with trains every day to Moscow . . . one in the morning, one in the evening. Take the evening train, when it's dark. If anyone asks you, say you're visiting an uncle. Never tell anyone you came from Estrov. Never use that word again. Promise me that."

"Where will I go in Moscow?" I asked. I didn't want to leave. I wanted to stay with her.

She reached out and took me in her arms, hugging me against her. "Don't be scared, Yasha. We have a good friend in Moscow. He's a biology professor and he worked with your father. You'll find him at the Moscow University. His name is Misha Dementyev. I'll try to telephone him, but I expect they'll have cut the lines. It doesn't matter. When you tell him who you are, he'll look after you."

Misha Dementyev. I clung on to the two words, my only lifeline.

My mother was still embracing me. I was looking at the curve of her neck, smelling her scent for the last time. "Why can't you come with me?" I sobbed.

"It would do no good. I'm infected. I want to stay with your father. But it's not so bad, knowing you've gotten away." She moved me away from her, still holding me, looking straight into my eyes. "Now, you have to be brave. You have to leave. Don't look back. Don't let anyone stop you."

"Mother . . ."

"I love you, my dear son. Now go!"

If I'd spoken to her again, I wouldn't have been able
to leave her. I knew that. We both did. I broke away. I ran.

The forest was on the other side of the house, to the north
and spreading to the east of Estrov. It stretched on for
about sixty-five kilometers, mainly pine trees but also
linden, birch, and spruce. It was a dark, tangled place and
none of us ever went into it, partly because we were afraid
of getting lost but also because there were rumored to be
wolves around, particularly in the winter. But somewhere
inside me I knew my mother was right. If there were
police or soldiers in the area, they would concentrate on
the main road. I would be safer out of sight. The highway
that she'd mentioned cut through the forest and they were
laying a new water pipe alongside it.

To begin with, I followed the track that wound
through the gardens, trying to keep out of sight, although
there was nobody around. In the distance, I saw a boy I
knew cycling past with a bundle under his arm, but he was
alone. I passed the village shop. It was closed. I continued
through the allotments where the villagers grew their own
food and stole everyone else's. I was already hot, wearing a
double set of clothes, and the air was suddenly warm and
thick. The clouds were gray and swollen, rolling in from
every side. It was definitely going to rain.

I had already decided that I was not going to do what
my mother had told me. Did she really think I could run
off and leave her on her own with my father lying dead

beside the car? No matter what had happened at the factory, and whatever she had said, I couldn't just abandon her. I would wait a few hours in the forest and see what happened. And then, once it was dark, I would return. She had talked about a weapon—anthrax. She had said the whole village was contaminated. But I refused to believe her. I was even angry with her for telling me these things. In truth, I do not think I was actually in my right mind.

And then I saw someone ahead of me, crouching down with their bottom in the air, pulling vegetables out of the ground. Even from this angle, I recognized him at once. It was Leo. He had been working on his family's vegetable patch, probably as a punishment for doing something wrong. He had two younger brothers, and whenever any of them fought, their father would take a belt to them and they would end up either mending fences or gardening. He was covered in mud with a bunch of very wrinkled carrots dangling from his hand, but seeing me approach, he broke into a grin.

"Hey, Yasha!" he called out. He did a double take, noticing my Pioneer clothes. "What are you doing?"

"Leo . . ." I was so glad to see him, but I didn't know what to say. How could I explain what had just happened?

"Did you hear the siren?" he said. "And there was shooting. I think something's happened over at the factory."

"Where are your parents?" I asked.

"Dad's working. Mom's at home."

"Leo, you have to come with me." The words came rushing out. I hadn't planned to ask him along, but suddenly it was the most important thing in the world. I couldn't leave without him.

"Where are you going?" He lowered the carrots and stood there with his legs slightly apart, one hand on his hip, his boots reaching up to his thighs. For a moment he looked like one of those old posters, the sort they had printed to get the peasants to work in the fields. He gave me a crooked smile. "What's the matter, Yasha? What's wrong?"

"My dad's dead," I said.

"What?"

Hadn't he understood anything? Hadn't he realized that something was wrong? But that was Leo for you. Gunshots, explosions, alarms . . . and he would just carry on weeding.

"He's been shot," I said. "That was what the siren was about. It was him. They tried to stop him from leaving. But he told me I have to go away and hide. Something terrible has happened at the factory." I was pleading with him. "Please, Leo. Come with me."

"I can't . . ."

He was going to argue. No matter what I told him, he would never have abandoned his family. But just then we became aware of a sound, something that neither of us had ever heard before. At the same time, we felt a slight pulsing in the air, beating against our skin. We looked around and saw five black dots in the sky, swooping low over the hills, heading toward the village. They were military helicopters, just like the ones in the pictures in my room. They were still too far away to see properly, but they were lined up in precise battle formation. It was that exactness that made them so menacing. Somehow I was certain that they weren't going to land. They weren't going to disgorge doctors and technicians who had come to help us. My parents had warned me that people were coming to Estrov to kill me, and I had no doubt at all that they had arrived.

"Leo! Come on! Now!"

There must have been something in my voice, or perhaps it was the sight of the helicopters themselves. But this time Leo dropped his carrots and obeyed. Together, without a single thought, we began to run up the slope, away from the village. The edge of the forest, an endless line of thick trunks, branches, pine needles, and shadows, stretched out before us. We were still about fifty meters away and now I found that my legs wouldn't work, that the soft mud was deliberately dragging me down. Behind me, the sound of the helicopters was getting louder. I didn't dare turn around but I could feel them getting closer and closer. And then—another shock—the bells of St. Nicholas began to ring, the sound echoing over the rooftops. We had no priest in the village. The church was empty. I had never heard the bells before.

I was sweating. My whole body felt as if it were

trapped inside an oven. Something hit me on the shoulder and for a crazy moment I thought one of the helicopters had fired a bullet. But it was nothing more than a fat rain-drop. The storm was about to break.

"Yasha!"

We stopped on the very edge of the forest and turned around just in time to see the helicopters deliver their first payload. They fired five missiles, one after the other. But they didn't hit anything, not like in an old war film. The pilots hadn't actually been aiming at any particular buildings. The missiles exploded randomly—in lanes, in peoples' gardens—but the destruction was much, much worse than anything I could have imagined. Huge fireballs erupted at the point of impact, spreading out instantly so that they joined up with one another, wiping out everything they touched. The flames were a brilliant orange, fiercer and more intense that any fire I had ever seen. They devoured my entire world, burning up the houses, the walls, the trees, the roads, the very soil. Nothing that touched those flames could possibly survive. The first five missiles wiped out almost the en-tire village, but they were followed by five more and then another five. We could feel the heat reaching out to us, so intense that even though we were some distance away, our eyes watered and we had to look away. I put up my hand to protect my face and felt the back of my fingers burn. In seconds, Estrov, the village where I had spent my entire life, was turned into hell. My father was already dead and I had no doubt at all that my mother had now joined him. And my grandmother. And Leo's mother and his brothers. It was impossible to see his house through the curtain of fire, but by now it would be nothing more than ash.

The helicopters were continuing, heading toward us. Now that they were closer, I recognized them at once. They were Mil Mi-24s, sometimes known as Crocodiles, developed for the Russian military for both missile support and troop movements. Each one could carry eight men at speeds of over 350 kilometers per hour. As well as the main and the tail rotors, the Mil had two wings stretching out of the main fuselage, each one equipped with a missile launcher that dangled beneath it. I had never seen anything that looked more deadly, more like a giant bird with claws outstretched, swooping out of the sky to snatch me up. They were getting closer and closer. I could actually see the nearest pilot, very low down in the glass bubble that was the cockpit window. Where had he come from? Had he once been a boy like me, dreaming of flying? How could he sit there and be responsible for so much killing? And yet he was without mercy. There could be no doubt at all that he was aiming the next salvo at me. I swear I saw him gazing straight at me as he fired. I saw the spurt of flame as the missiles were fired.

Fortunately, they fell short. A wall of flame erupted about thirty meters behind me. Even so, the heat was so intense that Leo screamed. I could smell the air burning.

A cloud of chemicals and smoke poured over us. It was only later that I realized it must have briefly shielded us from the pilot. Otherwise he would have fired again.

Leo and I plunged into the forest. The light was cut out behind us. Instantly we were surrounded by green, with leaves and branches all around us and soft moss beneath our feet. We had reached the top of the hill. The forest sloped down on the other side, and this proved our salvation. We lost our footing and tumbled down, rolling over roots and mud. It was already raining harder. Water was dripping down and maybe that helped us too. We were invisible. We were away from the flames. As I fell, I caught a glimpse through the trees of the red and black horror that I had left behind. I heard the roar of helicopter blades. Branches were whipping and shaking all around me. But then I was at the very bottom of the hollow. Leo was next to me, staring helplessly, completely terrified. But we were protected by the forest and by the earth. The helicopters could not reach us.

Well, perhaps the pilots could have tried again. Maybe they had exhausted their missile supply. Maybe they didn't think it was worth wasting more of their ammunition on two small boys. But even as I lay there, I knew that this wasn't over yet. They had seen us and they would radio ahead. Others would come to finish the work. It wasn't enough that the village had been destroyed. Everybody who had lived there would have to be killed. There could be nobody left to tell what had happened.

"Yasha," Leo gasped. He was crying. His face was a mess of mud and tears.

"We have to go," I said.

We struggled to our feet and plunged into the safety of the forest. Behind us, the sky was red, the helicopters hovering as Estrov continued to burn.

## ЛЕС

When I was a small boy, I had feared the forest with its ghosts and its demons. It had given me nightmares. My own parents had come from the city and didn't believe such things, but Leo's mother used to tell me stories about it, the same stories that her mother had doubtless told her. Every child in the village knew them and stayed away. But now I wanted it to draw me in, to swallow me up and never let me go. The deeper I went, the safer I felt, surrounded by huge, solid trunks with the sky blotted out and everything silent except for the drip of the rain on the canopy of leaves. The real nightmare was behind me. It was almost impossible to think of my village and the people who had lived there. Mr. Vladimov smoking his cigarettes until the stubs burned his fingers. Mrs. Bek, who ran the village shop and put up with everyone's complaints when there was nothing on the shelves. The twins, Irina and Olga, so alike that we could never tell them apart but always arguing and at each other's throats. My grandmother. My parents. My friends. They had all gone as if they had never existed, and nothing would remain of them, not even their names.

*Never tell anyone you came from Estrov. Never use that word again.*

My mother's warning to me. And of course she was

right. The place of my birth had now become a sentence of death.

I was in shock. So much had happened and it had happened so quickly that my brain simply wasn't able to cope with it all. I had seen very few American films—and computer games hadn't arrived in my corner of Russia yet—so the sort of violence I had just experienced was completely alien to me. Perhaps it was for the best. If I had really considered my situation, I might easily have gone mad. I was fourteen years old and suddenly I had nothing except a hundred rubles, the clothes I was wearing, and the name of a man I had never met in a city I had never visited. My best friend was with me, but it was as if his soul had flown out of him, leaving nothing but a shell behind. He was no longer crying but he was walking like a zombie. For the last hour, he had said nothing. We had been walking in silence with only the sound of our own footsteps and the rain hitting the leaves.

It wasn't over yet. We were both waiting for the next attack. Maybe the helicopters would return and bomb the forest. Maybe they would use poison gas next time. They knew we were here and they wouldn't let us get away.

"What was it all about, Yasha Gregorovich?" Leo asked. He used my full name in the formal way that we Russians do sometimes—when we want to make a point or when we are afraid. His face was puffy and I could see that his eyes were bright with tears although he had made a point of not crying in front of me.

"I don't know," I said. But that wasn't true. I knew

only too well. "There was an accident at the factory," I
went on. "Our parents lied to us. They weren't just making chemicals for farmers. They were also making weapons. Something went wrong and they had to close it down
very quickly."

"The helicopters . . ."

"I suppose they didn't want to tell anyone what had
happened. It's like that place we learned about. You
know . . . Chernobyl."

We all knew about Chernobyl in Ukraine. Not so long
ago, when Russia was still part of the Soviet Union, there
had been a huge explosion at a nuclear reactor. The whole
area had been covered with clouds of radioactive dust—
they had even reached parts of Europe. But at the time,
the authorities had done everything they could to cover
up what had happened. Even now it was uncertain how
many people had actually died. That was the way the Russian government worked back then. If they had admitted
there had been a catastrophe, it would have shown they
were weak. So it was easy to imagine what they would do
following an accident at a secret facility creating biological
weapons. If a hundred or even five hundred people were
murdered, what would it matter, so long as things were
kept quiet?

Leo was still trying to take it all in. It hurt me seeing him like this. This was a boy who had been afraid
of nothing, who had been rude to all the teachers and
who had never complained when he was beaten or sent on

forced marches. But it was as if he had become five years younger. He was lost. "They killed everyone," he said.

"They had to keep it a secret, Leo. My mother and father managed to get out of the factory. They told me to run away because they knew what was going to happen." My voice cracked. "They died too."

"I'm sorry, Yasha."

"Me too, Leo."

He was my best friend. He was all that I had left in the world. But I still wasn't telling him the whole truth. My arm was throbbing painfully and I was sure that he must have noticed the bloodstain on my sleeve, but I hadn't mentioned the syringe. My mother had inoculated me with the antidote against whatever had escaped into the air. She had said it would protect me. No one had done the same for Leo. Did that mean he was carrying the anthrax spores on him even now? Was he dying? I didn't want to think about it and, coward that I was, I certainly couldn't bring myself to talk about it with him.

We were still walking. The rain was getting heavier. Now it was making its way through the leaves and splashing down all around us. It was early in the afternoon, but most of the light was gone. I had taken out my compass and given it to Leo. I could of course have used it myself, but I thought it would be better for him to have his mind occupied—and anyway, he was better at finding directions than me. Not that the compass really helped. Every time we came to a particularly nasty knot of brambles or found a tangle of undergrowth blocking our path, we had to go another way. It was as if the forest itself were guiding us. Where? If it was feeling merciful, it would lead us to safety. But it might be just as likely to deliver us into our enemies' hands.

The forest began to slope upward, gently at first, then more steeply, and we found our feet kept slipping and we tripped over the roots. Leo looked dreadful, his clothes plastered across him, his face deadly white, his hair, soaking wet now, hanging lifelessly over his eyes. I felt guilty in my waterproof clothes, but it was too late to hand them over. Ahead of us, the trees began to thin out. This was doubly bad news. First, it meant that we were even less protected from the rain. But it would also be easier to spot us from the air if the helicopters returned.

"Over there!" I said.

I had seen an electricity pylon not too far away, poking out above the trees, part of the new construction. They had been laying all three together—the new highway, the water pipe, and electricity—all part of the modernization of the area, before the work had ground to a halt. But even without tarmac or lighting, the road would lead us straight to Kirsk. At least we knew which way to go.

I had very little memory of Kirsk. The last time I had been there had been about a year ago, on a school trip. Getting out of Estrov had been exciting enough, but when we had gotten there, we had spent half the time in a museum and by the afternoon I was bored stiff. When I was twelve, I had spent a week in Kirsk Hospital after I'd broken my leg. Both times, I had been taken there by bus and had no idea how to get around. But surely the station wouldn't be too difficult to find, and at least I would have enough money to buy two tickets for the train. A hundred rubles was worth a great deal. It was more than a month's salary for one of my teachers.

We trudged forward, making better progress. We were beginning to think that we had gotten away after all, that nobody was interested in us anymore. Of course it is just when you begin to think like that, when you relax your guard, that the worst happens. If I had been in the same situation now, I would have gone anywhere except toward the new highway. When you are in danger, you must always opt for what is least expected. Predictability kills.

We reached the first evidence of the construction: abandoned spools of wire, cement slabs, great piles of plastic tubing. Ahead of us, a brown ribbon of dug-up earth stretched out into the gloom. The town of Kirsk and the railway to Moscow lay at the other end.

"How far is it?" Leo asked.

"I don't know," I said. "About thirty kilometers, I think. Are you okay?"

Leo nodded, but the misery in his face told another story.

"We can do it," I said. "Five or six hours. And it can't rain forever."

It felt as if it was going to do just that. We could actually see the raindrops now, fat and relentless, slanting down in front of us and splattering on the ground. It was like a curtain hanging between the trees, and we could barely make out the road on the other side. There were more pipes scattered on both sides, and after a short while we came to a deep ditch that must have been cut as part of the water project. Was it really possible for an entire community to near the end of the twentieth century without running water? I had carried enough buckets down to the well to know the answer to that.

We walked for another ten minutes, neither of us speaking, our feet splashing in the puddles. And then we saw them. They were ahead of us, a long line of soldiers spread out across the forest, making steady progress toward us . . . like detectives looking for clues after a murder. They were spaced out so that nobody would be able to pass through the line without being seen. They had no faces. They were dressed in pale silver anti-biochemical uniforms with hoods and gas masks, and they carried semiautomatic machine guns. They had dogs with them, scrawny Alsatians, straining at the end of metal leashes. It was as if they had walked out of my worst nightmare. They didn't look human at all.

It should have been obvious from the start that whoever had sent the helicopters would follow it with infantry backup. First destroy the village, then put a noose around the place to make sure there are no survivors. The line of militiamen, if that's what they were, would have formed a huge circle around Estrov. They would close in from all sides. And they would have been told to shoot any stragglers—Leo and me—on sight. Nobody could be allowed to tell what had happened. And above all, the anthrax virus that we might be carrying could not break free.

They would have seen us at once but for the rain. And the dogs, too, would have smelled us if everything hadn't been so wet. In the darkness of the forest, the pale color of their protective gear stood out, but for a few precious seconds, we were invisible. I reached out and grabbed Leo's arm. We turned and ran the way we had come.

It was the worst thing to do. Since that time, long ago now, I have been taught survival techniques for exactly such situations. You do not break your pace. You do not panic. It is the very rhythm of your movement that will alert your enemy. We should have melted to one side, found cover, and then retreated as quickly but as steadily as we could. Instead, the sound of our shoes stamping on the wet ground signaled that we were there. One of the dogs began to bark ferociously, followed immediately by the rest of them. Somebody shouted. An instant later there was the deafening clamor of machine gun fire, a dozen weapons spraying bullets that sliced through the trees and the leaves, sending pieces of debris showering over our heads. We had been seen. The line began to move forward more urgently. We were perhaps thirty or forty meters ahead of them but we were already close to exhaustion, drenched, unarmed. We were children. We had no chance at all.

More machine gun fire. I saw mud splattering up centimeters from my feet. Leo was slightly ahead of me. His legs were shorter than mine and he had been more tired than me, but I was determined to keep him in front of me, not to leave him behind. If one went down, we both went down. The dogs were making a hideous sound. They had seen their prey. They wanted to be released.

And we stayed on the half-built highway! That was a killing ground if ever there was one, wide and exposed, an easy matter for a sniper to pick us off. I suppose we thought we could run faster with a flat surface beneath our feet. But every step I took, I was waiting for the bullet that would come smashing between my shoulders. I could hear the dogs, the guns, the blast of the whistles. I didn't look back but I could actually feel the men closing in behind me.

Still we had the advantage of distance. The line of soldiers would move more slowly than us. They wouldn't want to break rank and risk the chance of our doubling back and slipping through. I had perhaps one minute to work out some sort of scheme before they caught up with us. Climb a tree? No, it would take too long, and anyway, the dogs would sniff us out. Continue back down the hill? Pointless. There were probably more soldiers coming up the other side. I was still running, my heart pounding in my chest, the breath harsh in my throat. And then I saw

it—the ditch we had passed with the plastic tubes scattered about.

"This way, Leo!" I shouted.

At the same time, I threw myself off the road, skid-
ding down the deep bank and landing in a stream of water
that rose over my ankles.

"Yasha, what are you—?" Leo began, but he was
sensible enough not to hesitate, turning back and following me down, almost landing on top of me. And so there
we were, below the level of the road, and I was already
making my way back, heading _toward_ the line of soldiers,
looking for what I prayed must be there.

Hundreds of meters of the water pipe had already been
laid. The opening was in front of us: a perfect black circle
like the entrance to some futuristic cave. It was small. If I
hadn't been so thin and if Leo hadn't been so slight, neither of us would have fit into it, and it was unlikely that
many of the soldiers would be able to follow, certainly not
in their gas masks and protective gear. They would have
been mad to try. Would they really be prepared to bury
themselves alive, plunging into utter darkness with tons of
damp earth above their heads?

That was what we did. On our hands and knees, we
threw ourselves forward, our shoulders scraping against
the curve of the pipe. At least it was dry inside the tunnel.
But it was also pitch-black. When I looked back to see if
Leo was behind me, I caught a glimmer of soft light a few
meters behind me. But when I looked ahead . . . there

was nothing! I brought my hand up and touched my nose, but I couldn't see my fingers. For a moment, I found it difficult to breathe. I had to fight off the claustrophobia, the sense of being suffocated, of being squeezed to death. I wondered if it would be a good idea to go any farther. We could have stayed where we were and used the tunnel as a hiding place until everyone had gone—but that wasn't good enough for me. I could imagine a burst of machine gun fire killing me or, worse still, paralyzing me and leaving me to die slowly in the darkness. I could feel the Alsatians, sent after us, snapping and snarling their way down the tunnel and then tearing ferociously at our legs and thighs. I had to let the tunnel carry me away and it didn't matter where it took me. So I kept going with Leo behind me, the two of us burrowing ever farther beneath the wood.

To the soldiers it must have seemed as if we had disappeared by magic. They would have passed the ditch, but it's quite likely that they didn't see the pipeline—or, if they did, refused to believe that we had been foolhardy enough to enter it. Once again, the rain covered our tracks. The dogs failed to pick up our scent. Any footprints were washed away. And the soldiers were completely unaware that, as they moved forward, we were right underneath them, crawling like insects through the mud. When I looked back again, the entrance was no longer there. It was as if a shutter had come down, sealing us in. I could hear Leo very close to me, his breath sobbing. But any sound in the tunnel was strange and muted. I could feel the weight above me, pressing down.

We had swapped one hell for another.

We could only go forward. There wasn't enough room to turn around. I suppose we could have shuffled backward until we reached the tunnel entrance, but what would be the point of that? The soldiers would be looking for us, and once we emerged, the dogs would be onto us instantly. On the other hand, the farther we went forward, the worse our situation became. Suppose the tunnel simply ended? Suppose we ran out of air? Every centimeter that we continued was another centimeter into the grave and it took all my willpower to force myself on. I think Leo only followed because he didn't want to be left on his own. I was getting warmer. Once again I was sweating inside my clothes. I could feel the sweat mixed with rainwater in my armpits and under the palms of my hands. My knees were already hurting. Occasionally, I passed rivets where one section of the pipe had had been fastened into the next and I felt them tugging at my anorak, scratching across my back. And I was blind. It really was as if someone had switched off my eyes. The blackness was very physical. It was like a surgical operation.

"Yasha?" Leo's whispered voice came out of nowhere.

"It's all right, Leo," I said. My own voice didn't sound like me at all. "Not much farther."

But we continued for at least twenty minutes more. We were moving like robots with no sense of direction, no choice of where to go. We were simply functioning—one hand forward, then the next, knees following behind, blind and deaf. There was nothing to hear apart from ourselves. Suppose the tunnel went all the way to Kirsk? Would we have the strength to travel as much as thirty kilometers underground? Of course not. Between us, we had half a liter of water. We hadn't eaten for hours. I had to stop myself from imagining what might happen. If I wasn't careful, I would scare myself to death.

Hand and knee, hand and knee. Every part of me was hurting. I wanted to stand up and the fact that I couldn't almost made me cry out with frustration. My shoulders hit the curve of the ceiling again and again. My eyes were closed. What was the point of using them when I couldn't see? And then, quite suddenly, I was outside. I felt the breeze brush over my shoulders and the rain, lighter now, patter onto my head and the back of my neck. I opened my eyes. The workmen had constructed some sort of inspection hatch, and they had left this part of the pipe open. I was crouching in a V-shaped ditch with pieces of wire and rusting metal bolts all around. I pulled back my sleeve and looked at my watch. Amazingly, it was five o'clock. I thought only an hour had passed, but the whole day had gone.

Leo clambered out into the half-light and sat there, blinking. For a moment neither of us dared speak, but there were no sounds around us and it seemed fairly certain we were on our own.

"We're okay," I said. "We went under them. They don't know we're here."

"What next?" Leo asked.

"We can keep going . . . follow the road to Kirsk."

"They'll be looking for us there."

"I know. We can worry about that when we get there."

And just for one moment, I thought we were going to make it. We had escaped from the helicopters. We had outwitted the soldiers. I had a hundred rubles in my pocket. I would get us to Moscow and we would tell the whole world what had happened and we would be heroes. Right then, I really did think that despite what we had been through and all that we had lost, we might actually be all right.

But then Leo spoke.

"Yasha," he said, "I don't feel well."

## 4

## НОЧЬ

WE COULDN'T STAY WHERE we were. I was afraid that the soldiers would find the entrance to the pipeline and realize how we had managed to slip past them—in which case they would double back and find us. We had to put more distance between us while we still had the strength. But at the same time I saw that Leo couldn't go much farther. He had a headache and he was finding it difficult to breathe. Was it too much to hope that he had simply caught a cold, that he was in shock? He didn't have to be contaminated by the chemicals from the factory. I tried to convince myself that, like me, he was exhausted and if he could just get a night's rest he would be all right again.

Even so, I knew I had to find him somewhere warm to shelter. He needed food. Somehow I had to dry his clothes. As I looked around me at the spindly trees that rose up into an ever-darkening sky, I felt a sense of complete helplessness. How could I possibly manage on my own? I wanted my parents and I had to remind myself that they weren't going to come, that I was never going to see them again. I was sick with grief—but something inside me told me that I couldn't give in. Leo and I hadn't escaped from Estrov simply to die out here, a few kilometers away, in the middle of a forest.

We walked together for another hour, still following the road. They'd been able to afford asphalt for this section, which at least made it easier to find our way in the dark. I knew it was dangerous, that we had more chance of being spotted, but I didn't dare lose myself among the trees.

And in the end it was the right decision. We stumbled upon it quite by chance, a wooden hut that must have been built for the construction team and abandoned only recently. The door was padlocked, but I managed to kick it in, and once we were inside I was surprised to find two bunks, a table, cupboards, and even an iron stove. I checked the cupboards. There was no food or medicine, but the almost empty shelves did offer me a few rewards. Using my flashlight, I found some old newspapers, saucepans, tin mugs, and a fork. How glad I was now that I had thought to take a box of matches from my parents' kitchen and that my waterproof clothes had managed to keep them dry. There was no coal or firewood, so I tore off some of the cupboard doors and smashed them up with my foot, and ten minutes later I had a good fire blazing. I wasn't worried about the smoke being seen. It was too dark and I kept the door and the shutters closed to stop the light from escaping.

I helped Leo out of his wet clothes and hung them to dry. He stretched himself out on the nearest bunk and I covered him with newspaper and a rug from the floor. It might not be too clean, but at least it would help to keep him warm. I had the food that I had brought from my home and I took it out. Leo and I had drunk all our water, but that wasn't a problem. I carried a saucepan outside and filled it from the gutter that ran around the side of the building. After all the rain, it was full to overflowing and boiling it in the flames would get rid of any germs. I added the tea and the sugar and balanced the whole thing on the stove. I broke the chocolate bars into pieces and examined the cans. There were three of them and they all contained herring, but fool that I was, I had forgotten to bring a can opener.

While Leo drifted in and out of sleep, I spent the next half hour desperately trying to open the cans. In a way, it did me good to have to focus on a problem that was so small and so stupid. Forget the fact that you are alone, in hiding, that there are soldiers who want to kill you, that your best friend is ill, that everything has been taken from you. Open the can! In the end, I managed it with the fork that I had found, hammering at it with a heavy stone and piercing the lid so many times that eventually I was able to peel it away. The herring was gray and oily. I'm not sure that anyone eats it anymore, but it had always been a special treat when I was growing up. My mother would serve it with slabs of black, dry bread or sometimes potatoes. When I smelled the fish, I thought of her and I felt all the pain welling up once more, even though I was doing everything I could to block out what had happened.

I tried to feed some to Leo, but after all my effort, he

was too tired to eat and it was the best I could manage to force him to sip some tea. I was suddenly very hungry myself and gobbled down one of the cans, leaving the other two for him. I was still hopeful that he would be feeling better in the morning. It seemed to me that now that he was resting, he was breathing a little easier. Maybe all the rain would have washed away the anthrax spores. His clothes were still drying in front of the fire. Sitting there, watching his chest rise and fall below the covers, I tried to convince myself that everything would be all right.

It was the beginning of the longest night of my life. I took off my outer clothes and lay down on the second bunk, but I couldn't sleep. I was frightened that the fire would go out. I was frightened that the soldiers would find the hut and burst in. Actually, I was so filled with fears of one sort or another that I didn't need to define them. For hours I listened to the crackle of the flames and the rattle of Leo's breath in his throat. From time to time I drifted into a state where I was floating although still fully conscious. Half a dozen times, I got up and fed more of the furniture into the stove, doing my best to break the wood without making too much noise. Once, I went outside to urinate. It was no longer raining but a few drops of water were still falling from the trees. I could hear them but I couldn't see them. The sky was totally black. As I stood there, I heard the howl of a wolf. I had been holding the flashlight, but at that moment I almost dropped it into the undergrowth. So the wolves weren't just a bit of village gossip! This one could have been far away, but at the same time it could have been right next to me, the sound starting impossibly low then rising higher and higher as if the creature had somehow flown into the air. I buttoned myself up and ran back inside, determined that nothing would get me out again until it was light.

My own clothes were still damp. I took them off and knelt in front of the fire. If anything got me through that night, it was that stove. It kept me warm, and without its glow I wouldn't have been able to see, which would have made all my imaginings even worse. I had taken out the roll of ten-ruble notes that had been in the tin and at the same time I found the little black bag my mother had given me. I opened it. Inside, there was a pair of earrings, a necklace, and a ring. I had never seen them before and I wondered where she had gotten them from. Were they valuable? I made an oath to myself that whatever happened, I would never sell them. They were the only remains of my past life. They were all I had left. I wrapped them up again and climbed onto the other bunk. Almost naked and lying uncomfortably on the hard mattress, I dozed off again. When I next opened my eyes, the fire was nearly out, and when I pulled back the shutters, the very first streaks of pink were visible outside.

The sun seemed to take forever to rise. They call them the small hours, that time from four o'clock onward, and I know from experience that they are always the most miserable of the day. That is when you feel most vulnerable and alone. Leo was sound asleep. The hut was even more desolate than before—I had fed almost anything that was made of wood into the fire. The world outside was wet, cold, and threatening. As I got dressed again, I remembered that in a few hours I should have been going to school.

"Wake up, Yasha. Come on! Get your things together . . ."

I had to force my mother's voice out of my head. She wasn't there for me anymore. Nobody was. From now on, if I was to survive, I had to look after myself.

The two remaining cans of fish were still waiting, uneaten, on a shelf beside the fire. I was tempted to wolf them down myself, as I was really hungry, but I was still keeping them for Leo. I made some more tea and ate a little chocolate, then I went back outside. The sky was now a dirty off-white. The trees were more skeletal than ever. But at least there was nobody around. The soldiers hadn't come back. Walking around, I came across a shrub of bright red lingonberries. They were past their best but I knew they would be edible. We used to make them into a dish called *kissel,* a sort of jelly, and I stuffed some of them into my mouth. They were slightly sour, but I thought they would keep me going and I placed several more in my pockets.

"Yasha?"

As I returned to the hut, I heard Leo call my name. He had woken up. I was delighted to hear his voice and hurried over to him. "How are you feeling, Leo?" I asked.

"Where are we?"

"We found a shed. After the tunnel. Don't you re-member?"

"I'm very cold, Yasha."

He looked terrible. As much as I wanted to, I couldn't pretend otherwise. There was no color at all in his face and his eyes were burning, out of focus. I didn't know why he was cold. The one thing I had managed to do was to keep the hut reasonably warm and he was still tucked underneath the makeshift covers that I had put on the bed.

"Maybe you should eat something," I said.

I brought the open can of herring over, but he recoiled at the smell. "I don't want it," he said. His voice rattled in his chest. He sounded like an old man.

"All right. But you must have some tea."

I took the mug over and forced him to sip from it. As he strained his neck toward me, I noticed a red mark under his chin. Very slowly, trying not to let him know what I was doing, I folded back the covers to see what was going on. I was shocked by what I saw. The whole of Leo's neck and chest was covered by dreadful diamond-shaped sores. His skin looked as if it had been burned in a fire. I could easily imagine that his whole body was like this, and I didn't want to see any more. His face was the only part of him that had been spared. Underneath the covers he was a rotting corpse.

And at the same time, I knew that if it hadn't been for my parents, I would be exactly the same as him. They had injected me with something that protected me from the biochemical weapon that they had helped to build. They had said it acted quickly and here was the living—or perhaps the dying—proof. No wonder the authorities had been so quick to quarantine the area. If the anthrax or whatever it was had managed to do this to Leo in just a few hours, imagine what it would do to the rest of Russia as it spread.

"I'm sorry, Yasha," Leo whispered.

"There's nothing to be sorry about," I said. I was casting about, trying to find something to do. The fire, untended, had almost gone out. But there was no more wood to put in it anyway.

"I can't come with you," Leo said.

"Yes, you can. We're just going to have to wait. That's all. You'll feel better when the sun comes up."

He shook his head. He knew I was lying for his sake. "I don't mind. I'm glad you looked after me. I always liked being with you, Yasha."

He rested his head back. Despite the marks on his body, he didn't seem to be in pain. I sat beside him and after about ten minutes he began to mutter something. I leaned closer. He wasn't saying anything. He was singing. I recognized the words. "Close the door after me . . . I'm going." Everyone at school would have known the song. It was by a rock singer named Victor Tsoi and it had been the rage throughout the summer.

Perhaps Leo didn't even want to live—not without his family, not without the village. He got to the end of the line and he died. And the truth is that, apart from the silence, there wasn't a great deal of difference between Leo alive and Leo dead. He simply stopped. I closed his eyes. I drew the covers over his face. And then I began to cry. Is it shocking that I felt Leo's death even more than that of my own parents? Maybe it was because they had been snatched from me so suddenly. I hadn't even been given a chance to react. But it had taken Leo the whole of that long night to die and I was sitting with him even now, remembering everything he had been to me. I had been close to my parents but much closer to Leo. And he was so young . . . the same age as me.

In a way, I think I am writing this for Leo. I have decided to keep a record of my life because I suspect my life will be short. I do not particularly want to be remembered. After all, being unknown has been essential to my work. But I sometimes think of him and I would like him to understand what it was that made me what I am. After all, living as a boy of fourteen in a Russian village, it had never been my intention to become a contract killer.

His death may have been one step on my journey. But—believe me—it was not a major step. It did not change me in any meaningful way. That happened much later.

I set fire to the hut with Leo still inside it. I remembered the helicopters and knew that the flames might attract their attention, but it was the only way I could think of to prevent the disease from spreading. And if the soldiers were drawn here, perhaps it wasn't such a bad thing. They had their gas masks and protective suits. They would know how to decontaminate the area.

But that didn't mean I was going to hang around waiting for them to come. With the smoke billowing behind me, carrying Leo out of this world, I hurried away, along the road to Kirsk.

⊆

# КИРСК

I ENTERED KIRSK ON LEGS that were tired and feet that were sore and remembered that the last time I had been here, it had been on a school trip. Lenin had once been here. That was what we were told. The great Soviet leader had stopped briefly in the town on his way to somewhere more important because there was a problem with his train. He made a brief speech on the station platform, then went to the local café for a cup of tea and, happening to glance in the mirror, decided that his beard and mustache needed a trim. Not surprisingly, the local barber almost had a heart attack when the most powerful man in the Soviet Union walked into his shop. The cup that he drank from and the clippings of black hair were still on display in the History and Folklore Museum of Kirsk. I saw them when I was there on my school trip.

As I entered the town, on foot, I remembered the museum. It was a large reddish brown building filled with rooms that were filled with objects, and after only an hour my head was already pounding. From the outside, it looked like a railway station. Curiously, Kirsk railway station looked quite like a museum with wide stairs, pillars, and huge bronze doors that should have opened onto something more important than ticket offices, platforms, and waiting rooms. I had seen it the last time I was here, but of course I couldn't remember where it was. When you've been taken to a place in a coach and marched around shoulder to shoulder in a long line with no talking allowed, you don't really look where you're going. That hadn't been my only visit. My father had taken me to the cinema here once—a long, boring film about a girl being bullied at school. And then there had been my visit to the hospital. But all these buildings could have been on different planets. I had no idea where they were in relation to one another.

After Estrov, the place seemed enormous. I had forgotten how many buildings there were, how many shops, how many cars and buses racing up and down the wide, cobbled streets. Everywhere seemed to have electricity. There were wires zigzagging from pole to pole, crossing each other like a disastrous cat's cradle. But I'm not suggesting that Kirsk was anything special. I'd spent my whole life in a tiny village, so I was easily impressed. I didn't notice the crumbling plaster on the buildings, the empty construction sites, the pits in the road, and the dirty water running through the gutters.

It was late afternoon when I arrived and the light was already fading. My mother had said there were two trains a day to Moscow, and I hoped I was in time to catch the evening one. I had never spent a night in a hotel before, and even though I had money in my pocket, the idea of finding one and booking a room filled me with fear. How much would I have to pay? Would they even give a room to a boy on his own? I had been walking for seven hours nonstop, leaving the forest behind me just after midday. I was starving . Since leaving the shed, all I'd had to eat were the lingonberries I'd collected. I still had a handful of them in my pocket, but I couldn't eat any more because they were giving me stomach cramps. My feet were aching and soaking wet. I was wearing my leather boots, which had suddenly decided to leak. I felt filthy and wondered if they would let me onto the train. And what if they didn't? I had only one plan, to get to Moscow, and even that seemed daunting. I had seen pictures of the city at school, of course, but I had no real idea what it would be like.

Finding the station wasn't so difficult in the end. Somehow I stumbled onto the center of the town—I suppose every road led there if you walked enough. It was a wide area with an empty fountain and a Second World War monument, a slab of granite shaped like a slice of cake with the inscription WE SALUTE THE GLORIOUS DEAD OF KIRSK. I had always been brought up to respect all those who had lost their lives in the war, but I know now that there is nothing glorious about being dead. The monument was surrounded by statues of generals and soldiers, many of them on horseback. Was that how they had set off to face the German tanks?

The station was right in front of me, at the end of a wide, very straight boulevard with trees on both sides. I recognized it at once. It was surrounded by stalls selling everything from suitcases, blankets, and cushions to all sorts of food and drink. I could smell *shashlik*—skewers of meat—cooking on charcoal fires, and it made my mouth water. I was desperate to buy something, but that was when I realized I had a problem. Although I had a lot of money in my pocket, it was all in large notes. I had no coins. If I were to hand over a ten-ruble note for a snack that would cost no more than a few kopecks, I would only draw attention to myself. The stall holder would assume I was a thief. Better to wait until I was far away. And once I'd bought my train ticket, I would have change.

With these thoughts in my mind, I walked toward the main entrance of the station. I was so relieved to have gotten here and so anxious to be on my way that I was careless. I was keeping my head down, trying not to catch anyone's eye. I should have been looking all around me. In fact, if I had been sensible, I would have tried to enter the station from a completely different direction, around the side or the back. As it was, I hadn't taken more than a dozen steps before I found that my way was blocked. I looked up and saw two policemen standing in front of me, dressed in long gray coats with insignia around their collars and military caps. They were both young, in their twenties. They both had revolvers hanging from their belts.

"Where are you going?" one of them asked. He had bad skin, very raw, as if he had only started shaving recently and had used a blunt razor.

"To the station." I pointed, trying to sound casual.

"Why?"

"I work there. After school. I help clean the platform." I was making things up as I went along.

"Where have you come from?"

"Over there . . ." I pointed to one of the apartment blocks I had passed on my way into the town.

"Your name?"

"Leo Tretyakov." My poor dead friend. Why had I chosen him?

The two policemen hesitated, and for just a moment I thought they were going to let me pass. Surely there was no reason to stop me. I was just a boy, doing odd jobs after school. But then the second policeman spoke. "Your identity papers," he demanded. His eyes were cold.

I had used a false name because I was afraid the authorities would know who I was. After all, it had been my parents, Anton and Eva Gregorovich, who had escaped from the factory. But now I was trapped. The moment they looked at my passport, they would know I had lied to them. I should have been watching out for them from the start. Now that I looked around me, I realized that there were policemen everywhere. The entrance to the station was crawling with them. Obviously. The police would know what had happened at Estrov. They would have been told that two boys had escaped. They had been warned to look out for us at every station in the area . . . and I had simply walked into their arms.

"I don't have them," I stammered. I put a stupid look

on my face, as if I didn't realize how serious it was to be out without ID. "They're at home."

It might have worked. I was only fourteen and looked young for my age. But maybe the policemen had been given my description. Maybe one of the helicopter pilots had managed to take my photograph as he flew overhead. Either way, they knew. I could see it in their eyes, the way they glanced at each other. They were only in their twenties, at the start of their careers, and this was a huge moment for them. It could lead to a promotion, a pay raise, their names in the newspaper. They had just scored big-time. They had me.

"You will come with us," the first policeman said.

"But I've done nothing wrong. My mother will be worried." Why was I even bothering? Neither of them believed me.

"No arguments," the second man snapped.

I had no choice. If I argued, if I tried to run, they would grab me and call for backup. I would be bundled into a police van before I could blink. It was better, for the moment, to stick with them. At least they weren't armed. And if they were determined to bring me into the police station themselves, there might still be an opportunity for me to get away. The building could be on the other side of town. By going with them, I would at least buy myself a little time to think of a way out of this.

We walked slowly and all the time I was thinking, my eyes darting about, adding up the possibilities. There

were plenty of people around. The working day was coming to an end and they were on their way home. But they
wouldn't help me. They wouldn't want to get involved. I
glanced back at the two policemen, who were walking
about two steps behind me. What was it that I had noticed about them? They had clearly been pleased they had
caught me, no question of that—but at the same time they
were nervous. Well, that was understandable. This was a
big deal for them.

But there was something else. They were nervous for
another reason. I saw it now. They were walking very carefully, close enough to grab me if I tried to escape but not
so close that that could actually touch me. Why the distance between me and them? Why hadn't they put hand-
cuffs on me? Why were they giving me even the smallest
chance to run away? It made no sense.

Unless they knew.

That was it. It had to be.

I had supposedly been infected with a virus so deadly
that it had forced the authorities to wipe out my village. It
had killed Leo in less than twenty-four hours. The soldiers
in the forest had all been dressed in biochemical protective gear. The police in Kirsk—and in Rosna, for that matter—must have been told that I was dangerous, infected.
None of them could have guessed that my parents had
risked everything to inoculate me. They probably hadn't
been told that an antidote existed at all. There was nothing to protect the young officers who had arrested me. As

far as they were concerned, I was a walking time bomb. They wanted to bring me in. But they weren't going to come too close.

We continued walking, away from the station. A few people passed us but said nothing and looked the other way. The policemen were still hanging back and now I knew why. Although it didn't look like it, I had the upper hand. They were afraid of me! And I could use that.

Casually, I slipped my hand into my pocket. Because the two men were behind me, they didn't see the movement. I took it out and wiped my mouth. I sensed that we were drawing close to the police station. Our pace had quickened and there were police cars parked ahead.

"This way!" One of the policemen pointed. We were going to enter the station at the back, down a wide alley and across a deserted parking lot with overflowing trash cans lined up along a rusting fence. We turned off and suddenly we were on our own. It was exactly what I wanted.

I staggered slightly and let out a groan, clutching hold of my stomach. Neither of the policemen spoke. I stopped. One of them prodded me in the back. Just one finger. No contact with my skin.

"Keep moving," he commanded.

"I can't," I said. I put as much pain as I could manage into my voice.

I twisted around. At the same time, I began to cough, making horrible retching noises as if my lungs were tearing themselves apart. I sucked in, gasping for air, still holding my stomach. The policemen stared at me in horror. There was bright blood all around my lips, trickling down my chin. I coughed again and drops of blood splattered in their direction. I watched them fall back as if they had come face-to-face with a poisonous snake. And as far as they knew, my blood *was* poison. If any of it touched them, they would end up like me.

But it wasn't blood.

Just a minute ago, I had slipped some of the berries from the forest into my mouth and chewed them up. What I was spitting was red berry juice mixed with my own saliva.

"Please help me," I said. "I'm not well."

The two policemen had come to a dead halt, caught between two conflicting desires: one to hold on to me, the other to be as far away from me as possible. I was overacting like crazy, grimacing and staggering about like a drunk, but it didn't matter. Just as I'd suspected, they'd been told how dangerous I was. They knew the stakes. Their imagination was doing half the work for me.

"Everyone died," I went on. "They all died. Please . . . I don't want to be like them." I reached out imploringly. My hand was stained red. The two men stepped back. They weren't coming anywhere near. "So much pain!" I sobbed. I fell to my knees. The juice dripped onto my jacket.

The policemen made their decision. If they stayed where they were, if they tried to force me to my feet, it would kill them . . . quickly and unpleasantly. Yes, they wanted their promotion. But their lives mattered more. Maybe it occurred to them that the very fact that they had come into contact with me meant that they themselves would have to be eliminated. As far as they could see, I was dying anyway. I was lying on my side now, writhing on the ground, sobbing. My whole face was covered in blood. One of them spoke briefly to the other. I didn't hear what he said, but his colleague must have agreed, because a moment later they were gone, hurrying back the way they had come. I watched them turn a corner. I very much doubted that they would report what had just happened. After all, dereliction of duty would not be something they would wish to advertise. They would probably spend the rest of the day at the bathhouse, hoping that the steam and the hot water would wash away the disease.

I waited until I was sure they had gone, then got to my feet and wiped my face with my sleeve. At least the encounter had given me an advance warning. There was no way I was going to walk into the railway station at Kirsk. The moment I tried to buy a train ticket, there would be someone there to arrest me, and I very much doubted the same trick would work a second time. If I was going to get onto a train to Moscow, I was going to have to think of something else.

And I already had an idea.

There had been quite a few passengers arriving in taxis and coming off buses just before I had been arrested, and that suggested that the evening train might be coming soon. At the same time, I'd seen a number of porters running forward to help them with their luggage. Some of them had been boys dressed in loose-fitting blue jackets with red piping down the sleeves. I don't think they were employed officially. They were just trying to make a few kopecks on the side.

I made my way back toward the station—only this time I stayed behind the trees, close to the buildings, keeping an eye out for any policemen, mingling with the crowd. I soon found what I was looking for. One of the porters was sitting outside a café, smoking a cigarette. He was about my age even if he was trying to disguise it with the beginnings of a beard and a mustache. They were both made of that horrible wispy hair that doesn't really belong on a face. His jacket was hanging open. His cap sat crookedly on his head.

I sidled up to him and sat down next to him. After a while, he noticed me and nodded in my direction without smiling. Even so, it was enough.

"When's the next train to Moscow?" I asked.

He glanced at his watch. "Twenty minutes."

I pretended to consider this piece of information. "How would you like to make five rubles?" I asked.

His eyes narrowed. Five rubles was probably as much as he earned in a week.

"I'll be honest with you, friend," I said. "I'm in trouble with the police. I was almost arrested just now. I need to get on that train, and if you'll sell me your jacket and your cap, I'll give you the cash."

It was not such a big gamble. Somehow, I knew that this boy would be greedy. And anyway, most people in Russia would help you if you were trying to get away from the authorities. That was how we were.

"Why do the police want you?" he asked.

"I'm a thief."

He sucked lazily on his cigarette. "I will give you my jacket and my cap," he said. "But it will cost you ten rubles.

"Agreed."

I took out the money, taking care not to show him how much I had, and handed over a single note. Tonight, this porter would drink himself into a stupor. He might invite his friends to join him. He handed me his coat and his cap—but I did not go straight to the station. I stopped at one of the stalls and used another four rubles to buy a pair of secondhand suitcases from an old man who had a whole pile of them. Quickly, I took off my outer clothes and slipped them into one of the cases. I put on the jacket and cap. Then, carrying the suitcases, I made my way to the station.

It seemed now that the police were everywhere. Was it possible that the ones who had arrested me had talked after all? They had thrown a ring around the entire building. They were in front of the ticket office, on the platform. But not one of them noticed me. I waited until a smart-looking couple—some sort of local government of-

ficial and his wife—got out of a taxi and I followed them
into the station. They did not look around. But to the
police and to anyone else who glanced our way, it simply looked as if they had hired a porter and that the two
almost-empty cases I was carrying were theirs.

I had timed it perfectly. We had no sooner arrived
at the platform than a train drew in. The evening train
to Moscow. I followed my clients to their carriage and
climbed in behind them. They were completely unaware
of my presence, and although I was out there in plain
sight, nobody challenged me.

This is something that has not changed to this day.
People look at the clothes you are wearing without ever
thinking about the person who is inside. A man with his
collar turned back to front is a vicar. A woman in a white
coat with a stethoscope around her neck is a doctor. It is
as simple as that. You do not ask them for ID.

I stayed on the train, and a few minutes later it left,
very quickly picking up speed, carrying me into the darkness. I knew I would never return.

# 6

## MOCKBA

KAZANSKIY STATION. MOSCOW.

It is hard to remember my feelings as the train drew near to its final destination. On the one hand, I was elated. I had made it. I had traveled nine hundred sixty-five kilometers, leaving the police and all my other problems behind me. But what of this new world in which I was about to find myself? The train would stop. The doors would open. And what then?

Through the windows I had already seen apartment blocks, one after another, that must have been home to tens of thousands of people. How could they live like that, so many of them, piled up on top of each other? Then there were the churches with their golden domes, five times the size of poor St. Nicholas. The factories billowing smoke into a sky that was cloudless, sunless, a single sheet of gray. But all of these were dwarfed by the skyscrapers with their spires and glittering needles, thousands of windows, millions of bricks, rising up as if from some crazy dream. Of course I had been shown pictures of them at school. I knew they had been built by Stalin back in the forties and fifties. But seeing them for myself was different. Somehow I was shocked that they did actually exist and that they really were here, scattered around the city, watching over it.

I had been fortunate on the train. There was an empty compartment right at the back with a bunk bed that folded down. That was where I slept—not on the bunk but underneath it on the floor, out of sight of the ticket collectors. The strange thing was that I managed to sleep at all, but then I suppose I was exhausted. I woke up once or twice in the night and listened to the train rumbling through the darkness and I could almost feel the memories slipping away behind me . . . Estrov, Leo, my parents, my school. I knew that by the time I arrived in Moscow, I would be little more than an empty shell, a fourteen-year-old boy with no past and perhaps no future. There was even a small part of me that wished I hadn't escaped from the police. At least that way I wouldn't have to make any decisions. I wouldn't be on my own.

One name stayed with me, turning over and over in my head. Misha Dementyev. He worked in the biology department of Moscow University, and my mother had insisted that he would look after me. Surely it wouldn't be so hard to find him. The worst of my troubles might already be over. At least that was what I tried to tell myself.

The station was jammed. I had never seen so many people in one place. As I stepped down from the train, I found myself on a platform that seemed to stretch on forever with passengers milling about everywhere, carrying suitcases, packages, bundles of clothes, some of them chewing on sandwiches, others emptying their hip flasks. Everyone looked tired and grimy. There were policemen too, but I didn't think they were looking for me. I had taken off the porter's cap and jacket and abandoned the suitcases. Once again I was wearing my Young Pioneers outfit, although I thought of getting rid of that too. It was quite warm in Moscow. The air felt heavy and smelled of oil and smoke.

I allowed myself to be swept along, following the crowd through a vast ticket hall, larger than any room I had ever seen, and out into the street. I found myself standing on the edge of a square. Again, it was the size that struck me first. To my eyes, this one single space was as big as the whole of Kirsk with six lanes of traffic and cars, buses, trams roaring past in every direction. Traffic—the very notion of a traffic jam—was a new experience for me, and I was overwhelmed by the noise and the stench of the exhaust fumes. Even today it sometimes surprises me that people are willing to put up with it. The cars were every color imaginable. I had seen official Chaikas and Ladas, but it was as if these had driven here from every country in the world. Gray taxis with chessboard patterns on their hoods dodged in and out of the different lanes. There were subways built for pedestrians. It was just as well. Trying to cross on the surface would have been suicide.

There were actually three railway stations in the square, each one trying to outdo the other with soaring pillars, archways, and towers. Travelers were arriving from different parts of Russia, and as soon as they emerged, they were greeted by dozens of food stalls, mainly run by wrinkled old women in white aprons and hats. In fact, people were selling everything . . . food, vegetables, Chinese jeans and padded jackets, electrical goods, their own furniture. Some of them must have come off the train for no other reason. Nobody had any money. This was where you had to start.

My own needs were simple and immediate. I was dizzy with hunger. I headed to the nearest food stall and started with a small pie filled with cabbage and meat. I followed it with a currant bun—we called them *kalerikas* and they were specially made to fill you up. I bought a drink from a machine that squirted syrup and fizzy water into a glass. It still wasn't enough. I had another and then a raspberry ice cream that I bought for seven kopecks. The lady beamed at me as she handed it over as if she knew it was something special. I remember the taste of it to this day.

It was as I finished the last spoonful that I realized I was being watched. There was a boy of about seventeen or eighteen leaning against a lamppost, examining me. He was the same height as me but more thickly set, with muddy eyes and long, very straight, almost colorless hair. He would have been handsome but at some time his nose had been broken and it had set unevenly, giving his whole face an unnatural slant. He was wearing a leather jacket that was much too big for him, the sleeves rolled back so that they wouldn't cover his hands. Perhaps he had stolen it. Nobody was coming anywhere near him. Even the travelers seemed to avoid him. From the way he was standing there, you would think he owned the sidewalk and perhaps half the city. I quite liked that, the way he had nothing but pretended otherwise.

As I looked around, I realized that there were actually quite a lot of children outside Kazanskiy station, most of them huddling together in groups close to the entrance without daring to go inside. These children looked much less well off than the boy in the leather jacket, emaciated with pale skin and hollow eyes. Some of them were trying to beg from the arriving passengers, but they were doing it halfheartedly, as if they were nervous of being seen. I saw a couple of tiny boys who couldn't be more than ten years old, homeless and half starved. I felt ashamed. What would they have been thinking as they watched me gorge myself? I was tempted to go over and give them a few kopecks, but before I could move, the older boy suddenly walked forward and stood in front of me. There was something about his manner that unnerved me. He seemed to be smiling at some private joke. Did he know who I was, where I had come from? I got the feeling that he knew everything about me even though we had never met.

"Hello, soldier," he said. He was referring of course to my Pioneer outfit. "Where have you come from?"

"From Kirsk," I said.

"Never heard of it. Nice place?"

"It's all right."

"First time in Moscow?"

"No. I've been here before."

I had a feeling he knew straightaway, like the policemen in Kirsk, that I was lying. But he just smiled in that odd way of his. "You got somewhere to stay?"

"I have a friend . . ."

"It's good to have a friend. We all need friends." He looked around the square. "But I don't see anyone."

"He's not here."

It reminded me of my first day at senior school. I was trying to sound confident, but I was completely defenseless and he knew it. He examined me more closely, weighing up various possibilities, then suddenly he straightened up and stretched out a hand. "Relax, soldier," he said. "I don't want to give you any hassle. I'm Dimitry. You can call me Dima."

I took his hand. I couldn't really refuse it. "I'm Yasha," I said.

We shook.

"Welcome to Moscow," he said. "Welcome back, I should say. So when were you last here?"

"It was a while ago," I said. I knew that the more I spoke, the more I would give away. "It was with my parents," I added.

"But this time you're on your own."

"Yes."

The single word hung in the air.

It was hard to make out what Dima had in mind. On

the one hand he seemed friendly enough, but on the other I could sense him unraveling me. It was that broken nose of his. It made it very difficult to read his face. "This person I'm supposed to be meeting," I said. "He's a friend of my parents. He works at Moscow University. I don't suppose you know how to get there?"

"The university? It's a long way from this part of town, but it's quite easy. You can take the metro." His hand slipped over my shoulder. Before I knew it, we were walking together. "The entrance is over here. There's a direct line that runs all the way to the station. It's actually called Universitet. Do you have any money?"

"Not much," I said.

"It doesn't matter. The metro's cheap. In fact, I tell you what . . ." He reached out and a coin appeared at his fingertips as if he had plucked it out of the air. "Here's five kopecks. It's all you need. And don't worry about paying me back. Always happy to help someone new to town."

We had arrived at a staircase leading into the ground, and to my surprise he began to walk down with me. Was he going to come the whole way? His hand was still on my shoulder, and as we went he was telling me about the journey.

"Nine stops, maybe ten. Just stay on the train and you'll be there in no time . . ."

As he spoke, a set of swing doors opened in front of us and two more boys appeared, coming up the steps. They were about the same age as Dima, one dark, the other fair. I expected them to move aside—but they didn't. They barged into me and for a moment I was sandwiched between them with Dima still behind to me. I thought they were going to attack me, but they were gone as suddenly as they'd arrived.

"Watch out!" Dima shouted. He twisted around and called out after them, "Why don't you look where you're going?" He turned back to me. "That's how people are in this city. Always in a hurry and to hell with everyone else."

The boys were gone and we said no more about it. Dima took me as far as the barriers. "Good luck, soldier," he said. "I hope you find who you're looking for."

We shook hands again.

"Remember—Universitet." With a cheerful wave, he ambled away, leaving me on my own. I walked forward and stopped in front of the escalator.

I had never seen anything like it. Stairs that moved, that carried people up and down in an endless stream. They seemed to go on and on and I couldn't believe that the railway lines had been laid so deep. Cautiously, I stepped onto it and found myself clinging to the handrail, being carried down as if into the bowels of the earth. At the very bottom, there was a uniformed woman in a glass box. Her job was simply to watch the passengers, to make sure that nobody tripped over and hurt themselves. I couldn't imagine what it must be like to work here all day, buried underground, never seeing the sun.

The whole station was spectacular, with gold-colored

pillars, a mosaic floor, and dozens of glass spheres blazing with light. To the thousands of passengers who used it, it was nothing, simply a way of getting around, but I was amazed. A train came roaring out of the tunnel almost immediately. I got on and a moment later the doors slammed shut. With a jolt, the train moved off.

I took a spare seat—and it was as I sat down that I knew something was wrong. I reached back and patted my pants pocket. The pocket was empty. I had been robbed. All my money was gone apart from a few coins. I played back what had happened and realized that I had been set up from the start. Dima had seen me paying for the food. He knew I had cash. Somehow he must have signaled to the two other boys and sent them into the station through another entrance. He'd kept me talking just long enough and then he'd led me down the steps and straight into their arms. It was a professional job and one they had probably done a hundred times before. My anger was as black as the tunnel we'd plunged into. I had lost more than seventy rubles! My parents had saved that money. They had thought it would save me. But I had stupidly, blindly allowed it to be taken away from me. What a fool I was! I didn't deserve to survive.

But sitting there, being swept along beneath the city, I decided that perhaps it didn't matter too much after all. Even as the train was carrying me forward, I could put it all behind me. I was going to meet Misha Dementyev and he would look after me. I didn't actually need the money anymore. Looking back now, I would say that this was one of the first valuable lessons I learned, and one that would be useful in my future line of work. Sometimes things go wrong. It is inevitable. But it is a mistake to waste time and energy worrying about events that you cannot influence. Once they have happened, let them go.

What was I expecting the university to be like? In my mind, I had seen a single building like my school, only bigger. What I found instead, when I came out of the station, was a city within the city, an entire neighborhood devoted to learning. It was much more spacious and more elegant than what I had so far seen of Moscow. There were boulevards and parks, special buses to carry the students in and out, lawns and fountains and not one building but dozens of them, evenly spaced, each one in its own domain. It was all dominated by one of Stalin's skyscrapers, and as I stood in front of it, I saw how it had been designed to make you feel tiny, to remind you of the power and the majesty of the state. Standing in front of the steps that led to the front doors—hidden behind a row of columns—I felt like the world's worst sinner about to enter a church. But at the same time, the building had a sort of magnetic attraction. I had no idea where the biology department was. But this was the heart of the university. I would find Misha Dementyev here. I climbed the steps and went in.

The inside of the building didn't seem to fit what I had seen outside. It was like stepping into a submarine or a ship with no windows, no views. The ceilings were low.

It was too warm. Corridors led to more corridors. Doors opened onto other doors. Staircases sprouted in every direction. Students marched past me on all sides, carrying their books and their backpacks, and I forced myself to keep moving, knowing that if I stopped and looked lost it would be a sure way to get myself noticed. It seemed to me that if there were an administrative area, an office with the names of all the people working at the university, it would be somewhere close to the entrance. Surely the university wouldn't want casual visitors to plunge too far into the building or to take one of the elevators up to the fortieth or fiftieth floor? I tried a door. It was locked. The next one opened into a toilet. Next to it there was a bare room, occupied by a cleaner with a mop and a cigarette.

"What do you want?" she asked.

"The administration office."

She looked at me balefully. "The next corridor. On the left. Room 1117."

The next corridor went on for about a hundred meters, but the door marked 1117 was only halfway down. I knocked and went in.

There were two more women sitting at desks that were far too small for the typewriters, piles of paper, files, and ashtrays that covered them. One of the women was plugged into an old-fashioned telephone system, the sort with wires looping everywhere, but she looked up as I came in.

"Yes?" she demanded.

"Can you help me?" I asked. "I'm looking for some-one."

"You need the student office. That's room 1301."

"I'm not looking for a student. I need to speak to a professor. His name is Misha Dementyev."

"Room 2425—the twenty-fourth floor. Take the elevator at the end of the corridor."

I felt a surge of relief. He was here! He was in his office! At that moment, I saw the end of my journey and the start of a new life. This man had known my parents. Now he would help me.

I took the elevator to the twenty-fourth floor, sharing it with different groups of students who all looked purposefully grubby and disheveled. I had actually been in an elevator before and this old-fashioned steel box, which shuddered and stopped at least a dozen times, had none of the wonders of the escalator on the metro. Finally I found myself on the floor I wanted. I stepped out and followed a cream-colored corridor that, like the ground floor, had no windows. At least the offices were clearly labeled and I found the one I was looking for right at the corner. The door was open as I approached and I heard a man speaking on the telephone.

"Yes, of course, Mr. Sharkovsky," he was saying. "Yes, sir. Thank you, sir."

I knocked on the door.

"Come in!"

I entered a small, cluttered room with a single square window looking out over the main avenue and the steps that had first brought me into the building. There must have been five or six hundred books there, not just lined up along the shelves but stacked on the floor and every available surface. They were fighting for space with a whole range of laboratory equipment, different sized flasks, two microscopes, scales, Bunsen burners, and boxes that looked like miniature ovens or fridges. Most unnerving of all, a complete human skeleton stood in a frame in one corner as if it were here to guard all this paraphernalia while its owner was away.

There was a man sitting at his desk. He had just put down the phone as I came in. My first impression was that he was about the same age as my father, with thick black hair that only emphasized the round bald patch in the middle of his head. The skin there was stretched tight and polished, reflecting the ceiling light. He had a heavy beard and mustache, and as he examined me from behind a pair of glasses, I saw small, nervous eyes blinking at me as if he had never seen a boy before—or had certainly never allowed one into his office.

Actually, I was wrong about this. He was nervous because he knew who I was. He spoke my name immediately. "Yasha?"

"Are you Mr. Dementyev?" I asked.

"Professor Dementyev," he replied. "Please, come in. Close the door. Does anyone know you're here?"

"I asked in the administration room downstairs," I said.

"You spoke to Anna?" I had no idea what the woman

had been named. He didn't let me reply. "That's a great pity. It would have been much better if you had telephoned me before you came here. How *did* you get here?"

"I came by train. My parents . . ."

"I know what has happened in Estrov." He was agitated. Suddenly there were beads of sweat on the crown of his head. I could see them glistening. "You cannot stay here, Yasha," he said. "It's too dangerous."

I couldn't believe what I was hearing. "My parents said you'd look after me!"

"And I will! Of course I will!" He tried to smile at me, but he was full of nervous energy and he was allowing his different thought processes to tumble over each other. "Sit down, Yasha, please." He pointed to a chair. "I'm sorry, but you've taken me completely by surprise. Are you hungry? Are you thirsty? Can I get you something?" Before I could answer, he snatched up the telephone again. "There's somebody I know," he explained to me. "He's a friend. He can help you. I'm going to ask him to come."

He dialed a number, and as I sat down facing him, uncomfortably close to the skeleton, he spoke quickly into the receiver.

"It's Dementyev. The boy is here. Yes . . . here at the university." He paused while the person at the other end spoke to him. "We haven't had a chance to speak yet. I thought I should let you know at once." He was answering a question I hadn't heard. "He seems all right. Unharmed, yes. We'll wait for you here."

He put the phone down and it seemed to me that he was suddenly less agitated than he had been when I'd arrived—as if he had done what was expected of him. For some reason I was feeling uneasy. From the look of it, Professor Dementyev wasn't pleased to see me. I was a danger to him. This was my parents' closest friend, but I was beginning to wonder how much that friendship was worth.

"How did you know who I was?" I asked.

"I've been expecting you ever since I heard about what happened. And I recognized you, Yasha. You look very much like your mother. I saw the two of you together a few times when you were very young. You won't remember me. It was before your parents left Moscow."

"Why did they leave? What happened? You worked with them."

"I worked with your father. Yes."

"Do you know that he's dead?"

"I didn't know for certain. I'm sorry to hear it. He and I were friends."

"So tell me . . ."

"Are you sure I can't get you something?"

I had eaten and drunk everything I wanted at Kazanskiy station. Really what I wanted was to be away from here. I have to say that I was disappointed by Misha Dementyev. I'm not sure what I'd been expecting, but maybe he could have been more affectionate, more like a long-lost uncle or something? He hadn't even come out from behind his desk.

"What happened?" I asked again. "Why was my father sent to work in Estrov?"

"I can't go through all that now." He was flustered again. "Later—"

"Please, Professor Dementyev!"

"All right. All right." He looked at me as if he was wondering if he could trust me. Then he began. "Your father was a genius," he began. "He and I worked here together in this department. We were young students, idealists, excited. We were researching endospores . . . and one in particular. Anthrax. I don't suppose you know very much about that."

"I know about anthrax," I said.

"We thought we could change the world . . . your father in particular. He was looking at ways to prevent the infection of sheep and cattle. But there was an accident. Working in the laboratory together, we created a form of anthrax that was much faster and deadlier than anything anyone had ever known. It had no cure. Antibiotics were useless against it."

"It was a weapon."

"That wasn't our intention. That wasn't what we wanted. But—yes. It was the perfect biological weapon. And of course the government found out about it. Everything that happens in this place they know about. It was true then. It's true now. They heard about our work here and they came to us and ordered us to develop it for military use." Dementyev took out a handkerchief and used it to polish the lenses of his glasses. He put them back on. "Your father refused. It was the last thing he wanted. So they started to put the pressure on. They threatened him. And that was when he did something incredibly brave . . . or incredibly stupid. He went to a journalist and tried to get the story into the newspapers.

"Of course, he was arrested at once. I was here, in the laboratory, when they marched him away. They arrested your mother too."

"How old was I?" I asked.

"You were two. And—I'm sorry, Yasha—they used you to get at your parents. That was how they worked. It was very simple. If your parents didn't do what they were told, they would never see you again. What choice did they have? They were sent to Estrov to work in the factory. They were forced to produce the new anthrax. That was the deal. Stay silent. And live."

So everything—my parents' life or non-life in that remote village, the little house, the boredom, and the poverty—had been for me. I wasn't sure how that made me feel. Was I to blame for everything that had happened? Was I the one who had destroyed their lives?

"Yasha . . ." Dementyev stood up and came over to me. He was much taller than I had expected now that he was on his feet. He loomed over me. "Were you inoculated?" he asked.

I nodded. "My parents were killed when they escaped. But they stole a syringe. They injected me."

"I knew your father had been working on an antidote. Thank God! But I guessed it the moment I saw you. Otherwise you would have been dead a long time ago."

"My best friend died," I said.

"I'm so sorry. Anton and Eva—your parents—were my friends too."

We fell silent. He was still standing there, one hand on the back of my chair.

"What will happen to me?" I asked.

"You don't need to worry anymore, Yasha. You'll be well looked after."

"Who was that you called?"

"It was a friend. Someone we can trust. He'll be here very soon."

There was something wrong. Things that he'd told me just didn't add up. I was about to speak when I heard the sound of sirens, police cars approaching, still far away but drawing nearer. And I knew instantly that there was no friend, that Dementyev had called them. It wasn't detective work. I could have asked him why my parents had been sent to live in Estrov while he had been allowed to stay here. I could have played back the conversation he'd had on the telephone, how he had referred to me simply as "the boy." Not "Yasha." Not "Anton's son." The people at the other end knew who I was because they'd been expecting me to show up, waiting for me. I could have worked it out, but I didn't need to. I saw it all in his eyes.

"Why?" I asked.

He didn't even try to deny it. "I'm sorry, Yasha," he said. "But nobody can know. We have to keep it secret."

We. The factory managers. The helicopter pilots. The militia. The government. And Dementyev. They were all in it together.

I scrabbled to my feet—or tried to. But Dementyev was ahead of me. He pounced down, his hands on my shoulders, using his weight to pin me to the seat. For a moment his face was close to mine, the eyes staring at me through the thick lenses.

"There's nowhere you can go!" he hissed. "I promise you . . . they won't treat you badly."

"They'll kill me!" I shouted back. "They killed every-one!"

"I'll talk to them. They'll take you somewhere safe."

Yes. I saw it already. A prison or a mental asylum, somewhere I'd never be seen again.

I couldn't move. He was too strong for me. And the police cars were getting closer. We were twenty-four floors up, but I could hear the sirens cutting through the air. And then I had an idea. I forced myself to relax.

"You can't do this!" I exclaimed. "My father gave me something for you. He said it was very valuable. He said if I gave it to you, you'd have to help me."

"What is it?"

"I don't know. It's in a bag. It's in my pocket!"

"Show me."

He let go of one of my shoulders . . . but only one

of them. I still couldn't wrench myself free. I was sitting down. He was standing over me and he was twice my size.

"Take it out," he said.

The police had turned into the main university drive. If I had looked out the window, I would have been able to see them. I heard car doors slam shut.

Using my one free arm, I drew out the black bag that my mother had given me. At least Dima and his friends hadn't stolen it when they took my money. I placed it on the desk. And it worked just as I'd hoped. Dementyev still didn't let go of me, but his grip loosened as he reached out and opened the bag. I saw his face change as he tipped out the contents.

"What—" he began.

I jerked myself free, throwing the chair backward. As it toppled over, I managed to get to my feet. Dementyev swung around but he was too late to stop me from lashing out with my fist. I knocked the glasses off his face. He fell back against the desk but still he didn't release me. I needed a weapon and there was only one that I could see. I reached out and grabbed the arm of the skeleton, wrenching it free from the shoulder. The hand and the wrist dangled down, but I hung on to the upper bone, the humerus, and used it as a club, smashing it against Dementyev's head again and again until, with a howl, he fell back. I twisted away. Dementyev had crumpled over the desk. There was blood streaming down his face.

"It's too late," he snarled. "You won't get away."

I snatched back the jewelry and tumbled out of the office. There was nobody outside. Surely someone must have heard what had happened? I didn't want to know. I ran to the elevator. It was already on the way up and it took me a few seconds to work out that the police were almost certainly inside, traveling toward me. And I might have been caught standing there, waiting for them! I continued down the corridor and found a fire exit—twenty-four flights of stairs. I didn't stop until I reached the bottom, and it was only then that I realized I was still carrying the skeleton's arm. I found a trash can, pulled out some loose papers, and dropped the arm in.

As I walked down the steps at the front door, I saw three police cars parked there with their lights flashing. I pretended to be immersed in the papers I had taken. If there were any policemen outside, I would look like just one more of the dozens of students coming in and out.

But nobody stopped me. I hurried back to the station with just one thought in my head: I was alone in Moscow. My money had been stolen and I had nowhere to go.

# 7

# ТВЕРСКАЯ

I WENT BACK TO Kazanskiy station.

In a way, it was a mad decision. The police knew I was in Moscow and they would certainly be watching all the major stations—just as they had in Rosna and Kirsk. But I had no intention of leaving. The truth was that in the whole of Russia I had nowhere to go and no one to look after me. I couldn't go back to Estrov, obviously, and although I remembered my mother once telling me that she had relations in a city called Kazan, I had no idea where it was or how to get there.

No, it was much better to stay in Moscow, but first of all I would need to change my appearance. That was easy enough. I stripped off my Pioneer uniform and dumped it in a trash can. Then I got my hair cut short. Although the bulk of my money was gone, I had managed to find eighteen kopecks scattered through my pockets and I used nine of them at a barber's shop, a dank little place close to Universitet station with old hair strewn over the floor. As I stepped out again, feeling the unfamiliar cool of the breeze on my head and the back of my neck, a police car rushed past—but I wasn't worried. Even today, I am aware of how little you need to change to lose yourself in a city. A hair cut, different clothes, perhaps a pair of sunglasses . . . it is enough.

I still had enough kopecks for the return journey, and as I sat once again in the metro, I tried to work out some sort of plan. The most immediate problem was accommodation. Where would I sleep when night came? If I stayed out on the street, I would be at my most vulnerable. And then there was the question of food. Without money, I couldn't eat. Of course, I could steal, but the one thing I most dreaded was falling back into the hands of the police. If they recognized me, I was finished. And even if they didn't, I had heard enough stories about the prison camps all over Russia, built specially for children. Did I want to end up with the rest of my hair shaved off, stuck behind barbed wire in the middle of nowhere? There were thousands of Russian boys whose life was exactly that.

This time I barely even noticed the stations, no matter how superbly they were decorated. I was utterly miserable. My parents had believed in Misha Dementyev and they had sent me to him even though it had cost them their lives. But from the moment I had walked into his office, he had thought only of saving his own skin. It seemed to me that there was nobody in the world I could trust. Even Dima, the boy I had met when I got off the train, had only been interested in robbing me.

But perhaps Dima was the answer.

The more I thought about it, the more I decided he might not be all bad. Certainly, when we had met, he had been pleasant enough, smiling and friendly, even if he was simply setting me up for his friends. But maybe I was partly to blame for what had happened, coming off the train and flashing my money around all the different stalls. Dima was living on the street. He had to survive. I'd made myself an obvious target and he'd done what he had to.

At the same time, I remembered what he'd said to me. *It's good to have a friend. We all need friends.* Could it be possible that he actually meant it? He was, after all, only a few years older than me and we were both in the same situation. Part of me knew that I was fooling myself. Dima was probably kilometers away by now, laughing at me for being such a fool. But the truth was that he was the only person in the city I actually knew. If I could find him again, perhaps I could persuade him to help me.

And there was something else. I still had my mother's jewels.

Half an hour later, I climbed up to street level and found myself back where I had begun. The women were still there at their food stalls, but they almost seemed to be taunting me. Before, they had been my friends. Now, all their pies and ice creams were beyond my reach. I found a bench and sat down, watching the crowds around me. Stations are strange places. When you pass through them, traveling somewhere, you barely notice them. They simply help you on your way. But stand outside with nowhere to go and they make you feel worthless. You should not be here, they shout at you. If you are not a passenger, you do not belong here.

To start with, I did nothing at all. I just sat there,

staring at the traffic, letting people stream past me on all sides. The children I had seen were still dotted around and I wondered what they would do with themselves when night fell. That could be only a few hours away. The light was barely changing, the sun trapped behind unbroken cloud, but there were already commuters arriving at the station, on their way home, and I could feel the darkness pressing in. There was no sign of Dima. In the end, I went over to a couple of boys, the ten-year-olds that I had seen before.

"Excuse me," I said.

Two pairs of very sly and malevolent eyes turned on me. One of the children had snot running out of his nose. Both of them looked worn out, unhealthy.

"I'm looking for someone I was talking to earlier," I went on. "He was wearing a black leather jacket. His name is Dima."

The boys glanced at each other. "You got any money?" one of them asked.

"No."

"Then get lost!" Those weren't the words he used. This little boy, whose voice hadn't even broken, used the filthiest language I'd ever heard. I saw that he had terrible teeth with gaps where half of them had fallen out. His friend hissed at me like an animal and at that moment the two of them weren't children at all. They were like horrible old men, not even human. I was glad to leave them on their own.

I tried to ask some of the other street kids the same question, but as I approached them, they moved away. It was as if they all knew that I was from out of town, that I wasn't one of them, and for that reason they would have nothing to do with me. And now the sun really was beginning to disappear. The light was hardening. I was beginning to feel the threat of nightfall and knew that I couldn't stay here very much longer. I would have to find a doorway—or perhaps I could sleep in one of the crossings beneath the streets. I had four kopecks left in my pocket. Barely enough for a cup of hot tea.

And then, quite unexpectedly, I saw him. Dima— with his oversized leather jacket and his half-handsome, half-ugly face—had turned the corner, smoking a cigarette, flicking away the match. There was another boy with him and I recognized him too. He had been one of the two who had robbed me. Dima said something and they laughed. It looked as if they were heading for the metro, presumably on their way home.

I didn't hesitate. It was now or never. I crossed the concourse in front of the station and stood in their path.

Dima saw me first and stopped with the cigarette halfway to his lips. I had taken him by surprise and he thought I was going to make trouble. I could see it at once. He was tense, wary. But I was completely relaxed. I'd already worked it out. He'd tricked me. He'd robbed me. But I had to treat him as my friend.

"Hi, Dima." I greeted him as if the three of us had arranged to meet here for coffee.

He smiled a little but he was still suspicious. And there was something else. I wasn't quite sure what it was, but he was looking at me almost as if he had expected me to come back, as if there was something he knew that I didn't. "Soldier!" he exclaimed. "How are you doing? What happened to your hair?"

"I got it cut."

"Did you meet your friend?"

"No. He wasn't there. It seems he's left Moscow."

"That's too bad."

I nodded. "In fact, I've got a real problem. He was going to put me up, but now I don't have anywhere to go."

I was hoping he might offer to help. That was the idea, anyway. Why not? He was seventy rubles richer than me. Thanks to him, I had nothing. He could at least have offered me a bed for the night. But he didn't speak and I realized I was wasting my time. He was street hardened, the sort of person who had never helped anyone in his life. His friend muttered something and pushed past me, disappearing into the metro, but I stood my ground. "Can you help me?" I said. "I just need somewhere to stay for a few nights." And then—my last chance. "I can pay you."

"You've got money?" That surprised him. He thought he'd taken it all already.

"Not anymore," I said. I shrugged as if it didn't matter and I'd already forgotten about it. "But I've got this," I went on. I took out the black velvet bag that my parents had given me and which I'd used to trick Dementyev. I opened it and poured the contents—the necklace, the ring, and the earrings—into my hand. "There must be a pawnshop somewhere. I'll sell them and then I can pay you for a room."

Dima examined the jewelry, the brightly colored stones in their silver and gold settings, and I could already see the light stirring in his eyes as he made the calculations. How much were they worth and how was he going to separate them from me? He dropped his cigarette and reached out, picking up one of the earrings. He let it hang from his finger and thumb. "This won't get you much," he said. "It's cheap."

Right then, I thought of my mother and I could feel the anger rising in my blood. I wanted to punch him, but still I forced myself to stay calm. "I was told they were valuable," I said. "That's gold. And those stones are emeralds. Take me to a pawnshop and we can find out."

"I don't know . . ." He was pretending otherwise, but he knew that the jewels were worth as much as he had already stolen. "Give me the stuff and I'll take it to a pawnbroker for you. But I don't think you'll get more than five rubles."

He'd get fifty. I'd get five . . . if I was lucky. I could see how his mind worked. I held out my hand and, reluctantly, he gave me the earring back. "I can find a pawnbroker on my own," I said.

"There's no need to be like that, soldier! I'm only trying to help." He gave me a crooked smile, made all the more crooked by his broken nose. "Listen. I've got a room and you're welcome to stay with me if you like. You know . . . we're all friends here in Moscow, right? But you'll have to pay rent."

"How much rent?"

"Two rubles a week."

I pretended to consider. "I'll have to see it first."

"Whatever you say. We can go there now, if you like."

"Sure. Why not?"

He took me back down onto the metro. He even paid the fare for me again. I knew I was taking a risk. He could lead me to some faraway corner of the city, take me into an alleyway, put a knife into me, and steal the jewels. But I had a feeling that wasn't the way he worked. Dima was a hustler, a thief—but he just didn't have the look of someone who was ready to kill. He would get the jewelry in the end anyway. I would pay it to him as rent or he would steal it from me while I slept. My plan was simply to make myself useful to him, to become part of his gang. If I could do this quickly enough, he might let me stay with him even when I had nothing more to give. That was my hope.

He took me to a place just off Tverskaya Street, one of the main thoroughfares in Moscow, which leads all the way down to the Kremlin and Red Square. Today, there is a hotel on that same corner—the seven-story Marriott Grand, where American tourists stay in total luxury. But when I came there, following Dima and still wondering if I wasn't making another bad mistake, it was very different. Moscow has changed so much, so quickly. It was another world then.

Dima lived in what had once been a block of apartments but which had long been abandoned and left to rot. All the color had faded out of the brickwork, which was damp, moldy, and covered with graffiti—not artwork but political slogans, swearwords, the names of city football teams. The windows were so dirty that they looked more like rusting metal than glass. The building rose up ten stories, three more than the hotel that would one day replace it, and the whole thing seemed to be sagging in on itself, hardly bothering to stay upright. It was surrounded by other blocks that were similar; they were all like old men standing out in the cold, having a last cigarette together before they died. The streets here were so narrow that they were more like alleyways, twisting together in the darkness, covered with rubbish and mud. There were shops on the ground floor—an empty grocery store, a pharmacy, and a massage parlor—but the farther up you went, the more desolate it became. There were no elevators, of course. Just a concrete staircase that had been used as a toilet so many times that it stank. By the time you got to the top, there was no electricity, no proper heating. The only water came dribbling, cold, out of the taps.

We climbed up together. I noticed that Dima was wheezing by the time we got to the top and I wondered if he was ill—although it could just have been all those cigarettes. On the way, we passed a couple of people, a man and a woman, lying one on top of the other, unconscious. I couldn't even be sure they were actually alive. Dima just stepped over them and I did the same, wondering what I was getting myself into. My village had been a place full of poverty and hardship, but it was somehow more shocking here, in the middle of a city.

Dima's room was on the eighth floor. There was no lighting. He had taken out a flashlight and used it to find the way. We went down a corridor that was missing its carpet, with gaping holes showing the pipework and wiring. There were doors on either side, most of them locked, some of them reinforced with metal plating. Somewhere, I could hear a baby crying. A man shouted out a swearword. Somebody laughed. The sounds that echoed around me only added to the nightmare, the sense that I was being sucked into a dark and alien world.

"This is me," Dima said.

We'd come to a door marked with a number—83. Somebody had added DIMA'S PLACE in bright red letters that hadn't dried properly. They had trickled down like blood. Perhaps the effect was deliberate. There was a hole where the lock should have been, but Dima used a padlock and a chain to keep the place secure. At the moment, it was hanging open. His friends had arrived ahead of us.

"Welcome home!" he said to me. "This is my place. Come in and meet my mates . . ."

He pushed the door open. We went in.

The apartment was tiny. Most of it was contained in a single room, which he shared with the two boys who had robbed me. They slept on the floor. There were three mattresses and some filthy pillows on top of a carpet that was moldy and colorless. The place was lit by candles and my first thought was that if one of them toppled over in the night, we would all burn to death. A single table and four chairs stood on one side. Otherwise there was no furniture of any description. A few bits of the kitchen were still in place, but I could tell at a glance that the sink hadn't been used for years—there was no water—and without electricity the fridge was no more than a oversized cupboard. The smell in the room was unpleasant, a mixture of human sweat, unwashed clothes, dirt, and decay.

Dima waved me over to the table. "This is Yasha," he announced. "He's going to be staying with us for a while." His two friends were already sitting there playing Snap with a deck that was so worn that the cards hung limp in their hands. They didn't look pleased as I joined them. "He's going to pay," Dima added. "Two rubles a week."

He opened the fridge and took out a bottle of vodka and some black bread. He found some dirty glasses in the sink and poured drinks for us all. He lit a cigarette for himself, then offered me one, which I accepted gratefully. It wasn't that I wanted to smoke. It was a gesture of friendship and a way of fitting in. I needed them to trust me.

Dima introduced his friends. "This is Roman. That's Grigory." Roman was tall and thin. He looked as if he had been deliberately stretched. Grigory was round faced, pockmarked, with oily black hair. All three of them looked not just adult but old, as if they had forgotten their true age . . . which was about seventeen. Roman collected the cards and put them away. It was obvious who was the leader here. So long as Dima said I could stay, they weren't going to argue.

"Tell us about yourself, soldier," Dima said. "I'd like to know what brought you to Moscow." He winked at me. "And I'd particularly like to know why the police are so interested in you."

"What?"

So that was the difference I had noticed at the station. The police had been there, looking for me.

"That's right. Tell him, Grig." Grigory said nothing, so Dima went on. "They're looking for someone new to town. Someone who might have come into Kazanskiy station, dressed up like a Young Pioneer. They've been asking everyone." He tapped ash. "They're offering a reward for information."

My heart sank. I wondered if I had walked into another trap. Had Dima invited me here to have me arrested? But there was no sound coming from outside, no footsteps in the corridor, no sirens in the street.

"Don't worry, soldier! No one's going to turn you in. Not even for the money. They never pay up anyway."

"I hate the p . . . p . . . p . . . police." Roman had a stutter. I watched his face contort as he tried to spit out the last word.

"What do they want with you?" Grigory asked. He sounded hostile. Maybe he was afraid that I was bringing more trouble into his life. He probably had enough already.

I wasn't sure how to answer. I didn't want to lie, but I

was afraid of telling the truth. In the end, I kept it as short as I could. "They killed my parents," I said. "My dad knew something he wasn't meant to know. They wanted to kill me too. I escaped."

"What about your friend at the university?" Dima asked.

"He wasn't my friend." I was on safer ground here. I told them everything that had happened in Misha Dementyev's office. When I described how I had beaten Dementyev off using the arm of the skeleton, Dima laughed out loud. "I wish I'd seen that," he said. "You certainly gave him the elbow!"

It was a weak joke, but we all laughed. Dima refilled our glasses and once again we drank the Russian way, throwing the liquid back in a single gulp. It didn't take us long to finish the bottle and about an hour later we all went to bed . . . if you can call a square of carpet with a pile of old clothes as a pillow a bed. I was just glad to have a roof over my head, and helped by the vodka, I was asleep almost at once.

The next morning, Dima took me to the pawnbroker he had mentioned. It was a tiny shop with a cracked front window and an old, half-shaven man sitting behind a counter that was stacked with watches and jewelry. I handed across my mother's earrings and stood there, watching him examine them briefly through an eyeglass that he screwed into his face as if it were part of him. Right then, a little part of me died. It had been a pawnbroker that the hero had murdered in *Crime and Punishment*. I could almost have done the same.

He wanted to give me nine rubles for the earrings, but Dima talked him up to fifteen. The two of them knew each other well.

"You're a crook, Reznik." Dima scowled.

"And you're a thief, Dima," Reznik replied.

"One day someone will stick a knife in you."

"I don't mind. So long as they buy it from me first."

Dima took the money and we went back out into the sunlight. He gave me three rubles, keeping six for himself, and when I looked down reproachfully at the crumpled notes, he clapped me on the back. "That's three weeks' rent, soldier," he said.

"What about the other three rubles?"

"That's my commission. If you hadn't had me with you, that old crook would have ripped you off."

I'd been ripped off anyway, but I didn't complain. Dima had said I could stay with him for three weeks. It was exactly what I wanted to hear.

"Let's get some breakfast!" he said.

We ate breakfast in the smallest, grimiest restaurant it would be possible to imagine. Somehow, I ended up paying for that too.

So began my stay in Moscow. I adapted very quickly to the way of life. The truth is that nobody did anything very much. They stole, they ate, they survived. I spent long hours outside the station with Dima, Roman, and Grigory. The two boys didn't warm to me very much, but gradually they began to accept that I was there. At the same time, Dima had made me his special project. I wondered if he might have had a younger brother at some time. He never spoke about his past life, but that was how he treated me. When I write about him now, I still see him with the sleeves of his precious leather jacket falling over his hands, his smile, the way he swaggered along the street, and I wonder if he is alive or dead. Dead most probably. Homeless kids in Moscow never survive long.

Dima taught me how to beg. You had to be careful because if the police saw you, they would pick you up and throw you into jail. But my fair hair, and the fact that I looked so young, helped. If I stood outside the Bolshoi Ballet at night, I could earn as much as five rubles from the rich people coming out. There were tourists in Red Square and I would position myself outside St. Basil's Cathedral with its towers and twisting, multicolored domes. I didn't even have to speak. Once, an American gave me five dollars, which I passed on to Dima. He gave me fifty kopecks back, but that was his own special exchange rate. In truth, it was worth a lot more.

I got used to the city. Streets that had seemed huge and threatening became familiar. I could find my way around on the metro. I visited Lenin, lying dead in his tomb, although Dima told me that most of the body was made of wax. I also saw the grave of Yuri Gagarin, the first man in space. Not that he meant anything to me now. I went to the big stores—GUM and Yeliseev's Food Hall—and stared at all the amazing food I would never be able to afford. Just once, I visited a bathhouse near the Bolshoi and enjoyed the total luxury of sitting in the steam, breathing in the scent of eucalyptus leaves, and feeling warm and clean.

And I stole.

We needed to buy food, cigarettes, and—most important—vodka. It sometimes seemed that it was impossible to live in Tverskaya without alcohol, and every night there were terrible arguments when somebody's bottle was finished. We would hear the screams and the knife fights, and the next day there would often be fresh blood on the stairs. Those who couldn't afford vodka got high on the fumes of shoe polish.

No matter how much time I spent begging, we never had enough money, and I wasn't surprised to find myself back at Reznik, the pawnbroker. With Dima's help, I got fifteen rubles for my mother's necklace, more than the earrings but less than I'd hoped. I was determined not to part with her ring. It was the only memory of her that I had left.

And so, inevitably, I turned to crime. One of Dima's favorite tricks was to hang around outside an expensive shop, watching as the customers came out with their groceries. He would wait while they loaded up their car, then either Roman or Grigory would distract them while he snatched as much as he could out of the trunk and ran for it. I watched the operation a couple of times before Dima let me play the part of the decoy. Because I was so much younger than the other two boys, people were more sympathetic—and less suspicious. I would go up to them and pretend to be lost while Dima sneaked up to the back of their car.

The first three times, it worked perfectly and we found ourselves eating all sorts of things that we'd never tasted before. Roman and Grigory were getting used to me now. We'd begun playing cards together—a game that every Russian knows called *Durak,* or Fool. They'd even found a mattress for me. It wasn't a lot softer than the floor and it was infested with insects, but I still appreciated the gesture.

The fourth time, however, was almost a disaster. And it changed everything.

It was the usual setup. We were outside a shop on a quiet street. It was an area we hadn't been to before. Our target was a chauffeur, obviously working for some big businessman who could afford to entertain. His car was a Daimler and there was enough food in the back to keep us going for a month. As usual, I went up to the man and, looking as innocent as possible, tried to engage him in conversation.

"Can you help me? I'm looking for Pushkin Square."

Out of the corner of my eye, I saw Dima scurry up the sidewalk and disappear behind the raised hood of the trunk.

The chauffeur glared at me. "Get lost!"

"I am lost! I need to get to Pushkin Square . . ."

All I had to do was keep up the conversation for about thirty seconds. By the end of that time, Dima would have gone and two or three bags would have gone with him. But suddenly I heard him cry out and I saw, with complete horror, that a policeman had appeared out of nowhere. To this day I don't know where he had come from because we always checked the immediate area first, but I can only assume that he'd been expecting us, that the police must have decided to crack down on this sort of street theft, and that he had been lying in wait all along. He was a huge man with the neck and the shoulders of a professional weight lifter. Dima was squirming in his jacket like a fish caught in a net.

I saw the chauffeur making a grab for me, but I ducked under his arms and ran around the back of the car. There was nothing I could do for Dima. The only sensible thing was to run away and leave him and just be grateful I'd had a lucky escape. But I couldn't do it. Despite everything, I was grateful to him. I had been with him for six weeks now and he had protected me. I couldn't have survived without him. I owed him something.

I threw myself at the policeman, who reacted in astonishment. I was honestly less than half his size and I barely even knocked him off balance. He didn't let go of Dima—if anything, he tightened his grip, bellowing at the chauffeur to come and join in. Dima lashed out with a fist but the policeman didn't feel it. With his spare hand, he grabbed hold of my shirt so that we were both held captive, and seeing us unarmed and helpless, the chauffeur lumbered forward to help.

We would certainly have been taken prisoner and that would have been the end of my Moscow adventure. Indeed, if I was recognized, it might be the end of my life. But as I struggled, I saw that one of the shopping bags had fallen over, spilling out its contents. There was a plastic bag of red powder on the top. I snatched it up, split it open, and hurled it into the policeman's face, all in a single movement.

It was chili powder. The policeman was instantly blinded and howled in pain, both hands rushing to his face, covering his eyes. Dima was forgotten. In fact everything was forgotten. The policeman's head was covered in red powder. He was spinning around on his feet. I grabbed Dima and the two of us began to run. At the same moment, a police car appeared at the far end of the street, speeding toward us, its lights blazing. We ran across the pavement and down a narrow alleyway between two shops. It was a cul-de-sac, blocked at the far end by a wall. We didn't let it stop us, not for a second. We simply sprinted up the brickwork and over the top, crashing down onto an assortment of trash cans and cardboard boxes on the other side. Dima rolled over, then got back to his feet. We could hear the siren behind us and knew that the police were only seconds away. We kept running—down another alleyway and across a main road with six lanes of traffic and cars, trucks, motorbikes, and buses bearing down on us from every direction. It's a miracle we weren't killed. As it was, one car swerved out of our way and there was a screech and a crumpling of metal as a second car crashed into it. We didn't stop. We didn't look back. In fact we must have run three-quarters of a kilometer across Moscow, ducking into side roads, chasing behind buildings, doing everything we could to keep out of sight. Eventually we came to a metro entrance and dived into it, disappearing underground. There was a train waiting at the platform. We didn't care where it was going. We dived in and sank, exhausted, into two seats.

We didn't speak again until we got back to our own station and climbed back to our familiar streets. We didn't go to the apartment straightaway. Dima took me to a coffee house and we bought a couple of glasses of *kvass,* a sweet, watery drink that was actually made out of bread.

We sat next to the window. We were both still out of breath. I could hear Dima's lungs rattling. Climbing the stairs was enough exercise for him and he had just run a marathon.

"Thank you, soldier," he said eventually.

"We were unlucky," I said.

"I was lucky you were there. You could have just left me."

I didn't say anything.

"I hate this stupid city," Dima said. "I never wanted to come here."

"Why did you?"

"I don't know." He shrugged, then pointed to his broken nose. "My dad did this to me when I was six years old. He never wanted me. He threw me out when I was seven. I ended up in an orphanage in Yaroslav, and that was a horrible place . . . horrible. You don't want to know." He took out a cigarette and lit it. "They used to tie the kids down to the beds, the troublemakers. They left them there until they were covered in their own dirt. And the noise! The screaming, the crying . . . It never stopped. I think half of them were mad."

"Were you adopted?" I asked.

"Nobody wanted me. Not the way I looked. I ran away. Got out of Yaroslav and ended up on a train to Moscow . . . just like you."

He fell silent.

"There's something I want you to know," he said. "That first day we met, at Kazanskiy station." He took a drag on his cigarette and exhaled blue smoke. "We took your money. It was Roman, Grig, and me. We set you up."

"I knew," I said.

He looked at me. "I thought you must have. But now I'm admitting it . . . okay?"

"It doesn't matter," I went on. "I'd have done the same."

"I don't think so, soldier. You're not the same as us."

"I like being with you," I said. "But there's something I want to ask."

"Go ahead."

"Do you mind not calling me 'soldier'?"

He nodded. "Whatever you say, Yasha."

He patted me on the shoulder. We finished our drinks, stood up, and went home. And it seemed to me that I'd actually done what I'd set out to do. The two of us were friends.

# ФОРТОЧНИК

FOR THE NEXT FEW days, we barely left the apartment. Dima was worried the police would be looking for us and I also had my concerns. Forget Estrov. I was now wanted for theft and assaulting a police officer. It was better for us not to show our faces in the street and so we ate, we drank, we played cards . . . and we were bored. We were also running out of cash. I never asked Dima what he had done with the rubles he had taken from me, and it wasn't as if we were spending a lot of money, but somehow there was never enough for our basic needs. Roman and Grigory brought in a few rubles now and then, but the truth is that they were too unattractive to have much success begging and Roman's stutter made it hard for him to ask for money.

Even so, it was Roman who suggested it one night. "We should try b . . . b . . . b . . . burglary."

We were sitting around the table with vodka and cards. All we had eaten that day was a couple of slices of black bread. All four of us were looking ill. We needed proper food and sunlight. I had gotten used to the smell in the room by now—in fact I was part of it. But the place was looking grimier than ever and we all longed to be out.

"Who are we going to b . . . b . . . burgle?" Dima asked.

Roman shrugged.

"It's a good idea," Grigory said. He slapped down an attack card—we were having another bout of *Durak*. "Yasha is small enough. He could be our *fortochnik*."

"What's a *fortochnik*?" I asked.

Dima rolled his eyes. "It's someone who breaks in through a *fortochka*," he explained.

That, at least, I understood. A *fortochka* was a type of window. Many apartments in Moscow had them before air-conditioning took over. There would be a large window and then a much smaller one, set inside it, a bit like a cat flap. Even in the last months of autumn, people would open the *fortochkas* to let in the breeze, which of course was an invitation for thieves . . . provided they were small enough. Grigory was right. He was too fat and Roman was too ungainly to crawl through, but I could make it easily. I'd always been small for my age—and I'd lost even more weight in the past few weeks.

"It's a good idea," Dima agreed. "But we need an address. There's no point just breaking in anywhere, and anyway, it's too dangerous." His eyes brightened. "We can talk to Fagin!"

Fagin was an old soldier who lived three floors down in a room on his own. He had been a soldier in Afghanistan and had lost one eye and half his left arm—he claimed in action, although there was a rumor he had been run over be a trolleybus while he was home on leave. Fagin wasn't his real name, of course, but everyone called him that after a character in an English book, *Oliver Twist.* And the thing about Fagin was that he knew everything about everything. I never found out how he got his information, but if a bank was about to move a load of money or a diamond merchant was about to visit a smart hotel, somehow Fagin would catch wind of it and he would pass the information on—at a price. Everyone in the block respected him. I had seen him a couple of times, a short, plump man, shuffling along the corridors in a dirty coat with a huge beard bristling around his chin, and I had thought he looked more like a tramp than a master criminal.

But now that Dima had thought of him, the decision had been made, and the following day we gathered in his apartment, which was the same size as ours but furnished at least with a sofa and a few pictures on the wall. He had electricity too. Fagin himself was a disgusting old man. The way he looked at us, you didn't really want to think what was going on in his head. If Santa Claus had taken a dive into a sewer he would have come up looking much the same.

"You want to be *fortochniks*?" he asked, smiling to himself. "Then you want to do it soon before the winter comes and all the windows are closed! But you need an address. That's what you need, my boys. Somewhere worth the pickings!" He produced a leather notebook with old bus tickets and receipts sticking out of the pages. He opened it and began to thumb through.

"How much is your take?" Dima asked.

"Always straight to the point, Dimitry. That's what I like about you." Fagin smiled. "Whatever you take, you bring to me. No lying! I know a lie when I hear one, and believe me, I'll cut out your tongue." He leered at us, showing the yellow slabs that were his teeth. "Sixty percent for me, forty for you. Please don't argue with me, Dimitry, dear boy. You won't get better anywhere else. And I have the addresses. I know all the places where you won't have any difficulty. Nice, slim boys, slipping in at night . . ."

"Fifty fifty," Dima said.

"Fagin doesn't negotiate." He found a page in his notebook. "Now here's an address off Lubyanka Square. Ground-floor apartment." He looked up. "Shall I go on?"

Dima nodded. He had accepted the deal. "Where is it?"

"Mashkova Street. Number seven. It's owned by a rich banker. He collects stamps. Many of them valuable." He flicked the page over. "Maybe you'd prefer a house in Old Arbat. Lots of antiques. Mind you, it was done over last spring, and I'd say it was a bit early for a return visit." Another page. "Ah yes. I've had my eye on this place for a while. It's near Gorky Park . . . fourth floor and quite an easy climb. Mind you, it's owned by Vladimir Sharkovsky. Might be too much of a risk. How about Ilinka Street? Ah yes! That's perfect. Nice and easy. Number sixteen. Plenty of cash, jewelry . . ."

"Tell me about the apartment in Gorky Park," I said.

Dima turned to me, surprised. But it was the name

that had done it. Sharkovsky. I had heard it before. I remembered the moment when I entered Dementyev's office at Moscow University. I had heard him talking on the telephone.

*"Yes, of course, Mr. Sharkovsky. Yes, sir. Thank you, sir."*

"Who is Sharkovsky?" I asked.

"He's a businessman," Fagin said. "But rich. Very, very rich. And quite dangerous, so I'm told. Not the sort of man you'd want to meet on a dark night and certainly not if you were stealing from him."

"I want to go there," I said.

"Why?" Dima asked.

"Because I know him. At least . . . I heard his name."

At that moment, it seemed almost like a gift. Misha Dementyev was my enemy. He had tried to hand me over to the police. He had lied to my parents. And it sounded as if he was working for this man, Sharkovsky—assuming it was the same Sharkovsky. So robbing his apartment made perfect sense. It was like a miniature revenge.

Fagin snapped the notebook shut. We had made our decision and it didn't matter which address we chose. "It won't be so difficult," he muttered. "Fourth floor. Quiet street. Sharkovsky doesn't actually live there. He keeps the place for a friend, an actress." He leered at us in a way that suggested she was much more than a friend. "She's away a lot. It could be empty. I'll check."

Fagin was as good as his word. The following day he provided us with the information we needed. The actress was performing in a play called *The Cherry Orchard* and wouldn't be back in Moscow until the end of the month. The apartment was deserted but the *fortochka* was open.

"Go for the things you can carry," he suggested. "Jewelry. Furs. Mink and sable are easy to shift. TVs and stuff like that . . . leave them behind."

We set off that same night, skirting around the walls of the Kremlin and crossing the river on the Krimskiy Bridge. I thought I would be nervous. This was my first real crime—very different from the antics that Leo and I had got up to during the summer, setting off bombs outside the police station or pinching cigarettes. Even stealing from the back of parked cars wasn't in the same league. But the strange thing was that I was completely calm. It struck me that I might have found my destiny. If I could learn to survive in Moscow by being a thief, that was the way it would have to be.

Gorky Park is a huge area on the edge of the Moscow River. It's always been a favorite place for the people in the city, with a fairground, boating lakes, and even an open-air theater. Anyone who had an apartment here would have to be rich. The air was cleaner, and if you were high enough you'd get views across the trees and over to the river, with barges and pleasure boats cruising slowly past and the Foreign Ministry, another Stalin skyscraper, in the far distance. The apartment that Fagin had identified was right next to the park on a quiet street that hardly seemed to belong to the city at all. It was too elegant. Too expensive.

We got there just before midnight, but all the lamps

were lit and I was able to make out a very attractive building made from some sort of cream-colored stone, with arched doorways and windows and lots of decoration over the walls. It was smaller and neater than our apartment block, just four stories high, with a slanting roof made of orange tiles.

"That's the window—up there." Dima pointed.

The apartment was on the fourth floor, just as Fagin had said, and sure enough I could make out the *fortochka*, which was actually slightly ajar. The woman who lived there might have thought she was safe, being so high up, but I saw at once that it would be possible to climb in using the building's decorations as footholds. There were ledges, windowsills, carved pillars, and even a drainpipe that would act as one side of a ladder. It wouldn't be easy for me, but once I was inside, I would go back down and open the front door. I'd let the others in and the whole place would be ours.

There were no lights on inside the building. The other residents must have been asleep. Nor was there anyone in the street. We crossed as quickly as we could and grouped ourselves in the shadows, right up against the wall.

"What do you think, Yasha?" Dima asked.

I looked up and nodded. "I can do it." But still I hesitated. "Are you sure she's away?"

"Everyone says Fagin is reliable."

"Okay."

"We'll be waiting for you at the door. Make sure you don't make any noise coming down the stairs."

"Right. Good luck."

Dima cupped his hands to help me climb up to the first level, and as I raised my foot, our eyes met and he smiled at me. But at that moment I suddenly felt troubled. This might be my destiny, but what would my parents have said if they could have seen me now? They were honest people. That was the way I'd been brought up. I was amazed how quickly I'd become a burglar, a thief. And if I stayed in Moscow much longer? I wondered what I might become next.

I began the climb. The three boys scattered. We'd agreed that if a policeman happened to come along on patrol, Grigory would warn me by hooting like an owl. But right now we were alone, and at first it was easy. I had the drainpipe on one side and there were plenty of bricks and swirling plasterwork to give me a foothold. The architect or the artist who had built this place might have had plenty of ideas about style and elegance, but he had been less brilliant when it came to security.

Even so, the higher I went, the more dangerous it became. The pipe was quite loose. If I put too much weight onto it, I risked tearing it out of the wall. Some of the decorations were damp and had begun to deteriorate. I rested my foot briefly on a diamond-shaped brick, part of a running pattern, and to my horror it crumbled away. The sound of loose plaster hitting the pavement echoed ominously. I scrabbled against the face of the building, desperately trying to stop myself from plunging down. If I'd fallen from the first floor, I'd have broken an ankle.

From this height it was more likely to be my neck. Somehow I managed to steady myself. I looked down and saw Dima standing underneath one of the streetlamps. He had seen what had happened and waved a hand—either spurring me on or warning me to be more careful.

I took a deep breath to steady my nerves, then continued up—past the third floor and up to the fourth. At one stage I was right next to a window, and peeping in, I saw the vague shape of two people lying under a fur cover, in bed. I was lucky they were heavy sleepers. I pulled myself up as quickly as possible and finally reached the ledge that ran along the whole building just below the top floor. It was no more than fifteen centimeters wide and I had to squeeze myself flat against the wall, shuffling along with my toes touching the brickwork and my heels hanging in the air. If I had leaned back even slightly, I would have lost my balance and fallen. But I had come this far without killing myself. I was determined to see it through.

I got to the window with the smaller window set inside it and now I saw that I had two more problems. It was going to be an even tighter fit than I had imagined. And it was going to be awkward too. Somehow I had to lever myself up and in, but that would mean putting all my weight on the main sheet of glass. The windows were only separated by a narrow frame, and unless I was careful, there was a real chance they would shatter beneath me and I would end up cutting myself in half. Once again I looked for Dima, but this time there was no sign of him.

I reached out and held on to the edge with one hand. The *fortochka* was definitely unlocked. The room on the other side was dark but seemed to be a lounge with a dining area and a kitchen attached. I swung around and grabbed the glass with my other hand. I saw now that I was going to have to go in headfirst. It just wasn't possible to lever up my leg. Using my forehead, I pushed the little window open. I leaned forward, pushing my head inside. Now the glass was resting against the back of my neck, making me think of a prisoner in the old days, about to be decapitated by guillotine. Trying to keep as much of my weight off the glass as I could, I arched forward and in. The fit was very tight. The opening was barely more than forty centimeters square . . . a cat flap indeed. My shoulders only just passed through and I felt the loose end of the glass scraping against my back. I pushed harder and found myself wedged with the lower rim of the *fortochka* pressing into my back just above my buttocks. Suddenly I was trapped! I couldn't move in either direction and I had a nightmare vision of being stuck there all night, waiting for someone to discover me and call the police in the morning. The glass was creaking underneath me. I was sure it was going to break. I pushed again. It was like giving birth to myself. The edge cut into me but then, somehow, gravity took over. I plunged forward into the darkness and hit the floor. I was in!

If it hadn't been for the carpeted floor, I would have broken my nose and ended up looking like Dima. If there was anyone in the apartment, they would certainly have heard me. I lay there for a moment, waiting for the door to open and the lights to go on. It didn't happen. I remembered the people I had seen beneath their furs in the apartment below. Surely they would have heard the thump and wondered what it was. But there was no sound from below either. I waited another minute. My arm was sticking out at a strange angle and I wondered if I had dislocated my shoulder, but when I shifted my weight and got back into a sensible position, it seemed all right. Dima and the others would have seen me go in. They would be waiting for me to come down and open the front door. It was time to move.

First I examined my surroundings. As my eyes got used to the half-light, I saw that I was in the main living area and that the owner must be as wealthy as Fagin had said. I had never been anywhere like this. The furniture was modern and looked brand-new. Living in a wooden house in a village, I had never seen—I had never even imagined—glass and silver tables, leather sofas, beautiful cabinets with rings hanging off the drawers. Everything I had ever sat on or slept in had been old and shabby. There was a gorgeous rug in front of a fireplace and even to steal that would make this adventure worthwhile. How much more comfortable I would be lying on that than on the lumpy mattress back at the Tverskaya Street apartment!

Paintings in gold frames hung on the walls. I didn't really understand them. They seemed to be splashes of paint with no subject matter at all. There had been a few framed photographs in my house, a tapestry hanging in my parents' bedroom, pictures cut out of magazines, but nothing like this. Next to the sitting area there was a dining room table, an oval of wood partly covered by a lace cloth, with four chairs—and beyond it a kitchen that was so clean it had surely never been used. I ran my eye over the electric oven, the sink with its gleaming taps. No need to run down to any wells if you lived here. There was a fridge in one corner. I opened the door and found myself bathed in electric light, staring at shelves stacked with ham, cheese, fruit, salad, pickled mushrooms, and the little pancakes that we called *blinis*. I'm afraid I couldn't help myself. I reached in and stuffed as much food into my mouth as I could, not caring if it was salty or sweet.

And that was how I was, standing in the kitchen with food in my hands and in my mouth, when a key rattled in the lock, the main door of the apartment opened, and the lights came on.

Fagin had gotten it wrong after all.

A man stood staring at me. I saw his eyes turn instantly from surprise to understanding and then to black, seething fury. He was wearing a black fur coat, black gloves, and the sort of hat you might see on an American gangster. A white silk scarf hung around his shoulders. He was not a huge man, but he was solid and well built and he had a presence about him, a sense of power. I could see it in his extraordinarily intense eyes, heavily lidded, with thick black eyebrows. His flesh had the color and the vitality of a man lying dead in his coffin, and standing there framed in the doorway, he had that same heavy stillness. His face was unlined, his mouth a narrow gash. I could make out the edges of a tattoo on the side of his neck: red flames. It suggested that the whole of his body, underneath his shirt, was on fire. Without knowing anything about him, I knew I was in terrible trouble. If I had met the devil I could not have been more afraid.

"What is it, Vlad?" There was a woman standing behind him. I glimpsed a mink collar and blond hair.

"There is someone in the apartment," he said. "A boy."

His eyes briefly left me, darting across the room to the window. He didn't need to ask any questions. He knew how I had gotten in. He knew that I was alone.

"Do you want me to call the police?"

"No. There's no need for that."

His words were measured, uttered with a sort of dull certainty. And they told me the worst thing possible. If he wasn't calling the police, it was because he had decided to deal with me himself and he wasn't going to shake my hand and thank me for coming. He was going to kill me. Perhaps there was a gun in his coat pocket. Perhaps he would tear me apart with his bare hands. I had no doubt at all that he could do it.

I didn't know how to react. My one desire was to get out of the apartment, back onto the street. I wondered if Dima, Roman, and Grigory had seen what had happened, but I knew that even if they had, there was nothing they could do. The front door would be locked. If they were sensible, they would probably be halfway back to Tverskaya. I tried to collect my thoughts. All I had to do was to get past this man and out into the corridor. The woman wouldn't try to stop me. I looked around me and did perhaps the stupidest thing I could. There was a steak knife on the counter. I picked it up.

The man didn't move. He didn't speak. He glanced at the blade with outrage. How could I dare to pick up _his_ property and threaten him in _his_ home? That was what he said without actually saying anything. Holding the knife didn't make me feel any stronger. In fact, all the strength drained out of me the moment I had it in my hand, and the silver, jagged blade filled me with horror.

"I don't want any trouble," I said, and my voice didn't sound like my own. "Just let me go and nobody will be hurt."

He had no intention of doing that. He moved toward me and I jabbed out with the knife without thinking, not meaning to stab him, not really knowing what I was doing. He stopped. I saw the face of the girl behind him, frozen in shock. The man looked down. I followed his eyes and saw that the point of the blade had gone through his coat, into his chest. I was even more horrified. I stepped back, dropping the knife. It fell free and clattered to the floor.

The man didn't seem to have felt any pain. He brought up a hand and examined the gash in his coat as if it mattered more to him than the flesh underneath. When he brought his hand away, there was blood on the tips of his glove.

He gazed at me. I was unarmed now, trapped by those horrible eyes.

"What have you done?" he demanded.

"I . . ." I didn't know what to say.

He took one step forward and punched me in the face. I had never been struck so hard. I didn't even know it was possible for one human to hurt another human so much. It was like being hit by a rod of steel and I felt my cheekbone break. I heard the girl cry out. I was already falling, but as I went down, he hit me again with the other fist so that my head snapped back and my body collapsed in two directions at once. I remember a bolt of white light that seemed to be my own death. I was unconscious before I reached the floor.

I WOKE UP IN TOTAL darkness, lying in a cramped space with my legs hunched up, a gag in my mouth, and my hands tied. My first thought was that I was locked inside a box, that I had been buried alive—and for the next sixty seconds I was screaming without making any sound, my heart racing, my muscles straining against the ropes around my wrists, barely able to catch breath. Somehow I got myself under control. It wasn't a box. I was in the trunk of a car. We had been standing stationary a moment ago, but now I heard the throb of the engine and felt us move off. That still wasn't good. I was being allowed to live—but for how long?

I was in a bad way. My head was pounding—and by that I mean all of it, inside and out. The whole side of my face was swollen. It hurt me to move my mouth and I couldn't close one of my eyes. The man's fist had broken my cheekbone. I had no idea what I looked like, but what did that matter? I did not expect to live.

I presumed that the man was Vladimir Sharkovsky. Fagin had warned me that he was dangerous, but that was only half the story. I had seen enough of the man in the apartment to know that he was a psychopath. No ordinary person had eyes like that. He had been utterly cold when I had attacked him, but when his temper flared up, it had been like a demon leaping out of the craters of hell. *He hadn't called the police.* That was the worst of it. He was taking me somewhere and when he got there, he could do to me whatever he wanted. I dreaded to think what that might be. Was he planning to torture me as a punishment for what I had done? I had heard that many hundreds of children went missing from the streets of Moscow every year. It might well be my fate to become one of them.

I cannot say how long the journey took. I couldn't see my watch with my hands tied behind me and after a while I dozed off. I didn't sleep exactly. I simply drifted out of consciousness. It would have been nice to have dreamed of my parents and of my life in Estrov, to have spent my last hours on this planet reliving happier times, but I was in too much pain. Every few minutes, my eyes would blink open and I would once again find myself struggling for air in this almost airtight compartment, desperately wanting to straighten up, to go to the toilet, to be anywhere but there. The car just rumbled on.

Eventually, we arrived. First, I felt us slowing down. Then we stopped and I heard a man's voice, a command being given, followed by the click of a metal gate as it was activated. When we set off again, there was a different surface—gravel—beneath the tires. The car stopped and the engine was turned off. The driver's door opened and shut and I heard footsteps on the gravel. I tensed myself, waiting for the car trunk to be released, but it didn't happen. The footsteps disappeared into the distance and when, a long time later, they hadn't come back, I began to think that I was going to be left here all night, like a piece of baggage that nobody needed.

And so it was. I was left in the dark, in silence, with no idea how long it was going to last or what would happen when I was released. It was being done on purpose, of course, to break my spirit, to make me suffer. I was the victim of my own worst imaginings. I had nothing to do except to count every single painful minute. Unable to move, to stretch myself, my whole body was in torment. All I could do was try to sleep, fighting back all the dread that came from being tied up and left in this small space. It was a long, hideous night. By the time the trunk was opened, I was no longer afraid of death. I think I would have welcomed it. A short tunnel of horrors followed by release. It would be worth the journey.

There was a man leaning over me—not the one from the Moscow apartment. He was quite simply massive, with oversized shoulders and a thick neck, dressed in a cheap gray suit, a white shirt, and a black tie. His hair was blond and thickly oiled so that it stood up in spikes. He was wearing dark glasses and there was a radio transmitter behind his ear with a wire curling down to a throat mike. His skin was utterly white, as if he had never spent any time in the sun, and it occurred to me that he might have been in a prison or some other institution all his life.

He reached down and with a single movement dragged me out of the trunk, then stood me up so that I was balanced against the back of the car. I would have fallen otherwise. There was no strength in my legs. He looked at me with hardly any expression apart from disgust, and for that I couldn't blame him. I stank. My clothes were crumpled. My face was caked with blood. He reached into his jacket pocket and I winced as he produced a knife. I was quite ready for him to plunge it into my chest, but he simply leaned over me and cut the cords around my wrists. My hands fell free. They looked horrible. The flesh around my wrists was blue, covered in welts. I couldn't move my fingers but I felt the pins and needles as the blood supply was restored.

"You are to come with us," he said. He had a deep, gravelly voice. He spoke without emotion, as if he didn't actually enjoy speaking.

Us?

I glanced around and saw a second man standing at the side of the car. For a moment, I thought my brain was playing tricks on me after my long captivity. This second man was identical to the first—the same height, the same looks, the same clothes. They were twins . . . just like the two girls I had once known in Estrov. But it was almost as if these two had trained themselves to be indistinguishable. They had the same haircut, the same sunglasses. They even moved at exactly the same time, like mirror images.

The first twin hadn't asked me my name. He didn't want to know anything about me.

"Where are we?" I asked. The words came out clumsily because of the damage to my face.

"No questions. Do as you are told."

He gestured. I began to walk and for the first time I was able to take in my surroundings. I was in what looked like a large and very beautiful park with pathways, neatly cut grass, and trees. The park was surrounded by a brick wall, several meters high with razor wire around the top, and I could make out the tops of more trees on the other side. The car that I had been in was a black Lexus. It had been parked quite close to an arched gateway with a barrier that rose and fell, the only way out, I suspected. A guardhouse stood next to it. This was a wooden construction with a large glass window, and I could see a man in uniform watching us as we walked together. My first thought was that I had been brought to some sort of prison. There were arc lamps and security cameras set at intervals along the wall.

We were heading toward a cluster of eight wooden houses that had been tucked out of sight behind some fir trees, about a hundred meters from the gates. They'd been built on top of each other with external staircases connecting them, and there was a larger, brick building nearby. I looked behind me. Although I hadn't been given permission, I came to a stumbling halt. Where the hell was I? I had never seen anything like this.

A gravel drive with lamps and flower beds on each side led from the entrance through the parkland and up to a monumental white house. Not a house. A palace . . . and not one that had come out of any fairy tale. It was a modern building, perhaps only a year old, pure white, with two wings stretching out from a central block, which alone must have contained about fifty rooms. There were terraces with white balustrades, white columns with triple-height doorways opening behind, walkways and balconies and above it all a white dome like that of a planetarium or perhaps a cathedral. Half a dozen satellite dishes had been mounted on the roof as well as television antennas and a radio tower. A man stood there, watching me through binoculars. He was wearing the same uniform as the man at the gate—but with a difference. Even at this distance I could see that he had a machine gun strapped to his shoulder.

Closer to the house, the gardens became more orna-mental with statues on plinths, marble benches, beauti-fully tended walkways and arbors, bushes cut into fantastic shapes, more flower beds laid out in intricate patterns. An army of gardeners would have to work the whole year round to keep it all looking like this, and even as I stood there I saw some of them, pushing wheelbarrows or on their knees, weeding. The drive broke in two as it reached the front door, sweeping around a white marble fountain with gods and mermaids all tangled together and water splashing down. I saw two Rolls-Royces, a Bentley, and a Ferrari parked outside. But the owner didn't just have cars. His private helicopter was parked on a concrete square, discreetly located next to a summer house. It was under canvas with the blades tied down.

"Why are you waiting?" one of the twins demanded.

"Who lives here?" I asked.

His answer was a jab in the side of my stomach. It had been aimed around my kidney and it hurt. "I told you. No questions."

I was very quickly learning the rules of this place. I was worth nothing. Anyone could do anything to me. I swallowed a grunt of pain and continued to the smallest cabin, right on the edge of the complex. The door was open and I looked into a room with a narrow metal bed, a table, and a chair. There was no carpet, no curtains, nothing in the way of decoration. A second door led into a toilet and shower.

"You have five minutes," the man said. "Throw those clothes away. You will not need them. Wash yourself and make yourself presentable. Do not leave this room. If you do, the guards will shoot you down."

He left me on my own. I stripped off my clothes and went into the bathroom. First I used the toilet. Then I had a shower. I knew I was in danger. It was quite likely that I would soon be dead. But that shower was still a wonderful experience. The water was hot and there was enough pressure to soak me completely. There was even a bar of soap. It had been three weeks since I had last washed—that had been in the *banya,* the bathhouse in Moscow—and black dirt seemed to ooze out of my body, disappearing down the plug. Thinking of the bathhouse reminded me of Dima. What would he be doing now? Had he seen me being bundled into the car by Sharkovsky, and if so, might he come looking for me? At least that was something to give me hope.

My face still hurt, though, and when I examined myself in the mirror, it was as bad as I had feared. I barely recognized myself. One eye was half closed. There was a huge bruise all around it. My cheek looked like a rotting fruit with a gash where the man's fist had caught me. I was lucky I still had all my teeth. Looking at the damage, I was reminded of what lay ahead. I hadn't been brought here for my own comfort. I was being prepared for something. My punishment was still to come.

I went back into the bedroom. My own clothes had been taken away while I was washing, and with a jolt I realized that the last of my mother's jewelry had gone with them. Her ring had been in my back pocket. I knew at once that there would be no point asking for it back and I had to hold down a great wave of sadness, the sense that I had lost everything. She had worn that ring and, touching it, I had felt I was touching her. Now that had been taken from me and apart from my old watch, which I was still wearing, nothing of my old life remained.

I had been supplied with a black tracksuit, black socks, and black slip-on shoes. I dried myself using a towel that had been hanging in the bathroom and got dressed. The clothes fit me very well.

"Are you ready?" The twins were standing outside, calling to me. I left the cabin and joined them. They glanced at me, both of them still showing a complete lack of interest.

"Come with us," one of them said. They appeared to have a fairly limited vocabulary too.

We walked up the drive, all the way to the big house. As we went, we passed another security guard, this one with an Alsatian dog on a leash. Another camera mounted above the front door watched our approach. But we didn't go in that way. The twins took me in through a side door next to the garbage area and along a corridor. Here the walls were plain and the floor black and white tiles. The servants' entrance. We passed a laundry room, a boot room, a sort of pantry. I glimpsed a woman in a black dress with a white apron, polishing silver. She didn't notice me or, if she did, she pretended not to. My feet, in the soft shoes, made no sound as we continued through. I was feeling queasy and I knew why. I was afraid.

We passed through a hallway. This was the main entrance to the house, behind the front door. A magnificent staircase swept down to the front door, which stood with a marble pillar on each side. The hallway itself was huge. You could have parked a dozen cars there. A bowl of flowers stood on a table—it must have emptied a flower shop. The main light was from a chandelier, hundreds of crystals twinkling brilliantly like a fireworks display. It made the lights I had seen in the Moscow metro look cheap and gaudy. There were more doors on every side. It was all too much for me to take in. If a spaceship had grabbed me and deposited me on the moon, I would have felt as much at home.

"In here . . ."

One of the twins knocked on an oak door and opened it without waiting for a reply. I went in.

The man from the Moscow apartment was sitting behind an oversized antique desk. There were bookshelves behind him and on one side a globe that looked so old that quite a few modern-day countries were probably missing, as they wouldn't have been discovered yet. He was framed by two windows with red velvet curtains hanging down. There was a view out to the fountain and the drive. The room was very warm. One wall contained a stone fireplace—two crouching imps or demons supporting the mantelpiece on their shoulders—and there was a dog, a Dalmatian, stretched out in front of it. The walls were covered with paintings. The largest was a portrait of the man I was facing, and I have to say that the painted version was the more welcoming of the two. He had not looked up from his work. He was reading some sort of document, making notes in the margins with a black fountain pen.

There was a gun on the desk in front of him.

As I stood there, waiting to be told what to do, I found myself staring at it. It was a revolver, a very old-fashioned model, twelve centimeters long, with a stainless steel barrel and a black enamel grip. It wasn't like an automatic or a self-loading pistol where you feed the bullets into a clip. This one had a cylinder and six chambers. A single bullet lay beside it.

"Sit down," he said.

There was an empty chair in front of him. I stepped forward, although it felt more as if I was floating, and sat down. The door clicked shut behind me. Without being instructed, the twins had left.

I waited for the master of the house to speak. He was wearing a suit now and somehow I knew that it was expensive and that it hadn't been made in Russia. The material was too luxurious and it fit too well. He had a pale blue shirt and a brown tie. Now that he wasn't wearing his coat, I could see that he was very muscular. He must have spent hundreds of hours in the gym. He had also removed the hat and I saw that he was completely bald. He had not lost his hair. He had shaved it off, leaving a dark shadow that made him more deathlike than ever. I waited in dread for his heavy, ugly eyes to settle on me. My face was hurting badly and I wanted to go to the toilet again. But I didn't dare say anything. I didn't move.

At length he stopped and laid the pen down. "What is your name?" he asked.

"Yasha Gregorovich."

"Yassen?" He had misheard me. The side of my face was so swollen that I had mispronounced my own name. It would be very unusual to be called Yassen. It is Russian for "ash tree." But I did not correct him. I had decided it would be better not to say anything unless I had to. "How old are you?" he asked.

"I'm fourteen."

"Where are you from?"

I remembered my mother's warning. "A town called Kirsk," I said. "It's a long way away. You won't have heard of it."

The man thought for a moment, then he got up, walked around the desk, and stood next to me. He took his time, considering the situation, then suddenly and without warning slapped me across the face. The blow wasn't a particularly hard one, certainly not as hard as the night before, nor did it need to be. My cheekbone was already broken and the fresh pain almost knocked me off the chair. Black spots appeared in front of my eyes. I thought I was going to be sick.

By the time I had recovered, the man was back in his chair. "Never make assumptions," he said. "Never assume anything about me. And when you speak to me, call me 'sir.' Do you understand?"

"Yes, sir."

He nodded. "Do you have parents?"

"No, sir. They're both dead."

"And last night, when you broke into my apartment, were you alone?"

I had already decided that I wasn't going to tell him about Dima, Roman, and Grigory. If I told him their names, I had no doubt he would send his men around to

Tverskaya to kill them. I still assumed he was going to kill me. "Yes, sir," I replied. "I was on my own."

"How did you come to choose that apartment—as opposed to any other?"

"I was just walking past. I saw that the window was open and the lights were out. I didn't even think about it. I just went in."

The answer seemed to satisfy him. He took out a gold cigarette case. I noticed the initials V.S. on the cover. He removed a cigarette and lit it, then lay the case on the desk, close to the gun. "Vladimir Sharkovsky," he said. "That is my name."

I didn't tell him that I knew. I simply sat there and watched as he smoked in silence. My insides were churning.

"You must be wondering why you are still alive," he continued. "In truth, you should not be. Last night, as I drove over the bridge, I thought of dropping you in the Moscow River. I would quite have enjoyed watching you drown. When I drove you here, my intention was to give you to Josef and Karl, to be punished and then to be killed. Even now, I am undecided if you will live or if you will die." His eyes rested briefly on the revolver. "The fact that you are sitting in this room, talking to me, is down to one reason only. It is a question of timing. Perhaps you have been lucky. A week ago it would have been different. But right now . . ."

He trailed off, then took another drag on the cigarette, the blue smoke curling into the air. A log snapped in the fireplace and the dog stirred briefly, then went back to sleep. So far, Vladimir Sharkovsky had shown no emotion whatsoever. His voice was flat, entirely disinterested. If machines ever learned to speak, they would speak like him.

"I am a careful man," he went on. "One of the reasons I have been so successful is that I have always used everything that has been given to me. I never miss an opportunity. It may be an investment in a company, the chance to buy my way into a bank, the weakness of a government official who is open to bribery. Or it may be the chance appearance of a worthless thief and guttersnipe like yourself. But if it can be used, then I will use it. That is how I live.

"There is something you need to understand about me. I am extremely successful. Right now, Russia is changing. The old ways are being left behind. For those of us with the vision to see what is possible, the rewards are limitless. You have nothing. You steal because you are hungry and all you think about is your next pathetic meal. I have the world and everything in it. And now, Yassen Gregorovich, I have you.

"A large number of people work for me in this house. Because of the nature of my work and who I am, I have to be careful. Josef and Karl, the two men who brought you here, are my personal bodyguards. Right now they are standing outside, and I should perhaps warn you that there is a communication button underneath this desk. If you were to try anything, if you were to threaten me again, they would be in here in an instant. Be glad they were not with me in Moscow. That was the private apartment of a friend of mine. The moment you picked up that knife, your own life would have been over.

"I will not kill you—yet—because I think I can use you. As it happens, a position has arisen here, a vacancy which would not normally be easy to fill. You are, as I said, very fortunate with the timing. I have no doubt that you are stupid and uneducated. But even so you might be acceptable."

He paused and it took me a few seconds to realize that he was waiting for me to reply. I couldn't believe what he had just told me. He wasn't going to kill me. He was offering me a job!

"I'd be very happy to work for you, sir," I said.

His eyes settled on me, full of contempt. "Happy?" He repeated the word with a sneer. "You say stupid things without thinking. It is not my intention to make you 'happy.' Quite the opposite. You broke into my apartment. You attempted to hurt me and in doing so you ruined a perfectly good overcoat, a jacket, and a shirt. You even cut my flesh. For this, you must pay. You must be punished. If you decide to accept my proposal, you will spend every hour of the rest of your life wishing that the two of us had never met. I am not offering to pay you. I will own you. I will use you. And maybe, many years from now, if you work hard enough, I will let you go. Until then, I will expect your total obedience. You will do whatever I tell you. You will not hesitate." He gestured at the fireplace. "You see the dog? That is what you are now. That's all you mean to me."

He stubbed out the cigarette. I could see that he was bored of the interview, that he wanted it to be over.

"What do you want me to do?" I asked. "What sort of work?"

I had no choice. I had to survive. Let him employ me in whatever capacity and somehow I would find a way out of this place. In the back of a car, over the wall . . . I would find a way to escape.

"You will clean. You will carry messages. You will sweep floors. You will help in the garden. But that's just part of it. The main reason that I need you is something quite different." He paused. "You will be my food taster."

"Your . . . ?" I almost laughed out loud, and if I had, I am sure he would have shot me there and then. But it was ridiculous. At school, we had been taught about the Roman emperors—Julius Caesar and the others—who had employed slaves to taste everything they ate. But this was Russia in the twentieth century. He couldn't possibly mean what he had just said.

"It is unfortunately the case that I have many ene-mies," Sharkovsky explained. He was completely serious. "Some of them fear me. Some of them are jealous of me. All of them would benefit if I was no longer here. In the last year, there have been three attempts on my life. That is how things are now. Several of my associates have been less fortunate—which is to say, they have been less careful than me. And they have died.

"Outside my wife and my children, I can trust no one, and even my immediate family might be bribed one day to do me harm. I employ a great many people to protect me and I have to employ more people to watch over them. I trust none of them." His dark eyes bored into me. "Can I trust you?"

I was trying to make sense of all this. Was that really to be my fate? Sitting at his dining table, digging my fork into his blinis and caviar?

"I'll do whatever you want," I said.

"Will you?"

"Yes, sir."

"Anything?"

"Yes . . ." This time I was uneasy.

It was what he had been waiting for. It was the very worst thing I could have said.

"We will see." He reached out and took the gun. He jerked open the cylinder and showed me that it was empty. Then he picked up the bullet—a little cylinder of gleaming silver—and held it between his finger and thumb like a scientist giving a demonstration. I watched silently. I didn't know what was about to happen, but I could feel my heart pounding. He slid the bullet into one of the chambers and snapped the cylinder shut. Then he spun it several times so that the metal became a blur and it was impossible for either of us to tell where the bullet had lodged.

"You say you will do anything for me," he said. "So do this. The gun has six chambers. As you have seen, one of them now contains a live bullet. You do not know where the bullet is. Nor do I." He placed the gun back on the desk, right in front of me. "Put the gun in your mouth and pull the trigger."

I stared at him. "I don't understand."

"It's simple enough!" he said. "Point the gun at the back of your mouth and shoot."

"But why . . . ?"

"Because you said to me five seconds ago that you would do anything I asked you, and now I am asking you to prove it. I need to know that I can rely on you. Either you will pull the trigger or you will not. But let us consider the options, Yassen Gregorovich. If you will not do what I ask, then you have lied to me and I cannot use you after all. In that case, I can assure you that your death is certain. If you do as I have asked, then there are two possibilities that lie ahead of you. It is quite possible that you will kill yourself, that in a few minutes' time my cleaners will be wiping your brains off my carpet. That will be annoying. But there is also a very good chance that you will live, and from that moment on you will serve me. It is your decision and you must make it now. I don't have all day."

He was torturing me after all. He was asking me to play this horrible game to prove beyond any doubt that he had complete power over me. I would never argue with him. I would never refuse an order. If I did this, I would be accepting that my own life no longer belonged to me. That in every respect I was his.

What could I do? What choice did I have?

I picked up the gun. It was much heavier than I had expected, but at the same time, I had no strength at all. Nothing below my shoulder seemed to be working properly—not my wrist, not my hand, not my fingers. I could feel my pulse racing and I had to struggle even to breathe. What this man was demanding was horrific . . . beyond imagination. Six chambers. One containing a bullet. A one in six chance. When I pulled the trigger, nothing might happen. Or I might send a piece of metal traveling at three hundred twenty-five kilometers per hour into my own head. If I didn't do it, he would kill me. That was what it came down to. I felt hot tears brimming over my cheeks. It seemed impossible that my life could have come to this.

"Don't cry like a baby," Sharkovsky said. "Get on with it."

My arm and wrist were aching. I could feel the blood pumping through my veins. Almost involuntarily, my finger had curled around the trigger. The grip was pressed against the palm of my hand. For a crazy moment, I thought of firing at Sharkovsky, of emptying the chamber in his direction. But what good would that do me? He probably had a second gun concealed somewhere, and if I didn't find the bullet at the first attempt, he would have plenty of time to shoot me where I sat.

"Please, sir," I whispered.

"I am not interested in your tears or your pleading," he snapped. "I am interested only in your obedience."

"But . . ."

"Do it now!"

I touched the muzzle of the gun against the side of my head.

"In your mouth!"

I will never forget his insistence, that one obscene detail. I pushed the barrel of the gun between my teeth, feeling the muzzle grazing the roof of my mouth. I could taste the metal, cold and bitter. I was aware of the black hole, the muzzle, pointing at my throat with, perhaps, a bullet resting behind it, waiting to begin its short journey. Sharkovsky was gloating. I don't think he cared one way or another what the outcome would be. I couldn't breathe. The contents of my stomach were rising up. I pressed with my finger but I couldn't make it work. I could already hear the explosion. I could feel the scorching heat and see the blood splattering across the room from the back of my neck.

"Do it!" he snarled.

One chance in six.

I squeezed the trigger.

The hammer drew back. How far would it travel before it fell? I was quite certain that these were the last seconds of my life. And yet everything was happening horribly slowly. They seemed to stretch on forever.

I felt the mechanism release itself in my hand. The hammer fell with a heavy, thunderous click.

Nothing.

There had been no explosion. The chamber was empty.

Relief rushed through me but it did not feel good. It was as if I was being emptied, as if my entire life and all the good things I had ever experienced were being taken from me. From this moment on, I belonged to Sharkovsky. That was what he had demonstrated. I dropped the gun. It fell heavily against the surface of the desk and lay there between us. The muzzle was wet with my saliva.

"You can leave now," he said.

He must have pressed a communication button somewhere behind his desk, because although I hadn't heard them, the men who had brought me here had returned. Perhaps the twins had actually been present and had seen what had just happened. I didn't know.

I stood up. My whole body felt foreign to me. I might not have killed myself, but even so, something inside me had died.

"Yassen Gregorovich is working for me now," Sharvovsky continued. "Take him downstairs and show him."

The two men led me out of the study and back into the corridor we had come through together. But this time we took a staircase down into a basement area. There was an oversized fridge door that led into a cold storage room and I watched as one twin opened it and the other went inside. He wheeled out a trolley. There was a dead body on it, covered by a sheet. He lifted it up and I saw a naked man. He couldn't have been more than ten years older than me when he died. It had happened very recently. His face was distorted with pain. His hands seemed to be scrabbling at his throat.

I understood without being told. The old food taster.

*"A position has arisen here."* That was what Vladimir Sharkovsky had said to me. Now I knew why.

# СЕРЕБРЯНЫЙ БОР

I MADE MY FIRST ESCAPE attempt that same day.

I knew I couldn't stay here. I wasn't going to play any more of Sharkovsky's sadistic games and I certainly wasn't going to swallow his food . . . not when there was a real chance of my ending up on a metal slab. I had been left alone for the rest of the day. Perhaps they thought I needed time to recover from my ordeal and they were certainly right. The moment I got back to my room, I was sick. After that, I slept for about three hours. One of the twins visited me during the afternoon. He brought with him more clothes: overalls, boots, an apron, a suit. Each piece of clothing related to a different task I would be expected to perform. I left them on the floor. I wasn't going to be part of this. I was out.

As soon as the night had come, I left my room and set out to explore the grounds, now empty of gardeners, although there were still guards patrolling close to the wall. It was clear to me that the wall completely surrounded the complex and there was no possibility of my climbing it. It was too high, and anyway, the razor wire would cut me to shreds. The simple truth was that the archway was the only way in and out—but at least that meant I could focus my attention on that one avenue. And looking at it, I wasn't sure that it was as secure as it seemed. Three uniformed guards sat inside a wooden cabin with a glass window that allowed them to look out over the driveway. They had television monitors too. There was a red-and-white pole that they had to raise, and they searched every vehicle that came in, one of them looking underneath with a flat mirror on wheels while another checked the driver's ID. But when there were no cars, they did nothing. One of them read a newspaper. The others sat back looking bored. I could simply slip out. It wouldn't be difficult at all.

That was my plan. It was about seven o'clock and I assumed everyone was eating. I'd had no food all day but I was in no mood to eat. Still wearing the black tracksuit—the color would help to conceal me in the darkness—I slipped outside. When I was sure there was nobody around, I sprinted to the edge of the cabin and then crept around, crouching underneath the window and keeping close to the wall. The road back to Moscow lay in front of me. I couldn't believe it was this easy.

It wasn't. I only found out about the infrared sensors when I passed through one of them, immediately setting off a deafening alarm. At once the whole area exploded into brilliant light as arc lamps sliced into me and I found myself trapped between the beams. There was no point running. I would have been shot before I had taken ten steps, and I could only stand there looking foolish as the guards seized hold of me and dragged me back.

Punishment was immediate and it was hideous. I was given to the twins, who simply beat me up as if I were a punching bag in a gym. It wasn't just the pain that left its mark on me. It was their complete indifference. I know they were being paid by Sharkovsky. They were following his orders. But what sort of man can do this to a child and live with himself the next day? They were careful not to break any more bones, but by the time they dragged me back to my room, I was barely conscious. They threw me onto my bed and left me. I was unconscious before they closed the door.

I made my second attempt as soon as I was able to move again, the next day. It was certainly foolish, but it seemed to me that it was the last thing they would expect and so they might briefly lower their guard. They thought I was broken, exhausted. Both of these things were true, but I was also determined. This time, a delivery truck provided the opportunity. I'd eaten breakfast in my room— one of the twins had brought it on a tray—but after I'd finished, I was ordered up to the house to help unload about fifty crates of wine and champagne that Sharkovsky had bought. It didn't matter that I could feel my shirt sticking to my open wounds and that every movement caused me pain. While the driver waited, I carried the crates in through the back door and down the steps that led to the cold storage room. There was a wine cellar next to it, a cavernous space that housed hundreds of bottles facing each other in custom-built racks. It took me about two hours to carry them all down, and when I'd finished, I noticed that there were a lot of empty boxes in the back of the van. It seemed simple enough to hide myself behind a pile of them. Surely they wouldn't bother searching the van on the way out?

The driver closed the door. Crouching behind the boxes, I heard him start the engine. We drove back down to the drive and slowed down. I waited for the moment of truth, the acceleration that meant we had passed through the barrier and were outside the compound. It never came. The door was thrown open again and a voice called out to me.

"Get out!"

Again, it was one of the twins. I don't know how he was so certain that I was there. Maybe I had been caught by one of the security cameras. Maybe he had been expecting it all along. I felt a weakness in my stomach as I stood up and showed myself. I wasn't sure I could take another beating. But even as I climbed down, I was determined not to give in. I wasn't going to let him see I was scared.

"Come with me," he instructed.

His face gave nothing away. I followed him to the house, but this time he took me around the back. There was a conservatory on the other side, although actually it was more like a pavilion, constructed mainly out of glass with white wooden panels, at least fifty meters long. It had a series of folding doors so that in the full heat of the summer the whole thing could be opened out, but this was late October and they were all closed. The twin opened a single door and led me inside. I found myself in front of an enormous swimming pool, almost Olympic sized. The water was heated. I could see the steam rising over the surface. It had blue tiles. Sun loungers had been arranged around the edge and there was a well-stocked bar with a mirrored counter and leather stools.

Sharkovsky was doing laps. We stood there, watching, while he went from one end to the other and back again, performing a rhythmic, steady butterfly stroke. I counted eighteen laps and he never stopped once. Nor did he look my way. This was how he liked to keep himself fit, and as he continued, I couldn't help but notice the extraordinarily well developed muscles in his back and shoulders. I also saw his tattoos. There was a Jewish Star of David in the center of his back—but it wasn't a religious symbol. On the contrary, it was on fire, with the words DEATH TO ZIONISM engraved below. It was these flames that I had seen reaching up to his neck. When he finally finished swimming and climbed out, I saw a huge eagle with outstretched wings, perched on a Nazi swastika, all of it tattooed across his chest. He had a slight paunch, but even this was solid rather than flabby. There was a bandage just underneath one of his nipples and I realized that this was where I must have cut him with the knife. He was wearing tiny swimming trunks. His whole appearance was somehow very horrible.

At last he noticed me. He picked up a towel and walked over to me. I was trembling. I couldn't stop myself. I was expecting the worst.

"Yassen Gregorovich," he said, "I understand that you tried to leave this place last night. You were punished for this, but it didn't prevent you from making a second attempt today. Is that right?"

"Yes, sir." There was no point denying it.

"It is understandable. It shows spirit. At the same time, it goes against the contract that you and I made between us in my study yesterday. You agreed to work for me. You agreed you were mine. Have you forgotten so soon?"

"No, sir."

"Very well. Then hear this. You cannot escape from here. It is not possible. Should you try again, there will be no further discussion, no punishment. I will simply have you killed. Do you understand?"

"Yes, sir."

He turned to the twin. "Josef, take Yassen away. Give him another beating—this time use a cane—and then lock him up on his own without food. Let me know when he has recovered enough to start work. That's all."

But we didn't leave. The twin wouldn't let me. And Sharkovsky was waiting for me to say something.

"Thank you, sir," I said.

Sharkovsky smiled. "That's right, Yassen. It's my pleasure."

I was to spend the next four years with Vladimir Sharkovsky.

I could not risk another escape attempt—not unless I was prepared to commit suicide. It took me a week to recover from the beating I received that day. I will not say that it broke my spirit. But by the end of it I knew that when I had picked up that gun and pointed it at my own head, I had signed a deal with the devil. I was not just his servant. I was his possession. You might even say I was his slave.

The place where I found myself, the huge white house, was his *dacha*—which is the name we use for a second home outside Moscow. It was in Serebryanyy Bor—"Silver Forest"—not that far from the center. This was an area well suited to wealthy families. The air was cleaner in the forest. It was quieter and more private. There were lakes and wooded walkways outside the complex where you could exercise the dogs or go hunting and fishing . . . not that these activities were available to me, of course, because I was never once allowed outside. I was restricted to the same few faces, the same menial tasks. My life was to have no rewards and no prospect of advancement or release. It was a terrible thing to do to anyone—even worse when you consider that I was so young.

And yet slowly, inevitably perhaps, I accepted my destiny. The injury to my face healed and fortunately it left no mark. I began to get used to my new life.

I worked all the time at the dacha—fifteen hours a day, seven days a week. I never had a vacation, and as Sharkovsky had promised, I didn't receive one kopeck.

The fact that I was being allowed to live was payment enough. Christmas, Easter, Victory Day, my birthdays— all these simply disappeared into each other. Sharkovsky had told me I would be his food taster, but he had also made it clear to me that this was only a small part of my work. He was true to his word. I chopped and carried firewood. I cleaned bathrooms and toilets. I helped in the laundry and the kitchen. I washed dishes. I painted walls. I looked after the dog, picking up after it when it fouled. I lifted suitcases. I unblocked drains. I washed cars. I polished shoes. I never complained. I understood that there was no point in complaining. The work never stopped.

Sharkovsky lived in the big house with his wife, Maya, and his two children, Ivan and Svetlana. Maya had very little to do with me. She spent most of her time reading magazines and paperbacks—she liked romances—or shopping in Moscow. She had once been a model and she was still attractive, but life with Sharkovsky was beginning to take its toll and I would sometimes catch her looking anxiously in the mirror, tracking a finger along a wrinkle or a wisp of gray hair. I wondered if she knew about the apartment in Gorky Park and the actress who lived there. In a way, she was as much a prisoner as I was, and maybe that was why she avoided me. I reminded her of herself.

The family was seldom together. Sharkovsky had business interests all over the world. As well as the helicopter, he kept a private jet at Moscow airport. It was on permanent standby, ready to take him to London, New York, Hong Kong, or wherever. I once glimpsed him on television, standing next to the president of the United States. He also took his vacations in the Bahamas or the South of France, where he kept a 150-meter yacht with twenty-one guest cabins, two swimming pools, and its own submarine. His son, Ivan, was at Harrow School in the UK. If there was one thing that all wealthy Russians wanted, it was an English education for their children. Svetlana was only seven when I arrived, but she was kept busy too. There were always private tutors coming to the house to teach dance, piano, horse riding, tennis (they had their own tennis court), foreign languages, poetry . . . When they were small, each child had had two nannies, one for the day, one for the night. Now they had two full-time housekeepers . . . and me.

Sixteen staff members lived full-time on the estate. They all slept in wooden cabins similar to mine, apart from Josef and Karl, who lived in the big house. There were two housekeepers—bossy women who were always in a hurry, always scowling. One of them was named Nina and she had it in for me from the start. She used to carry a wooden spoon in her apron, and whenever she got the chance she would clout me over the head with it. She didn't seem to have noticed that we were both servants, on the same level, but I didn't dare complain. I have a feeling that she hated working for Sharkovsky as much as I did. The only trouble was, she'd decided to take it out on me.

Then there was Pavel, about fifty years old, short, twitchy, always dressed in whites. He was very important to me because he was the chef and it was his cooking that I would be tasting. I'll say this for him. He was good at his job. All the food he prepared was delicious and I was given things that I had never known existed. Until I came to the dacha, I had never eaten salmon, pheasant, veal, asparagus, French cheese . . . or even such a thing as a chocolate éclair. Pavel only used the very best and the freshest ingredients, which were flown in from all over the world. I remember a cake he made for Maya's birthday. It was shaped like a Russian cathedral, complete with gold leaf icing on the domes. Heaven knows how much he was given to spend.

I never got to know Pavel very well, even though he slept in the cabin next to me. He was hard of hearing, so he never talked very much. He was unmarried. He had no children. All he cared about was his work.

The other staff was made up of a personal trainer and two chauffeurs. Sharkovsky had a huge fleet of cars and he was always buying more. Six armed guards patrolled the grounds and took turns manning the gatehouse. There was a general maintenance man who was always smoking, always coughing. He looked after the tennis court and the heated swimming pool in the conservatory. I will not waste time describing them or the gardeners, who turned up every morning and worked ten hours a day. They are not really part of my story. They were simply there.

But I must mention the helicopter pilot, a very quiet man in his forties with silver hair cut short in a military style. His name was Arkady Zelin and he had once flown with the VVS—the Soviet Air Force. He neither drank nor smoked. Sharkovsky would never have put his life in the hands of a man who was not utterly dependable. He was always on standby in case his master needed to get somewhere in a hurry, so he might spend weeks at the dacha between flights, and once the helicopter had been tied down, there was little for him to do. Just like Maya, he read books. He also kept himself fit, doing push-ups and running around the grounds. Sharkovsky had a gymnasium as well as the pool, but Zelin wasn't allowed to use either of them.

Zelin was one of the few people who bothered to introduce himself to me, and I was quick to let him know of my old love of helicopters. He piloted a twin-bladed Bell Jet Ranger with seating for four passengers—Sharkovsky had ordered it from Canada—and although I wasn't allowed near it, I often found myself gazing at it across the lawn. Escape was too dangerous to consider, but even so, in my wilder moments, it sometimes occurred to me that the helicopter might be my only way out. I couldn't hide in it. I'd have been spotted at once unless I crawled into the luggage compartment, and that was always kept locked. But maybe, one day, would I be able to persuade Zelin to take me with him—if he was flying alone? It was a foolish thought, but I had to keep some sort of hope alive in my head or I'd go mad. And so I stayed close to him. The two of us sometimes played *Durak* together, the same game that I had played with Dima, Roman, and Grigory. Sometimes I wondered what had happened to them. But as time went on, I thought about them less and less.

One other member of the staff was important to me. His name was Nigel Brown and he was English, a thin, elderly man with straggly ginger hair and a pinched face. He had once been the headmaster of a prep school in Norfolk and still dressed as if he worked there, with corduroy pants and, every day, the same tweed jacket with leather patches on the elbows. Zelin told me there had been some sort of scandal at the school and he had been forced to take early retirement. It was certainly true that Mr. Brown never talked about his time there. Sharkovsky had hired him as a private tutor, to help Ivan and Svetlana pass their exams. Other tutors came and went, but he lived at the dacha permanently.

We met every evening. Just as I had thought, the brick building that I had seen beside the cabins was a recreation room with a kitchen and dining area where we ate our meals. There were a few battered sofas and chairs, a billiard table, a television, a coffee machine, and a public telephone—although all calls were monitored and I wasn't allowed to use it at all. After dinner, the guards who weren't on duty, the chauffeurs, and sometimes the chef would sit and smoke. Mr. Brown had nothing to say to any of them, but perhaps because I was so young, he took an interest in me and decided for no good reason to teach me English. It soon became a very personal project and he took delight in my progress. It turned out that I had a natural aptitude for language, and after a while he began to teach me French and German too. Most of the languages I speak today I owe to him.

While he taught me, he drank. Maybe this was what had led to his downfall in Norfolk; at the start of each lesson he would open a bottle of vodka, and by the end of it I could hardly work out what he was saying no matter what the language. By midnight he was usually unconscious, and there were many occasions when I had to carry him back to his room. There was, however, one aspect of this that was useful to me. He was not a careful man, and under the influence of alcohol, he didn't care what he said.

It was Nigel Brown who told me what little I knew about Sharkovsky.

"How did he make all his money?" I once asked. It was a warm evening about six months after I had arrived. There was no breeze and the mosquitoes were whining beneath the electric lights.

"Ah, well, that's all politics," he replied. We had been talking in English, but now he slipped back into Russian, which he spoke fluently. "The end of Communism in your country created a sort of vacuum. A few men stepped in and he was one of them. They've sucked all the money out of your country, every last ruble. Some of them have made billions! Mr. Sharkovsky invested in companies. Scrap metal, chemicals, cars . . . he bought and he sold and the money flowed in."

"But why does he need so much protection?"

"Because he's an evil bastard." He smiled as if he was surprised by what he had just said but decided to continue anyway. "Mr. Sharkovsky is connected to the police. He's connected to the politicians. He's connected to the mafia. He's a very dangerous man. God knows how many people he's killed to get to where he is. But the trouble is, you can't go on like that without making enemies. He really is a *shark*." He repeated the last word in English. "Do you know the word *shark*, Yassen? It's a big fish. A dangerous fish. It will gobble you up. Now, let's get back to these irregular verbs, past tense. I buy, you bought. I see, you saw. I speak, you spoke . . ."

Sharkovsky must have had plenty of enemies. We lived our life under siege at the dacha and as I had discovered—painfully—there was no way in or out. There were X-rays and metal detectors at the main gates—just like a modern airport—and nobody was allowed in or out without being searched. The gardeners were expected to leave their tools behind when they finished work. They arrived empty-handed. The tutors, the drivers, the housekeepers . . . everyone's background had been checked except for mine, but then my background didn't matter. Josef and Karl always stayed close to their boss. The security cameras were always on. Everyone watched everyone else.

Other businessmen in Russia were careful but none of them went to these extremes. Sharkovsky was paranoid, but as I had seen for myself in that basement refrigerator, he had good reason to be.

He was extremely careful about what he ate and drank. For example, he only accepted mineral water from bottles that he had opened himself after checking that the seal had not been broken. The bottles always had to be glass. His enemies might be able to contaminate a plastic one using a hypodermic syringe. He sometimes ate food straight from the packet or the can, pronging it into his mouth with no sign of pleasure, but if it arrived on a plate, I would have to taste it first.

Most times, I would report to the kitchen before the meals were sent out and I would eat straight out of the pans, with Josef or Karl watching over me and Pavel standing nervously to one side. It's hard to describe how I felt about this. On one level, I have to admit that there was a part of me that enjoyed it. As I have said, the food was superb. But at the same time, it was still an unpleasant experience. First of all, one mouthful was all I was allowed and I was always aware that one mouthful might be enough to kill me. In a way, every tasting session was the same as the Russian roulette I had been forced to play on my first night. I learned to attune my senses to look out for the acrid taste of poison or simply the suspicion that something might not be right. The trouble was, by the time I detected it, it might well have killed me.

After a while, I put the whole thing out of my mind. I simply did what I was told robotically, without complaining. You might say that I had a very strange relationship with death. The two of us were constantly together, side by side. And yet we ignored each other. In this way, we were able to get by.

What I most dreaded were the formal dinners that I was forced to attend in the huge dining room with its brilliant chandeliers, gold and white curtains, antique French table and chairs, and dozens of flickering candles. Sharkovsky often invited business associates and friends—people he knew well. To begin with, I was worried that Misha Dementyev, the professor from Moscow University, might show up. He knew Sharkovsky. Indeed, he—along with my own stupidity—was the reason I was here. What would happen if he recognized me? Would it actually make my situation worse? But he never did appear and it occurred to me that he was probably a minor employee in Sharkovsky's empire and that it was very unlikely that he would receive an invitation. Nearly all the guests arrived in expensive cars. Some even came in their own helicopters. They were as rich and as vicious as Sharkovsky himself.

I had been given a gray suit with a white shirt and a black tie for these events—the same uniform as his bodyguards—and I would stand behind him as I had been instructed, looking down at the floor with my hands held behind my back. I was not allowed to speak. As each course was served, I would step forward and, using my own cutlery, take a sample directly from his plate, eat it, nod, and step back again. There was no doubt that Sharkovsky was afraid for his life, but at the same time he was enjoying himself. He loved playing the Roman emperor, showing me off to his other guests, deliberately humiliating me in front of them.

But if the father was bad, his son was much, much worse. Ivan Sharkovsky first became aware of me at one of those dinners, and although I wasn't supposed to look at the guests, out of the corner of my eye, I noticed him examining me. Ivan, a year older than me, resembled his father in many ways. He had the same dark qualities, but they had been distributed differently—in his black, curly hair, his heavy jowls, his downturned mouth. He seemed to be constantly brooding about something. His father was solid and muscular. He was fat with puffy cheeks, thick lips, and eyelids that were slightly too large for his eyes. Sitting hunched over the table, spooning food into his mouth, he had something brutish about him.

"Papa?" he asked. "Where did you get him from?"

"Who?" Sharkovsky was at the head of the table with Maya sitting next to him. She was wearing a huge diamond necklace that sparkled in the light. Whenever there were guests, he insisted that she smother herself in jewelry.

"The food taster!"

"From Moscow." Sharkovsky dismissed the question as if he had simply picked me up in a shop.

"Can he taste my food?"

Sharkovsky leaned forward and jabbed a fork in the direction of his son. He had been drinking heavily— champagne and vodka—and although he wasn't drunk, there was a looseness about the way he spoke. "You don't need a food taster. You're not important. Nobody would want to kill you."

The other guests all took this as a joke and laughed uproariously, but Ivan scowled and I knew that I would be hearing from him soon.

And the very next day, he came outside and found me. It was a cold afternoon. I was washing one of his father's cars, spraying it with a hose. As soon as I saw him coming, I stopped my work and looked down. This was what I had been taught. We had to treat the whole family as if they were royalty. Part of me hoped he would simply walk on, but at the same time I could see it wasn't going to happen. I knew straightaway that I was in trouble.

"What is your name?" he asked, although of course he knew.

"Yassen Gregorovich," I answered. That was the name I always used now.

"I'm Ivan."

"Yes," I said. "I know."

He looked at me questioningly and I could feel the sense of menace hanging in the air. "But you don't call me that, do you?"

"No . . . sir." It made me sick having to say the words, but I knew that was what he wanted.

He glanced at the car. "How long has it taken you to clean that?" he asked.

"An hour," I said. It was true. The car was the Bentley and it had been filthy. When I finished with it, it would have to look as if it had just come out of the showroom.

"Let me help you."

He gestured for the hose, which was still spouting water onto the ground, and dreading what was to come, I handed it to him. First he pointed it at the car. He placed his thumb over the end so that the water rushed out in a jet. It poured over the windshield and down over the doors. Then he turned it on me . . . my head, my chest, my arms, my legs. I could only stand there uselessly as he soaked me. Had this happened in my village, I would have knocked him to the ground. Right then I had to use all my self-restraint to stop myself from punching him in the face. But that was exactly what he was showing me. He had complete power over me. He could do anything to me that he wanted.

When he had finished, he smirked and handed the hose back to me. Finally, he noticed the bucket of muddy water beside the car. He kicked out, sending the contents spraying over the bodywork.

"Bad luck, Yassen," he said. "You're going to have to start again."

I stood there, dripping wet, as he turned and walked away.

After that, he tormented me all the time. His father must have known what was happening—Ivan would have never acted in this way without his authority—but he allowed it to carry on. And so I would get an order, usually transmitted by Josef, Karl, or one of the housekeepers. It didn't matter if it was morning or the middle of the night. I would go up to the big house and there he would be with football boots that needed cleaning, suitcases that needed carrying, or even crumpled clothes that needed ironing. He liked me to see his room, so spacious and comfortable, filled with so many nice things, because he knew I lived in a small wooden cabin with nothing. And despite what Sharkovsky had said, Ivan sometimes got me to taste his food for him, watching with delight as I leaned over his plate. Often he would play tricks on me. I would discover that he had deliberately filled the food with salt or chili powder so that it would make me sick. I used to long for the day he would return to his school in England and I would finally be left alone.

Four years . . .

I grew taller and stronger. I learned to speak different languages. But otherwise I might have been dead. I saw nothing of the world except what was shown on the television news. The horror of my situation was not the drudgery of my work nor the daily humiliations I received. It was in the dawning realization that I might be here for the rest of my life, that even as an old man I might be cleaning toilets and corridors and, worse still, that I might be grateful. Already, I could feel part of myself accepting what I had become. I no longer thought about escaping. I didn't even think about what might exist on the other side of the wall. Once, I found myself looking in the mirror because there was a stain on my shirt. There was to be a dinner that night and I was genuinely embarrassed, afraid I would let my master down. At that moment I was disgusted with myself. I saw, quite clearly, what I was becoming . . . perhaps what I had already become.

I never thought of Estrov. It was as if my parents had not existed. Even my time in Moscow seemed far behind me. It was obvious that Dima would never find me, and even if he did, I would be out of his reach. All I could think of was the work I would do the next day. This was Sharkovsky's revenge. He had allowed me to keep my life but he had taken away my humanity.

And so it might have continued.

But things changed quite suddenly in the early summer of my fourth year of captivity. Ivan had just finished his last year at Harrow and was due back any time. Svetlana was staying with friends at the Black Sea. Sharkovsky was having another dinner party and I had been told to report to the dining room to help with the preparations.

For some reason, I arrived early. As I walked up to the house, a car passed me and stopped at the front door. A man got out, rang the bell, and hurried inside. I had seen him before. His name was Brodsky and he was one of Sharkovsky's business associates from Moscow. The two of them owned several companies together and they were connected in other ways it was probably best not to know. I went into the kitchen, and a few moments later, the telephone rang. Mr. Brodsky wanted tea. Pavel was busy preparing the dinner—a broiled Atlantic salmon that he was decorating with red and black caviar. The housekeepers were laying the table. I was there and in my suit, so I made the tea and carried it up.

I crossed the hallway, which was now so familiar to me that I could have made my way blindfolded. The sweeping staircase, the marble pillars, the huge vases of flowers, and the chandeliers no longer meant anything to me. I had seen them too often. The door to the study was half open as I approached, and normally I would have knocked and entered, set the tray down on a table, and left as quickly as I could. But this time, just as I drew close, I heard a single word that stopped me in my tracks and rooted me to the floor.

"Estrov . . . they're asking questions about it again. We're going to have to do something before the situation gets out of hand."

Estrov.

My village.

It had been Brodsky who had spoken. Estrov. What could he possibly know about Estrov? Hardly daring to breathe, I waited for Sharkovsky to reply.

"You can deal with it, Mikhail."

"It's not as easy as that, Vladimir. These are Western journalists, working in London. If they connect you to what happened . . ."

"Why should they?"

"They're not stupid. They've already discovered you were a shareholder."

"So what?" Sharkovsky didn't sound concerned. "There were lots of shareholders. What exactly am I supposed to have done?"

"You wanted them to raise productivity. You wanted more profit. You ordered them to change the safety procedures."

"Are you accusing me, Mikhail?"

"No. Of course not. I'm your closest adviser and your friend, and why should I care if a few peasants got killed? But these people smell a story. And it would be seriously damaging to us if the name of Estrov were to be mentioned in the British press or anywhere else."

"It was all taken care of at the time," Sharkovsky replied. "There was no evidence left. Our friends in the ministry made sure of that. It never happened! Let these stupid journalists sniff around and ask questions. They won't find anything. And if I do come to believe that they are dangerous to me or to my business, then I'll deal with them. Even in London there are car accidents. Now stop worrying and have a drink."

"I ordered tea."

"It should be here. I'll call down."

It was a miracle I hadn't been caught listening outside. If Karl or Josef had come down the stairs and seen me, I would have been beaten. But I couldn't go in quite yet. I had to wait for the echoes of the conversation to die away. I counted to ten, then knocked on the door and entered. I kept my face blank. It was vital that they should not know that I had heard them talking. But as I crossed the carpet to where the visitor was sitting, the cup and the saucer rattled on the silver tray, and I'm sure there can't have been any color in my face.

Sharkovsky barely glanced at me. "What took you so long, Yassen?" he asked.

"I'm sorry, sir," I said. "I had to wait for the kettle to boil."

"Very well. Get out."

I bowed and left as quickly as I could.

I was shaking by the time I returned to the hall. It was as if all the pain and misery I had suffered in the last four years had been bundled together and then been slammed into me, delivering one final, knockout blow. It wasn't enough that Vladimir Sharkovsky had been endlessly cruel to me. It wasn't enough that he had reduced me to the role of his mindless slave. He was also directly implicated in the deaths of my mother and father, of Leo and everyone else in the village.

Was it really such a surprise? When I had first heard his name, it had been at the university in Moscow. He had been talking to Misha Dementyev on the telephone, and Dementyev had been directly implicated in what had happened. Nigel Brown had warned me too. He had told me that Sharkovsky invested in chemicals. I should have made the connection. And yet how could I have? It was almost beyond belief.

That night, as I stood at the table watching him tear apart the salmon that I had just tasted in front of all the other guests, I swore that I would kill him. It was surely the reason why fate had brought me here, and it no longer mattered if I lived or died.

I would kill him. I swore it to myself.

I would kill him.

I would kill.

## МЕХАНИК

I BARELY SLEPT THAT NIGHT. Every time I closed my eyes, my thoughts turned to guns, to kitchen knives, to the forks and shovels that I used in the garden, to hammers and fire axes. The truth was that I was surrounded by weapons. Sharkovsky was used to having me around. I could reach him and have my revenge for Estrov before anyone knew what had happened.

But what good would it do? Josef and Karl—of course I knew which was which by now—were always nearby, and even assuming I could reach Sharkovsky before they stopped me, they would deal with me immediately afterward. Lying in my simple wooden bed, in my empty room, looking at the cold light of another day, I saw that any action on my part would only lead to my own death. There had to be another way.

I felt sick and unhappy. I remembered Fagin with his leather notebook, reading out the different names and addresses in Moscow. What was it that had made me make this choice? How could I have been so foolish?

Once again, and for the first time in a very long time, my thoughts turned to escape. I knew what the stakes were. If I tried and failed, I would die. But it no longer mattered. One way or another, this had to end.

I had just one advantage. By now I knew everything

about the dacha, and that included all the security arrangements. I took out one of the exercise books that Nigel Brown had given me—it was full of English vocabulary—and turned to an empty page at the back. Then, using a pencil, I drew a sketch of the compound and, resting it on my knees, I began to consider the best way out.

There wasn't one.

Security cameras covered every inch of the gardens. Climbing the wall was impossible. Quite apart from the razor wire, there were sensors buried under the lawn and they would register my footfall before I got close. Could I approach one of the guards? No. They were all far too afraid of Sharkovsky. What about his wife, Maya? Could I somehow persuade her to take me on one of her shopping trips to Moscow? It was a ridiculous idea. She had no reason to help me.

Even if I did miraculously make it to the other side, what was I to do next? I was surrounded by countryside—the Silver Forest—with no idea how near I was to the nearest bus stop or station. If I made it to Moscow, I could go back to Tverskaya. I had no doubt that Dima would hide me . . . assuming he was still there. But Sharkovsky would use all his police and underworld contacts to hunt me down. It wouldn't bother him that he had been keeping me a prisoner for more than four years and he had treated me in a way that was certainly illegal. It was just that we had made a deal and he would make sure I kept it. I worked for him or I was dead.

For the next few weeks, everything went on as before.

I cleaned, I washed, I bowed, I scraped. But for me, nothing was the same. I could hardly bear to be in the same room as Sharkovsky. Tasting his food made me physically sick. This was the man responsible for what had happened to Estrov, the unnamed investor my parents had been complaining about the night before they died. If I couldn't escape from him, I would go mad. I would kill him or I would kill myself. I simply couldn't stay here anymore.

I had hidden the exercise book under my mattress and every night I took it out and jotted down my thoughts. Slowly, I realized that I had been right from the very start. There was only one way out of this place—and that was the Bell Jet Ranger helicopter. I turned to a new page and wrote down the name of the pilot, Arkady Zelin, then underlined it twice. What did I know about him? How could I persuade him to take me out of here? Did he have any weaknesses, anything I could exploit?

We had known each other for four years but I wouldn't say we were friends. Zelin was a very solitary person, often preferring to eat alone. Even so, it was impossible to live in such close confinement without giving things away, and the fact was that we did talk to each other, particularly when we were playing cards. Zelin liked that I was interested in helicopters. He'd even let me examine the workings of the engine once or twice, when he was stripping it down for general maintenance, although he had drawn the line at allowing me to sit in the cockpit. The security guards wouldn't have been happy about that. And then there was Nigel Brown. He knew a bit about Zelin too, and when he'd had a few drinks, he would share it with me.

*Arkady Zelin*

*Russian Air Force. Gambling?*
*Saratov.*
*Wife? Son.*
*Skiing . . . France/Switzerland. Retire?*

This was about the total knowledge that I had of the man who might fly me out of the dacha. I wrote it down in my exercise book and stared at the useless words, sitting there on the empty page.

What did they add up to?

Zelin had been in the Russian Air Force, but he'd been caught stealing money from a friend. There had been a court-martial and he had been forced to leave. He was still bitter about the whole thing and claimed that he was innocent, that he had been set up, but the truth was he was always broke. It was possible that he was addicted to gambling. I often saw him looking at the racing pages in the newspapers, and once or twice I heard him making bets over the phone.

He owned a crummy apartment in the city of Saratov, on the Volga River, but he hardly ever went there. He had three weeks' vacation a year—he often complained it wasn't enough—and he liked to travel abroad, to Switzerland or France in the winter. He loved skiing. He'd once told me that he would like to work in a ski resort. He'd talked briefly about heli-skiing, flying rich people to the top of glaciers and watching them ski down. He had been married and he carried a photograph in his wallet . . . a boy who was about eleven or twelve years old, presumably his son. I remembered the day when I had come into the rec room once with a huge bruise on my face. I had done a bad job polishing the silver and Josef had lost control and almost knocked me out. Zelin had seen me, and although he had said nothing, I could tell he was shocked. Perhaps I could appeal to him as a father? On the other hand, he never spoke about his son . . . or his wife, for that matter. He never saw either of them . . . perhaps they had cut him out of their life. He was quite lonely. He was the sort of person who looks after number one simply because there is nobody else.

I could scribble until I had filled the entire exercise book, but it wasn't going to help very much. Sharkovsky had a number of trips abroad that summer, and each time he left in the helicopter, I would stop whatever I was do- ing and watch the machine rise from the launch pad and hover over the trees before disappearing into the sky. I had nothing I could offer—no money, no bribe. I knew that there was no way Zelin was going to fall out with his employer. In the end I forgot about him and began to think of other plans.

We came to the end of another summer, and I swore

to myself that it would be my last at the dacha, that by Christmas I would be gone. And yet August bled into September and nothing changed. I was feeling sick and angry with myself. Not only had I not escaped, I hadn't even tried. Worse still, Ivan Sharkovsky had returned. He had left Harrow by now and was on his way to Oxford University. Presumably his father had offered to pay for a new library or a swimming pool because I'm not sure there was any other way he'd have gotten in.

I was in the garden pushing a wheelbarrow full of leaves, taking it down to the compost heap, when I first saw him. Suddenly he was standing there in front of me, blocking my path. Age had not improved him. He was still overweight. We were both about the same height but he was much heavier than me. I stopped at once and bowed my head.

"Yassen!" he said, spitting out the two syllables in a singsong voice. "Are you glad to see me?"

"Yes, sir," I lied.

"Still slaving for my dad?"

"Yes, sir."

He smirked at me. Then he reached down and picked up a handful of filthy leaves from the wheelbarrow. I was wearing a tracksuit, and very deliberately, he shoved the leaves down the front of my chest. Then he laughed and walked away.

From that moment on, there was a new, very disturbing edge to his behavior. His attacks on me became more physical. If he was angry with me, he would slap me or punch me, which was something he had never done before. Once, at the dinner table, I spilled some of his wine and he picked up a fork and jabbed it into my thigh. His father saw this but said nothing. In a way, the two of them were equally mad. I was afraid that Ivan wouldn't be satisfied until I was dead.

That was the month that Nigel Brown was fired. He wasn't particularly surprised. He was no longer tutoring Ivan, and his sister, Svetlana, had been accepted into Cheltenham Ladies' College in England, so there was nothing left for him to do. Mr. Brown was sixty by now and his teaching days were over. He talked about going back to Norfolk but he didn't seem to have any fondness for the place. It's often interested me how some people can follow a single path through life that takes them to somewhere they don't want to be. It was hard to believe that this crumpled old man with his vodka and his tweed jacket had once been a child, full of hopes and dreams. Was this what he had been born to be?

I was having dinner with him one evening, shortly before he went. Arkady Zelin had joined us. He had returned from Moscow that morning with Sharkovsky, who had flown in from the United States. Mr. Brown hadn't begun drinking yet. At least, he'd only had a couple of glasses—and he was in a reflective mood.

"You're going to have to keep up your languages, Yassen, once I'm gone," he was saying. "Maybe they'll let me send you books. There are very good tapes these days."

He was being kind, but I knew he didn't really mean what he was saying. Once he was gone, I would never hear from him again.

"What about you, Arkady?" he went on. "Are you going to stay working here?"

"I have no reason to leave," Zelin said.

"No. I can see you're doing well for yourself. Nice new watch!"

It was typical of my teacher to notice a detail like that. When we were doing exercises together, he could instantly spot a single misspelled word in the middle of a whole page. I glanced at Zelin's wrist just in time to see him draw it away, covering it with his sleeve.

"It was given to me," he said. "It's nothing."

"A Rolex?"

"Why do you interest yourself in things that don't concern you? Why don't you mind your own business?"

For the rest of the meal, Zelin barely spoke—and when he had finished eating, he left the room even though we'd agreed to play cards. I did an hour's German with Mr. Brown, but my mind wasn't into it and in the end he gave up, dragged the bottle off the table, and went and plumped himself into an armchair in the corner. I was left on my own, thinking. It was a small detail. A new Rolex. But it was strange the way Zelin had tried to conceal it, and why had it made him so angry?

I might have forgotten all about it, but the next day something else happened that brought it back to my mind. Sharkovsky was leaving for Leningrad at the end of the week. It was an important visit and he much preferred to fly than to take the roads. During the course of the morning, I saw Zelin working on the helicopter, carrying out a routine inspection. There was nothing unusual about that. But just before lunch, he presented himself at the house. I happened to be close by, cleaning the ground-floor windows, and I heard every word that was said.

"I'm very sorry, sir," he said. "We can't use the helicopter."

Sharkovsky had come to the front door, dressed in riding gear. He had taken up riding the year before and had bought two horses—one for himself, one for his wife. He'd also built a stable close to the tennis court and employed one of the gardeners as a groom. Zelin was standing in his overalls, wiping his hands on a white handkerchief that was smeared with oil.

"What's wrong with it?" Sharkovsky snapped. He had been very short-tempered recently. There was a rumor that things hadn't been going too well with his business. Maybe that was why he had been traveling so much.

"There's been a servo actuator malfunction, sir," Zelin said. "One of the piston rods shows signs of cracking. It's going to have to be replaced."

"Can you do it?"

"No, sir. Not really. Anyway, we have to order the part . . ."

Sharkovsky was in a hurry. "Well, why don't you call in the mechanic . . . what's his name . . . Borodin?"

"I called his office just now. It's annoying, but he's ill." He paused. "They can send someone else."

"Reliable?"

"Yes, sir. His name is Rykov. I've worked with him."

"All right. See to it."

Maya was waiting for him. He stormed off without saying another word.

I didn't know for certain that Zelin was lying, but I had a feeling that something was wrong. Every day at the dacha was the same. When I say that life went like clockwork, I mean it had that same dull, mechanical quality. But now there were three coincidences and they had all happened at the same time. The helicopter had been fine the day before, but suddenly it was broken. The usual mechanic—a brisk, talkative man who turned up every couple of months—was mysteriously ill. And then there was that new watch and the strange way that Zelin had behaved.

There was something else. It occurred to me that it really wasn't so difficult to replace a piston rod. I had been reading helicopter magazines all my life and knew almost as much as if I'd actually been flying myself. I was sure that Zelin would have a spare and should have been able to fix it himself.

So what was he up to? I said nothing, but for the rest of the day, I kept my eye on him. When the new mechanic arrived that same afternoon, I made sure I was there.

He came in a green van marked MVZ Helicopters, and I saw him step out to have his passport and employment papers checked by the guards. He was a short, plump man with a mop of gray hair that sprawled over his head and several folds of fat around his chin. He was dressed in green overalls with the same initials, MVZ, on the top pocket. He had to wait while the guards searched his van—for once, their metal detectors weren't going to help them. The back was jammed with spare parts. He didn't seem to mind, though. He stood there smoking a cigarette, and when they finally let him through, he gave them a friendly wave and drove straight across to the helicopter pad. Arkady Zelin was waiting for him there and they spent the rest of the day working together, stripping down the engine and doing whatever it was they had to do.

It was a warm afternoon, perfect weather to be outside, and at four o'clock one of the housekeepers sent me over to the helicopter with a tray of lemonade and sandwiches. The mechanic—Rykov—came strutting toward me with a smile on his face.

"Who are you?" he demanded.

"My name is Yassen, sir."

"And what's in these sandwiches?" He pried one open with a grimy thumb. "Ham and cheese. I see they look after you well here, Yassen. That's very nice of you." He was already eating, talking with his mouth full. Then he signaled to Zelin and the two of them went back to work.

I saw him a second time when I came back to pick

up the tray. Once again he was pleased to see me, but I thought that Zelin was more restrained. He was quieter than I had ever known him and this was a man I knew fairly well. You cannot play cards with someone and not get a sense of the way they think. I would have said he was nervous. I wondered why he wasn't wearing his new watch today. By now, the helicopter was almost completely reassembled. I lingered with the two men, waiting to take back the tray. And it seemed only natural to chat.

"Do you fly these?" I asked the mechanic.

"Not me," he said. "I just take them take them apart and put them back together."

"Is it difficult?"

"You have to know what you're doing."

"Wouldn't you like to fly?"

He shook his head. "Not really." He took out a cigarette and lit it. "I wouldn't know what to do with a joystick between my legs. I prefer to keep my feet safely on the ground."

"That's enough, Yassen," Zelin growled. "Don't you have work to do? Go and do it."

"Yes, Mr. Zelin."

I picked up the tray with the dirty glasses and carried them back to the house. But I'd already discovered everything I needed to know. The mechanic knew nothing about helicopters. Even I could have told him that a Bell helicopter doesn't have a joystick. It has a cyclic control that transmits instructions to the rotor blades. And it's not in front of you. It's to one side. Zelin had lied about the malfunction just as he had lied about the usual mechanic, Borodin, being sick. I was sure of it.

From that moment, I didn't let them out of my sight. I knew I would get into trouble. There were ten pairs of shoes I was meant to polish and a whole pile of crates to be broken up down in the cellar. But there was no way I was going to disappear inside. Zelin was planning something. If Rykov wasn't a helicopter mechanic, what was he? A thief? A spy? It didn't matter. Zelin had brought him into the compound and had to be part of it. This was the opportunity I'd been waiting for. I could blackmail him. Suddenly I saw him with his hand on the cyclic. He could fly me out.

My biggest worry was that Ivan would return to the dacha. He'd gone into Moscow for the day, driving the new Mercedes sports car that his father had bought him for his birthday, but if he came back and saw me, chances were that he would find some task for me to do. At five o'clock there was still no sign of him, but Sharkovsky and his wife returned from a ride and I helped them down from their saddles and walked the horses around to the stable. All the gardeners were gone. There were just the usual guards, walking in pairs, unaware that anything unusual was going on.

As I got back, I heard the helicopter start up, the whine of the engine rising as the rotors picked up speed. There was no sign of Rykov, but the van with the MVZ logo was still parked close by, so I knew he couldn't have left. I pretended to walk into the house, but at the last minute I hurried forward and ducked behind one of the cars. It was actually the Lexus that had first brought me here. If anyone found me there, I would pretend I was cleaning it.

I could see Arkady Zelin inside the cockpit, checking the controls, and suddenly the mechanic emerged from the other side of the helicopter and began to walk toward me, toward the house, carrying a sheaf of papers. If the guards had seen him, it would have looked completely natural. He had finished the job and he needed someone to sign the documentation. But he was being careful. He kept to the shadows. Nobody except me saw him go in through the back door.

I followed. I didn't know what I was going to do because I still hadn't worked out what was happening. All I knew was it wasn't what it seemed.

I crept down the corridor past the service rooms— the laundry and the boot room where I had spent so many hundreds of hours, day and night, in mindless drudgery. There was nobody around and that was very unusual. The mechanic couldn't have just walked into the house. One of the housekeepers would have challenged him and then made him wait while she went to fetch Josef or Karl. Rykov had entered only a few seconds ahead of me. He should have been here now. I felt the silence all around me. None of the lights were on. I glanced into the kitchen. There was a pot of soup or stew bubbling away on top of the hearth, but no sign of Pavel.

I was tempted to call out, but something told me to

stay quiet. I continued past the pantry. The door was ajar and that too was strange, as it was always kept locked in case the dog went in. I pushed it open, and at that moment everything made sense. It should have been obvious from the start. How could I have been so slow not to see it?

The housekeeper was there, lying on the floor. I had lost count of the number of times that Nina had snapped at me, scolding me for being too slow or too clumsy, hitting me on the head whenever she got the chance. I could see the wooden spoon still tucked into her apron, but she wasn't going to be using it. She had been shot at close range, obviously with a silencer, because I hadn't heard the sound of the gun. She was on her back with her hands spread out, as if in surprise. There was a pool of blood around her shoulders.

Arkady Zelin had been bribed. There was no other explanation. He never had any money but suddenly he had an expensive new watch. Rykov was an assassin who had come here to kill Sharkovsky. The safest way to smuggle a gun into the compound, perhaps the only way to get past the metal detectors and X-ray machines, was to bring it in a truck packed with metal equipment. It would have been easy enough to dismantle it and to scatter the separate parts among the other machinery. And the fastest way out after he had done his work was the helicopter, which was waiting even now, with the rotors at full velocity.

My mouth was dry. My every instinct was to turn and run. I couldn't help Sharkovsky. I didn't even want to. If

Rykov saw me, he would kill me without even thinking about it, just as he had killed Nina. But I didn't leave. I couldn't. This was the only chance I would ever get and I had to use it. There was a small ax hanging in the pantry. I had used it until there were blisters all over my hands, chopping kindling for the fire in Sharkovsky's study. Making as little noise as possible and doing my best not to look at the dead woman, I unhooked it. An ax would be little use against a gun, but even so, I felt safer having some sort of weapon. I continued to the door that led into the main hall. It was half open. Hardly daring to breathe, I looked through.

I had arrived just in time for the endgame.

The hall was in shadow. The sun was setting behind the house and its last rays were unable to reach the windows. The lights were out. I could hear the shrill whine of the helicopter outside in the distance, but a curtain of silence seemed to have fallen on the house. Josef was lying on the stairs where he had been gunned down. Rykov was standing in front of me, edging forward, an automatic pistol with a silencer attached in his hand. He was creeping toward the study, his feet making no sound on the thick carpet. But even as I watched, the door of the study opened and Vladimir Sharkovsky came out dressed in a suit and tie but with his jacket off. He must have heard the disturbance, the body tumbling down the stairs, and had come out to see what was happening.

"What—?" he began.

Rykov didn't say anything. He stepped forward and shot my employer three times, the bullets thudding into his chest and stomach so quietly that I barely heard them. The effect was catastrophic. Sharkovsky was thrown backward . . . off his feet. His head hit the carpet first. If the bullets hadn't killed him, he would surely have broken his own neck. His legs jerked, then became still.

What did I feel at that moment? Nothing. Of course I wasn't going to waste any tears on Sharkovsky. I was glad he was dead. But I couldn't find it in myself to celebrate the death of another human being. I was frightened. I was still wondering how I could turn this to my advantage. Everything was happening so quickly that I didn't have time to work out my emotions. I suppose I was in a state of shock.

And then a voice came floating out of the darkness.

"Don't turn around. Put the gun down!"

Rykov twisted his head but saw nothing. I was hiding behind the door, out of sight. It was Karl. He had come up from the cellar. Maybe he had been looking for me, wanting someone to help him move the crates. He was behind Rykov and over to one side, edging into the hall with a gun clasped in both hands, holding it at the same level as his head.

Rykov froze. He was still holding the gun he had used to kill Sharkovsky and I wondered if he'd had time to reload. He had fired at least five bullets. Rykov couldn't see where the order had come from, but he remained completely calm. "I will pay you one hundred thousand rubles to let me leave here," he said. He sounded very different from the mechanic I had spoken to. His voice was younger, more cultivated.

"Who sent you?"

"Scorpia."

The word meant nothing to me. Nor did it seem to have any significance for Karl. "Lower your gun very slowly," he said. "Put it on the carpet where I can see it . . . in front of you."

There was nothing Rykov could do. If he couldn't see the bodyguard, he couldn't kill him. He lowered the gun to the floor.

"Kick it away."

"If it hadn't been me, it would have been someone else," Rykov said. "Do yourself a favor. You're out of a job. Take the money and go."

Silence. Rykov knew he had to do what he was told. He kicked the gun across the carpet. It came to a halt a few centimeters away from the dead man.

Karl stepped farther into the hall, still holding his gun in both hands. It was aimed at the back of Rykov's neck. He glanced to the right and saw Josef lying spread-eagle on the stairs. Something flickered across his face and I had no doubt that he was going to shoot down the man who had been responsible for the death of his brother. As he moved forward, his path took him in front of the door where I was standing, and suddenly I was behind him.

"One hundred and fifty thousand rubles," Rykov said. "More money than you will ever see in your life."

"You have killed my brother."

Rykov understood. There was no point in arguing. In Russia, the blood tie, particularly between brothers, is a strong one.

Karl was very close to him now, and without really thinking about it I made the decision, probably the most momentous of my life. I slipped through the door and, raising the ax, took three steps into the hall. The body-guard heard me at the very last moment, but it was too late. Using the blunt end, I brought the ax swinging down and hit him on the back of the head. He collapsed in front of me, his arms, his legs, his entire body suddenly limp. The mechanic moved incredibly fast. He didn't know what had happened, but he dived forward, reaching out for the gun he had just kicked away. But I was faster. Before he could reach it, I had dropped the ax and swept up Karl's gun, and already I was aiming it straight at him, doing my best to stop my hand from shaking.

Rykov saw me and stared. He was unarmed. He couldn't believe what had just happened. "You!" he ex-claimed.

"Listen to me," I said. "I could shoot you now. If I fire a single shot, everyone will come. You'll never get away."

"What do you want?" he demanded.

"I want to get out of here."

"I can't do that."

"Yes, you can. You have to help me!" I scrabbled for words. "I knew you weren't really a mechanic. I knew you and Zelin were working together. But I didn't say anything. It's thanks to me that you managed to do what you came for." I nodded at the body of Vladimir Sharkovsky.

"I will give you money—"

"I don't want money. I want you to take me with you. I never asked to come here. I'm a prisoner. I'm their slave. All I'm asking is for you to take me as far away as you can and then to leave me. I don't care about you or about Scorpia. I'm glad he's dead. Do you understand? Is it a deal?"

He pretended to think . . . but only very briefly. The helicopter was still whining outside and very soon one of the guards might ask what was happening. Arkady Zelin might panic and take off without him. He didn't have any time. "Let me get my gun," he said. He stretched out his hand.

"No!" I tightened my grip. "We'll leave together. It'll be better that way for you. The guards know me and they're less likely to ask questions." He still seemed to be hesitating, so I added, "You do it my way or you never leave."

He nodded once. "Very well. Let's go."

We left together, back down the corridor, past the room with the dead woman. I was terrified. I was with a man who had just killed three people without even blinking and I knew that he would make me the fourth if I gave him the slightest chance. I made sure I didn't get too close to him. If he hit out at me or tried to grab me, I would fire the gun. This one wasn't silenced. The sound of the explosion would act as a general alarm.

Rykov didn't seem at all concerned. He didn't speak as we left the house and walked through the half-darkness together, skirting the fountain and making our way across the lawn toward the helicopter. And it had been true, what I had told him. One of the guards saw us but did nothing. The fact that I was walking with him meant that everything had to be okay.

But Zelin was shocked when he saw the two of us together. "What is he doing?" he shouted.

I could barely hear a word he said, but the meaning was obvious. I was struggling to keep the gun steady, feeling the wind from the rotors buffeting my arms. I knew that this was the most dangerous part. As we climbed in, the mechanic could wrench the gun away and kill me with it. He could probably kill me with his bare hands. I wasn't sure if I should go in first or second. What if he had another gun hidden under one of the seats?

I made my decision. "I'm getting in first!" I shouted. "You follow!"

As I climbed into the backseat, I kept the gun pointed at Zelin, not the mechanic. I knew that Rykov couldn't fly. If he tried anything, I would shoot the pilot and we would both be stuck. I think he understood my strategy. There was actually something close to a smile on his face as he climbed into the seat next to the pilot.

Zelin shouted something else. The mechanic leaned forward and shouted back into his ear. Again, it was impossible to hear. For all I knew, he was sentencing me to death. I might have the advantage now, but their moment would come while we were flying or perhaps when we landed. I wouldn't be able to keep them both covered and one of them would get me.

An alarm went off in the house, even louder than the scream of the helicopter. At once, the arc lamps all exploded into life. Two of the guards started running toward us, lifting their weapons. At the same time, a jeep appeared from the gatehouse, its headlights blazing, tearing across the grass. The mechanic slammed the door and Zelin hit the controls. The muzzles of the automatic machine guns were flashing in the darkness. Machine gun bullets were strafing past. One of them hit the cockpit but ricocheted away uselessly, and I realized that, of course, it must be armored glass.

The helicopter rose. It turned. It rocked above the lawn as if anchored there, unable to lift off. Bullets filled the air like fireflies.

And then Zelin jerked the cyclic. The helicopter twisted around one last time, and carrying me with it, it soared away, over the wall, over the forest, and into the darkening sky.

# БОЛТИНО

I HAD DONE IT. FOR the first time in four long years I was outside the compound. Even if I hadn't been sitting in a helicopter, I would have felt as if I were flying.

Sharkovsky was dead. It was nothing less than he deserved and I was glad that he would not be able to come after me. Would I be blamed for his death? The guards had seen me leave with Rykov. They knew I was part of what had happened. But I had not been the one who had invited the mechanic into the house. That had been Zelin. With a bit of luck, Sharkovsky's people would concentrate on the two of them and they would forget about me.

I was not safe yet. Far from it.

Both Zelin and Rykov had put on headphones, and although the blast of the rotors made conversation impossible for me, they were able to talk freely. What were they planning? I knew Zelin had been angry to see me but he was not the one in charge. Everything depended on Rykov. It might well be that he had already radioed ahead. There could be people waiting for me when we landed. I could be dragged out of my seat and shot. I knew already that human life meant nothing to the so-called mechanic. He had killed Nina, Josef, and Sharkovsky without batting an eyelid. It would make no difference to him if he added an unknown teenager to the score.

But I didn't care. I hated myself at the dacha. I was eighteen years old, still cleaning toilets and sweeping corridors, kneeling in front of Ivan to polish his shoes or, worse, still performing like a trained monkey at his father's dinner parties. It had been necessary to do these things to live, but what was the point of a life so debased? If I were to die now, at least it would be on my own terms. I had grabbed hold of the opportunity. I had escaped. I had proved to myself that I was not beaten after all.

And there were so many other things I was experiencing for the first time. I had never flown before. Even to sit in the luxurious leather seat of the Bell Jet Ranger was extraordinary. It had once been my dream to fly helicopters and here I was, gazing over Zelin's shoulder, watching him as he manipulated the controls. I wished I could see more of the countryside, but it was already dark and the outskirts of Moscow were little more than a scattering of electric lights. I didn't mind if I was being taken to my death. I was happy! Sharkovsky was finished. I had got away. I was flying.

After about ten minutes, Rykov turned around with a plastic bottle of water in his hand. He was offering it to me. I shook my head. At the same time, I retreated into the farthest corner, once again raising the gun. I was afraid of a trick. Rykov shrugged as if to say that I was making a mistake but he understood and turned back again. We continued for another half hour, then began to descend. It was only the pressure in my ears that warned me. Looking out of the window, I got the idea we must be above water; everything seemed to be black. Gently, we touched down. Zelin hit the controls and the engine stopped, the rotors slowing down.

Rykov took off his headphones and hung them up. Then he turned and faced me. "What now?" he asked.

"Where are we?" I demanded.

"On the edge of a town called Boltino. To the north of Moscow." He unfastened his seat belt. "You have your wish, Yassen. You have escaped from Vladimir Sharkovsky. I'm sure we all agree that the world is a better place without him. As for Arkady and me, we have a plane waiting to take us on the next leg of our journey. I'm afraid we have to say good-bye."

Ignoring the gun, almost forgetting I was there, Rykov opened the door and let himself out of the helicopter.

Arkady Zelin turned to me. "You shouldn't have done this," he hissed. "You don't know these people."

"Who are they?" I asked. I remembered the name I had heard. "Scorpia."

"They will kill you." He undid his own belt and scrambled out, following the mechanic.

Suddenly, I didn't want to be left on my own. I went after them. Looking around me, I had no idea why we had landed here. The helicopter was resting on a strip of mud that was so light colored that on second thought I realized it must be sand. An expanse of water stretched out next to it with about thirty sailing boats and cruisers moored to a jetty. There were trees on either side of us and what looked like wooden hangars or warehouses behind. The mechanic had been doing something to himself as I climbed down, and by the time I reached him, I was astonished to see that he had completely changed his appearance. The tangled gray hair was a wig. Underneath, his hair was the same color as mine, short and neatly cut. There had been something in his mouth that had changed the shape of his face, and the folds of flesh around his chin were gone. He was suddenly slimmer and younger. He stripped out of his oily overalls. Underneath he was wearing a black T-shirt and jeans. The man who had come to the dacha in a green van marked MVZ Helicopters had disappeared. Nobody would ever see him again.

"Where are you going?" I asked.

"We are leaving the country."

"In a boat?"

"In a plane, Yassen."

I looked around me, confused. How could a plane possibly land here?

"A seaplane," he went on. "Don't you see it?"

And there it was, sitting flat in the water with a pilot already in the cockpit, waiting to fly them to their next destination. The seaplane was white. It had two propellers perched high up on the wings and a tail that was higher still so that, even without moving, it looked as if it were trying to lift itself into the air.

"Take me with you," I said.

The mechanic who was no longer a mechanic smiled once again. "Why should I do that?"

I still had the gun. I could have forced him to take me . . . or tried to. But I knew that was a bad idea, that it would only end up getting me killed. Instead, I had to make a gesture, to show them I could be trusted. It was a terrible risk but I knew there was no other way. I turned the gun around in my hand and gave it to him. He looked genuinely surprised. He could shoot me where I stood and no one would be any the wiser. Apart from Zelin and the waiting pilot, there was nobody near.

"I saved your life," I said. "And I don't know why you killed Sharkovsky, but you couldn't have hated him more than I did. We're on the same side."

He weighed the gun. Zelin watched the two of us, his face pale.

"I'm not on any side. I was paid to kill him," Rykov said.

"Then take me with you. It doesn't matter where you're going. Maybe I can work for you. I can be useful to you. I'll do anything you tell me. I speak four languages. I . . ." My voice trailed away.

Rykov was still holding the gun. Perhaps he was amused. Perhaps he was wondering where to fire the next bullet. It was impossible to tell what was going on in his head. Eventually he spoke—but not to me. "What do you think, Arkady?" asked.

"I think we should leave," Zelin said.

"With or without our extra passenger?"

There was a pause and I knew my life was hanging in the balance. Arkady Zelin had known me for four years. He had played cards with me. I had never been a threat to him. Surely he wouldn't abandon me now.

At last he made up his mind. "With him, if you like. He's not so bad. And they treated him like a dog."

"Very well." Rykov slid the gun into his waistband. "It may well be that my employers have a use for you. They can make the final decision. But until then, you do exactly as you're told."

"Yes, sir."

"There's no need to call me that."

He was already walking down the jetty to the plane. The pilot saw him and flicked on the engine. It sounded like one of the gas lawnmowers at the dacha, and looking at the tiny propellers, the ungainly wings, I wondered how it could possibly separate itself from the water and fly. Arkady Zelin was carrying a travel bag that he had brought from the helicopter. It occurred to me that everything he owned must be inside it. He was leaving Russia, and if he was wise, he would never come back. Sharkovsky's people might leave me alone but they would certainly be looking for him. It was impossible to say how much Zelin had been paid for his part in all this, but I hoped the price included a completely new identity.

We got into the plane, a four-seater. I was lucky there was room for me. The new pilot ignored me. He knew better than to ask unnecessary questions.

But I had to know. "Where are we going?" I asked for a second time.

"To Venice," Rykov said.

*And to Scorpia,* he might have added. The most dangerous criminal organization in the world.

I was about to walk right into its arms.

# ⊕≡13⊟

## ВЕНЕЦИЯ

IT WAS NIGHTTIME when we landed.

Once again we came plunging out of the darkness with only the sound of the engine and the rising feeling in my stomach to tell me we had reached the end of our journey. The seaplane hit the water, bounced, then skimmed along the surface before finally coming to rest. The pilot turned off the engine and we were suddenly sitting in complete silence, rocking gently on the water. Looking out of the window, I could make out a few lights twinkling in the distance. I glanced at Rykov, his face illuminated by the glow of the control panels, trying to work out what was going on in his mind. I was still afraid he would turn around and shoot me. He gave nothing away.

What next?

Although I didn't know it at the time, Venice was surrounded by water, a perfect destination for those traveling by seaplane, particularly if they wished to arrive without being seen. It is possible, of course, that the Italian police and air traffic control had been bribed, but nobody seemed to have noticed that we had landed. For about two minutes, nobody spoke. Then I heard the deep throb of an engine and, with my face pressed against the window, I saw a motor launch slip out of the darkness and draw up next to us. The captain opened the door and we climbed out.

The motor launch was about ten meters long, made of wood, with a cabin at the front and leather seats behind. There were two men on board, a captain and a deckhand who helped us climb down. If they were surprised to find themselves with an extra passenger, they didn't show it. They said nothing. Rykov gestured and I sat out in the open at the back of the launch, even though the night was chilly. Zelin sat opposite me. He was clutching his travel bag, deep in thought.

We set off and as we went I heard the seaplane start up and take off again. I was already impressed. Everything about this operation had been well planned and executed down to the last detail. There had only been one mistake . . . and that was me. It took us about ten minutes to make the crossing, pulling into a ramshackle wooden jetty with striped poles slanting in different directions. Rykov dismounted and waited for me to follow, but Zelin stayed where he was and I realized he was not coming with us.

I held out a hand to the helicopter pilot. "Thank you," I said. "Thank you for letting me come with you."

"That place was horrible and Sharkovsky was beneath contempt," Zelin replied. "All those things they did to you . . . I'm sorry I didn't help."

"It's over now."

"For both of us." He shook my hand. "I hope it works out for you, Yassen. Take care."

I climbed onto the jetty and the boat pulled away. Moments later it had disappeared over the lagoon.

Rykov and I continued on foot. He took me to an apartment in the largest quarter of Venice, an area called Castello, near the old dockyards where we had disembarked. Why do I call him Rykov? As I was soon to discover, it was not his name. He was not a mechanic. I'm not even sure that he was Russian, although he spoke my language fluently. He told me nothing about himself in the time I was with him and I was wise enough not to ask. When you are in his sort of business—now my business—you are not defined by who you are but by who you are not. If you want to stay ahead of the police and the investigation agencies, you must never leave a trace of yourself behind.

We reached a doorway between two shops on an anonymous street. Rykov unlocked it and we entered a hallway with a narrow, twisting staircase leading up. His apartment was on the fourth floor. He unlocked a second door and turned on the light. I found myself in a square, whitewashed room with a high ceiling and exposed beams. It had very little personality and I guessed it was merely somewhere he stayed when he was in Venice rather than a home. The furniture looked new. There was a sofa facing a television, a dining table with four chairs, and a small kitchen. The pictures on the wall were views of the city, probably the same views you could see if you opened the shutters. It did not feel as if anyone had been here for some time.

"Are you hungry?" Rykov asked.

I shook my head. "No. I'm okay."

"There are some cans in the cupboard if you want."

I was hungry. But I was tired too. In fact, I was exhausted as all the suffering of the last four years suddenly drained out of me. It had all ended so quickly. I still couldn't quite accept it. "What happens now?" I asked.

Rykov pointed at a door that I hadn't noticed, next to the fridge. "There's only one bedroom here," he said. "You can sleep on the couch. I have to go out but I'll be back later. Don't try to leave here. Do you understand me? You're to stay in this room. And don't use the telephone either. If you do, I'll know."

"I don't have anyone to call," I said. "And I don't have anywhere to go either."

He nodded. "Good. I'll get you some blankets before I leave. Help yourself to anything you need."

A short while later, he left. I drank some water, then made up a bed on the couch and lay down without getting undressed. I was asleep instantly. It was the first time I had slept outside my small wooden cabin in four years.

I didn't hear Rykov come back, but I was woken up by him the following morning as he folded back the shutters and let in the sun. He had changed once again and it took me a few moments to remember who he was. He was wearing a suit and sunglasses. There was a gold chain around his neck. He looked slim and very fit, ten years younger than the mechanic who had come to mend the Bell Jet Ranger.

"It's nine o'clock," he said. "I can't believe Sharkovsky let you sleep this long. Is that when you started work?"

"No," I replied. At the dacha, I'd woken every morning at six.

"You can use my shower. I've left you a fresh shirt. I think it's your size. Don't take too long. I want to get some breakfast."

Ten minutes later, I was washed and dried, wearing a pale blue T-shirt that fit me well. Rykov took me out and for the first time I saw Venice in the light of an autumn day.

There is simply nowhere in the world like it. Even today, when I am not working, this is somewhere I will come to unwind. I love to sit outside while the sun sets, watching the seagulls circling and the traffic crossing back and forth across the lagoon . . . the water taxis, the water ambulances, the classic speedboats, the vaporettos, and of course the gondolas. I can walk for hours through the streets and alleyways that seem to play cat and mouse with the canals, suddenly bringing you to a church, a fountain, a statue, a tiny humpback bridge . . . or perhaps depositing you in a great square with bands playing, waiters circling, and tourists everywhere. Every corner has another surprise. Every street is a work of art. I am glad I have never killed anyone there.

Rykov took me to a café around the corner from his apartment, an old-fashioned place with a tiled floor, a long counter, and a giant-sized coffee machine that blew out clouds of steam. We sat together at a little antique table and he ordered cappuccinos, orange juice, and *tre-mezzini*—little sandwiches made out of soft bread with smoked ham and cheese. I hadn't eaten for about twenty hours and this was my first taste of Italian food. I wolfed them down and didn't complain when he ordered a second plate. There was a canal running past outside and I was fascinated to see the different boats passing so close to the window.

"So your name is Yassen Gregorovich," he said. He had been speaking in English ever since we had arrived in Venice. Perhaps he was testing me—although it was more likely that he had decided to leave the Russian language behind, along with the rest of the character he had been. "How old are you?"

"Eighteen," I said. I thought for a moment. "Almost nineteen."

"Sharkovsky kidnapped you in Moscow. He kept you his prisoner for more than four years. You were his food taster. Is that true?"

"Yes."

"You're lucky. We tried to poison him once and we were considering a second attempt. Your parents are dead?"

"Yes."

"Arkady Zelin told me about you in the helicopter. And about Sharkovsky. I don't know why you put up with it so long. Why didn't you just put a knife into the bastard?"

"Because I wanted to live," I said. "Karl or Josef would have killed me if I'd tried."

"You were prepared to spend the rest of your life working for him?"

"I did what I had to to survive. Now he's dead and I'm here."

"That's true."

Rykov took out a cigarette and lit it. He did not offer me one, nor did I want it. This was the one good thing that had come out of my time at the dacha. I had not been allowed to have cigarettes and so I had been forced to give up smoking. I have never smoked since.

"Who are you?" I asked. "And who are Scorpia? Did they pay you to kill Sharkovsky?"

"I'll give you a piece of advice, Yassen. Don't ask questions and never mention that name again. Certainly not in public."

"I'd like to know why I'm here. When we were in Boltino, it would have been easier for you to kill me."

"Don't think I wasn't tempted. As it is, it may be that I've made a bad mistake. We'll see." He drew on the cigarette. "The only reason I didn't kill you is because I owed you. It was stupid of me not to see the second bodyguard. I don't usually make mistakes and I'd be dead if it wasn't for you. But before you get any fancy ideas, we're quits. The debt is canceled. From now on, you're nothing to me. You're not going to work for me. And whatever happens to you, I don't really care."

"So why am I here?"

Because the people I work for want to see you. We're going there now."

"There?"

"The Widow's Palace. We'll get a boat."

From the name, I expected somewhere somber, an old, dark building with black curtains drawn across the windows. But in fact the Widow's Palace was an astonishing place, like something out the storybooks I had read as a child, built out of pink and white bricks, with dozens of windows glittering in the sun. There was a covered walkway on the level of the first floor, stretching from one end to the other, held up by slender pillars with archways below. And the palace wasn't standing beside the canal. It was actually sinking into it. The water was lapping at the front door with the white marble steps disappearing below the murky surface.

We pulled in and entered. There was a man standing at the entrance, bald with thick shoulders, wearing a white shirt and a black suit. Briefly, he examined us, then nodded for us to continue forward. Already I was regretting this. As I passed from the sunlight to the shadows of the interior, I was thinking of what Zelin had said as he left the helicopter. *You don't know these people. They will kill you.* Maybe four long years taking orders from Vladimir Sharkovsky had clouded my judgment. I was no longer used to making decisions.

A massive spiral staircase—white marble with wrought iron banisters—rose up, twisting over itself. Rykov went first and I followed a few steps behind, neither of us speaking. I was nervous but he was completely at ease, one hand in his pants pocket, taking his time. We came to a corridor lined with paintings: portraits of men and women who must have died centuries before. They stood in their gold frames, watching us pass. We walked down to a pair of doors, and before he opened them, Rykov turned and spoke briefly, quietly.

"Say nothing until you are spoken to. Tell the truth. She will know if you're lying."

She? The widow?

He knocked and without waiting for an answer opened the doors and went through.

The woman who was waiting for us was surely too young to have married and lost a husband. She couldn't have been more than twenty-six or twenty-seven, and my first thought was that she was very beautiful. My second was that she was dangerous. She was quite short, with long, black hair, tied back. It contrasted with the paleness of her skin. She wore no makeup apart from a smear of crimson lipstick that was so bright it was almost cruel. She was dressed in a black silk shirt, open at the neck. A simple gold necklace twisted around her neck. She could have been a model or an actress, but there was something that danced in her eyes and told me she was neither.

She was sitting behind a very elegant, ornate table with a line of windows behind her, looking out on the Grand Canal. Two chairs had been placed in front of her and we took our places without waiting to be told. She had not been doing anything when we came in. It was clear that she had simply been waiting for us.

"Mr. Grant," she said, and it took me a moment to realize she was talking to Rykov. "How did it go?" Her voice was very young. She spoke English with a strange accent that I couldn't place.

"There was no problem, Mrs. Rothman," Rykov—or Grant—replied.

"You killed Sharkovsky?"

"Three bullets. I got into the compound thanks to the helicopter pilot. He flew me out again. Everything went according to plan."

"Not quite." She smiled and her eyes were bright, but I knew something bad was coming and I was right. Slowly she turned to face me as if noticing me for the first time. Her eyes lingered on me. I couldn't tell what was in her mind. "I do not remember asking you to bring me a Russian boy."

Grant shrugged. "He helped me and I brought him here because it seemed the easiest thing to do. It occurred to me that he might be useful to you . . . and to Scorpia. He has no background, no family, no identity. He's shown himself to have a certain amount of courage. But if you don't need him, I'll get rid of him for you. And of course there'll be no extra charge."

I had been struggling to follow all this. My teacher, Nigel Brown, had done a good job. My English was very advanced—but still it was the first time I had heard it spoken by other people. There were one or two words I didn't understand. Nor did I need to. I fully understood the offer that Grant had just made and knew that once again my life was in the balance. The worst of it was, there was nothing I could do. I had nothing to say. I'd never be able to fight my way out of this house. I could only sit there and see what this woman decided.

She took her time. I felt her examining me and tried not to show how afraid I was. "That's very generous of you, Mr. Grant," she said at last. "But what gives you the idea that I can't deal with this myself?"

I hadn't seen her lower her hand beneath the surface of the table, but when she raised it she was holding a gun, a silver revolver that had been polished until it shone. She held it almost like a fashion accessory, a perfectly manicured finger curling around the trigger. It was pointing at me and I could see that she was deadly serious. She intended to use it.

I tried to speak. No words came out.

"It's rather a shame," Mrs. Rothman went on. "I don't actually enjoy killing, but you know how it is. Scorpia will not accept the second rate." Her hand hadn't moved but her eyes slid back to Grant. "Sharkovsky isn't dead."

"What?" Grant was shocked.

Mrs. Rothman moved her arm so that the gun was facing him. She pulled the trigger. Grant was killed instantly, propelled backward in his chair, crashing onto the floor.

I stared. The noise of the explosion was ringing in my ears. She swung the gun back to me.

"What do you have to say for yourself?" she asked.

"Sharkovsky's dead!" I gasped. It was all I could think to say. "He was shot three times."

"That may well be true. Unfortunately, our intelligence

is that he survived. He's in a hospital in Moscow. He's critical. But the doctors say he'll pull through."

I didn't know how to react to this information. It seemed impossible. The shots had been fired at close range. I had seen him thrown off his feet. And yet I had always said he was the devil. Perhaps it would take more than bullets to end his life.

The gun was still pointing at me. I waited for Mrs. Rothman to fire again. But suddenly she smiled as if nothing had happened, put the gun down, and stood up.

"Would you like a glass of Coke?" she asked.

"I'm sorry?"

"Please don't ask me to repeat myself, Yassen. I find it very boring. We can't sit and talk here, with a dead body in the room. It isn't dignified. Let's go next door."

She slid out from behind the desk and I followed her through a door that I hadn't noticed before—it was part of a bookshelf covered with fake books so as not to spoil the pattern. There was a much larger living room next door with two plump sofas on either side of a glass table and a massive stone fireplace, though no fire. Fresh flowers had been arranged in a vase and the scent of them hung in the air. Drinks—Coke for me, iced tea for her—had already been served.

We sat down.

"Were you shocked by that, Yassen?" she asked.

I shook my head, not quite daring yet to speak.

"It was very unpleasant but I'm afraid you can't allow

anyone too many chances in our line of work. It sends out the wrong message. This wasn't the first time Mr. Grant had made mistakes. Even bringing you here and not disposing of you when you were in Boltino frankly makes me question his judgment. But never mind that now. Here you are and I want to talk about you. I know a little about you, but I'd like to hear the rest. Your parents are dead, I understand."

"Yes."

"Tell me how it happened. Tell me all of it. See if you can keep it brief, though. I'm only interested in the bare essentials. I have a long day . . ."

So I told her everything. Estrov, the factory, Moscow, Dima, Sharkovsky . . . even I was surprised how my whole life could boil down to so few words. She listened with what I can only describe as polite interest. You would have thought that some of the things that had happened to me would have caused an expression of concern or sympathy. She really didn't care.

"It's an interesting story," she said when I had finished. "And you told it very well." She sipped her tea. I noticed that her lipstick left bright red marks on the glass. "The strange thing is that the late Mr. Grant was actually quite right. You could be very useful to us."

"Who are you?" I asked. Then I added, "Scorpia."

"Ah yes. Scorpia. I'm not entirely sure about the name, if you want the truth. The letters stand for *sabotage, corruption, intelligence,* and *assassination,* but that's only a few of the things we get up to. They could have added kidnapping, blackmail, terrorism, drug trafficking, and vice, but that wouldn't make a word. Anyway, we've got to be called something and I suppose Scorpia has a nice ring to it.

"I'm on the executive board. Right now there are twelve of us. Please don't get the idea that we're monsters. We're not even criminals. In fact, quite a few of us used to work in the intelligence services . . . England, France, Israel, Japan . . . but it's a fast-changing world and we realized that we could do much better if we went into business for ourselves. You'd be amazed how many governments need to subcontract their dirty work. Think about it. Why risk your own people spying on your enemies, when you can simply pay us to do it for you? Why start a war when you can pick up the phone and get someone to kill the head of state? It's cheaper. Fewer people get hurt. In a way, Scorpia has actually been quite helpful when it comes to world peace. We still work for virtually all the intelligence services, and that must tell you something about us. A lot of the time we're doing exactly the same jobs that we were doing before. Just at a higher price."

"You were a spy?" I asked.

"Actually, Yassen, I wasn't. I'm from Wales. Do you know where that is? Believe it or not, I was brought up in a tiny mining community. My parents used to sing in the local choir. They're in jail now and I was in an orphanage when I was six years old. My life has been quite similar to yours in some ways. But as you can see, I've been rather more successful."

It was warm in the room. The sun was streaming in through the windows, dazzling me. I waited for her to continue.

"I'll get straight to the point," she said. "There's something quite special about you, Yassen, even if you probably don't even appreciate yourself. Do you see what I'm getting at? You're a survivor, yes. But you're more than that. In your own way, you're unique!

"You see, pretty much everyone in the world is in a database somewhere. The moment you're born, your details get put into a computer, and computers are getting more and more powerful by the day. Right now I could pick up the telephone and in half an hour I would know anything and everything about anyone you care to name. And it's not just names and that sort of thing. You break into a house and leave a fingerprint or one tiny little piece of DNA and the international police will track you down no matter where in the world you are. A crime committed in Rio de Janeiro can be solved overnight at Scotland Yard, and believe me, as the technology changes, it's going to get much, much worse.

"But you're different. The Russian authorities have actually done you a great favor. They've wiped you out. The village you were brought up in no longer exists. You have no parents. I would imagine that every last piece of information about you and everyone you ever knew in

Estrov has been destroyed. And do you know what that's done? It's made you a nonperson. From this moment on, you can be completely invisible. You can go anywhere and do anything and nobody will be able to find you."

She reached for her glass, turning it between her finger and her thumb. Her nails were long and sharp. She didn't drink.

"We are always on the lookout for assassins," she said. "Contract killers like Mr. Grant. As you have seen, the price of failure in our organization is a high one, but so are the rewards of success. It is actually a very attractive life. You travel the world. You stay in the best hotels, eat in the best restaurants, shop in Paris and New York. You meet interesting people . . . and some of them you kill."

I must have looked alarmed, because she raised a hand, stopping me.

"Let me finish. You were brought up by your parents, who, I am sure, were good people. So were mine! You are thinking that you could never murder someone for money. You could never be like Mr. Grant. But you're wrong. We will train you. We have a facility not very far from here, on an island called Malagosto. We run a school there . . . a very special school. If you go there, you will work harder than you have ever worked in your life, even harder than in that dacha where you were kept.

"You will be given training in weapons and martial arts. You will learn the techniques of poisoning, shooting, explosives, and hand-to-hand combat. We will show you how to pick locks, how to disguise yourself, how to talk your way in and out of any given situation. Every week there will be psychological and physical evaluations. We will teach you not only how to act like a killer but how to think like one. There will also be formal schooling. You need to have math and science. Your English is excellent but you still speak with a Russian accent. You must lose it. You should learn Arabic as we have many operations in the Middle East.

"I can promise you that you will be more exhausted than you would have thought possible, but if you last the course, you will be perfect. The perfect killer. And you will work for us.

"The alternative? You can leave here now. Believe it or not, I really mean it. I won't stop you. I'll even give you the money for the train fare if you like. You have nothing. You have nowhere to go. If you tell the police about me, they won't believe you. My guess is that you will end up back in Russia. Sharkovsky will be looking for you. Without our help, believe me, he will find you.

"So there you have it, Yassen. That's what it comes down to."

She smiled and finished her drink.

"What do you say?"

# 14

# OCTPOB

THEY TAUGHT ME how to kill.

In fact, during the time that I spent on the island of Malagosto, they taught me a great deal more than that. There was no school in the world that was anything like the Training and Assessment Center that Scorpia had created. How do I begin to describe all the differences? It was, of course, highly secret. Nobody chose to go there . . . they chose you. It was surely the only school in the world where there were more teachers than students. There were no holidays, no sports days, no uniforms, no punishments, no visitors, no prizes, and no exams. And yet it was in its own way a school. You could call it the Harvard of murder.

What was strange about Malagosto was how close it was to mainland Venice. Here was this city full of rich tourists drifting between jazz bars and restaurants, five-star hotels and gorgeous palazzos—and less than three-quarters of a kilometer away, across a strip of dark water, there were activities going on that would have made their hair stand on end. The island had been a plague center once. There was an old Venetian saying: "Sneeze in Venice and wipe your nose in Malagosto"—the last thing you could afford in a tightly packed medieval city with its sweating crowds and stinking canals was an outbreak of the plague. The rich merchants had built a monastery, a hospital, living quarters, and a cemetery for the infected. They would house them, look after them, pray for them, and bury them. But they would never have them back.

The island was small. I could walk around it in forty minutes. Even in the summer the sand was a dirty yellow, covered with shingle, and the water was an unappealing gray. All the woodland was tangled together as if it been hit by a violent storm. There was a clearing in the middle with a few gravestones, the names worn away by time, leaning together as if whispering the secrets of the past. The monastery had a bell tower made out of dark red bricks and it slanted at a strange angle . . . it appeared sure to collapse at any moment. The whole building looked dilapidated, half the windows broken, the courtyards pitted with cracks, weeds everywhere.

But the actual truth was quite surprising. Scorpia hadn't just watched the place fall into disrepair, they had helped it on its way. They had removed anything that looked too attractive: fountains, statues, frescoes, stained glass windows, ornamental doors. They had even gone so far as to insert a hydraulic arm into the tower, deliberately tilting it. The whole point was that Malagosto was not meant to be beautiful. It was off limits anyway, but they didn't want a single tourist or archaeologist to feel it was worth hiring a boat and risking the crossing. The last time anyone had tried had been six years before, when a group of nuns had taken a ferry from Murano, following in the footsteps of some minor saint. They had still been singing when the ferry had inexplicably blown up. The cause was never found.

Inside, the buildings were much more modern and comfortable than anyone would have guessed. There were two classrooms, warm and soundproofed, with brand-new furniture and banks of audiovisual equipment that would have had my old teachers in Rosna staring in envy. All they'd had was chalk and blackboards. We had both indoor and outdoor shooting ranges, a superbly equipped gymnasium with an area devoted exclusively to fighting—judo, karate, kickboxing, and above all *ninjutsu*—and a swimming pool, although most of the time we used the sea. If the temperature was close to freezing, that only made the training more worthwhile. My own rooms, on the second floor of the accommodation block, were very comfortable. I had a bedroom, a living room, and even my own bathroom with a huge marble bath that took only seconds to fill, the steaming hot water jetting out of a monster brass tap shaped like a lion's head. I had my own desk, my own TV, and a private fridge that was always kept stocked up with bottled water and soft drinks. All of this came at a price. Once I left the facility, I would be tied into a five-year contract working exclusively for Scorpia, and the cost of my training would be taken from my salary. This was made clear to me from the start.

After I had met Julia Rothman and accepted her offer, I was taken straight to the island in the back of a water ambulance. It seemed an odd choice of vessel, but of course it would have been completely inconspicuous in the middle of all the other traffic, and I did not travel alone. Mr. Grant came with me, lying on a stretcher. I have to say that I felt sorry for him. In his own way he had been kind to me. I turned my thoughts to Vladimir Sharkovsky, probably lying in a Moscow hospital, surrounded by fresh bodyguards watching over him just as the machines would be watching over his heart rate, his blood pressure, all his vital signs. Who would be tasting his food for him now?

It was midday when I arrived.

The water ambulance pulled up to a jetty that was much less dilapidated than it looked and I saw a young woman waiting for me. In fact, from a distance, I had mistaken her for a man. Her dark hair was cut short and she was wearing a loose white shirt, a waistcoat, and jeans. But as we drew closer, I saw that she was quite attractive, about two or three years older than me, quite serious looking. She wore no makeup. She reached out and gave me a hand off the boat and suddenly we were standing together, weighing each other up.

"I'm Colette," she said.

"I'm Yassen."

"Welcome to Malagosto. Do you have any luggage?"

I shook my head. I had brought nothing with me. I had no possessions in the world.

"I've been asked to show you around. Mr. Nye will want to see you later on."

"Mr. Nye?"

"You could say he's the principal. He runs this place."

"Are you a teacher?"

She smiled. "No. I'm a student. The same as you. Come on—I'll start by showing you your room."

I spent the next two hours with Colette. There were only three students there at the time. I would be the fourth. The others were on the mainland, involved in some sort of exercise. As we stood on the beach, looking out across the water, Colette told me a little about them.

"There's Marat. He's from Poland. And Sam. He only got here a few weeks ago . . . from Israel. Neither of them talk very much, but Sam came out of the army. He was going to join Mossad—Israeli intelligence—but Scorpia made him a better offer."

"What about you?" I asked. "Where have you come from?"

"I'm French."

We had been speaking in English, but I had been aware she had a slight accent. I waited for her to tell me more, but she was silent. "Is that all?" I asked.

"What else is there? You and me . . . we're here. That's all that matters."

"How did you get chosen?"

"I didn't get chosen. I volunteered." She thought for a moment. "I wouldn't ask personal questions if I were you. People can be a bit touchy around here."

"I just thought it was strange, that's all. A woman learning how to kill . . ."

She raised an eyebrow at that. "You are old fashioned, aren't you, Yassen! And here's another piece of advice. Maybe you should keep your opinions to yourself." She looked at her watch, then drew a thin book out of her back pocket. "And now I'm afraid I'm going to have to leave you on your own. I've got to finish this."

I glanced at the cover. _Modern Interrogation Techniques_ by Dr. Three.

"You might get to meet him one day," Colette said. "And if you do, be careful what you say. You wouldn't want to end up as a chapter in his book."

I spent the rest of the day alone in my room, lying on my bed with all sorts of thoughts going through my head. Much later on, at about eight o'clock in the evening, I was summoned to the headmaster's office, and it was there that I met the man who was in charge of all the training on Malagosto.

His name was Desmond Nye and my first thought was that he had the darkest skin I had ever seen. His glistening bald head showed off eyes that were extraordinarily large and animated and he had brilliant white teeth, which he displayed often. He had an astonishing smile. He dressed very carefully—he liked well-cut blazers, obviously expensive. His shoes were always polished to perfection. He was originally from Somalia. His family were modern-day pirates, holding up luxury yachts, cruise ships, and even on one occasion an oil tanker that had strayed too close to the shore. They were utterly ruthless . . . I saw framed newspaper articles in the office describing their exploits.

Nye himself had a very loud voice. Everything about him was larger than life.

"Yassen Gregorovich!" he exclaimed, pointing me to a chair in the office, which was almost circular with eight sides and an iron chandelier in the middle. There were floor-to-ceiling bookshelves, two windows looking out onto woodland, and half a dozen clocks, each one showing a different time. A pair of solid iron filing cabinets stood against one wall. Mr. Nye wore the key that opened them around his neck. "Welcome to Malagosto," he went on. "Welcome indeed. I always take the greatest pleasure in meeting the new recruits because, you see, when you leave here, you will not be the same. We are going to turn you into something very special, and when I meet you after that, it may well be that I do not want to. You will be dangerous. I will be afraid of you. Everyone who meets you, even without knowing why, will be afraid of you. I hope that thought does not distress you, Yassen, because if it does, you should not be here. You are going to become a contract killer, and although you will be rich and you will be comfortable, I am telling you now, it is a very lonely path."

There was a knock at the door and a second man appeared, barely half the height of the headmaster, dressed in a linen suit and brown shoes, with a round face and a small beard. He seemed quite nervous of Mr. Nye, his eyes blinking behind his tortoiseshell glasses. "You wanted to see me, headmaster?" he inquired. He had a French accent, much more distinct than Colette's.

"Ah yes, Oliver!" He gestured in my direction. "This is our newest recruit. His name is Yassen Gregorovich. Mrs. Rothman sent him over from the Casa Vedova."

"Delighted." The little man nodded at me.

"This is Oliver D'Arc. He will be your personal tutor and he will also be taking many of your classes. If you're unhappy, if you have any problems, you go to him."

"Thank you," I said, but I had already decided that if I had any problems I would most certainly keep them to myself. This was the sort of place where any weakness would only be used against you.

"I am here for you anytime you need me," D'Arc assured me.

I would spend a lot of time with Oliver D'Arc while I was at Malagosto, but I never completely trusted him. I don't think I ever knew him. Everything about him—his appearance, the way he spoke, even his name, probably—was an act put on for the students' benefit. Later on, after Nye was killed by one of his own students, D'Arc became the headmaster, and by all accounts he was very good at the job.

"Do you have any questions, Yassen?" he asked me.

"No, sir," I said.

"That's good. But before you turn in for the night, there's something I want you to do for me; I hope you don't mind. It shouldn't take more than a couple of hours."

That was when I noticed that Oliver D'Arc was holding a spade.

My first job on Malagosto was to bury Mr. Grant in

the little cemetery in the wood. It was a final resting place that he would share with plague victims who had died four hundred years before him, although I had no doubt that there were other more recent arrivals too, men and women who had failed Scorpia just like him. It was an unpleasant, grisly task, digging on my own in the darkness. Even Sharkovsky had never asked me to do such a thing—but it's possible that it was meant to be a warning to me. Julia Rothman had let me live. She had even recruited me. But this is what I could look forward to if I let her down.

As I dragged Mr. Grant off the stretcher and tipped him into the hole I had dug, I couldn't help but wonder if someone would do the same for me one day. For what it's worth, it is the only time I have ever had such thoughts. When your business is death, the only death you should never consider is your own.

It had begun to rain slightly, a thin drizzle that only made my task more unpleasant. I filled in the grave, flattened it with the spade, then carried the stretcher back to the main complex. Oliver D'Arc was waiting for me. He escorted me to my room and even insisted on running a bath for me, adding a good measure of Floris of London bath oil to the foaming water. I was glad when he finally left. I was afraid he was going to offer to scrub my back.

Five months . . .

No two days were ever exactly the same, although we were always woken at half past five in the morning for a one-hour run around the island followed by a forty-minute swim—out to a stump of rock and back again. Breakfast was at half past seven, served in a beautiful dining room with a sixteenth-century mosaic on the floor, wooden angels carved around the windows, and a faded view of heaven painted on the domed ceiling above our heads. The food was always excellent. All four students ate together and I usually found myself sitting next to Colette. As she had warned me, Marat and Sam weren't exactly unfriendly, but they hardly ever spoke to me. Sam was dark and very intense. Marat seemed more laid-back, sitting in class with his legs crossed and his hands behind his back. After they had graduated, they decided to work together as a team and were extremely successful, but I never saw them again.

Morning lessons took place in the classrooms. We learned about guns and knives, how to create a booby trap, how to make a bomb using seven different ingredients that you could find in any supermarket. There was one teacher—he was redheaded, scrawny, with tattoos all over his upper body—who brought in a different weapon for us to practice with every day: not just guns and knives but swords, throwing spikes, ninja fighting fans, and even a medieval crossbow . . . he actually insisted on firing an apple off Marat's head. His name was Gordon Ross and he came from a city called Glasgow, in Scotland. He had briefly been assistant to the chief armorer at MI6 until Scorpia had tempted him away at five times his original salary.

The first time we met, I impressed him by stripping down an AK7 machine gun in eighteen seconds. My old friend Leo, of course, would have done it faster. Ross was actually a knife man. His two great heroes were William Fairbairn and Eric Sykes, who had together created the ultimate fighting knife for British commandos during the Second World War. He was an expert with throwing knives and he'd had a set specially designed and weighted for his hand. Put him twenty meters from a target and there wasn't a student on the island who could beat him for speed or accuracy, even when he was competing against guns.

Ross also had a fascination with gadgets. He didn't manufacture any himself, but he had made a study of the secret weaponry provided by all the different intelligence services and he had managed to steal several items, which he brought in for us to examine. There was a credit card developed by the CIA. One edge was razor sharp. The French had come up with a string of onions—several of them were grenades. His own employers, MI6, had provided an antiseptic cream that could eat through metals, a fountain pen that fired a poisoned nib, and a Power Plus battery that concealed a radio transmitter. You simply gave the whole thing a half twist and it would set off a beacon to summon immediate help. All these devices amused him, but at the end of the day he dismissed them as toys. He preferred his knives.

Weapons and self-defense were only part of my training. I was surprised to find myself going back to school in the old-fashioned sense; I learned math, English, science—even classical music, art, and cooking. Oliver D'Arc took some of these classes. However, I will never forget the day I was introduced to the unsmiling Italian woman who never told anyone her name but called herself the Countess. It may well be that she was a true aristocrat. She certainly behaved like one, insisting that we stand when she entered and always address her as "ma'am." She was about fifty, exquisitely dressed, with expensive jewelry and perfect manners. When she stood up, she expected us to do so too. The Countess took us shopping and to art galleries in Venice. She made us read newspapers and celebrity magazines and often talked about the people in the photographs. At first, I had absolutely no idea what she was doing on the island.

It was only later that I understood. A killer is not just someone who lies on a roof with a 12.7mm sniper rifle, waiting for his prey to walk out of a restaurant. Sometimes it is necessary to be inside that restaurant. To pin down your target, you have to get close to him. You have to wear the right clothes, walk in the right way, demand a good table, understand the food and the wine. Do you think a boy from a poor Russian village would have been able to do any of these things if he had not been taught? I have been to art auctions, to operas, to fashion shows, and to horse races. I have sipped champagne with bankers, professors, designers, and multimillionaires. I have always felt comfortable and nobody has ever thought I was out of place. For this, I have the Countess to thank.

The toughest part of the day came after lunch. The afternoons were devoted to hand-to-hand combat, and three-hour classes were taught either by the headmaster, Mr. Nye, or a Japanese instructor, Hatsumi Saburo. We all called him HS and he was an extraordinary man. He must have been seventy years old, but he moved faster than a teenager, certainly faster than I did. If you weren't concentrating, he would knock you down so hard and so fast that you simply wouldn't be aware of what had happened until you were on the floor and he was standing above you, gazing at the ceiling, as if it had been nothing to do with him. Desmond Nye taught judo and karate, but it was Hatsumi Saburo who introduced me to a third martial art, *ninjutsu,* and it is this that has always stayed with me.

*Ninjutsu* was the fighting method developed by the ninjas, the spies, and the assassins who roamed across Japan in the fifteenth century. It was taught to them by the priests and the warriors who were in hiding in the mountains. What I learned from HS over the next five months was what I can only describe as a total fighting system that encompassed every part of my body, including my feet, my knees, my elbows, my fists, my head, even my teeth. And it was more than that. He used to talk about *nagare,* the flow of technique: knowing when to move from one form of attack to the next. At the end of the day, everything came down to mental attitude. "You cannot win if you do not believe you will win," he once said to me. He had a very heavy Japanese accent and barked like a dog. "You must control your emotions. You must control your feelings. If there is any fear or insecurity, you must destroy it before it destroys you. It is not the size or the strength of your opponent that matters. These can be measured. It is what cannot be measured . . . courage, determination . . . that count."

I felt great reverence for Hatsumi Saburo, but I did not like him. Sometimes we would fight each other with wooden swords that were known as _boken_. He never held back. When I went to bed that night, my whole body would be black and blue while I had never so much as touched him. "You have too many emotions, Yass-sen!" he would crow as he stood over me. "All that sadness. All that anger. It is the smoke that gets into your eyes. If you do not blow it away, how can you hope to see?"

Was I sad about what had happened to me? Was I angry? I suppose Scorpia would know better than me because, just as Mrs. Rothman had promised, I was given regular psychological examinations by a doctor named Karl Steiner, who, despite his name, actually came from South Africa. I disliked him from the start, the way he looked at me, his eyes always boring into mine as if he suspected that everything I said was a lie. I don't think I ever heard Dr. Steiner say anything that wasn't a question. He was a very neat man, always dressed in a suit with a carnation in his lapel. He would sit there with one leg crossed over the other, occasionally glancing at a gold pocket watch to check on the time. His office was completely bare . . . just a white space with two armchairs. It had a window that looked out over the firing range and I would sometimes hear the crack of the rifles outside as he fired his own questions my way.

I regretted now that I had told Julia Rothman so much about myself. She had passed all the information to him and he wanted me to talk about my parents, my grandmother, my childhood in Estrov. The more we talked, the less I wanted to say. I felt empty, as if the life I was describing was something that no longer belonged to me. And the strange thing is, I think that was exactly what he wanted. In his own way he was exactly like Hatsumi Saburo. My old life was smoke. It had to be blown away.

We were given a couple of hours' rest before dinner, but we were always expected to use the time productively. My tutor, Oliver, insisted that I read books . . . and in English, not Russian. Some evenings we had political discussions. I learned more about my own country while I was on the island than I had the whole time I was living there.

We also had guest lecturers. They were brought to Malagosto in blindfolds and many of them had been in prison, but they were all experts in their own fields. One was a pickpocket—he shook hands with each one of us before he began and then started his lecture by returning our watches. Another showed us how to pick locks. There was one really brilliant lecture by an elderly Hungarian man with terrible scars down the side of his face.

He had lost his sight in a car accident. He talked to us for two hours about disguise and false identities, and then revealed that he was actually a thirty-two-year-old Belgian woman and could see as well as any of us.

You never knew what was going to happen. The school loved to throw surprises our way. Sometimes, in the middle of the night, a whistle would blow and we would find ourselves called out to the assault course, crawling through the rain and the mud, climbing nets, and swinging on ropes while Mr. Ross fired live ammunition at our heels. Once, we were told to swim to the mainland, to steal clothes and money when we got there, and then to make our own way back.

Scorpia did not want us to become too cut off, too removed from the real world. As well as the expeditions with the Countess, they often gave us half a day off to visit Venice. Marat and Sam kept themselves to themselves, so I usually found myself with Colette. We would go to the markets together and walk the streets. She was always stopping to take photographs. She loved little details . . . an iron door handle, a gargoyle, a cat asleep on a windowsill. I had never been out with a girl before—I had never really had the chance—and I found myself being drawn to her in a way I could not completely understand. All the time, I was being taught to hide my feelings. When I was with her, I wanted to do the opposite.

She never told me very much about herself other than what she had that first time we had met, and I was sensible enough not to ask. She did let slip that she had once lived in Paris, that her father was something to do with the French government, and that she hadn't spoken to him for years. She had left home when she was very young and had somehow survived on her own since then. She never explained how she had found out about Scorpia. But I did learn that her training would be over very soon. Like all recruits, she was going to be sent on her first solo kill—a real job with a real target.

"Do you ever think about it?" I asked her.

We were sitting outside a café on the Riva degli Schia-voni with a great expanse of water in front of us and hundreds of tourists streaming past. They gave us privacy.

"What?" she asked.

I lowered my voice. "Killing. Taking another person's life."

She looked at me over the top of her coffee. She was wearing sunglasses that hid her eyes, but I could tell she was annoyed. "You should ask Dr. Steiner about that."

I held her gaze. "I'm asking you."

"Why do you even want to know?" she snapped. She stirred the coffee. It was very black, served in a tiny cup. "It's a job. There are all sorts of people who don't deserve to live. Rich people. Powerful people. Take one of them out, maybe you're doing the world a favor."

"What if they're married?"

"Who cares?"

"What if they have children?"

"If you think like that, you shouldn't be here. You shouldn't even be talking like this. If you were to say any of this to Marat or Sam, they'd go straight to Mr. Nye."

"I wouldn't talk to them," I said. "They're not my friends."

"And you think I am?"

I still remember that moment. Colette was leaning toward me and she was wearing a jacket with a very soft, close-fitting jersey beneath. She unhooked her sunglasses and looked at me with brown eyes that, I'm sure, had more warmth in them than she intended. Right then, I wished that we could just be like all the other people streaming past us, a Russian boy and a French girl who had just happened to bump into each other in one of the most romantic places on the earth. But of course it couldn't be. It would never be.

"I'm not your friend," she said. "We'll never have friends, Yassen. Either of us."

She finished her coffee, stood up, and walked away.

Colette left a few weeks later, and after that there were just the three of us continuing with the training, day and night.

None of the instructors ever said as much, but I knew I was doing well. I was the fastest across the assault course. On the shooting range, my targets always came whirring back with the bullets grouped neatly inside the head. I had mastered all sixteen body strikes—the so-called "secret fists"—that are essential to *ninjutsu*, and in one memorable training session I even managed to land a blow on Hatsumi Saburo. I could see the old man was pleased . . . although he flattened me half a second later. After hours in the gym, I was in peak physical condition. I could run five times around the island and I wouldn't be out of breath.

And yet I couldn't forget what I had talked about with Colette. When I fired at a target, I would always imagine a real human being and not the cutout soldier with his blank, snarling face in front of me. Instead of the quick snap, the little round hole that appeared in the paper as the bullet passed through, there would be the explosion of bone fragmenting, blood splashing out. The paper soldier's eyes ignored me. He felt nothing. But what would a man be thinking as he died? He would never see his wife again. He would never feel the warmth of the sun. Everything that he had and everything he was would have been stolen away by me. Could I really do that to someone and not hate myself forever?

I had not chosen this. There was a time when I'd thought I was going to work in a factory making pesticides. I was going to live in a village that nobody had ever heard of, dreaming of being a helicopter pilot, pinning pictures to the wall. Looking back, it felt as if some evil force had been manipulating me every inch of the way to bring me here. From the moment my parents had been killed, my own life had no longer been mine to control. And yet, it occurred to me, it was still not too late. Scorpia had taught me how to fight, how to change my identity, how to hide, and how to survive. Once I left Malagosto, I could use these skills to escape from them. I could steal money and go anywhere in the world that I wanted, change my name, begin a new life. Lying in bed at night, I would think about this, but at the same time I knew, with a sense of despair, that I was wrong. Scorpia was too powerful. No matter how far I ran, eventually they would find me and there was no escaping what the result would be. I would die young. But wasn't that better than becoming what they wanted? At least I would have stayed true to myself.

I was terrified of giving any of this away with Dr. Steiner. I always thought before I answered any of his questions and tried to tell him what he wanted to hear, not what I really thought. I was afraid that if he caught sight of my weakness, my training would be canceled and the next recruit would end up burying me in the woods. The secret was to be completely emotionless. Sometimes he showed me horrible pictures—scenes of war and violence. I tried not to look at the dead and mutilated bodies, but then he would ask me questions about them and I would find myself having to describe everything in detail, trying to keep the quiver out of my voice. And yet I thought I was getting away with it. At the end of each session, he would take my hand—cupping it in both of his own—and purr at me, "Well done, Yassen. That was very, very good." As far as I could tell, he had no idea at all what was really going on in my head.

And then, at last, the day came when Oliver D'Arc

called me to his study. As I entered, he was tuning the cello, which was an instrument he played occasionally. The room was a mess with books everywhere and papers spilling out of drawers. It smelled of tobacco, although I never saw him smoke.

"Ah, Yassen!" he exclaimed. "I'm afraid you're going to miss evening training. Mrs. Rothman is back in Venice. You're to have dinner with her. Make sure you wear your best clothes. A launch will pick you up at seven o'clock."

When I had first come to the island, I might have asked why she wanted to see me, but by now I knew that I would always be given all the information I needed and to ask for more was only to show weakness.

"It looks like you're going to be leaving us," he went on.

"My training is finished."

"Yes."

He plucked one of the strings. "You've done very well, my dear boy," he said. "And I must say, I've thoroughly enjoyed tutoring you. And now your moment has come. Good luck!"

From this, I understood that my final test had arrived . . . the solo kill. My training was over. My life as an assassin was about to begin.

And that night, I met Julia Rothman for the second time. She had sent her personal launch to collect me, a beautiful vessel that was all teak and chrome with a silver scorpion molded into the bow. It carried me beneath the

famous Bridge of Sighs—I hoped that was not an omen—
and on to the Widow's Palace where we had first met. She
was dressed, once again, in black; this time a very low-cut
dress with a zip down one side, which I recognized at once
as the work of the designer Gianni Versace. We ate in her
private dining room, a long table lit by candles and surrounded by paintings—Picasso, Cézanne, van Gogh—all
of them worth millions. We began with soup, then lobster,
finally a creamy custard mixed with wine that the Italians
call *zabaglione*. The food was delicious, but as I ate I was
aware of her examining me, watching every mouthful, and
I knew that I was still being tested.

"I'm very pleased with you, Yassen," she said as the
coffee was poured. The whole meal had been served by
two men in white jackets and black pants, her personal
waiters. "Do you think you're ready?"

"Yes, Mrs. Rothman," I replied.

"You can stop calling me that now." She smiled at
me and I was once again struck by her film-star looks. "I
prefer Julia."

There was a file on the table beside her. It hadn't been
there when we started. One of the waiters had brought
it in with the coffee. She opened it. First she took out a
printed report.

"You're naturally gifted . . . an excellent marksman.
Hatsumi Saburo speaks very highly of your abilities. I see
also that you have learned from the Countess. Your manners are faultless. Six months ago you wouldn't have been

able to sit at a table like this without giving yourself away, but you are very different from the street urchin I met back then."

I nodded but said nothing. Another lesson. Never show gratitude unless you hope to gain something from it.

"But now we must see if you can actually put into practice everything that we have taught you in theory." She took out a passport and slid it across the table. "This is yours," she said. "We have kept your family name. There was no reason not to, particularly as your first name had changed anyway. Yassen Gregorovich is what you are now and will always be . . . unless of course we feel the need for you to travel undercover." An envelope followed. "You'll find the details of your bank account inside," she said. "You are a client of the European Finance Group. It's a private bank based in Geneva. There are fifty thousand American dollars, fifty thousand euros, and fifty thousand pounds in the account, and no matter how much you spend, these figures will always remain the same. Of course, we will be watching your expenses."

She was enjoying this, sending me out for the first time, almost challenging me to show reluctance or any sign of fear. She took out a second envelope, thicker than the first. This one was sealed with a strip of black tape. There was a scorpion symbol stamped in the middle.

"This envelope contains a return air ticket to New York, which is where your first assignment will take place. There is another thousand dollars in here too, petty cash to get you started. You are flying economy."

That didn't surprise me. I was young and I was entering the USA on my own. Traveling in business or first class might draw attention to myself.

"You will be met at the airport and taken to your hotel. You will report back to me here in Venice in one week's time. Do you want to know who you are going to kill?"

"I'm sure you'll tell me when you want to," I said.

"That's right." She smiled. "You'll get all the information that you need once you arrive. A weapon will also be delivered to you. Is that all understood?"

"Yes," I said. Of course I had questions. Above all I wanted a name, a face. Somewhere on the other side of the world, a man was going about his business with no knowledge that I was on my way. What had he done to anger Scorpia? Why did he have to lose his life? But I stayed silent. I was being very careful not to show any signs of weakness.

"Then I think our evening is almost over," Mrs. Rothman said. She reached out and, just for a moment, her fingers brushed against the back of my hand. "You know, Yassen," she said, "you are incredibly good-looking. I thought that the moment I saw you, and your five months on Malagosto have done nothing but improve you." She sighed and drew her hand away. "Russian boys aren't quite my thing," she continued. "Or else who knows what we might get up to? But it will certainly help you in your work. Death should always come smartly dressed."

She got up as if about to leave. But then she had second thoughts and turned back to me. "You were fond of that girl, Colette, weren't you?"

"We spent a bit of time together," I said. "We came into Venice once or twice." Julia Rothman would know that anyway.

"Yes," she murmured. "I had a feeling the two of you would hit it off."

She was daring me to ask. So I did.

"How is she?"

"She's dead." Mrs. Rothman brushed some imaginary dust from the sleeve of her dress. "Her first assignment went very wrong. It wasn't entirely her fault. She took out the target, but she was shot dead by the Argentinian police."

And that was when I knew what she had done to me. That was when I knew exactly what Scorpia had made me.

I said nothing. If I was sad, I didn't show it. I simply watched impassively as she left the room.

# 15

## Н Ь Ю - Й О Р К

I HAD NEVER SPENT SO long in an airplane.

Nine hours in the air! I found the entire experience fascinating: the size of the plane, the number of people crammed together, the unpleasant food served in plastic trays, night and day refusing to behave as they should outside the small round windows. I also experienced jet lag for the first time. It was a strange sensation, like being dragged backward down a hill. But I was in excellent shape. I was full of excitement about my mission. I was able to fight it off.

I was entering the United States under my own name and with a cover story that Scorpia had supplied. I was a student on a scholarship from Moscow University, studying literature. I was here to attend a series of lectures on famous American writers being given at the New York Public Library. The lectures really were taking place. I carried with me a letter of introduction from my professor, a copy of my thesis, and an NYPL program. I would be staying with my uncle and aunt, a Mr. and Mrs. Kirov, who had an apartment in Brooklyn. I also had a letter from them.

I joined the long queue in the immigration hall and watched the uniformed men and women in their booths stamping the passports of the people in front of me. At last it was my turn. I was annoyed to find that my heart was thumping as I faced a scowling black officer who seemed suspicious of me before I had even opened my mouth.

"What's your business in the States?" he asked.

"I'm studying American literature. I'm here to attend some lectures."

"How long are you staying"—he squinted at my name in the passport—"Yassen?"

"Two weeks."

I thought that would be it. I was waiting for him to pick up the stamp and allow me in. Instead, he suddenly asked: "So how do you like Scott Fitzgerald?"

I knew the name. F. Scott Fitzgerald had been one of the greatest American writers of the twentieth century. "I really enjoyed *The Great Gatsby,*" I said. "I think it's his best book. Although his next one, *Tender Is the Night,* was fantastic too."

He nodded. "Enjoy your stay."

The stamp came down. I was in.

I had one suitcase with me. Both the suitcase and all the clothes inside it had been purchased in Moscow. Of course I carried no weapon. It might have been possible to conceal a pistol somewhere in my luggage, but it wasn't a risk worth taking. Thanks to America's absurd gun laws, it would be much easier to arm myself once I arrived. I waited by the carousel for it. I knew at once that nobody had looked inside the case either at Venice airport or here. If the police or airport authorities had opened one of the catches, they would have broken an electrical circuit that ran through the handle. The blue luggage tag attached would have changed color, giving me advance warning of what had happened. The tag was still blue. I grabbed the case and went out.

My contact was waiting for me in the arrivals hall, holding up my name on a piece of white card. He looked like all the other limo drivers: tired and uninterested, dressed in a suit with a white shirt and sunglasses, even though it was early evening and there was little sign of the sun. He had misspelled my name. The card read YASSEN GREGORIVICH. This was not a mistake. It was an agreed signal between the two of us. It told me that he was who he said he was and that it was safe for us to meet.

He did not tell me his name. Nor did I ask. I doubted that the two of us would meet again. We walked to the car park—or the parking garage, as the Americans called it—without speaking. He had parked his car, a black Daimler, close to the exit and held the door open for me as I slid into the backseat. He climbed into the front, then handed me another envelope. This one was also marked with a scorpion.

"You'll find your instructions inside," he said. "You can read them in the car. The drive is about forty minutes. I'm taking you to the SoHo Plaza Hotel, where a room has been reserved in your name. You are to stay there this evening. There'll be a delivery at exactly ten o'clock. The man will knock three times and will introduce himself as Marcus. Do you understand?"

"Yes."

"Good. There's a bottle of water in the side pocket if you need it."

He started the engine and a moment later we set off.

Nothing quite prepares you for the view of New York as you come over the Brooklyn Bridge, the twinkling lights behind thousands and thousands of windows, the sky-scrapers presenting themselves to you like toys in a shop window, so much life crammed into so little space. The Empire State Building, the Chrysler Building, Rockefeller Center, the Beekman, the Waldorf-Astoria . . . your eye travels from one to the other, but all too soon you're over-whelmed. You cannot separate them. They merge together to become one island, one city. Every time you return you will be amazed. But the first time you will never forget.

I saw none of it. Of course I looked out as I was car-ried over the East River, but I couldn't make the images connect with my brain. It was as if I was sitting in some sort of prison and the tinted glass of the car window was a silent television screen that I was glimpsing out of the cor-ner of my eye. If you had told me a year ago that I would one day arrive here in a chauffeur-driven car, I would have laughed in your face. But the view meant nothing. I had torn open the envelope. I had taken out a few sheets of paper and two photographs. I was looking at the face of the person I had come to kill. My first thoughts had been wrong. My target was not a man.

Her name was Kathryn Davis and she was a lawyer,

a senior partner in a firm called Clarke Davenport based on Fifth Avenue. I suspected that the address was an expensive one. The first photograph was in black and white and had been taken as she stood beside a traffic light. She was a serious-looking woman with a square face and light brown hair cut in a fringe. I would have guessed she was in her midthirties. She was wearing glasses that only made her look more severe. There was something quite bullish about her. I could easily imagine her tearing someone apart in court. In the second photograph she was smiling. This one was in color and generally she was more relaxed, waving at someone who was not in the shot. I wondered which Kathryn Davis I would meet. Which one would be easier to kill?

There was a newspaper article attached:

## NY LAWYER THREATENED

In Red Knot Valley, Nevada, she's a hero—but New York lawyer Kathryn Davis claims she has received death threats in Manhattan, where she lives and works.

Ms. Davis represents 212 residents of the Red Knot community who have come together in a class action against the multinational Pacific Ridge Mining Company. They claim that millions of tons of mining waste have seeped into their ecosystem, killing their fish, poisoning their crops, and causing widespread flooding. Pacific Ridge, which has denied the claim, owns several "open pit" gold mines in the area, and when traces of arsenic were found in the food chain, local people were quick to cry foul. It has taken

37-year-old Ms. Davis two years to gather her evidence, but she believes that her clients will be awarded damages in excess of one billion dollars when the case comes to court next month.

It's not been an easy journey, says Ms. Davis, a mother of two. "My telephone has been bugged. I have been followed in the street. I have received hate mail that makes threats against me and which I have passed to the police. But I am not going to let myself be intimidated. What happened in Red Knot is a national scandal and I am determined to get to the truth."

I had also been supplied with the woman's home address—which was on West Eighty-Fifth Street—and a photograph of her house, a handsome-looking building that looked out over a tree-lined street. According to her biography, she was married to a doctor. She had two children and a dog, a spaniel. She was a member of several clubs and a gym. There was a blank card at the bottom of the envelope. It contained just four words.

MUGGING. BEFORE THE WEEKEND.

It is embarrassing to remember this, but I did not understand the word *mugging*—I had simply never come across it—and I spent the rest of the journey worrying that the driver or Marcus would discover that I had no idea what I was meant to do. I looked up the word the next day in a bookshop and realized that Scorpia wanted this to look like a street crime. As well as killing her, I would

steal money from her. That way there would be no connection with Scorpia or the gold mines at Pacific Ridge.

The driver barely spoke to me again. He pulled up in
front of an old-fashioned hotel where there were porters
waiting to lift out my case and help carry it into reception.
I showed my passport and handed over the credit card I
had been given.

"You have a room for five nights, Mr. Gregorovich,"
the receptionist confirmed. That would take me to Saturday. My plane back to Venice left John F. Kennedy airport
at eleven o'clock in the morning that day.

"Thank you," I said.

"You're in room 605 on the sixth floor. Have a nice
day."

During my training, Oliver D'Arc had told me the
story of an Israeli agent working undercover in Dubai.
He had gotten into an elevator with seven people. One of
them had been his best friend. The others were an elderly
French woman who was staying at the hotel, a blind man,
a young honeymooning couple, a woman in a burka, and
a chambermaid. The elevator doors had closed and that
was the moment when he discovered that all of them—
including his friend—were working for Al Qaeda. When
the elevator doors opened again, he was dead. I took the
stairs to my floor and waited for my case to be brought up.

The room was small, clean, functional. I sat on the
bed until the case came, tipped the porter, and unpacked.
Before I left Malagosto, Gordon Ross had supplied me

with a couple of the items that he had shown us during our lessons and he hoped would help me with my work. The first of these was a travel alarm clock. I took it out of my suitcase and flicked a switch concealed in the back. It scanned the entire room, searching for electromagnetic signals . . . in other words, bugs. There weren't any. The room was clean. Next, I took out a small tape recorder, which I stuck to the back of the fridge. When I left the room, it would record anyone who came in.

At ten o'clock exactly, there were three knocks on the door. I went over and opened it to find an elderly, gray-haired man, smartly dressed in a suit with his coat hanging open. He had a neat beard, also gray. If you had met him in the street, you might have thought he was a professor or perhaps an official in a foreign embassy.

"Mr. Gregorovich?" he asked.

It was all so strange. I was still getting used to being called "Mr." I nodded. "You're Marcus?"

He didn't answer that. "This is for you," he said, handing me a parcel wrapped in brown paper. "I'll call back tomorrow night at the same time. By then, I hope, you'll have everything planned out. Okay?"

"Right," I said.

"Nice meeting you."

He left. I took the parcel over to the bed and opened it. The size and weight had already told me what I was going to find inside, and sure enough, there it was—a Smith & Wesson 4546, an ugly but efficient semiautomatic that looked old and well-used. The serial number had been filed off, making it impossible to trace. I checked the clip. It had been delivered with six bullets. So there it was. I had the target. I had the weapon. And I had just four days to make the kill.

The following morning, I stood outside the offices of Clarke Davenport, which were located on the nineteenth floor of a skyscraper in upper Midtown, quite close to the huge white marble structure of St. Patrick's Cathedral. This was quite useful to me. A church is one of the few places in a city where it is possible to linger without looking out of place. From the steps, I was able to examine the building opposite at leisure, watching the people streaming in and out of the three revolving doors, wondering if I might catch sight of Kathryn Davis among them. I was glad she did not appear. I was not sure if I was ready for this yet. Part of me was worried that I never would be.

The secret of a successful kill is to know your target. That was what I had been taught. You have to learn their movements, their daily routine, the restaurants where they eat, the friends they meet, their tastes, their weaknesses, their secrets. The more you know, the easier it will be to find a time and an opportunity and the less chance there will be of making a mistake. You might not think I would learn a great deal from staring at a building for five hours, but at the end of that time I felt myself connected to it. I had taken note of the security cameras. I had counted how many policemen had walked past on patrol. I had seen the

maintenance men go in and had noted which company
they worked for.

At half past five that evening, just as the rush to get
home had begun and when everyone would be at their
most tired and impatient, I presented myself at the main
reception desk, wearing the overalls of an engineer from
Bedford (Long Island) Electricity. I had visited the company that afternoon—it was actually in Brooklyn—pretending that I was looking for a job, and it had been
simple enough to steal a uniform and an assortment of
documents. I had then returned to my hotel, where I had
manufactured an ID tag for myself using a square cut out
of a company newsletter and a picture of myself that I had
taken in a photo booth. The whole thing was contained in
a plastic holder that I had deliberately scratched and made
dirty so that it would be difficult to see. Maintaining a
false identity is mainly about mental attitude. You simply
have to believe you are who you say you are. You can show
someone a travel card and they will accept it as police ID
if you do it with enough authority. Another lesson from
Malagosto.

The receptionist was a very plump woman with her
eye already fixed on the oversized clock that was built into
the wall opposite her. There was a security man, in uniform, standing nearby.

"BLI Electrics," I said. I spoke with a New York accent, which had taken me many hours, working with
tapes, to acquire. "We've got a heating unit down . . ." I

pretended to consult my worksheet. "Clarke Davenport."

"I don't think I've seen you before," the woman said.

"That's right, ma'am." I showed her my pass, at the same time holding her eye so she wouldn't look at it too closely. "It's my first week on the job. *And* it's my first job," I added proudly. "I only graduated this past summer."

She smiled at me. I guessed that she had children of her own. "It's the nineteenth floor," she said.

The security man even called the elevator for me.

I took it as far as the eighteenth floor, then got out and made my way to the stairwell. It was still too early and I had a feeling lawyers wouldn't keep normal office hours. I waited an hour, listening to the sounds in the building, people saying good-bye to each other, the chimes of the elevators as the doors opened and shut. It was dark by now and with a bit of luck the building would be empty apart from the cleaners. I walked up one floor and found myself in the reception area of Clarke Davenport, with two silver letters—*C* and *D*—on the wall. There was no one there. The lights were burning low. A pair of frosted glass doors opened onto a long corridor, a length of plush blue carpet leading clients past conference rooms with leather chairs and tables polished like mirrors. My feet made no sound as I continued through an open-plan area filled with desks, computers, and photocopying machines, but as I reached the far end, I saw a movement out of the corner of my eye, and suddenly I was being challenged.

"Can I help you?"

I hadn't seen the young black woman who had been bending down beside a filing cabinet. She was wearing a coat and scarf, about to leave, but she hadn't gone yet and I had allowed her to see me. My heart sank at such carelessness. I could almost hear Desmond Nye shouting at me.

"The water cooler," I muttered, pointing down the corridor.

"Oh. Sure." She had found the file she was looking for and straightened up.

I continued walking. With a bit of luck, she wouldn't even remember we'd met.

All the offices at Clarke Davenport had the names of their occupants printed next to the doors. That was helpful. Kathryn Davis was at the far end. She must have been important to the company, as she had been given a corner office with views over Fifth Avenue and the cathedral. The door was locked but that was no longer a problem for me. Using a pick and a tension wrench, I had it open in five seconds and let myself into a typical lawyer's office with an antique desk, two chairs facing it, a shelf full of books, a leather sofa with a coffee table, and various pictures of mountain scenery. I turned on her desk lamp. It might have been safer to use a flashlight, but I didn't intend to stay here long and having proper light would make everything easier.

I went straight to the desk. There was a framed photograph of the woman with her two children, a girl and a boy, aged about fourteen and twelve. They were all wearing hiking gear. There was nothing of any interest in her drawers. I opened her diary. She had client meetings all week, lunches booked the following day and on Thursday, and on Friday some sort of evening engagement. The entry read:

*MET 7:00 pm*
*D home*

I got what I had come for. I knew when and where the killing would take place.

I was back in my hotel room, and at exactly ten o'clock there was a knock at the door. The man who called himself Marcus had returned. This time he came in.

"Well?" He waited for me to speak.

"Friday night," I said. "Central Park."

It hadn't taken me long to work out the diary entry, even without a detailed knowledge of the city. The art books on the table had been the clue. *MET* obviously meant the Metropolitan Museum of Art, a New York landmark. I had already telephoned them and discovered that there was indeed a private function at the museum that night for the American Bar Association . . . Kathryn Davis would certainly be a member. The *D* in the diary was her husband, David. He was going to be home, babysitting. She would be there on her own.

I explained this to Marcus. His face gave nothing away, but he seemed to approve of the idea. "You're going to shoot her in the park?" he asked. "How do you know she won't take a cab?"

"She likes walking," I said. The hiking gear and the mountain photographs had told me that. "And look at the map. She lives on West Eighty-Fifth Street. That's just a ten-minute stroll across the park."

"What if it's raining?"

"Then I'll have to do it when she comes out. But I've looked at the forecast and it's going to be unusually warm and dry."

"You're lucky. This time last year it was snowing." Marcus nodded. "All right. It sounds as if you've got it all worked out. If things go according to plan, you won't see me again. Throw the gun into the Hudson. Make sure you're on that Saturday plane. Good luck."

You should never rely on luck. Nine times out of ten it will be your enemy, and if you need it, it means you've been careless with your planning.

I was back outside St. Patrick's Cathedral the next day, and this time I did glimpse Kathryn Davis as she got out of a taxi and went into the building. She was shorter than I had guessed from her photographs. She was wearing a smart, beige-colored wool coat and carried a leather briefcase so full of files that she wasn't able to close it. Seeing her jolted me in a strange way. I wasn't afraid. It seemed to me that Scorpia had deliberately chosen an easy target for my first assignment. But somehow the stakes had been raised. I began to think about what I was going to do, about taking the life of a person I had never met and who meant nothing to me. Today was Wednesday. By the end of the week, my life would have changed and nothing would ever be the same again. I would be a killer. After that, there could be no going back.

The next two days passed in a blur. New York was such an amazing city with its soaring architecture, the noise and the traffic, the shop windows filled with treasures, the steam rising out of the street . . . I wish I could say I enjoyed my time there. But all I could think about was the job, the moment of truth that was getting closer and closer. I continued to make preparations. I examined the house on West Eighty-Fifth Street. I saw where the children went to school. I went to the Metropolitan Museum of Art and found the room where the private function would take place, checking out all the entrances and exits. I bought a silicone cloth and some degreaser, stripped the gun down, and made sure it was in perfect working order. I meditated using methods I had learned at Malagosto, keeping my stress levels down.

Friday evening was dry, just as the weather office had predicted. I was standing outside the office on Fifth Avenue when Kathryn Davis left, and I saw her hail a cab. That didn't surprise me. It was 6:45 and her destination was thirty blocks away. I hailed a second cab and followed. It took us twenty minutes to weave our way through the traffic, and when we arrived, there were crowds of smartly dressed people making their way in through the front entrance of the museum. Somehow we had managed to overtake the taxi carrying Kathryn Davis, and it took me a few anxious moments to find her again. She had just met a woman she knew and the two of them were kissing in the manner of two professionals rather than close friends, not actually touching each other.

As I stood watching, they went in together. I very much hoped that the women would not leave together too. It had always been my assumption that Kathryn Davis would walk home alone. What if her friend offered to accompany her? What if there was a whole group of them? I could see now that I had made a mistake leaving the killing until my last evening in New York. I had to be on a plane at eleven o'clock the following morning. If anything went wrong tonight, there could be no backup. I wouldn't get a second chance.

It was too late to worry about that now. There was a long plaza in front of the museum with an ornamental pool and three sets of steps running up to the main door. I found a place in the shadows and waited there while more taxis and limousines arrived and the guests went in. I could hear piano music playing inside.

Nobody saw me. I was wearing a dark coat that I had bought in a thrift shop and was one size too large for me. I had chosen it for the pockets, which were big enough to conceal both the gun and my hand, which was curved around it. It was an easy draw—I had already checked. I would get rid of the coat at the same time as the gun. I was very calm. I knew exactly what I was going to do. I had actually played out the scene in my mind. I didn't let it trouble me.

At 9:30, the guests began to leave. She was one of the first of them, talking to the same woman she had met when she had arrived. It seemed that they were going to set off together. Did it really matter, the death of two women instead of one? I was about to embark on a life where dozens, maybe hundreds of men and women would die because of me. There would always be innocent bystanders. There would be policemen—and policewomen—who might try to stop me. I could almost hear Oliver D'Arc talking to me.

*"The moment you start worrying about them, the moment you question what you are doing—good-bye, Yassen! You're dead!"*

I put my hand in my pocket and found the gun. One woman. Two women. It made no difference at all.

In fact, Kathryn Davis walked off on her own. She said something to her friend, then turned and left. Just as I had expected, she went around the side of the museum and into Central Park. I followed.

Almost at once we were on our own, cut off from the traffic on Fifth Avenue, the other guests searching for their cars and taxis. The way ahead was clear. Light was spilling out from a huge conservatory at the back of the museum, throwing dark green shadows between the shrubs and trees. We crossed a smaller road—this one closed to traffic—that ran through the park. Over to the left, a stone obelisk rose up in a clearing. It was called Cleopatra's Needle. I had stood in front of it that afternoon. A couple of joggers ran past, two young men in tracksuits, their Nike sneakers hitting the track in unison. I turned away, making sure they didn't see my face. The moon had come out, pale and listless. It didn't add much light to the scene. It was more like a distant witness.

Kathryn Davis had taken one of the paths that circled the softball fields, with a large pond on her left. She knew exactly where she was going, as if she had done this walk often. I was about ten paces behind her, slowly catching up, trying to pretend that I had nothing to do with her. We were already halfway across. I was beginning to hear the traffic noise on the other side. And then, quite suddenly, she turned around and looked at me. I would not say that she was scared, but she was aggressive. She was using her body language to assert herself, to tell me that she wasn't afraid of me. There was an electric lamp nearby and it reflected in her glasses.

"Excuse me," she said. "Are you following me?"

The two of us were quite alone. The joggers were gone. There were no other walkers anywhere near. What she had done was really quite stupid. If she had become aware of me, which she clearly had, she would have done better to increase her pace, to reach the safety of the streets. Instead, she had signed her death warrant. I could shoot her here and now. We were less than ten paces apart.

"What do you want?" she demanded.

I was trying to take out the gun. But I couldn't. It was just like when I had played Russian roulette with Vladimir Sharkovsky. My hand wouldn't obey me. I felt sick. I had planned everything so carefully, every last detail. In the last four days, I had done nothing else. But all that time I had ignored my own feelings, and it was only now, here, that I realized the truth. I was not, after all, a killer. This woman was about the same age as my own mother. She had two children of her own. If I shot her down, simply for money, what sort of monster would that make me?

*If you don't kill her, Scorpia will kill you,* a voice whispered in my ear.

*Let them,* I replied. *It would be better to be dead than to become what they want.*

"Who are you?" Kathryn Davis asked.

"I'm no one," I said. I took my hands out of my coat pockets, showing that they were empty. "I was just walking."

She relaxed a little. "Well, maybe you should keep your distance."

"Sure. I'm sorry. I didn't mean to scare you."

"Yeah—okay."

She stood there, watching me, waiting for me to go. I quickly walked past her, then turned off in another direction.

I didn't look back. Inside, I felt glad. That was the simple truth. I was glad that she was still alive. I was aware of a sense of huge relief, as if I had just fought a battle with myself and won. I saw now that from the moment I had climbed into the helicopter with Rykov—or Mr. Grant—I had been sinking into some sort of mental quicksand. Mrs. Rothman in Venice. Desmond Nye, Hatsumi Saburo, and Oliver D'Arc in Malagosto . . . they had all been drawing me into it. They were like a disease. And I had come so close to being infected. I had been about to kill somebody! If Kathryn Davis had not turned and spoken to me, I might well have done what I had been told. I might have committed murder.

The sound of the gunshot was not loud, but it was close, and my first thought was that I had been targeted. But even as I dropped to one knee, drawing out the Smith & Wesson, I knew that the direction was wrong, that the bullet had not come close. At that moment I was helpless. I had lost my focus, the vital self-knowledge—who I am, where I am, what is around me—that Saburo had drummed into me a hundred times. Anyone could have picked me off.

Kathryn Davis was dead. I saw it at once. She had been shot in the back of the head and lay on a circle of dark grass, her arms and legs stretched out in the shape of a star. There was someone walking toward her, wearing a coat and black gloves, a gun in his hand. I recognized the neat beard, the unworried eyes. It was Marcus, the man who had met me at the hotel.

He checked the body, nodded to himself. Then he saw me. He had his gun. I had mine. But I saw at once that there was no question of our firing at each other. He looked at me almost sadly.

"Make sure you're on that plane tomorrow," he said.

I wanted to talk to him. I wanted to explain what had happened, how I felt, but he had already turned his back on me and was walking away into the shadows. In the distance I heard the wail of a police siren. It might have nothing to do with what had happened here. Even if some-one had heard the shot, they wouldn't know where it had come from. But it still warned me that it was time to go.

I walked out of the park and all the way to the Hud-son River with the darkened mass of New Jersey in front of me. I took out the gun and weighed it in my hand, feeling nothing but loathing . . . for it and for myself. At the same time, I was aware of the first stirrings of fear. I would pay for this.

I threw the gun into the river. Then I went back to the hotel.

The following day, I left for Venice.

# 16

# ВТОРОЙ ШАНС

"I HAVE TO SAY, Yassen, we are extremely disappointed with you."

Desmond Nye was sitting behind the desk in his darkened office, his hands coming together in a peak in front of his face as if he were at prayer. A single light shone above his head, reflecting in the polished brass buttons on the sleeves of his blazer. His heavy white eyes were fixed on me. He was surrounded by photographs of leering pirates, trapped in the headlines of the world news. His family. He was as ruthless as they were and I wondered why I was still alive. In Silver Forest, an assassin sent by Scorpia had made one mistake. He had emptied his gun into Vladimir Sharkovsky but had failed to finish him, and for that he had been executed, instantly, in front of my eyes. But I was still here. Oliver D'Arc was also in the room, his hands folded in his lap. He had chosen a chair close to the door, as if he wanted to keep as far away from me as possible.

"What do you have to say?" Nye asked.

I had prepared for this scene, on the plane to Rome, the train to Venice, the boat across the lagoon. But now that I was actually sitting here, now that it was happening, it was very hard to keep hold of everything I had rehearsed.

"You knew I wasn't ready," I said. I was careful to keep my voice very matter-of-fact. I didn't want them to think I was accusing them. The important thing was to defend myself without seeming to do so. That was my plan. If I tried to make excuses, it would all be over and Marat or Sam would spend the evening burying me in the wood. I was here for a reason. I still had to prove myself. "Your agent followed me," I went on. "There was no other reason for him to be in Central Park. And I was never needed. He would have done the job . . . which is exactly what happened. I think you knew I would fail."

D'Arc twitched slightly. Nye said nothing. His eyes were still boring into me. "It is true that Dr. Steiner was not satisfied with your progress," he intoned at last. "He warned us that there was a seventy percent probability that you would be unable to fulfill your assignment."

I suppose I shouldn't have been surprised. Dr. Steiner had been hired because he knew what he was doing, and despite my attempts to fool him, he had read me like a book. "If I wasn't ready, why did you let me go?" I asked.

Very slowly, Nye nodded his head. "You have a point, Yassen. Part of the reason we sent you to New York was an experiment. We wanted to see how you would operate under pressure and in some respects you handled yourself quite well. You successfully broke into the offices of Clarke Davenport, although it might have been wise to change your appearance . . . perhaps the color of your hair. Also, you were seen by a junior partner. That was

careless. However, we can overlook that. You did well to
work out the movements of your target and Central Park
was a sensible choice."

"But you didn't kill her!" D'Arc muttered. He sounded
angry, like an old lady who had been kept waiting for her
afternoon tea.

"Why did you fail?" Nye asked me.

I thought for a moment. "I think it was because she
spoke to me," I said. "I had seen her photograph. I had followed her from the office. But when she spoke to me . . .
suddenly everything changed. She became human."

"Do you think you will ever be able to do this work?"

"Of course. Next time will be different."

"What makes you think there will be a next time?"

Another silence. The two men were making me sweat,
but I didn't think they were going to kill me. I already had
a sense of how Scorpia operated. If they had decided I was
no use to them, they wouldn't have bothered bringing me
back to the island. Marcus could have shot me down with
the same gun he had used on Kathryn Davis. I could have
been stabbed or strangled on the boat and dropped overboard. These were people who didn't waste their time.

Nye could see that I had worked it out. "All right," he
said. "We will draw a red line under this disappointing
event. You are very fortunate, Yassen, that Mrs. Rothman
has taken a personal liking to you. It's also to your advantage that you've had such excellent reports from your
instructors. Even Dr. Steiner believes there is something

special about you. We believe that you may one day become the very best in your profession—and whatever the reputation of our organization, we haven't forgotten that you are very young. Everyone deserves a second chance. Just be aware that there won't be a third."

I didn't thank him. It would only have annoyed him.

"We have decided to take your training up a notch. We are aware that you need to make a mental adjustment, and so we want you to go back out into the field as soon as possible—but this time in the company of another agent, a new recruit. He is a man who has already killed for us on two occasions. By staying close to him, you will learn survival techniques, but more than that, we hope he will be able to provide you with the edge that you seem to lack."

"He is a remarkable man," D'Arc added. "A British soldier who has seen action in Ireland and Africa. I think the two of you will get on famously."

"You will have dinner with him tonight in Venice," Nye said. "And you will spend a few weeks training with him, here on the island. As soon as he agrees that you are ready, the two of you will leave together. First you will be going to South America, to Peru. He has a target there and we're just arranging the final details. Assuming that goes well, you will return to Europe and there will be a second assignment, in Paris. The more time you spend together, the better. There's only so much you can achieve in the classroom. I think you will find this experience to be invaluable."

"What's his name?" I asked.

"When you are traveling together, you will address each other using code names only," Nye replied. "We have chosen a good one for you. You will be Cossack. There was a time when the Cossacks were famous soldiers and they were much feared. I hope it will inspire you."

I nodded. "And his?"

A man stepped forward. He had been standing in the room, observing me all the time, lost in the shadows. It seemed incredible to me that I hadn't noticed him, but at the same moment I understood that he must be a master in the ninja techniques taught by Hatsumi Saburo, that he was able to hide in plain sight. He was in his late twenties and still looked like a soldier in his physique, in the way he carried himself, in his close-cut brown hair. His eyes were also brown, watchful and serious, yet with just a hint of humor. He was wearing a sweatshirt and jeans. Even as he walked toward me, I saw that he was more relaxed than anyone I had met on the island. Both Nye and Oliver D'Arc seemed almost nervous of him. He was totally in control.

He reached out a hand. I shook it. He had a firm clasp.

"Hello, Yassen," he said. "I'm John Rider. The code name they've given me is Hunter."

# 17

# ОХОТНИК

I DON'T KNOW WHY, BUT I often think of Alex Rider.

We first crossed paths during the Stormbreaker business, but it sometimes seems to me that our lives were like two mirrors placed opposite each other, reflecting endless possibilities. It's strange that when I met his father, Alex hadn't even been born. That was still a few months away. But those months, my time with John Rider, made a huge difference to me. He wasn't even ten years older than me, but from the very start I knew that he had come from a completely different world and that we would never be on the same level. I would always look up to him.

We had dinner that night at a restaurant he knew near the Arsenale, a dark, quiet place run by a scowling woman who spoke no English and dressed in black. The food was excellent. Hunter had chosen a booth in the corner, tucked away behind a pillar, somewhere we would not be overheard. I call him that because it was the name he told me to use from the very start. He had good reason to hide his identity—there had been stories written about him in the British press—and there was less chance of my letting it slip out if it never once crossed my lips.

He ordered drinks—not alcohol but a red fruit syrup made from pomegranates called grenadine, which I had

never tasted before. He spoke good Italian, though with
an accent. And just as I had noted at our first meeting,
he had an extraordinary ease about him, that quiet confidence. He was the sort of man you couldn't help liking.
Even the elderly owner warmed up a little as she took the
order.

"I want you to tell me about yourself," he said as the
first course, pink slivers of prosciutto ham and chilled
melon, was served. "I've read your file. I know what's happened to you. But I don't know you."

"I don't know where to start," I said.

"What was the best present anyone ever gave you?"

The question surprised me. It was the last thing anyone in Malagosto would have asked or would have wanted
to know. I had to think for a moment. "I'm not sure," I
said. "Maybe it was the bicycle I was given when I was
eleven. It was important to me because everyone in the
village had one. It put me on the same level as all the other
boys and it set me free." I thought again. "No. It was this."
I slid back the cuff of my jacket. I was still wearing my
Pobeda watch. After the loss of my mother's ring, it was
the only part of my old life that had remained with me. In
a way, it was quite extraordinary that I still had it, that I
hadn't been forced to pawn it in Moscow or had it stolen
from me by Ivan at the dacha. After everything I had been
through, it was still working, ticking away and never losing a minute. "It was my grandfather's," I explained. "He'd
given it to my father and my father passed it on to me. I

was nine years old. I was very proud that he thought I was ready for it, and now, when I look at it, it reminds me of him."

"Tell me about your grandfather."

"I don't really remember him. I only knew him when we were in Moscow and we left when I was two. He only came to Estrov a few times and he died when I was young." I thought of the wife he had left behind. My grandmother. The last time I had seen her, she had been at the sink, peeling potatoes. Almost certainly she would have been standing there when the flames engulfed the house. "My father said he was a great man," I recalled. "He was there at Stalingrad in 1943. He fought against the Nazis."

"You admire him for that?"

"Of course."

"What is your favorite food?"

I wondered if he was being serious. Was he playing psychological games with me, like Dr. Steiner? "Caviar," I replied. I had tasted it at dinner parties at the dacha. Vladimir Sharkovsky used to eat mounds of it, washed down with iced vodka.

"Which shoelace do you tie first?"

"Why are you asking me these questions?" I snapped.

"Are you angry?"

I didn't deny it. "What does it matter which shoelace I tie first?" I said. I glanced briefly at my sneakers. "My right foot. okay? I'm right-handed. Now are you going to explain what exactly that tells you about who I am?"

"Relax, Cossack." He smiled at me and although I was still puzzled, I found it difficult to be annoyed with him for very long. Perhaps he was playing with me, but there didn't seem to be anything malicious about it. I waited to hear what he would ask next. Again, he took me by surprise. "Why do you think you were unable to kill that woman in New York?" he asked.

"You already know," I said. "You were in the study when I told Desmond Nye."

"You said it was because she spoke to you. But I don't think I believe you . . . not completely. From what I understand, you could have gunned her down at any time. You could have done it when she turned the corner from the museum. You were certainly close enough to her when you were at Cleopatra's Needle."

"I couldn't do it then. There were two people running, joggers . . ."

"I know. I was one of them."

"What?" I was startled.

"Don't worry about it, Cossack. Desmond Nye asked me to take a look at you, so I was there. We actually flew here on the same plane." He raised his glass as if he was toasting me and drank. "The fact is that you had plenty of opportunities. You know that. You waited until she turned around and talked to you. I think you wanted her to talk to you because it would give you an excuse. I think you'd already made up your mind."

He wasn't exactly accusing me. There was nothing

in his face that suggested he was doing anything more than stating the obvious. But I found myself reddening. Although I would never have admitted it to Nye or D'Arc, it was possible he was right.

"I won't fail again," I said.

"I know," he replied. "And let's not talk about it anymore. You're not being punished. I'm here to try and help. So tell me about Venice. I haven't had a chance to explore it yet. And I'd be interested to hear what you think about Julia Rothman. Quite a woman, wouldn't you say?"

The second course arrived, a plate of homemade spaghetti with fresh sardines. In my time at Malagosto, I had come to love Italian food and I said so. Hunter smiled, but I got the strange feeling that, once again, I had said the wrong thing.

For the next hour we talked together, avoiding anything to do with Malagosto, my training, Scorpia, or anything else. He didn't tell me very much about himself, but he mentioned that he lived in London and I asked him lots of questions about the city, which I had always hoped to visit. The one thing he let slip was that he had been married—although I should have noticed myself. He had a plain gold ring on his third finger. He didn't say anything about his wife and I wondered if he was divorced.

The bill arrived. "It's time to go back," Hunter said as he counted out the cash. "But before we go, I think I should tell you something, Cossack. Scorpia have high hopes for you. They think you have the makings of a first-rate assassin. I don't agree. I would say you have a long way to go before you're ready. It's possible you never will be."

"How can you say that?" I replied. I was completely thrown. I had enjoyed the evening and thought there was some sort of understanding between the two of us. It was as if he had turned around and slapped me in the face. "You hardly know me," I said.

"You've told me enough." He leaned toward me and suddenly he was deadly serious. At that moment I knew that he was dangerous, that I could never relax completely when I was with him. "You want to be a contract killer?" he asked. "Every answer you gave me was wrong. You tie your shoelaces with your right hand. You are right-handed. A successful assassin will be as comfortable shooting with his right hand as with his left. He has to be invisible. He has no habits. Everything he does in his life, right down to the smallest detail, he does differently every time. The moment his enemies learn something about him, the easier it is to find him, to profile him, to trap him.

"So that means you can't have preferences. Not French food, not Italian food. If you have a favorite meal, a favorite drink, a favorite anything, that gives your enemy ammunition. Cossack is fond of caviar. Do you know how many shops there are in London that sell caviar, how many restaurants that serve it? Not many. The intelligence services may not know your name. They may not know what you look like. But if they discover what you like, they'll be watching, and you'll have made it that much easier for them to find you.

"You talk to me about your grandfather. Forget him. He's dead and you have nothing more to do with him. If he's anything to you, he's your enemy because if the intelligence services can find him, they'll dig him up and take his DNA and that will lead them to you. Why are you so proud of the fact that he fought against the Nazis? Is it because they're the bad guys? Forget it! You're the bad guy now . . . as bad as any of them. In fact, you're worse, because you have no beliefs. You kill simply because you're paid. And while you're at it, you might as well stop talking about Nazis, Communists, Fascists, the Ku Klux Klan . . . as far as you're concerned, you have no politics and every political party is the same. You no longer believe in anything, Cossack. You don't even believe in God. That is the choice you've made."

He paused.

"Why did you blush when I asked you about New York?"

"Because you were right." What else could I say?

"You showed your feelings to me here, at this table. You're embarrassed, so you blush. You got angry when I asked you about your laces, and you showed that too. Are you going to cry when you meet your next target? Are you going to tremble when you're interviewed by the police? If you cannot learn to hide your emotions, you might as well give up now. And then there's your watch."

I knew he would come to that. I wished now that I hadn't mentioned it.

"You are Cossack, the invisible killer. You've been successful in New York, in Paris, in Peru. But the police examine the security footage and what do they see? Somebody was there at all three scenes and—guess what?—he was wearing a Russian watch, a Pobeda. You might as well leave a visiting card next to the body." He shook his head. "If you want to be in this business, sentimentality is the last thing you can afford. Trust me, it will kill you."

"I understand," I said.

"I'm glad. Did you enjoy the meal?"

I was about to answer. Then I had second thoughts. "Perhaps it's better if I don't tell you," I said.

Hunter nodded and got to his feet. "Well, you wolfed it down fast enough. Let's get back to the island. Tomorrow I want to see you fight."


He made me fight like no one else.

The next morning, at nine o'clock, we met in the gymnasium. When there were monks on the island, this might have been where they took their meals, sitting in silence and contemplation. The room was long and narrow with walls that curved overhead and windows that were too high up to provide a view. But since then it had been adapted with arc lights, stadium seating, and a fighting area fifteen meters square made up of a tatami mat that offered little comfort when you fell. We were both dressed in *karategi,* the white, loose-fitting tunics and pants used in karate. Hatsumi Saburo was watching from one of the stands. I could tell that he was not happy. He was sitting with his legs apart, his hands on his knees, almost challenging the new arrival to take him on. Marat and Sam were also there, along with a new student who had just arrived, a young Chinese guy who never spoke a word to me and whose name I never learned.

We walked onto the mat together and stood face-to-face. Hunter was about eight centimeters taller than me and heavier, more muscular. I knew he would have an advantage over me both in his physical reach and in the fact that he was more experienced. He began by bowing toward me, the traditional *rei* that is the first thing every combatant learns at judo school. I bowed back. And that was my first mistake. I didn't even see the move. Something slammed into the side of my face and suddenly I was on my back, tasting blood where I had bitten my tongue.

Hunter leaned over me. "What do you think this is?" he demanded. "You think we're here to play games, to be polite to each other? That's your first mistake, Cossack. You shouldn't trust me. Don't trust anyone."

He reached out a hand to help me to my feet. I took it—but instead of getting up, I suddenly changed my grip, pulling him toward me and pressing down on his wrist. I'd adapted a *ninjutsu* move known as *ura gyaku,* or the inside twist, and it should have brought him spinning onto the mat. I thought I heard a grunt of satisfaction from

HS, but it might just as well have been derision because Hunter had been expecting my move and slammed his knee into my upper arm. If I hadn't let go, he'd have broken it. Instantly, I rolled aside, just missing a foot strike that whistled past my head. A second later, I was on my feet. The two of us squared up again, both of us taking the number one posture—arms raised, our bodies turned so as to provide the smallest target possible.

I learned more in the next twenty minutes than I had in my entire time in Malagosto. No. That's not quite true. With HS and Mr. Nye I had acquired a thorough grounding in judo, karate and *ninjutsu*. In an incredibly short amount of time, they had taken me all the way from novice to third or second *kyu*—which is to say, green or blue belt. I would spend the rest of my life building on what they had given me, and they were both far ahead of Hunter when it came to basic martial arts technique. But he had something they hadn't. As Oliver D'Arc had told me, he had seen action as a soldier in Africa and Ireland. I would later learn that he had been with the Parachute Regiment, a rapid intervention strike force and one of the toughest outfits in the British army. He knew how to fight in a way that they didn't. They taught me the rules, but he broke them. In that first fight we had together, he did things that simply shouldn't have worked but somehow did. Once or twice I glimpsed HS shaking his head in disbelief, watching his own training manual being torn up. I was knocked down half a dozen times and not once did I see the move coming. Nothing I had been taught seemed to work against him.

After twenty minutes, he stepped back and signaled that the fight was over. "All right, Cossack, that will do for now." He smiled and held out a hand—as if to say "no hard feelings." I reached out and took it, but this time I was ready. Before he could throw me, which of course was what he intended, I twisted around, using his own weight against him. Hunter disappeared over my shoulder and crashed down onto the mat. He had landed on his back but sprang up at once.

"You're learning." He smiled his approval, then walked away, snatching up a bottle of water. I watched him, grateful that in the very last moment of the fight I had at least done something right and hadn't made a complete fool of myself in front of my teachers. At the same time it crossed my mind that he might actually have allowed me to bring him down, simply to let me save face. I had liked and admired Hunter when I had eaten with him the night before. But now I felt a sort of closeness to him. I was determined not to let him down.

We spent a lot of time together over the next few weeks—running, swimming, competing on the assault course, facing each other with more hand-to-hand combat in the gym. He was also training the other recruits and I know that they felt exactly the same way about him as I did. He was a natural teacher. Whether it was target practice or nighttime scuba diving, he brought out the best in us. Julia Rothman was also an admirer. The two of them had dinner several times when she returned to Venice, although I was never invited.

I have to say that I was not very comfortable on Malagosto. It was as if I had left school after taking my exams only to find myself inexplicably back again. Everyone knew that I had failed in New York. And time was moving on. My nineteenth birthday had come and gone without anyone noticing it . . . including me. It was time to stand up on my own two feet.

So I was very glad when Desmond Nye called me to his office one last time and told me that I would be leaving in a few days. "We all agree that the last time was too early," he said. "But on this occasion you will be traveling with John Rider. He is taking care of some business for us and you will be there strictly as his assistant. You will do everything he says. Do you understand?"

"Yes."

He had been holding my latest report, all the work of the last five weeks. I watched him as he got up from his desk and slid it into the filing cabinet against the wall. "It is very unusual for anyone to be given a second chance in this organization," he added. His twisted around and suddenly he was gazing at me, his great white eyes challenging me. "We can put New York behind us. John Rider speaks very highly of you and that's what matters. It's good to learn from your mistakes, but I will give you one piece of advice, Yassen. Don't make any more."

I could not sleep that night. There was a storm over Venice—no wind or rain but huge sheets of lightning that flared across the sky, turning the domes and the towers of the city into black cutouts. As I lay in bed, the curtains flapping, I could almost feel the air currents spinning around me. I was excited about the mission. I was flying all the way to Peru—and if that went well, I would find myself in Paris. But there was something else. John Rider had told me almost nothing about himself. I was expected to follow him across the world, to obey him without question, and yet the man was a complete mystery to me. Was he a criminal? He might have been in the British army, but why had he left? How had he found his way into Scorpia?

Suddenly I wanted to know more about John Rider. It didn't seem fair. After all, he'd been given my files. He knew everything about me. How could we travel together when everything was so one-sided? How could I ever face him on even terms?

I slipped out of bed and got dressed. I'd made a decision without even thinking it through. It was stupid and it might be dangerous, but what was my new life about if it wasn't about taking risks? Nye kept files on everyone in his office. I had seen him lock mine away only a few hours ago. He would also have a file on John Rider. His office was on the other side of the quadrangle, just a few meters from where I was standing now. Breaking in would be easy. After all, I'd been trained.

Everyone was asleep. Nobody saw me as I left the accommodation block and crossed the cloisters of what had once been the monastery. The door to Nye's office wasn't even locked. There were some on the island who would have regarded that as an unforgivable breach of security and it puzzled me—but at the same time I suppose he felt he was safe enough. It would have been impossible to reach Malagosto from the mainland without being detected and he knew everything about everyone who was here. Who would even have considered breaking in? The lightning flashed silently and for a brief moment I saw the iron chandelier, the books, the different clocks, the pirate faces—all of them stark white, frozen. It was as if the storm were warning me, urging me to leave while I still could. I felt a pulse of warm air pushing against me. This was madness. I shouldn't be here.

But still I was determined. The next day I was leaving with John Rider. We were going to be together for a week or more and I would feel more comfortable—less unequal—if I knew something of his background. I'll admit that I was curious, but it also made sense. I had been encouraged to learn everything I could about my targets. It seemed only right that I should apply the same rule to a man who was taking me into danger and on whom my life might depend.

I went over to the cabinet—the one where Nye had deposited my personal file. I had brought the tools I would need from my bedroom, although, examining the lock, I saw it was much more sophisticated than anything I had opened before. Another dazzling burst of lightning. My own shadow seemed to leap over my shoulder. I focused on the lock, testing it with the first pick.

And then, with shocking violence, I felt myself seized from behind in a headlock, two fists crossed behind my neck, and although I immediately brought my hands up in a countermove, reaching out for the wrists, I knew I was too late and that one sudden wrench would snap my spinal cord, killing me instantly. How could it have happened? I was certain nobody had followed me in.

For perhaps three seconds I stayed where I was, kneeling there, caught in the death grip, waiting for the crack that would be the sound of my own neck breaking. It didn't come. I felt the hands relax. I twisted around. Hunter was standing over me.

"Cossack!" he said.

"Hunter . . ."

"What are you doing here?" The lightning flickered but perhaps the worst of the storm had passed. "Let's go outside," Hunter said. "You don't want to be found in here."

We went back out and stood beneath the bell tower. I could feel that strange mixture of hot and cold in the air. We were enclosed by the walls of the monastery. We were alone but we spoke in low voices.

"Tell me what you were doing," Hunter said. His face was in shadow but I could feel his eyes probing me.

I had already decided what I was going to say. I

couldn't tell him the truth. "Nye had my file this morning," I said. "I wanted to read it."

"Why?"

"I wanted to know I was ready. After what happened
in New York, I didn't want to let you down."

"And you thought your report would tell you that?"

I nodded.

"You're an idiot, Cossack." That was what he said,
but there was no anger in his voice. If anything, he was
amused. "I saw you go in and I followed you," he explained.
"I didn't know who you were. I could have killed you."

"I didn't hear you," I said.

He ignored that. "If I didn't think you were ready, I
wouldn't be taking you," he said. He thought for a moment. "I have a feeling it would be better if neither of us
said anything about this little incident. If Desmond Nye
knew you'd been creeping about in his study, he might get
the wrong idea. I suggest you go back to bed. We've got an
early start. The boat's coming tomorrow at seven o'clock."

"Thanks, Hunter."

"Don't thank me. Just don't pull a stunt like this
again." He turned and walked away. "And get some sleep!"

I was up before sunrise. My gear was packed. I had my
passport and credit cards along with the dollars I'd saved
from New York. All my visas had been arranged.

There was no one around as I walked down to the
edge of the lagoon, my feet crunching on the gravel. For
a long time I stood there, watching the sun climb over

Venice, different shades of pink, orange, and finally blue rippling through the sky. I knew that my training was over and that I would not be coming back to Malagosto, at least not as a student.

I thought about Hunter, all the lessons he had taught me. He would be with me very soon and the two of us were going to travel together. He was going to give me the one thing that I had been unable to find in all my time on the island. I suppose you could call it the killer instinct. It was all I lacked.

I trusted him completely. There was something I had to do.

I took off my watch, my old Pobeda. As I weighed it in my hand, I saw my father giving it to me. I heard his voice. I was just nine years old, so young, still in short pants, living in the house in Estrov.

My grandfather's watch.

I held it one last time, then swung my arm and threw it into the lagoon.

# 18

# КОМАНДУЮЩИЙ

HIS NAME WAS GABRIEL Sweetman and he was a drug lord, sometimes known as the Sugar Man, more often as the Commander.

He was born in the slums of Mexico City. Nothing is known about his parents, but he first came to the attention of the police when he was eight years old, selling missing car parts to motorists. The reason the parts were missing was because he had stolen them, helped by his twelve-year-old sister, Maria. When he was twelve, he sold his sister. By then, it was said that he had killed for the first time. He moved into the drugs business when he was thirteen, first dealing on the street, then working his way up until he became the lieutenant to "Sunny" Gomez, one of the biggest traffickers in Mexico. At the time, it was estimated that Gomez was smuggling three million dollars' worth of heroin and cocaine into America every day.

Sweetman murdered Gomez and took over his business. He also married Gomez's wife, a former Miss Acapulco named Tracey. Thirty years later, it was rumored that Sweetman was worth twenty-five billion dollars. He was transporting cocaine all over the world, using a fleet of Boeing 727 jet aircraft that he also owned. He had murdered over two thousand people, including fifteen judges and two hundred police officers. Sweetman would kill anyone who crossed his path and he liked to do it slowly. Some of his enemies he buried alive. It was well known that he was mad, but only his family doctor had been brave enough to say so. He had killed the family doctor.

I do not know how or why he had come to the attention of Scorpia. It is possible that they had been hired to take him out by another drug lord. It might even have been the Mexican or the American government. He certainly was not being executed because he was bad. Scorpia was occasionally involved in drug trafficking itself, although it was a dirty and unpleasant business. People who spend large amounts of money doing harm to themselves and to their customers are not usually very reliable. Sweetman had to die because someone had paid. That was all it came down to.

And it was going to be expensive because this was not an easy kill. Sweetman looked after himself. In fact he made Vladimir Sharkovsky look clumsy and careless by comparison.

Sweetman kept a permanent retinue around him— not just six bodyguards but an entire platoon. This was how he had gotten the name the Commander. He had houses in Los Angeles, Miami, and Mexico City, each one as well fortified as an army command post. The houses were kept in twenty-four-hour readiness, and once he had arrived he seldom went outside, avoiding restaurants or any other public places. When he did travel it was first by private jet and then in an armor-plated, bulletproof limousine with two outriders on motorbikes and more bodyguards in front and behind. He had four food tasters, one in each of his properties.

The house where he spent most of his time was in the middle of the Amazon jungle, one hundred sixty kilometers south of Iquitos. This is one of the few cities in the world that cannot be reached by road, and there were no roads going anywhere near the house either. Trying to approach on foot would be to risk attacks from jaguars, vipers, anacondas, black caimans, piranhas, tarantulas, or any other of the fifty deadly creatures that inhabited the rain forest . . . assuming you weren't bitten to death by mosquitoes first. Sweetman himself came and went by helicopter. He had complete faith in the pilot, largely because the pilot's elderly parents were his permanent guests and he had given instructions for them to suffer very horribly if anything ever happened to him.

Scorpia had looked into the situation and had decided that he was at his most vulnerable in the rain forest. It is interesting that they had a permanent team of advisers— strategy planners and specialists—who had prepared a consultation document for them. The house in Los Angeles was too close to its neighbors, the one in Miami too well protected. In Mexico City, Sweetman had too many friends. It was another measure of the man that he spent ten million dollars a year on bribes. He had friends in the police, the army, and the government, and if anyone asked questions about him or tried to get too close, he would know about it at once.

In the jungle, he was alone and—like so many successful men—he had a weakness. He was punctual. He ate his breakfast at exactly seven fifteen. He worked with a personal trainer from eight o'clock until nine. He went to bed at eleven. If he said he was going to leave at midday, then that would be when he would go. This is exactly what Hunter had tried to explain to me the night we met in Venice. Sweetman had told us something about himself. He had a habit and we could use it against him.

Hunter and I had flown first from Rome to Lima and from there we had taken a smaller plane to Iquitos, an extraordinary city on the west bank of the Amazon with Spanish cathedrals, French villas, colorful markets, and straw huts built on stilts, all tangled up together along the narrow streets. The whole place seemed to live and breathe for the river. It was hot and humid. You could taste the muddy water in the air.

We stayed two days in a run-down hotel in the downtown area, surrounded by backpackers and tourists and plagued by cockroaches and mosquitoes. Since so many of the travelers were from Britain and America, we communicated only in French. I spoke the language quite badly at this stage and the practice was good for me. Hunter used the time to buy a few more supplies and to book our passage downriver on a cargo boat. We were pretending to be bird-watchers. We were going to camp on the edge of the jungle for two weeks and then return to Iquitos. That was our cover story and while I was in Malagosto I had learned the names of two hundred different species—from the white-fronted Amazon parrot to the scarlet macaw. I believe I could still identify them to this day. Not that anybody asked too many questions. The captain would have been happy to drop us anywhere—provided we were able to pay.

We did not camp. As soon as the boat had dropped us off on a small beach with a few Indian houses scattered in the distance and children playing in the sand, we set off into the undergrowth. We were both equipped with the five items which are the difference between life and death in the rain forest: a machete, a compass, insect nets, water purification tablets, and waterproof shoes. This last may sound unlikely, but the massive rainfall and the dense humidity can rot your flesh in no time at all, and should anyone ever crash-land in the rain forest, I would advise them to keep their feet dry. Hunter had said it would take six days to reach the compound where Sweetman lived. In fact, we made it in five.

I will never forget my journey though that vast, suffocating landscape . . . I do not know whether to call it a heaven or hell. The world cannot live without its so-called green lungs and yet the environment was as hostile as it is possible to imagine, with thousands of unseen dangers every step of the way. I could not gauge our progress. We were two tiny specks in an area that encompassed one billion acres, hacking our way through leaves and branches, always with fresh barriers in our way. We were surrounded by all manner of different life-forms and the noise was endless: the screaming of birds, the croaking of frogs, the murmur of the river, the sudden snapping of branches as some large predator hurried past. We were lucky. We glimpsed a red-and-yellow coral snake . . . much deadlier than its red-and-black cousin. In the night, a jaguar came close and I heard its awful, throaty whisper. But all the things that could have killed us left us alone and neither of us became sick. That is something that has been true of my whole life, by the way. I am never ill. I sometimes wonder if it is a side effect of the injection my mother gave me. It protected me from the anthrax. Perhaps it still protects me from everything else.

We did not speak to each other as we walked. It would have been a waste of energy and all our attention was focused on the way ahead. But even so, I felt a sort of kinship with Hunter. He seemed to find the way almost instinctively. My life depended on him. I also admired his fitness and stamina as well as his general knowledge of survival techniques. He knew exactly which roots and berries to eat, how to follow the birds and insects to water holes or, failing that, how to extract water from vines. He never once lost his temper. The jungle can play with your mind. It is hot and oppressive. It always seems to stand in your way. The insects attack you no matter how much cream you put on. You are dirty and tired. But Hunter remained good-natured throughout. I sensed that he was pleased with our progress and satisfied that I was able to keep up.

We slept for only five hours at night, using the moon to guide us after the sun had set. We slept in hammocks. It was safer to be above the ground. After we'd eaten our jungle rations—what we'd found or what we'd brought with us—we'd climb in, and I always looked forward to the brief conversation, the moment of companionship we would have before we slept.

On the fourth night we set up camp in an area which we called the Log. It was a circular clearing dominated by a fallen tree. When I had sat on it, I had almost fallen right through as it was completely rotten and crawling with termites. "You've done very well so far," Hunter said. "It may not be so easy coming back."

"Why's that?"

"It's possible we'll be pursued. We may have to move more quickly."

"The red pins . . ."

"That's right."

Whenever we came to a particular landmark, a place with a choice of more than one route, I had seen Hunter pressing a red pin close to the base of a tree trunk. He must have positioned more than a hundred of them. Nobody else would notice them, but they would provide us with a series of pointers if we needed to move in a hurry.

"What will we do if he isn't there?" I asked. "Sweetman may have left."

"According to our intelligence, he's not leaving until the end of the week. And never call him by his name, Cossack. It personalizes him. We need to think of him as an object . . . as dead meat. That's all he is to us." His voice floated out of the darkness. Overhead, a parrot began to screech. "Call him the Commander. That's how he likes to see himself."

"When will we be there?"

"Tomorrow afternoon. I want to get there before sunset . . . to give us time to reconnoiter the place. I need to find a position to make the kill."

"I could shoot him for you."

"No, Cossack, thanks all the same. This time you're strictly here for the ride."

We were up again at first light, the sky silver, the trees and undergrowth dark. We sipped some water and took energy tablets. We folded up our hammocks, packed our rucksacks, and left.

Sure enough, we reached the compound in the late afternoon. As we folded back the vegetation, we were suddenly aware of the sun glinting off a metal fence and crouched down, keeping out of sight. It was always possible that there would be guards patrolling outside the perimeter, although after half an hour we realized that the Commander had failed to take this elementary precaution. Presumably he felt he was safe enough inside.

Moving very carefully, we circled around, always staying in the cover of the jungle some distance from the fence. Hunter was afraid that there would be radar, trip wires, and all sorts of other devices that we might activate if we got too close. Looking through the gaps in the trees, we could see that the fence was electrified and contained a collection of colonial buildings spread out over a pale green lawn. They were similar in style to the ones we had seen in Iquitos. There were a lot of guards in dark green uniforms patrolling the area or standing with binoculars and assault rifles in rusting metal towers. Their long isolation had done them no good. They were shabby and listless. Although Hunter and I were both wearing jungle camouflage with our faces painted in streaks, they barely looked our way, and even if we'd been in bright red, they might not have noticed us.

The compound had begun life twenty years before as a research center for an environmental group studying the damage being done to the rain forest. They had all died from a mysterious sickness and a week later the Commander had moved in. Since then, he had adapted it to his own needs, adding huts for his soldiers and bodyguards, a helicopter landing pad, a private cinema, and all the devices he needed for his security. In some ways it reminded me of the dacha in the Silver Forest, although the two could not have been more different. It was only their purpose that was the same.

The Commander lived in the largest house, which was raised off the ground, with a veranda and electric fans. Presumably there would be a generator somewhere inside the complex. We had been watching through field glasses for more than an hour when suddenly he emerged, oddly dressed in a silk bathrobe and pajamas. It was still early evening. He went over to speak to a second man in faded blue overalls. His pilot? The helicopter was parked nearby, a four-seater Robinson R44. The two of them exchanged a few words. Then the Commander went back into the house.

"It's a shame we can't hear them," I said.

"The Commander is leaving at eight o'clock tomorrow morning," Hunter replied.

I stared at him. "How do you know?"

"I can lip-read, Cossack. It comes in quite useful sometimes. Maybe you should learn to do the same."

I hardly slept that night. We retreated back into the undergrowth and hooked up our hammocks once more, but we couldn't risk the luxury of a campfire and didn't speak a word. We swallowed down some cold rations and closed our eyes. But I lay there for a long time, all sorts of thoughts running through my head.

I really had hoped that Hunter might let me make the kill. My old psychiatrist, Dr. Steiner, would not have been happy if I had told him this, but I thought it would be much easier to assassinate a drug lord, an obviously evil human being, than a defenseless woman in New York. It would have been a good test for me . . . my first kill. But I could see now that it was out of the question. The position of the helicopter in relation to the main house meant that we would have, at most, ten seconds to make the shot.

Just ten steps and the Commander would be safely inside. If I hesitated or, worse still, missed, we would not have a second opportunity. Desmond Nye had already told me. I was here to assist and to observe and I knew I had to accept it. Hunter was the one in charge.

We were in position much earlier than we needed to be—at seven o'clock. Hunter had been carrying the weapon he was going to use ever since we had left Iquitos. It was a .308 Winchester sniper rifle, a very good weapon, perfect for long-range shooting with minimal recoil. I watched as he loaded it with a single cartridge and adjusted the sniper scope. It seemed to me that he and the weapon were one. I had noticed this already on the shooting range at Malagosto. When Hunter held a gun, it became part of him.

The minutes ticked away. I used my field glasses to scan the compound, waiting for the Commander to reappear. The soldiers were in their towers or patrolling the fence, but the atmosphere inside the compound was lazy. They were really only half awake. At ten to eight, the pilot came out of his quarters, yawning and stretching. We watched as he climbed into the helicopter, went through his checks, and started the rotors. Very quickly they began to turn, then disappeared in a blur. All around us, birds and monkeys scattered through the branches, frightened away by the noise. The Commander had still not stepped out at two minutes to eight and I began to wonder if he had changed his mind. I knew the time from the ordinary but efficient watch that I had bought for myself at Rome airport. I was sweating. I wondered if it was nerves or the close, stifling heat of the morning.

Something touched my shoulder.

My first thought was that it was a leaf that had fallen from a tree—but I knew at once that it was too heavy for a leaf.

It moved.

My hand twitched and it was all I could do to stop myself from reaching out and attempting to flick this . . . thing, whatever it was, away. I felt its weight shift as it went from my shoulder onto my neck and I realized that it was alive and that it was moving. It reached the top of my shirt and I shuddered as it legs prickled delicately against my skin. Even without seeing it, I knew that it was some sort of spider, a large one. It had lowered itself onto me while I crouched behind Hunter.

My mouth had gone dry. I could feel the blood pounding in the jugular vein that ran up the side of my neck and knew that the creature would have been drawn to that area, fascinated by the warmth and by the movement. And that was where it remained, clinging to me like some hideous growth. Hunter had not seen what had happened. He was still focused on the compound, his eye pressed against the sniper scope. I didn't dare call out. I had to keep my breath steady without turning my head. Straining, I looked out of the corner of my eye and saw it. I recognized it at once. A black widow. One of the most venomous spiders in the Amazon.

It still refused to move. Why wouldn't it continue on its way? I tensed myself, waiting for it to continue its journey across my face and into my hair, but still it stayed where it was. I didn't know if Hunter had brought antivenom with him but it would make no difference if he had. If it bit me in the neck, I would die very quickly. Maybe it was waiting to strike even now, savoring the moment. The spider was huge. My skin was recoiling, my whole body sending out alarm signals that my brain could not ignore.

I wanted to call to Hunter, but even speaking one word might be enough to alarm the spider. I was filled with rage. After the failure of New York, I had been determined that I would make a good account of myself in Peru, and so far I hadn't put a foot wrong. I couldn't believe that this had happened to me . . . and now! I searched desperately for a stick, something I could throw at Hunter. There was no further movement in the compound. Everyone was waiting for the Commander to make his appearance. I knew it would happen at any moment. It was strangely ironic that I might die at exactly the same time as him.

In the end, I whistled. It was such an odd thing to do that it would surely attract Hunter's attention. It did. He turned and saw me standing there, paralyzed, no color in my face. He saw the spider.

And it was right then that the door of the house opened and the Commander came out, wearing an olive green tunic and carrying a briefcase, followed by two men, with a third walking ahead. I knew at that moment that I was dead. There was nothing Hunter could do for me. He had his instructions from Scorpia and less than ten seconds in which to carry them out. I had almost forgotten about the helicopter, but now the whine of its rotors enveloped me. The Commander was walking steadily toward the cockpit.

Hunter made an instant decision. He sprang to his feet and moved behind me. Was he really going to abort the mission and save my life? Surely it had to be one or the other. Shoot the Commander or get rid of the spider. He couldn't do both, and after everything he had told me, his choice was obvious.

I didn't know what he was doing. He had positioned himself behind me. The Commander had almost reached the helicopter, his hand stretching out toward the door. Then, with no warning at all, Hunter fired. I heard the explosion and felt a streak of pain across my neck, as if I had been sliced with a red-hot sword. The Commander grabbed hold of his chest and crumpled, blood oozing over his clenched fingers. He had been shot in the heart. The men surrounding him threw themselves flat, afraid they would be targeted next. I was also bleeding. Blood was pouring down the side of my neck. But the spider was gone.

That was when I understood what had happened. Hunter had aimed through the spider and at the Commander. He had shot them both with the same bullet.

"Let's move," he whispered.

There was no time to discuss what had happened. The bodyguards were already panicking, shouting and pointing in our direction. One of them opened fire, sending bullets randomly into the rain forest. The guards in the towers were searching for us. More men were running out of the huts.

We snatched up our equipment and ran, allowing the mass of leaves and branches to swallow us up. We left behind us a dead drug lord with a single bullet and a hundred tiny fragments of black widow in his heart.

"You saved my life," I said.

Hunter smiled. "Taking a life and saving a life . . . and with just one bullet. That's not bad going," he said.

We had put twenty-five kilometers between ourselves and the compound, following the little red pins until the fading light made it impossible to continue and we had to stop for fear of losing our way. We had reached the Log, the campsite where we had spent the night before, and this time I was careful not to sit on the hollow tree. Hunter spent ten minutes stretching out trip wires all around us. These were almost invisible, connected to little black boxes that he screwed into the trunks of the trees. Once again, we didn't dare light a fire. After we had hooked up our hammocks, we ate our dinner straight out of the can. It amused me that Hunter insisted on carrying the empty cans with us. He had just killed a man, but he wouldn't litter the rain forest.

Neither of us was ready for sleep. We set cross-legged

on the ground, listening out for the sound of approaching feet. It was a bright night. The moon was shining and everything around us was a strange silver green. To my surprise, Hunter had produced a quarter bottle of malt whiskey. It was the last thing I would have expected him to bring along. I watched him as he held it to his lips.

"It's a little tradition of mine," he explained in a low voice. "A good malt whiskey after a kill. This is a twenty-five-year-old Glenmorangie. Older than you!" He held it out to me. "Have some, Cossack. I expect your nerves need it after that little incident. That spider certainly chose its moment."

"I can't believe what you did," I said. There was a bandage around my neck, already stained with sweat and blood. It hurt a lot and I knew that I would always have a scar where Hunter's bullet had cut me, but in a strange way I was glad. I did not want to forget this night. I sipped the whiskey. It burned the back of my throat but in a good way. "What now?" I asked.

"A slog back to Iquitos and then Paris. At least it'll be a little cooler over there. And no damn mosquitoes!" He slapped one on the side of his neck.

We were both at peace. The Commander was dead, killed in extraordinary circumstances. We had the whiskey. The moon was shining. And we were alone in the rain forest. That's the only way that I can explain the conversation that followed. At least, that was how it seemed at the time.

"Hunter," I said, "why are you with Scorpia?" I would

never normally have asked. It was wrong. It was insolent. But out here, it didn't seem to matter.

I thought he might snap at me, but he reached out for the bottle and answered quietly, "Why does anyone join Scorpia? Why did you?"

"You know why," I said. "I didn't really have any choice."

"We all make choices, Cossack. Who we are in this world, what we do in it. Generous or selfish. Happy or sad. Good or evil. It's all down to choice."

"And you chose this?"

"I'm not sure it was the right choice, but I've got nobody else to blame, if that's what you mean." He paused, holding the bottle in front of him. "I was in a pub," he said. "It was in the middle of London . . . in Soho. Me and a couple of friends. We were just having a drink, minding our own business. But there was a man in there, a taxi driver as it turned out, a big, fat guy in a sheepskin coat. He overheard us talking, realized we were all army, and began to make obnoxious remarks. Stupid things. I should have just ignored him or walked out. That was what my friends wanted to do.

"But I'd been drinking myself and the two of us got into an argument. It was so bloody stupid. The next thing I knew, I'd knocked him to the ground. Even then, there were a dozen ways I could have hit him. But I'd let my training get the better of me. He didn't get up and suddenly the police were there and I realized what I'd done." He paused. "I'd killed him."

He fell silent. All around us, the insects continued their chatter. There wasn't a breath of wind.

"I was dismissed from the army and thrown into jail," he went on. "As it happened, I wasn't locked up for very long. My old regiment pulled a few strings and I had a good lawyer. He managed to put in a claim of self-defense and I was let out on appeal. But after that I was finished. No one was going to employ me, and even if they did, you think I wanted to spend the rest of my life as a security guard or behind a desk? I didn't know what to do. And then Scorpia came along and offered me this. And I said yes."

"Are you married?" I asked.

He nodded. "Yeah. I've been married three years and there's a kid on the way. At least I'm going to have enough money to be able to look after him." He paused. "If it is a boy. You see what I mean? My choice."

The whiskey bottle passed between us one last time. It was almost empty.

"Maybe it's not too late for you to change your mind," he said.

I was startled. "What do you mean?"

"I'm thinking about New York. I'm thinking about the last few weeks . . . and today. You seem like a nice kid to me, Cossack. Not one of Scorpia's usual recruits at all. I wonder if you've really got it in you to be like me. Marat and Sam . . . they don't give a damn. They've got no imagination. But you?"

"I can do this," I said.

"But do you really *want* to? I'm not trying to dissuade you. That's the last thing I want to do. I just want you to be aware that once you start, there's no going back. After the first kill—that's it."

He paused. We both did. I wasn't sure how to respond.

"If I backed out now, Scorpia would kill me."

"I rather doubt it. They'd be annoyed, of course. But I think you're exaggerating your own importance. They'd very quickly forget you. Anyway, you've learned enough to keep away from them. You could change your identity, your appearance, start somewhere new. The world is a big place—and there are all sorts of different things you could be doing in it."

"Is that what you're advising me?" I asked.

"I'm not advising you anything. I'm just laying out the options."

I'm not sure what I would have said if the conversation had continued, but just then we heard something: the croaking of a frog at the edge of the clearing. At least, that was what it would have sounded like to anyone approaching, but it wasn't a frog that was native to the Amazon rain forest. One of the wires that Hunter had set down had just been tripped and what we were hearing was a recording, a warning. Hunter was on his feet instantly, crouching down, signaling to me with an outstretched hand. I had a gun. It had been supplied to me when we were in Iquitos—a Browning 9mm semiautomatic, popular with the Peruvian army and unusual in that it held thirteen rounds of ammunition. It was fully loaded.

I heard something. The single crack of a branch breaking, about twenty meters away. A beam of light flickered between the trees, thrown by a powerful flashlight. There was no time to gather up our things and no point in wondering who they were, how they had followed us here. We had already planned what to do if this happened. We got up and began to move.

They came in from all sides. Six of the Commander's men had taken it upon themselves to follow us into the rain forest. Why? Their employer was dead and there was going to be no reward for bringing in his killers. Perhaps they were genuinely angry. We had, after all, removed the source of their livelihood. I saw all of them as they arrived. The moon was so bright, they barely had any need of their flashlights. They were high on drugs, dirty and disheveled, with hollow faces, bright eyes, and straggly beards. Two of them had cigarettes dangling from their mouths. They were wearing bits and pieces of military uniforms with machine guns slung over their shoulders. One of them had a dog, a pit bull terrier, on a chain. The dog had brought them here. It began to bark, straining against the leash, knowing we were close.

But the men saw nothing. They had arrived at an empty clearing with a tree lying on its side, nobody in front of it, nobody behind, termites crawling over the bark. Our empty hammocks were in front of them. Perhaps their flashlights picked up the empty whiskey bottle on the ground.

"*Vamos a hacerlo!*" One of them gave the order in Spanish, his voice deep and guttural.

As one, the men opened fire, spraying the clearing with bullets, shooting into the surrounding jungle. After the peace of the night, the noise was deafening. For at least thirty seconds the clearing blazed white and the surrounding leaves and branches were chopped to smithereens. None of the men knew what they were doing. They didn't care that they had no target.

We waited until their clips had run out and then we stood up, dead wood cascading off our shoulders. We had been right next to the soldiers, lying facedown inside the fallen tree. We were covered with termites, which were crawling over our backs and into our clothes. But termites do not bite you. They do not sting. We had disturbed their habitat and they were all over us, but we didn't care.

We opened fire. The soldiers saw us too late. I was not sure what happened next, whether I actually killed any of them. There was a blaze of gunfire, again incredibly loud, and I saw the ragged figures being blown off their feet. One of them managed to fire again but the bullets went nowhere, into the air. I was firing wildly but Hunter was utterly precise and mechanical, choosing his targets and then squeezing the trigger again and again. It was all over very quickly. The six men were dead. There didn't seem to be any more on the way.

I brushed termites off my shoulders and out of my hair. "Are there any more of them?" I whispered.

"I don't think so," Hunter said. "But we'd better get moving."

We collected our things.

"I shot them," I said. "What you were saying to me . . . you were wrong. I was with you. I killed some of them." I wasn't even sure it was true. Hunter could have taken out all six himself. But we weren't going to argue about it now.

He shook his head. "*If* you killed . . ." He put the emphasis on the first word. "You did it in the dark, in self-defense. That doesn't make you a murderer. It's not the same."

"Why not?" I couldn't understand him. What was he trying to achieve?

He turned and suddenly there was a real darkness in his eyes. "You want to know what the difference is, Yassen?" He had used my real name for the first time. "We have another job in Paris, very different from this one. You want to know what it's really like to kill? You're about to find out."

# 19

# ПАРИЖ

Our target in Paris was a man named Christophe Vosque, a senior officer in the Police Nationale. He was, as it happens, totally corrupt. He had received many payments from Scorpia in return for which he had turned a blind eye to many of their operations in France. But recently he had gotten greedy. He had demanded more payments, and worse still, he had been in secret talks with the DGSE, the French secret service. He was planning a double cross and Scorpia had decided to make an example of him by taking him out. This was to be a punishment killing. It had to make headlines.

However, for once Scorpia had gotten their intelligence wrong. No sooner had we arrived at Charles de Gaulle airport than we were informed that Vosque was not in the city after all. He had gone on a five-day training course, meaning that we had the entire week to ourselves. Hunter wasn't at all put out.

"We need a rest," he said. "And since Scorpia's paying, we might as well check ourselves in somewhere decent. I can show you around Paris. I'm sure you'll like it."

He booked us into the luxurious Hotel George V, close to the Champs-Élysées. It was far more than decent. In fact, I had never stayed anywhere like this. The hotel was all velvet curtains, chandeliers, thick carpets, tinkling pianos, and massive flower displays. My bathroom was marble. The bath had gold taps. Everyone who stayed here was rich and they weren't afraid to show it. I wondered if Hunter had brought me here for a reason. Normally we would have stayed somewhere more discreet and out of the way, but I suspected that he was testing me, throwing me into this gorgeous, alien environment to see how I would cope. He spoke excellent French. Mine was rudimentary. He was in his late twenties and already well traveled. I was nineteen. I think it amused him to see me dealing with the receptionists, the managers, and the waiters in their stiff collars and black ties, trying to convince them that I had as much right to be there as anyone . . . trying to convince myself.

It was certainly true that we both deserved a rest. The journey into the rain forest and out again, the death of the Commander, the shoot-out that had followed, our time in Iquitos, even the long flight back to Europe had exhausted us and we both had to be in first-rate condition when we came up against Vosque. And if that meant eating the best food and waking up in five-star luxury, I certainly wasn't going to argue.

We had adjoining rooms on the third floor and both spent the first twenty-four hours asleep. When I woke up, I ordered room service . . . the biggest breakfast I have ever eaten, even though it was the middle of the afternoon. I had a hot bath with the foam spilling over the edges. I sprawled on the bed and watched TV. They had English and Russian channels, but I forced myself to listen in French, trying to attune myself to the language.

The next day, Hunter showed me the city. I had done more traveling in the past few weeks—Venice, New York, Peru—than I had in my entire life, but I loved every minute of my time in Paris. A few of the things we did were obvious. We went up the Eiffel Tower. We visited Notre-Dame. But he also took me to lots of unexpected places: the sewers, the flea markets, Père-Lachaise cemetery with its bizarre mausoleums and famous residents.

Spring had still not arrived, but the sun was shining and although the days were cold, there was a sparkle in the air. We drifted in and out of coffeehouses. We browsed in antique shops and bought clothes on the Avenue Montaigne. We ate fantastic ice cream at the Maison Berthillon on the Île St-Louis. Curiously, this was where the founding members of Scorpia had first come together—but perhaps wisely there was no blue plaque to commemorate the event.

We ate extremely well in restaurants that were empty of tourists. Hunter didn't like to spend a fortune on food and never ordered alcohol. He preferred grenadine, the red syrup he had introduced me to in Venice. I drink it to this day.

We never once discussed the business that had brought us here, but we were quietly preparing for it. At six o'clock that very morning we went on a two-hour run together; it was a spectacular circuit down the Champs-

Élysées, through the Jardins des Tuileries, and across the Seine. There was a pool and a gym at the hotel, and we swam and worked out for two hours more. I sometimes wondered what people made of us. We could have been friends on vacation or perhaps, given our age difference, an older and a younger brother. That was how it felt sometimes. Nor did Hunter ever refer back to our conversation in the jungle, although some of the things he had said remained in my mind.

We had arrived on a Monday. On the Thursday, Hunter received a note from the concierge as we were leaving the hotel and read it quickly without showing it to me. After that, I sensed that something had changed. We took the metro to Montmartre that day and walked around the narrow streets with all the artists' studios and drank coffee in one of the squares. It was just warm enough to sit outside. By now we were relaxed in each other's company, but I sensed that Hunter was still agitated. It was only when we reached the great white church of Sacré-Coeur with its astonishing views of Paris that he turned to me.

"I need to have some time on my own," he said. "Do you mind?"

"Of course not." I was surprised that he even needed to ask.

"There's someone I have to meet," he went on. He was more uneasy than I had ever seen him. "But I'm breaking the rules. We're both undercover. We're working. Do you understand what I'm saying? If Julia Rothman found out about this, she wouldn't be pleased."

"I won't tell her anything," I said. And I meant it. I would never have betrayed Hunter.

"Thank you," he said. "We can meet back at the hotel."

I walked away but I was still curious. The more I knew about Hunter, the more I wanted to know. I always got the feeling that there was so much more that he wasn't telling me. So when I reached the street corner, I turned back. I wanted to know what he was going to do.

And that was when I saw her.

She was standing on the terrace in front of the main entrance of the church. There were quite a few tourists around, but she stood out because she was alone and she was pregnant. She was quite small—the French would say *petite*—with long fair hair and pale skin. She was wearing a loose, baggy jacket with her hands tucked into her pockets. She was pretty.

Hunter was walking toward her. She saw him and turned. I saw her face light up with joy. She hurried over to him. And then the two of them were in each other's arms. Her head was pressed against his chest. He was stroking her hair. Two lovers on the steps of Sacré-Coeur . . . what could be more Parisian? I turned the corner and walked away.

The next day, Vosque returned.

He lived in the fifth arrondissement, in a quiet street of apartments and houses not far from the Panthéon, the elaborate church that had been modeled on a similar

building in Rome and where many of the great and good
of France were buried. Hunter had received a full briefing
in an envelope sealed with a scorpion. I guessed it had
been delivered to his hotel room by someone like Marcus,
who had done the same for me in New York. The two of
us went to a café on the Champs-Élysées. It might have
seemed odd to discuss this sort of business in a public
place, but in fact it was safer to choose somewhere completely random. We could make sure we weren't being followed. And we knew it couldn't be bugged.

Vosque provided a very different challenge from that
of the Commander. He might be easier to reach, but he
probably knew we were coming, so there was a good
chance he had taken precautions. He would carry a gun.
He could expect protection from the French police. As far
as they were concerned, he was one of them, a senior officer and a man to be respected. If he was gunned down
in the street, there would be an immediate outcry. Ports
and airports would be closed. We would find ourselves at
the center of an international manhunt.

He lived alone. Hunter produced some photographs
of his address. They had been provided by Scorpia and
showed a ground-floor apartment with glass doors and
double-height windows on the far side of a courtyard
shared by two more apartments. Although one of these
was empty, the other was occupied by a young artist, a
potential witness. An archway opened onto the street.
There was no other way in and an armed policeman—a

*gendarme*—had been stationed in the little room that had once been the porter's lodge. To reach Vosque, we had to get past him.

In all our discussions, we called Vosque "the Cop." As always, it was easier to depersonalize him. On the Saturday, we watched him leave the apartment and walk to his local supermarket, two blocks away. He was a short, bullish man in his late forties. As he walked, he swung his fists and you could imagine him lashing out at anyone who got in his way. He was almost bald with a thick mustache that didn't quite stretch to the end of his lip. He was wearing an old-fashioned suit but no tie. After he had done his shopping, he stopped at a café for a cigar and a *demi pression* of beer. Nobody had escorted him, and I thought it would be a simple matter to shoot him where he sat. We could do it without being seen.

But Hunter wasn't having any of it. "That's not what Scorpia wants," he said. "He has to be killed in his home."

"Why?"

"You'll see."

I didn't like the sound of that, but I knew better than to ask anything more.

Our Paris vacation was over. Even the weather had changed. On Sunday morning it rained and the whole city seemed to be sulking, the water spitting off the sidewalks and forming puddles in the roads. This was the day when Vosque was going to die. If we wanted to find him alone in his apartment, it made sense. Monday to Friday he would be in his office, which was situated inside the Interior Ministry. According to his file, most evenings he went out drinking or ate with friends in cheap restaurants around the Gare Saint-Lazare. Sunday for him was dead time—in more than one sense.

That morning, Annabelle Finnan, the artist who lived next door to Vosque, received a telephone call from the town of Orléans, telling her that her elderly mother had been run over by a van and was unlikely to survive. This was untrue, but Annabelle left at once. We were waiting in the street and saw her flag down a taxi. Then we moved forward.

We were both wearing cheap suits, white shirts, and black ties. We were carrying Bibles. The disguise had been Hunter's idea and it was a brilliant one. We had come as Jehovah's Witnesses. There had been real ones, apparently, working in the area and nobody would have noticed two more following in their wake. The gendarme in the porter's lodge saw us and dismissed us in the same instant. We were the last thing he needed on a wet Sunday morning, two Bible-bashers come to preach to him about the end of the world.

"Not here!" the gendarme grunted. "Thank you very much, my friends. We're not interested."

"But, monsieur . . . ," Hunter began.

"Just move along."

Hunter was holding his Bible at a strange angle and I saw him press down on the spine. There was a soft hissing sound, and the gendarme jerked backward and collapsed. The Bible must have been supplied by Gordon Ross, all the way from Malagosto. It had fired a knockout dart. I could see the little tuft sticking out of the man's neck.

"And on the seventh day, he rested," Hunter muttered, and I recognized the quotation from the second chapter of Genesis.

The two of us moved into the office. Hunter had brought rope and tape with him. "Tie him up," he said. "We'll be gone long before he wakes up, but it's best not to take chances."

I did as I was told, securely fastening his wrists and ankles and using the tape and a balled-up handkerchief to gag his mouth. After everything Hunter had told me, I was a little surprised that he hadn't simply shot the policeman. Wouldn't that have been easier? But perhaps, despite everything he had said, he preferred not to take a life unless it was really necessary.

With the gendarme hidden away, we walked across the courtyard, our Bibles in our hands. I thought we would go straight to Vosque's door, but instead Hunter steered us over to the artist's apartment and rang the bell there. It was a nice touch. She wasn't in, of course, but if Vosque happened to be watching out of his window, the fact that we were patiently waiting there would make us look completely innocent. We stood outside for a minute or two, ignoring the thin drizzle that was slanting down onto the cobblestones. Hunter pretended to slip a note through the letter box. Then we went over to Vosque's place and rang the bell.

He must have seen us coming and he didn't suspect a thing. He was already in a bad mood as he opened the door, wearing a sleeveless undershirt and boxers with a striped bathrobe falling off his shoulders. He hadn't shaved yet.

"Get the hell out of here," he snarled. "I haven't—"

That was as far as he got. Hunter didn't use another anesthetic dart. He hit him, very hard, under the chin. It wasn't a killer blow, although it could have been. He caught the Cop as he fell and dragged him into the house. I closed the door behind us. We were in.

The apartment was almost bare. The floor was uncarpeted, the furniture minimal. There were no pictures on the walls. It was private. Net curtains hung over the windows and although there was a glass door leading into a tiny back garden—unusual for a Paris property—nobody could see in. A bedroom led off to one side. There was an open-plan kitchen where, from the looks of it, Vosque hardly ever cooked anything much more than a boiled egg.

Hunter had manhandled the Cop across the floor and onto a wooden chair. "Find something to tie him up with," he said. "He should have some ties in the bedroom. If you can't find any, use a sheet off the bed. Tear it into strips."

I was mystified. What were we doing? Our orders were to kill the man, not threaten or interrogate him. Why wasn't he already dead? But once again I didn't argue. In

fact, Vosque had quite a collection of ties. I took five of
them from his wardrobe and used them to tie his arms
and legs, keeping the last one to gag his mouth. Hunter
said nothing while I worked. I had already seen that intense concentration of his when we were in the jungle, but
this time there was something else. I was aware that he
had something in his mind and for some reason it made
me afraid.

He checked that the Cop was secure, then went
over to the sink, filled a glass of water, and threw it in
his face. The Cop's eyes flickered open. I saw the jolt as
he returned to consciousness and the fear as he took in
his predicament. He began to struggle violently, rocking
back and forth, as if there was any chance of him breaking
free. Hunter signaled at him to stop. The Cop swore and
shouted at him but the words were muffled, incomprehen-
sible beneath the gag. Eventually, he stopped fighting. He
could see it would do no good.

I didn't dare speak. I wasn't even sure what language
I would be expected to use.

Hunter turned to me.

"You want to be an assassin," he said, speaking in Russian now. "When you were in the jungle, you told me you
killed some of the men who came after us. I'm not so sure
about that. It was dark and I have a feeling I was the one
who knocked all of them down. But that doesn't matter.
You said you were ready to kill. I didn't believe you. Well,
now's your chance to prove it. I want you to kill Vosque."

I looked at him. Then I turned to the Cop. I'm not sure that the Frenchman had understood what we were saying. He was silent, gazing straight ahead as if he was outraged, as if we had no right to be here.

"You want me to kill him," I said in Russian.

"Yes. With this."

He held out a knife. He had brought it with him and I stared at it with complete horror. I couldn't believe what I was seeing. The knife was razor sharp. There could be no doubt of that. I had never seen anything quite so evil. But it was tiny. The blade was more like an old-fashioned safety razor. It couldn't have been more than five centimeters long.

"That's crazy," I said. I was clinging to the thought that perhaps this was some sort of joke, although there could be no chance of that. Hunter was deadly serious. "Give me a gun. I'll shoot him."

"That's not what I'm asking, Yassen. This is meant to be a punishment killing. I want you to use the knife."

He had named me in front of the victim. Even though he was speaking in Russian, there could be no going back.

"Why?"

"Why are you arguing? You know how we work. Do as you're told."

He pressed the knife into my hand. It was terribly light, barely more than a slither of sharpened metal in a plastic handle. And at that moment I understood the point of all this. If I killed Vosque with this weapon, it would be slow and it would be painful. I would feel every cut that I made. And it might take several cuts. This wasn't going to be just a quick stab to the heart. However I did it, I would end up drenched in the man's blood.

A punishment killing. For both of us.

Something deep inside me rose to the surface. I was shocked, disgusted that he could behave this way. We'd just had six amazing days in Paris. In a way, they'd wiped out everything bad that had happened to me before. He'd been almost like a brother to me. Certainly, he had been my friend. And now, suddenly, he was utterly cold. From the way he was standing there, I could see that I meant nothing to him. And he was asking me to do something unspeakable.

Butchery.

And yet he was right. At the end of the day it was a lesson I had to learn if I was going to do this work. Not every assassination would take place from the top of a building or the other side of a perimeter fence. I had to get my hands dirty.

I examined the Cop. He was struggling again, his stomach heaving underneath his shirt, jerking the chair from side to side, whimpering. His whole face had gone red. He had seen the knife. I balanced it in my hand, once again feeling the flimsy weight. Where was I to start? I supposed the only answer was to cut his throat. Gordon Ross had even given us a demonstration once, but he had used a plastic dummy.

"You need to get on with it, Yassen," Hunter said. "We haven't got all day."

"I can't."

I had spoken the words without realizing it. They had simply slipped out of my mouth.

"Why can't you?"

"Because . . ."

I didn't want to answer. I couldn't explain. Vosque might not be a good man. He was corrupt. He took bribes. But he was a man nonetheless. Not a paper target. He was right here, in front of me, terrified. I could see the sweat on his forehead and I could smell him. I just didn't have it in me to take his life . . . and certainly not with this hideous, pathetic knife.

"Are you sure?"

I nodded, not trusting myself to speak.

"All right. Go outside. Wait for me there."

This time I did what I was told without questioning. If I had stayed there a minute longer, I'd have been sick. As I opened the front door I heard the soft thud of a bullet fired from a silenced pistol and knew that Hunter had taken care of matters himself. I was still holding the knife. I couldn't leave it behind. It was covered in forensic evidence that might lead the police to me. I carefully slid it into the top pocket of my jacket, where it nestled, the blade over my heart.

Hunter came out. "Let's go," he said. He didn't seem angry. He showed no emotion at all.

Walking back across the city, I told him my decision.

"I'm taking your advice," I said. "I don't want to be an assassin. I'm leaving Paris. I'm not coming back to Rome. I'm going to disappear."

"I didn't give you that advice," Hunter said. "But I think it's a good idea."

"Scorpia will find me."

"Go back to Russia, Yassen. It's a huge country. Russian is your first language and now you have skills. Find somewhere to hide. Start again."

"Yes." I felt a sense of sadness and had to express it. "I let you down," I said.

"No, you didn't. I'm glad it worked out this way. The moment I first saw you, I had a feeling that you weren't suited to this sort of work, and I'm glad you've proved me right. Don't be like me, Yassen. Have a life. Start a family. Keep away from the shadows. Forget all this ever happened."

We came to a bridge. I took out the knife and dropped it into the Seine. Then we walked on together, making our way back to the hotel.

# 20

# МОЩНОСТЬ ПЛЮС

WE WENT TO THE airport, sitting together in the back of a taxi with our luggage in the trunk. Hunter was returning to Venice, reporting to Julia Rothman. I was heading for Berlin. It would have been madness to take a plane to Moscow or anywhere in Russia. It would provide Scorpia with a giant arrow pointing in the right direction to come after me. Berlin was at the hub of Europe and gave me a host of different options . . . I could head west to the Netherlands or east to Poland. I would be only a few hours from the Czech Republic. I could travel by train or by bus. I could buy a car. I could even go on foot. There were dozens of border crossing points where I could pass myself off as a student and where they probably wouldn't even bother to check my ID. It was Hunter who had suggested it. There was no better place from which to disappear.

I was aware of all sorts of different feelings fighting inside me as we drove out through the shabby and depressing suburbs to the north of Paris. I still felt that I had let Hunter down although he had assured me otherwise. He had been friendly but businesslike when we met for breakfast that morning, keen to be on his way. He called me Yassen all the time, as if I had been stripped of my code name, although I was still using his. And that morning he had run by himself. Alone in my room, I had really missed our sprint around the city and felt excluded. It reminded me of the time when I'd broken my leg when I was twelve and had been forced out of a trip with the Young Pioneers.

I wondered if I would miss all this luxury: the five-star hotel, the international travel, buying clothes in high-class boutiques. It was very unlikely that I would be visiting Paris again, and if I did, it certainly wouldn't have the pleasure and the excitement of the last week. I had thought that I was becoming something, turning into something special. But now it was all over.

I had already begun to consider my future and had even come to a decision. There were still parts of my training that I could put to good use. I had learned languages. My English was excellent. The Countess had shown me how to hold my own with people much wealthier than me. And even Sharkovsky, in his own way, had been helpful. I knew how to iron shirts, polish shoes, make beds. The answer was obvious. I would find work in a hotel just like the George V. New hotels were being built all over Russia and I was certain I'd be able to get a job in one, starting as a bellboy or washing dishes in the kitchen and then working my way up. Moscow was too dangerous for me. It would have to be St. Petersburg or somewhere farther afield. But I would be able to support myself. I had no doubt of it.

I did not tell Hunter this. I would have been too

ashamed. Anyway, we had already agreed that we would not discuss my plans. It was better for both of us if he didn't know.

I was not sorry. I was relieved.

From the moment I had met Julia Rothman in Venice, I had been drawn into something very deadly, and deep down I had worried that I had no place there. What would my parents have said if I had chosen to become a paid killer? It was true that they had not been entirely innocent themselves. They had worked in a factory that produced weapons of death. But they had been forced into it and in a sense they had spent their whole lives protecting me from having to do the same. They had fed the dream of my becoming a university student, a helicopter pilot . . . whatever. Anything to get me out of Estrov. And what of Leo, a boy who had never hurt anyone in his life? He would say I'd had a lucky escape.

For better or for worse, it was over. That was what I told myself. At least I had some cash in my pocket. Only that morning I had drawn a thousand francs out of my bank account, knowing that the moment Scorpia discovered I was gone they would freeze it. I had my freedom. However I looked at it, my situation was a lot better than it had been four and a half years ago. I shouldn't complain.

We arrived at the airport and checked in. As it happened, my flight was leaving just thirty minutes after Hunter's, and we had a bit of time to kill. So we went through passport control and sat together in the departure lounge. We did not speak very much. Hunter was reading a paperback book. I had a magazine.

"I fancy a coffee," Hunter said suddenly. "Can I get you one?"

"No. I'm all right, thanks."

He got up. "It may take a while. There's a bit of a queue. Will you keep an eye on my things?"

"Sure."

After all we had been through, we were like two strangers . . . casual acquaintances at best.

He moved away, disappearing in the direction of the cafeteria. He hadn't checked in any luggage and was carrying two bags—a small suitcase and a canvas duffel bag. They were both on the floor and for no good reason I picked up the duffel and placed it on the empty seat next to me. As I did so, I noticed that one of the zips was partially undone. I went back to my magazine. Then I stopped. Something had caught my eye. What was it?

Moving the duffel bag had folded back the canvas, causing a side pocket to bulge open. Inside, there was a wallet, a mobile telephone, Hunter's boarding pass, a battery, and a pair of sunglasses. It was the battery that had caught my attention. The brand was Power Plus. Where had I seen the name before and why did it mean something to me? I remembered. A few months ago, when I was on Malagosto, Gordon Ross had shown us all a number of gadgets supplied by the different intelligence services around the world. One of them had been a Power

Plus battery that actually concealed a radio transmitter that agents could use to summon help.

But it was a British gadget, supplied by the British secret service. What was it doing in Hunter's bag?

I looked around me. There was no sign of Hunter. Quickly, I plucked the battery out and examined it, still hoping that it was perfectly ordinary and that I was making a mistake. I pressed the positive terminal, the little gold button on the top. Sure enough, there was a spring underneath. Pushing it down released a mechanism inside, allowing the battery to separate into two connected parts. If I gave the whole thing a half twist, I would instantly summon British Intelligence to Terminal Two of Charles de Gaulle airport.

British Intelligence . . .

Horrible thoughts were already going through my mind. At the same time, something else occurred to me. Hunter had said he was going to get a coffee. Perhaps I was reading too much into it, but he had left his wallet behind. How was he going to pay?

I got to my feet and moved away from the seats, ignoring the rows of waiting passengers, leaving the luggage behind. I felt light-headed, disconnected, as if I had been torn out of my own body. I turned a corner and saw the cafeteria. There wasn't a line at all and Hunter certainly wasn't there. He'd lied to me. Where was he? I looked around and then I saw him. He was some distance away with his back partly turned to me, but I wasn't mistaken.

It was him. He was talking on the telephone . . . an urgent, serious conversation. I might not be able to read his lips, but I could tell that he didn't want to be overheard.

I turned and went back to my seat, afraid that the luggage would be stolen if I didn't keep an eye on it—and how would I explain that? I was still holding the battery. I had almost forgotten it was in my hand. I unclicked the terminal and returned it to the duffel, then put the whole thing back on the floor. I didn't zip it up. Hunter would have spotted a detail like that. But I pressed the canvas with my foot so that the side pocket appeared closed. Then I opened my magazine.

But I didn't read it.

I knew. Without a shred of doubt. John Rider— Hunter—was a double agent, a spy sent in by MI6. Now that I thought about it, it was obvious and I should have seen it long ago. On that last night in Malagosto, when we had met in Desmond Nye's office, I had been quite certain he hadn't followed me in, and I was right. He had arrived *before* me. He had been there all along. Nye hadn't left his door open. Hunter must have unlocked it moments before I arrived. He had gone in there for exactly the same reason as me—to get access to Nye's files. But in his case, he had been searching for information about Scorpia to pass on to his bosses. No wonder he had been so keen to get me out of there. He hadn't reported me to Nye, not because he was protecting me, but because he didn't want anyone asking questions about him.

Now I understood why he hadn't killed the young policeman at Vosque's apartment. A real assassin wouldn't have thought twice about it, but a British agent couldn't possibly behave the same way. He had shot the Commander. There was no doubt about that. But Gabriel Sweetman had been a monster, a major drug trafficker, and the British and American governments would have been delighted to see him executed. What of Vosque himself? He was a senior French officer, no matter what his failings. And it suddenly occurred to me that I only had Hunter's word for it that he was dead. I hadn't actually been in the room when the shot was fired. Right now, Vosque could be anywhere. In jail, out of the country . . . but alive!

At the same time I saw, with icy clarity, that John Rider had been sent to do more than spy on Scorpia. He had also been sent to sabotage them. He had been deceiving me, almost from the very start. On the one hand he had been pretending to teach me. I couldn't deny that I had learned from him. But all the time he had been undermining my confidence. In the jungle, everything he had told me about himself was untrue. He hadn't killed a man in a pub. He hadn't been in jail. He had used the story to gain my sympathy and then he had twisted it against me, telling me that I wasn't cut out to be like him. It was John Rider who had planted the idea that I should run away.

He had done the same thing in Paris. The way he had suddenly turned on me when we were in Vosque's apartment, asking me to do something that nobody in their right mind would ever do whether they were being paid or not. He had given me that hideous little knife. And he had called Vosque by his real name. Not "the victim." Not "the Cop." He had wanted me to think about what I was doing so that I wouldn't be able to do it. And the result? All the training Scorpia had given me would have been wasted. They would have lost their newest recruit.

Of course Scorpia would have tracked me down. Of course they would have killed me. John Rider had tried to convince me otherwise, but he was probably on the telephone to them even now, warning them I was about to abscond. Why would he risk leaving me alive? Scorpia would have someone waiting for me at Berlin airport. After all, Berlin had been his idea. A taxi would pull up. I would get in. And I would never be seen again.

I was barely breathing. My hands were gripping the magazine so tightly that I was almost tearing it in half. What hurt the most, what filled me with a black, unrelenting hatred, was the knowledge that it had all been fake. It had all been lies. After everything I had been through, the loss of everyone I loved, my daily humiliation at the hands of Vladimir Sharkovsky, the poverty, the hopelessness, I thought I had finally found a friend. I had trusted John Rider and I would have done anything for him. But in a way he was worse than any of them. I was nothing to him. He had secretly been laughing at me—all the time.

I looked up. He was walking toward me.

"Everything okay?" he asked.

"Yes," I said. "You didn't get your coffee?"

"The queue was too long. Anyway, they've just called my flight."

I glanced at the television screen. That, at least, was true. The flight to Venice was blinking.

"Well, it looks as if it's good-bye, Yassen. I wish you luck . . . wherever you decide to go."

"Thank you, Hunter. I'll never forget you."

We shook hands. My face gave nothing away.

He picked up his bags and I watched him join the queue and board the flight. He didn't turn around again. As soon as he was gone, I took my own case and left the airport. I didn't fly to Berlin. Any flight with the passenger's names listed on a computer screen would be too dangerous for me. I took the train back into Paris and joined a group of students and backpackers on a Magic Bus to Hamburg. From there, I caught a train to Hanover with a connection to Moscow. It was a journey that would take me thirty-six hours, but that didn't bother me.

I knew exactly what I had to do.

# 21

# УБИЙЦА

I HAD NOT SEEN THE dacha at Serebryanyy Bor for six months. I had thought I would never see it again.

It had been strange to find myself back at Kazanskiy station in Moscow. I remembered stepping off the train in my Young Pioneers uniform. It seemed like a lifetime ago. There was no sign of Dima, Roman, or Grigory, which was probably just as well. I have no idea what I would have said to them if I had seen them. On the one hand, I would have liked them to know that I was safe and well. But perhaps it was best that we did not renew our acquaintance. My world was very different now.

It seemed to me that there were now fewer homeless children than there had been in the square outside the station. Perhaps the new government was finally getting its act together and looking after them. It is possible, I suppose, that they were all in jail. The food stalls were gone too. I thought of the raspberry ice cream I had devoured. Had it really been me that day? Or had it been Yasha Gregorovich, a boy who had disappeared and who would never be spoken about again?

I traveled on the metro to Shchukinskaya station and from there I took a trolleybus to the park. After that, I walked. It was strange that I had never actually seen the dacha from outside. I had arrived in the trunk of a car. I had left, in the darkness, in a helicopter. But I knew exactly where I was going. All the papers relating to the planning and construction of Sharkovsky's home along with the necessary licenses and permits had been lodged, as I suspected, with the Moscow Architecture and City Planning Committee. I had visited their offices in Triumfal'naya Square—curiously, they were very close to Tverskaya, where Dima had lived—very early in the morning. Breaking in had presented no problem. They were not expecting thieves.

Now I understood why Sharkovsky had chosen to live here. The landscape—flat and green with its pine forests, lakes, and beaches—was very beautiful. I saw a few riders on horseback. It was hard to believe that I had been so close to the city during my four years here but the noise of the traffic had been replaced by soft breezes and birdsong. There were no tall buildings breaking the skyline.

A narrow private road led to the dacha. I followed it for a while, then slipped behind the trees that grew on either side. It was unlikely that Sharkovsky had planted sensors underneath the concrete and there was no sign of any cameras, but I could not be sure. Eventually, the outer wall came into sight. I recognized the shape of it, the razor wire and the brickwork. They were of course much the same from whichever side they were viewed.

It was not going to be difficult to break in. Sharkovsky prided himself on his security network, but he knew nothing, while I had been trained by experts. His men went through the same procedures day in and day out. They acted mechanically, without thinking. And how many times had it been drummed into me on Malagosto? Habit is a weakness. It is what gets you killed. Certain cars and delivery trucks always arrived at the dacha at a given time. I remembered noting them down in my former life, scribbling in the back of an exercise book. Madness! It was a gift to the enemy.

The laundry van arrived shortly after five o'clock, by which time it was already dark. I knew it would come. I had lost count of the number of times I had helped to empty it, carrying fresh linens in and dirty sheets out. As the driver approached the main gate, he became aware of a branch that seemed to have fallen from a tree, blocking the way. He stopped the van, got out, and moved it. When he got back in again, he was unaware that he had an extra passenger. The back door hadn't been locked. Why should it have been? It was only carrying sheets and towels.

The van reached the barrier and stopped. Again, I knew exactly what would happen. I had seen it often enough and it imprinted in my mind. There were three guards inside the security hut. One of them was meant to be monitoring the TV cameras, but he was old and lazy and was more likely to have his head buried in a newspaper. The second man would stay on the left-hand side of the van to check the driver's ID while the third searched underneath the vehicle, using a flat mirror on wheels. I timed the moment exactly, then slipped out of the back and hid on the left-hand side, right next to the security hut, lost in the shadows. Now the first guard opened the back and checked inside. He was too late. I was gone. I heard him rummaging around inside. Eventually, he emerged.

"All right," he called out. "You can move on."

It was very kind of him to let me know when it was safe. I started forward, still shielded by the van, and climbed back inside. The driver started the van and we rolled forward, on our way to the house.

It was a simple matter to slip out again once we had stopped. I knew exactly where we would be, next to the side door that all the servants and delivery people used. I was careful not to step on the grass. I remembered where the sensors were positioned. I was also careful to avoid the security cameras as I edged forward. Even so, I was astonished to find that the door was not locked. Sharkovsky was a fool! I would have advised him to re-think all his security arrangements after a paid assassin had made it into the house—and certainly after Arkady Zelin and I had disappeared. That made three people who knew his weaknesses. But then again, he had been in the hospital for a very long time. His mind had been on other things.

I found myself inside, back in those familiar corridors. The laundry man had gone ahead and the housekeeper had gone with him. I passed the kitchen. Pavel was still there. The chef was bending over the stove, putting the finishing touches on the pie that he was planning to serve that evening. I knew I didn't have to worry about him. He was slightly deaf and absorbed in his work. However, there was something I needed. I reached out and unhooked the key to Sharkovsky's Lexus. Had I been in charge here, I would have suggested that all the keys should themselves be kept locked up somewhere more safe. But that was not my concern. It seemed only right that the car which had brought me here would also provide my means of escape. It was bulletproof. I would be able to smash through the barrier and nobody would be able to stop me.

How easy it all was. And yet I had been here all that time without seeing it. It was a disheartening thought.

I continued forward, knowing that I would have to be more careful from this point on. Things must have changed inside the house. For a start, the two bodyguards—Karl and Josef—would have been replaced, one of them buried and the other fired. Sharkovsky might have a new, more efficient team around him. But the hall was silent. Everything was as I remembered it, right down to the flower display on the central table. I tiptoed across and slipped through the door that led down to the basement. This was where I would wait until dinner had been served, in the same room where I had been shown the body of the dead food taster.

I did not climb upstairs again until eleven o'clock, by which time I imagined everyone would be in bed. I had been able to make out some of the sounds coming from above and it was clear to me that there had been no formal dinner party that night. The lights were out. There was nobody in sight. I went straight into Sharkovsky's study. I was concerned that the Dalmatian might be there but thought it would remember me and probably wouldn't bark. In fact there was no sign of it. Perhaps Sharkovsky had gotten rid of it. There was a fire burning low in the hearth and the glow guided me across the room as I approached the desk. I was looking for something and found it in the bottom drawer. Now all that remained was to climb upstairs to the bedroom at the end of the corridor where Sharkovsky slept.

But as it turned out, it was not necessary. To my surprise, the door opened and the lights in the room were turned on. It was Sharkovsky, on his own. He did not see me. I was hidden behind the desk, but I watched as he closed the door and, with difficulty, maneuvered himself into the room.

He was no longer walking. He was in a wheelchair, dressed in a silk bathrobe and pajamas. Either he was now sleeping downstairs or he had built himself an elevator. He was more gaunt than I remembered. His head was still shaved, his eyes dark and vengeful, but now they seemed to sparkle with the memory of pain. His mouth was twisted downward in a permanent grimace and his skin was gray, stretched over the bones of his face. Even the colors of his tattoo seemed to have faded. I could just make out the eagle's wings beneath his pajama top, on his chest. Every movement was difficult for him. I guessed that he had indeed broken his own neck when he had fallen. And although the bullets had not killed him, they had done catastrophic harm, leaving him a wreck.

The door was shut. We were alone. I had quickly taken out a pair of wire cutters and used them, but now I stood up, revealing myself. I was holding the gun, the revolver that he had handed to me the first time I had come to this room. In my other hand was a box of bullets.

"Yassen Gregorovich!" he exclaimed. His voice was very weak, as if something inside his throat had been severed. His face showed only surprise. Even though I was holding a gun, he did not think himself to be in any danger. "I didn't expect to see you again." He sneered at me. "Have you come back for your old job?"

"No," I said. "That's not why I'm here."

He wheeled himself forward, heading for his side of the desk. I moved away, making room for him. It was right that it should be this way . . . as it had been all those years before.

"What happened to Arkady Zelin?" he asked.

"I don't know," I replied.

"They were in it together, weren't they? He and the mechanic." I didn't say anything, so he went on. "I will find them eventually. I have people looking for them all over the world. They've been looking for you too." He was rasping and his voice was thick with hatred. He didn't need to tell me what they would have done with me if they'd found me. "Did you help them?" he asked. "Were you part of the plot?"

"No."

"But you left with them."

"I persuaded them to take me."

"So why have you come back?"

"We have unfinished business. We have to talk about Estrov."

"Estrov?" The name took him by surprise.

"I used to live there."

"But you said . . ." He thought back and somehow he remembered. "You said you came from Kirsk."

"My parents, all my friends died. You were responsible."

He smiled. It was a horrible death's-head smile with more malevolence in it than I would have thought possible. "Well, well, well," he croaked. "I have to say, I'm surprised. And you came here for revenge? That's not very civil of you, Yassen. I looked after you. I took you into my house. I fed you and gave you a job. Where's your gratitude?"

He had been fiddling around as he spoke, reaching for something underneath the desk. But I had already found what he was looking for.

"I've disconnected the alarm button," I told him. "If you're calling for help, it won't come."

For the first time, he looked uncertain. "What do you want?" he snapped.

"Not revenge," I said. "Completion. We have to finish the business that started here."

I placed the gun on the desk in front of him and spilled out some of the bullets.

"When you brought me here, you made me play a game," I said. "It was a horrible, vicious thing to do. I was fourteen years old! I cannot think of any other human being who would do that to a child. Well, now we are going to play it again—but this time according to my rules."

Sharkovsky could only watch, fascinated, as I picked up the gun, flicked open the cylinder and placed a bullet inside. I paused, then followed it with a second bullet, a third, a fourth, and a fifth. Only then did I shut it. I spun the cylinder.

Five bullets. One empty chamber.

The exact reverse of the odds that Sharkovsky had offered me.

He had worked it out for himself. "Russian roulette? You think I'm going to play?" he snarled. "I'm not going to commit suicide in front of you, Yassen Gregorovich. You can kill me if you want to, but otherwise you can go to hell."

"That's exactly where you kept me," I said. I was holding the gun, remembering the feel of it. I could even remember its taste. "I blame you for everything that has happened to me, Vladimir Sharkovsky. If it wasn't for you, I would still be in my village with my family and friends. But from the moment you came into my life, I was sent on a journey. I was given a destiny that I was unable to avoid.

"I do not want to be a killer. And this is my last chance . . . my last chance to avoid exactly that." I felt something hot trickling down the side of my face. A tear. I did not want to show weakness in front of him. I did not wipe it away. "Do you understand what I am saying to you? What you want, what Scorpia wants, what everyone wants . . . it is not what I want."

"I don't know what you're talking about," Sharkovsky said. "I'm tired and I've had enough of this. I'm going to bed."

"I didn't come here to kill you," I said. "I came here to die."

I raised the gun. Five bullets. One empty chamber.

I pressed it against my head.

Sharkovsky stared at me.

I pulled the trigger.

In its own way, the click was as loud as an explosion would have been. Against all the odds, I was still alive. And yet, I had expected it. I had been chosen. My future lay ahead of me and there was to be no escape.

"You're mad!" Sharkovsky whispered.

"I am what you made me," I said.

I swung the gun around and shot him between the eyes. The wheelchair was propelled backward, crashing into the wall. Blood splattered onto the desk. His hands jerked uselessly, then went limp.

I heard footsteps in the hallway outside and a moment

later the door crashed open. I had expected to see the
new bodyguards, but it was Ivan Sharkovsky who stood
there, wearing a dinner jacket with a black tie hanging
loose around his neck. He saw his father. Then he saw me.

"Yassen!" he exclaimed in the voice I knew so well.

I shot him three times. Once in the head, twice in the
heart.

Then I left.

# EPILOGUE

## THE KILL

KING'S CROSS, LONDON. Three o'clock in the morning.

The station was closed and silent. The streets were almost empty. A few shops were still open—a kebab restaurant and a minicab office, their plastic signs garishly bright. But there were no customers.

Inside his hotel room, Yassen Gregorovich took out the memory stick and turned off the computer. He had read enough. He was still sitting at the desk. The tray with the dirty dishes from his supper was on the carpet beside him. He looked at the blank screen, then yawned. He needed to sleep. He stripped off his clothes and left them folded on a chair. Then he showered, dried himself, and went to bed. He was asleep almost immediately. He did not dream. Since that final night in the Silver Forest, he had never dreamed.

He woke again at exactly seven o'clock. It was a Saturday and the street was quieter than it had been the day before. The sun was shining, but he could see from the flag on the building opposite that there was a certain amount of wind. He quickly scanned the sidewalks, looking for anything out of place, anyone who shouldn't be there. Everything seemed normal. He showered again, then shaved and got dressed. The computer was where he had left it on the table and he powered it up so that he could check for any new messages. He knew that the order he had received the day before would still be active. Scorpia was not in the habit of changing its mind. The screen told him that he had received a single e-mail and he opened it. As usual, it had been encrypted and sent to an account that could not be traced to him. He read it, considering its contents. He planned the day ahead.

He went downstairs and had breakfast—tea, yogurt, fresh fruit. There was a gym at the hotel, but it was too small and ill equipped to be worth using, and anyway, he wouldn't have felt safe in the confined space down in the basement. It was almost as bad as the elevator. After breakfast, he returned to his room, checking the door handle one last time, packed the few items he had brought with him, and left.

"Good-bye, Mr. Reddy. I hope you enjoyed your stay."

"Thank you."

The girl at the checkout desk was Romanian, quite attractive. Yassen had no girlfriend, of course. Any such relationship was out of the question, but for a brief moment he felt a twinge of regret. He thought of Colette, the girl who had died in Argentina. At once, he was annoyed with himself. He shouldn't have spent so much time reading the diary.

He paid the bill—using a credit card connected to the same gymnasium where he supposedly worked. He took the receipt, but later on he would burn it. A receipt was the beginning of a paper trail. It was the last thing he needed.

As he left the hotel, he noticed a man reading a newspaper. The headlines screamed out at him.

# SHOOTING AT SCIENCE MUSEUM

# PRIME MINISTER INVOLVED

# "NOBODY HURT," SAYS MI6

It was interesting that there was no mention of either Herod Sayle or Alex Rider. Nobody would want to suggest that a billionaire and major benefactor in the UK had been involved in an assassination attempt. As for Alex Rider, the secret service would have kept him well away from the press. They had recruited a fourteen-year-old schoolboy. That was one story that would never see the light of day.

Yassen passed through the revolving doors and walked around to the parking lot. He had hired a car, a Renault Clio, charging it to the same company as the hotel room. He put his things in the trunk, then drove west, all the way across London and over to a street in Chelsea, not far from the river. He parked not far away from a handsome terraced house with ivy growing up the front, a small, square garden in the front, and a wrought iron gate.

So this was where Alex Rider lived! Yassen assumed he would be somewhere inside, perhaps still asleep. There would be no school today, of course, but even if there had been, it was unlikely that Alex would have attended. Only the day before, he had hijacked a cargo plane in Cornwall and forced the pilot to fly him to London. He had parachuted into the Science Museum in Kensington and shot Herod Sayle, wounding him seconds before he could press the button that would activate the Stormbreaker computers. There had been a furor. Just as the newspapers had reported, the prime minister had been present. The police, the SAS, and MI6 had been involved. Yassen tried to imagine the scene. It must have been chaos.

He sat behind the wheel, still watching the house.

Yes. Alex Rider most certainly deserved a few extra hours in bed.

About an hour later, the front door opened and a young woman came out. She was wearing jeans and a loose-fitting jersey with red hair tumbling down to her shoulders. Yassen had never met her, but he knew who she was: Jack Starbright, Alex's housekeeper. It must have been rather odd, the two of them living together, but there was no one else. John Rider had died a long time ago. There had been an uncle, Ian Rider, who had become Alex's guardian, but he was dead too. Yassen knew because he had been personally responsible for that killing. How had he become so tangled up with this family? Would they never leave him alone?

Jack Starbright was carrying a straw bag. She was going shopping. While she was away, Yassen could slip into the house and tiptoe upstairs. If Alex Rider was in bed asleep, it would all be over very quickly. It would be easier for him that way. He simply wouldn't wake up.

But Yassen had already decided against it. There were too many uncertainties. He hadn't yet checked out the layout of the house. He didn't know if there were alarms. The housekeeper could return at any time. And then there was the e-mail that he had received. It presented him with a new priority. The Stormbreaker business wasn't quite over. Dealing with Alex Rider now might compromise what lay ahead. He reached down and turned the engine back on. It was useful to know where Alex lived, to acquaint himself with the territory. He could return another day.

He drove off.

Yassen spent the rest of the day doing very little. Is was one of the stranger aspects of his work. He'd had to learn how to fill long gaps of inactivity, effectively how to kill time. He had often found himself waiting in hotel rooms for days or even weeks. The secret was to put yourself in neutral gear, to keep yourself alert but without wasting physical or mental energy. There were meditation techniques that he had been taught when he was in Malagosto. He used them now.

Later that afternoon, he drove into the Battersea Heliport, which is situated between Battersea and Wandsworth Bridges. It is the only place in London where businessmen can arrive or leave by helicopter. The machine that he had ordered was waiting for him—a red-and-yellow Colibri

EC120B, which he liked because it was so remarkably silent. He had received his helicopter pilot's license five years ago, finally realizing a dream that he had had as a child, although he had never worked in air-sea rescue. It was just another skill that was useful to his line of work. He kept moving. He kept adapting. That was how he survived.

He had telephoned ahead. The helicopter was fueled and ready. All the necessary clearances had been arranged. Taking his case with him, Yassen climbed into the cockpit and a few minutes later he was airborne, following the River Thames east toward the City. The e-mail that he had received had specified a time and a place. He saw the place ahead of him, an office building thirty stories high with a flat roof and a radio mast. There was a cross, painted bright red, signaling where he should land.

Herod Sayle was there, waiting for him.

It was Sayle who had sent him the e-mail that morning and who had arranged all this, paying an extra one million euros into the special account that Yassen had in Geneva. The police were looking for the billionaire all over Britain. All the airports and main railway stations were being watched. There were extra policemen all around the coast. Sayle had paid Yassen to fly him out of the country. They would land outside Paris, where a private jet was waiting for him. From there he would be flown to a hideout in South America.

Hovering in the air, still some distance away, Yassen

recognized Sayle . . . even though the man was dressed almost comically in an ill-fitting cardigan and corduroy pants, very different from the suits he usually favored and presumably some sort of disguise. But the dark skin, the bald head, and the smallness of his stature were unmistakable. Sayle liked to wear a gold signet ring and there it was, flashing in the afternoon sun. He was holding a gun. And he was not alone. Yassen's eyes narrowed. There was a boy standing opposite him, close to the edge of the roof. It was Alex Rider! The gun was being aimed at Alex. Sayle was talking and it was obvious to Yassen that he was about to fire. He had somehow managed to capture the boy and had brought him here—to kill him before he left. Yassen wondered how Alex had allowed himself to fall into Sayle's hands.

He came to a decision. It wasn't easy, sliding open the cockpit door, reaching into his case, and keeping control of the Colibri, all at same time—but he managed it. He took out the gun he had brought with him. It was a Glock long-range shooting pistol, accurate at up to two hundred meters. In fact, Yassen was much nearer than that, which was just as well. This wasn't going to be easy.

It was time to make the kill.

He aimed carefully, the gun in one hand, the cyclic rod in the other. The helicopter was steady, hanging in the air. He gently squeezed the trigger and fired twice. Even before the bullets had reached their target, he knew he hadn't missed.

Herod Sayle twisted and fell. He hit the ground and lay quite still, unaware of the pool of blood spreading around him.

The boy didn't move. Yassen admired him for that. If Alex had tried to run, he would have received a bullet in the back before he had taken two paces. Much better to talk. The two of them had unfinished business.

Yassen landed the helicopter as quickly as he could, never once taking his eyes off Alex. The gun that had just killed Sayle was still resting in his lap. The landing skid touched the roof of the building and settled. Yassen switched off the engine and got out.

The two of them stood face-to-face.

It was extraordinary how similar he was to his father. Alex's hair was longer and it was lighter in color, reminding Yassen of the woman he had glimpsed with John Rider at Sacré-Coeur. He had the same brown eyes and there was something about the way he stood with exactly the same composure and self-confidence. He had just seen a man die but he wasn't afraid. It seemed remarkable— and strangely appropriate—that he was only fourteen, the same age that Yassen had been when those other helicopters had come to his village.

Alex's parents were dead, just like his. They had been killed by a bomb planted in an airplane on the orders of Scorpia. Yassen was glad that he'd had nothing to do with it. He had never told Julia Rothman what he knew about John Rider. By the time he returned to Venice, Hunter had already left, traveling with one of the other recruits. What was the point of sentencing him to death? Yassen had already decided. Whoever he might be and whatever he might have done, there could be no denying that Hunter had saved his life in the Peruvian rain forest, and that had created a debt of honor. Yassen would simply blot out the knowledge in his mind. He would pretend he hadn't seen the battery, that it had never happened. And what if Rider caused more damage to Scorpia? It didn't matter. Yassen owed no loyalty to them or to anyone else. In this new life of his, he would owe loyalty to no one.

He would still have his revenge. John Rider had betrayed him, and in return, Yassen would become the most efficient, the most cold-blooded assassin in the world. Vladimir and Ivan Sharkovsky had just been the start. Since then, there had been . . . how many of them? A hundred? Almost certainly more. And every time Yassen had walked away from another victim, he had proved that John Rider was wrong. He had become exactly what he was meant to be.

And here was John Rider's son. It was somehow inevitable that the two of them should finally meet. How much did Alex know about the past, Yassen wondered. Did he have any idea what his father had been?

"You're Yassen Gregorovich," Alex said.

Yassen nodded.

"Why did you kill him?" Alex glanced at the body of Herod Sayle.

"Those were my instructions," Yassen replied, but in fact he was lying. Scorpia had not ordered him to kill Sayle. He had made an instant decision, acting on his own initiative. He knew, however, that they would be pleased. Sayle had become an embarrassment. He had failed. It was better that he was dealt with once and for all.

"What about me?" Alex asked.

Yassen paused before replying. "I have no instructions concerning you."

It was another lie. The message on his computer could not have been clearer. But Yassen knew that he could not kill Alex Rider. The bond of honor that had once existed with the father extended to the son. Very briefly, he thought back to Paris. It was hard to explain, but there was a sort of parallel. He saw it now and it was why, at the last minute, he had diverted his aim. How he had been to John Rider when the two of them were together, in some way Alex Rider was to him now. There would be no more killing today.

"You killed Ian Rider," Alex said. "He was my uncle."

Ian Rider. John Rider's younger brother. It was true—Yassen had shot him as he tried to escape from Herod Sayle's compound in Cornwall. That was how this had all begun. It was the reason Alex Rider was here.

Yassen shrugged. "I kill a lot of people."

"One day I'll kill you."

"A lot of people have tried," Yassen said. "Believe me, it would be better if we didn't meet again. Go back to school. Go back to your life. And the next time they ask you, say no. Killing is for grown-ups and you're still a child."

It was the same advice that Alex's father had once given him. But Yassen was offering it for a very different reason.

The two of them had come from different worlds, but they had so much in common. At the same age, they had lost everything that mattered to them. They had found themselves alone. And they had both been chosen. In Alex's case it had been the British secret service, MI6 Special Operations, who had come calling. For Yassen it had been Scorpia. Had either of them ever had any choice?

It might still not be too late. Yassen thought about his life, the diary he had read the night before. If only someone could have reached out and taken hold of him . . . before he got on the train to Moscow, before he broke into the apartment near Gorky Park, before he reached Malagosto. For him, there had been nobody. But for Alex Rider, it didn't need to be the same.

He had given Alex a chance.

It was enough. There was nothing more to say. Yassen turned around and walked back to the helicopter. Alex didn't move. Yassen flicked on the engine, waited until the blades had reached full velocity, and took off a second time. At the last moment, he raised a hand in a gesture of farewell. Alex did the same.

The two of them looked at each other, both of them

trapped in different ways, on opposite sides of the glass.

Finally Yassen pulled at the controls and the helicopter lifted off the ground. He would have to report to Scorpia, explain to them why he had done what he had done. Would they kill him because of it? Yassen didn't think so. He was too valuable to them. They would already have another name in another envelope waiting for him. Someone whose turn had come to die.

He couldn't stop himself. High above the Thames with the sun setting over the water, he spun the cockpit around and glanced back one last time. But now the roof was empty apart from the body stretched out beside the red cross.

Alex Rider was gone.

NEED MORE

# ALEX RIDER?

READ A PREVIEW FROM THE BOOK

THAT STARTED IT ALL!

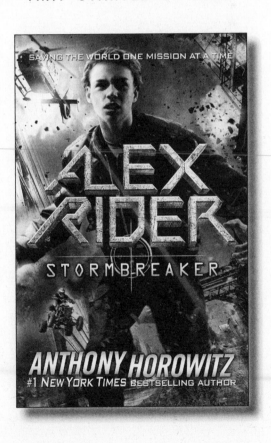

# 1
## FUNERAL VOICES

WHEN THE DOORBELL rings at three in the morning, it's never good news.

Alex Rider was woken by the first chime. His eyes flickered open, but for a moment he stayed completely still in his bed, lying on his back with his head resting on the pillow. He heard a bedroom door open and a creak of wood as somebody went downstairs. The bell rang a second time, and he looked at the alarm clock glowing beside him. There was a rattle as someone slid the security chain off the front door.

He rolled out of bed and walked over to the open window, his bare feet pressing down the carpet pile. The moonlight spilled onto his chest and shoulders. Alex was fourteen, already well built, with the body of an athlete. His hair, cut short apart from two thick strands hanging over his forehead, was fair. His eyes were brown and serious. For a moment he stood silently, half hidden in the shadow, looking out. There was a police car parked outside. From his second-floor window Alex could see the black ID number on the roof and the caps of the two men who were standing in front of the door. The porch light went on and, at the same time, the door opened.

"Mrs. Rider?"

"No. I'm the housekeeper. What is it? What's happened?"

"This is the home of Mr. Ian Rider?"

"Yes."

"I wonder if we could come in . . ."

And Alex already knew. He knew from the way the police stood there, awkward and unhappy. But he also knew from the tone of their voices. Funeral voices . . . that was how he would describe them later. The sort of voices people use when they come to tell you that someone close to you has died.

He went to his door and opened it. He could hear the two policemen talking down in the hall, but only some of the words reached him.

". . . a car accident . . . called the ambulance . . . intensive care . . . nothing anyone could do . . . so sorry."

It was only hours later, sitting in the kitchen, watching as the gray light of morning bled slowly through the West London streets, that Alex could try to make sense of what had happened. His uncle—Ian Rider—was dead. Driving home, his car had been hit by a truck at Old Street roundabout and he had been killed almost instantly. He hadn't been wearing a seat belt, the police said. Otherwise, he might have had a chance.

Alex thought of the man who had been his only relation for as long as he could remember. He had never known his own parents. They had both died in another accident, this one a plane crash, a few weeks after he had been born. He had been brought up by his father's brother (never "uncle"—Ian Rider had hated that word) and had spent fourteen years in the same terraced house in Chelsea, London, between the King's Road and the river. The two of them had always been close. Alex remembered the vacations they'd taken together, the many sports they'd played, the movies they'd seen. They hadn't just been relations, they'd been friends. It was almost impossible to imagine that he would never again see the man, hear his laughter, or twist his arm to get help with his science homework.

Alex sighed, fighting against the sense of grief that was suddenly overwhelming. But what saddened him the most was the realization—too late now—that despite everything, he had hardly known his uncle at all.

He was a banker. People said Alex looked a little like him. Ian Rider was always traveling. A quiet, private man who liked good wine, classical music, and books. Who didn't seem to have any girlfriends . . . in fact, he didn't have any friends at all. He had kept himself fit, had never smoked, and had dressed expensively. But that wasn't enough. It wasn't a picture of a life. It was only a thumbnail sketch.

"Are you all right, Alex?" A young woman had come into the room. She was in her late twenties with a sprawl of red hair and a round, boyish face. Jack Starbright was American. She had come to London as a student seven years ago, rented a room in the house—in return for light housework and babysitting duties—and had stayed on to become housekeeper and one of Alex's closest companions. Sometimes he wondered what the Jack was short for. Jackie? Jacqueline? Neither of them suited her and although he had once asked, she had never said.

Alex nodded. "What do you think will happen?" he asked.

"What do you mean?"

"To the house. To me. To you."

"I don't know." She shrugged. "I guess Ian would have made a will," she said. "He'll have left instructions."

"Maybe we should look in his office."

"Yeah. But not today, Alex. Let's take it one step at a time."

Ian's office was a room running the full length of the house, high up on the top. It was the only room that was always locked—Alex had only been in there three or four times, and never on his own. When he was younger, he had fantasized that there might be something strange up there . . . a time machine or a UFO. But it was merely an office with a desk, a couple of filing cabinets, shelves full of papers and books. Bank stuff—that's what Ian said. Even so, Alex wanted to go up there now.

"The police said he wasn't wearing his seat belt." Alex turned to look at Jack.

She nodded. "Yeah. That's what they said."

"Doesn't that seem strange to you? You know how careful he was. He always wore his seat belt. He wouldn't even drive me around the corner without making me put mine on."

Jack thought for a moment, then shrugged. "Yeah, it is strange," she said. "But that must have been the way it was. Why would the police have lied?"

TURN THE PAGE

FOR AN EXCLUSIVE BONUS

# ALEX RIDER

SHORT STORY!

# London Down

# Chapter One

## Teething Problems

ALEX RIDER HATED missing school.

One day would have been fine—a whole week, even, with a touch of flu, in bed with hot chocolate and homemade brownies and (if his strength was up to it) an hour or two on his PS4. Jack Starbright, his ever-cheerful housekeeper and closest friend, loved fussing over him. When he was small, he'd only have to cough and she'd be out with the thermometer and the hot water bottle, wrapping him up as if he were a special gift—although one for her alone.

But in the last couple of months, Alex had been away from Brookland School more than he'd been in it. It had started with the funeral of his uncle, Ian Rider, who had been killed, supposedly, in a car accident in Cornwall. Alex had found out soon enough that the accident, like almost everything else in his uncle's life, had been a lie. Ian Rider was a spy, an undercover agent working for the Special Operations division of MI6. That was the incredible truth. And once that secret door had opened and Alex had stepped through it, there had been no going back. MI6—the British secret service—had discovered that they had a use for him. And as they had quickly made clear, they were going to do everything they could to hang on to him.

Alex had been sent for two weeks' training with the Special Air Service in the Brecon Beacons. It had included assault courses, unarmed combat, forced marches, and survival in the so-called Killing House, a mock-up of an embassy used to practice techniques in hostage release. Alex had found himself up to his eyes in freezing mud and water, stumbling up and down hills, being shouted at by sergeants in khaki whose entire vocabulary seemed to be made up of four-letter words, swallowing down meals out of mess tins, and desperately snatching a few minutes of sleep when the exercises finally ended in the middle of the night. It was hardly surprising that, after a few days, he found himself missing the peace and quiet of geography and double maths.

As soon as he had finished his training, he had been sent to the

Port Tallon headquarters of Sayle Enterprises, where the so-called Stormbreaker computer was being mass-produced for free distribution to every school in the UK. Herod Sayle had turned out to be a psychopath and the computers deadly, and after Alex had managed to dismantle the whole operation, he had hoped he would be left alone.

Of course, it hadn't worked like that. He had barely been back at school a week when Alan Blunt, the head of MI6 Special Operations, had come calling a second time. In part, it was Alex's own fault. He should never have taken off after a couple of drug dealers, destroying their mobile laboratory but causing about half a million dollars of damage to the neighborhood of Putney in the process. He had played the hero—and it gave Blunt the opportunity to force him into a second mission, this time providing him with the alias of Alex Friend, son of a multimillionaire supermarket owner, and sending him to the lethal Point Blanc Academy high up in the Alps. That had been Alex's introduction to psychopath number two: Dr. Hugo Grief. Alex knew that he had been lucky to escape alive.

That mission had finished three weeks ago. Finally, Alex was back at school and enjoying himself. He was catching up on the work he had missed. He had been chosen to play left wing for the school's first soccer team. He had struck up a friendship with a boy of his own age—Tom Harris—and the two of them were talking about spending the summer together in Italy. Tom's older brother had an apartment in Naples. Even the weather was improving as May slipped past and the first day of June approached.

So another day off school was an annoyance, but this time it couldn't be helped, and—for a change—there was a genuine excuse. Alex had to go to the dentist.

The note had come through in one of those envelopes that look like bad news even before you open them. It was time for his annual examination, and although he had complained and tried to put it off, Jack had insisted. It wasn't that Alex was afraid of dentists. Only a short while before, he had been tied up by Dr. Grief and threatened with live dissection as a demonstration in a biology class, so visiting the dentist came fairly low on the terror scale. But it was boring and uncomfortable. Alex didn't enjoy having latex-clad fingers and silver needles poking around in his mouth. Did anyone? He was fairly sure that his teeth were in good condition anyway. At least, the last time he looked, they were all there.

Jack had managed to get the first appointment at nine o'clock, and they set off together after breakfast, at eight. Mr. Sweetman—perhaps an unfortunate name for a dentist—had offices in Soho and they walked down the King's Road to take the tube from Sloane Square.

"Why are you in such a bad mood?" Jack asked as the carriage doors slid shut behind them.

"I'm not," Alex replied.

"It's only once a year, and if you don't look after your teeth now, you'll regret it when you're older."

"Now you sound like my nanny!"

"I am your nanny. Sort of . . ."

"Well, you certainly didn't need to come with me. I could find my way there on my own."

"Of course I had to come with you, Alex. And if you don't stop complaining, I'm going to insist on holding your hand when we get to the office."

Alex spent the rest of the journey in grumpy silence. He had decided that Jack was as bad in her own way as the hideous Nadia Vole (last seen being stung to death beneath a giant jellyfish), while in his view Mr. Sweetman had all the charm and attractiveness of the hired killer Yassen Gregorovich. Meanwhile, Jack was refusing to sympathize. She had buried herself in the morning paper, and glancing in her direction, Alex was confronted by the headline sprawled over the front page: MR. MILLIONS GOES ON TRIAL.

Frank Curtis. They called him Mr. Millions because he'd been the chairman of one of the country's leading banks, and every day, they'd missed a million. In total, more than a hundred million dollars had disappeared. Even Alex had been unable to avoid the story on TV and in the news. Curtis had finally been caught with his fingers in the till . . . all eleven of them. He had been born with an extra finger on his left hand, and of course the newspapers had gone to town with that. Somehow it seemed so appropriate. The banker had been quietly stealing money from his clients—channeling it into private accounts in Switzerland, Monaco, and the Cayman Islands. The plan had only gone wrong at the last minute when he had been arrested at

Heathrow Airport, on his way out of the country. The money was still missing and Curtis had refused to say where it could be found. His trial—with maximum security—was about to start at the Old Bailey in London.

The small, round face of the banker, complete with glasses and a mustache, stared at Alex from the front page. *You're off to the dentist,* he seemed to be saying. *Sooner you than me.* Alex turned away, plugged himself into his iPlayer, and spent the rest of the journey listening to Eminem.

They reached Oxford Circus in good time and climbed the escalator back into the daylight. It was ten to nine, and the intersection where Regent Street met Oxford Street was packed with commuters. The dentist was about a five-minute walk away.

"Free cake! Try a Cadbury's Caramel Sponge! They're free today. Try one now . . . !"

There were young men and women covering all the station entrances with trays around their necks and little cubes of cake in silver wrapping piled up in front of them. There was nothing new about this, and Alex guessed that there would be similar distributors all over London. It often happened when there was a new product. The big companies gave away free samples at all the main stations. Almost without thinking, he reached out and took one.

"Forget it, Alex," Jack protested. "You can't eat chocolate cake five minutes before you go into the dentist."

Alex's heart sank. When he had been training with the SAS, he had been treated almost as an equal. Certainly, nobody had made allowances for his age. But here he was in the middle of London with Jack and she was talking to him as if he was . . . well, fourteen. And just because he was fourteen, that didn't make any difference. "I'm only taking it for later," he said.

"You may not be able to eat it after you've been drilled!"

"I bet you a fiver I don't need a filling."

"I'll bet you the cake." She took it from him and examined the packaging. "Delicious milk chocolate, caramel, and sponge cake . . ." She stopped. "That's funny."

"What?"

"Cadbury's."

"What about it?"

"Well, it's ridiculous, and I don't suppose anyone else would have noticed. But . . ."

"Go on, Jack."

"It's just that they've written the word *Cadbury's* on the packaging. It ought to read *Cadbury* without the *s*! It's odd . . . that's all."

"New product, new typing error," Alex suggested.

"I suppose so." Jack looked at her watch. "Come on. We won't want to be late."

They crossed the road and were about to turn off toward Cadogan Square when Alex noticed a white van pull in and park on a yellow line. The driver got out and went around to open the back door.

And Alex recognized him.

In his twenties but already beginning to lose his hair. An upturned nose and a weak chin. The face of a man who has spent his whole life going nowhere and somehow knows it. Alex was jolted. It was quite extraordinary that the man should be here, in the middle of London, but he knew he wasn't mistaken. It's never hard to remember someone who has threatened to kill you.

And that was just what this man had done—in the secret research center underneath Sayle Enterprises. He had been a guard, employed by Herod Sayle, and he had surprised Alex just as he came out of the disused mine.

*"If you make any sudden moves, I'll shoot you in the head."*

Alex remembered his voice, the surly arrogance of almost any man with a gun in his hands. But the guard had been less than efficient. He hadn't believed that any danger could come from a fourteen-year-old boy, and he had looked away long enough to allow Alex to take him out with a well-placed karate move, an *empi*, or elbow strike, below the ear.

Alex watched as the man took out a large cardboard box and walked to the area where the sidewalk widened in front of the NikeTown store, which was where the cake distributors were hard at work. They seemed to know him, took the box, and began to unload more of the silver cubes. So that was the setup. A hired killer from Sayle Enterprises had now become a cake delivery man in the center of London. Was that completely impossible? But there was something else. These cakes were supposed to be made by Cadbury, but someone had made an elementary mistake with the packaging.

Perhaps it was something he had inherited from Ian Rider. Or maybe it had been knocked into him when he was with the SAS, moving through the dark and silent passageways of the Killing House. But Alex had learned to trust his instincts. And right now there was a warning bell jangling madly in his head. It might well be that he was about to make a complete fool of himself. But that didn't matter. He knew he had to act.

"Jack," he said, "I want you to contact Alan Blunt."

"I don't have his telephone number, Alex."

"It doesn't matter. Find him somehow. Or call the police. But I think there's something going on."

"What are you talking about?"

"The cakes!"

The man with the cardboard box was still waiting for the distributor to finish emptying it. Alex ran across the road, weaving between the traffic. There was the screech of a horn and a dispatch rider on a black BMW swerved around him, the driver swearing beneath his helmet. Alex reached the white van. He looked inside. It was empty. This must be the last delivery. But there were a few blankets bundled up on the floor. That would do. He took one quick glance around, then climbed in and pulled some of the blankets over himself.

For Jack, it had all happened too quickly. She had heard what Alex said and had watched him hurl himself across Upper Regent Street, almost getting mown down by a motorbike. She had seen him climb into the back of the van and stood there staring as the driver returned and casually swung the door shut without even looking inside. The man climbed into the front, and a moment later the van drove off.

Jack was left there, still holding the cake, and with Alex's last words ringing in her ears.

*"Contact Alan Blunt . . . Or call the police."*

The van reached a green traffic light and went through. Suddenly Alex was gone. Jack shook her head, dazed. It was certainly quite a performance to avoid visiting the dentist!

# Chapter Two
## The Meat Market

A WOODEN PANEL divided the back of the white van from the driver's seat, but fortunately there was a knot in it, which provided Alex with an eyehole he could use to see out the front window. He had to be careful not to shift his weight while the van was standing still. Any movement would have told the driver that he was carrying an uninvited passenger. And it felt strange to be only inches away from a man who had once tried to take him prisoner, separated only by a thin sheet of wood. For a brief moment, Alex doubted the wisdom of what he was doing. The man had once worked for Herod Sayle. But Sayle was dead. Wasn't it reasonable enough that he would have gotten himself another job? And if he couldn't find another madman trying to destroy England, why not a confectionary company that needed chocolate cakes to be delivered for an advertising campaign? But there was still the spelling mistake on the packaging. If Alex was wrong, the worst that could happen was that he'd make a complete fool of himself. He might as well see this through to the end.

They drove through London, heading east. Alex had limited vision, but he was able to make out the Dominion Theatre on the corner of Tottenham Court Road and, a few minutes later, Holborn Station. As they lingered at the traffic lights, he noticed more young distributors with their trays, giving out free samples of cake. The commuters were snatching them up, but then, he thought, chocolate is one of the few things that unites adults and kids. It's a taste that stays with you all your life.

They continued past the huge building site that Farringdon had become with the construction of the new railway link and turned onto a narrower street. Ahead of him, Alex saw what looked like a solid pavilion, an elegant construction of stone, brick, and iron decorated with sculpted dragons and knights. A raised archway opened onto a cobbled street that allowed vehicles to drive through the middle. It was like a throwback to another century, and Alex recognized it at once. He had walked here with Jack only a few Sundays before . . .

she'd taken to doing London walks on the weekend and had dragged him along too.

It was the meat market at Smithfield. He remembered her saying that there had been a market here for over eight hundred years. It was one of the oldest in London, and unlike Billingsgate (fish) or Covent Garden (vegetables), it had refused to move out. At two in the morning, huge trucks would park and hundreds of carcasses, dangling on hooks, would trundle slowly forward, whole sheep and pigs making their final, undignified journey to the restaurants and supermarkets that had bought them.

Still gazing through the eyehole, Alex saw a couple of workers crossing the road, wearing bloodstained white overalls. A huge truck—PETE'S MEAT—pulled away. Several sections of the market had been closed. These were the more modern storage facilities, built after the war—soon to be demolished—and they stopped in front of one of them with a green sliding door blocking their way. Almost at once it opened, activated from inside. The white van drove forward and stopped. Alex heard the click of an electric motor and the door slid shut behind him. The van's engine was turned off. The driver opened the door and got out. Alex was left alone.

He was lucky. The back of the van could be opened from the inside, and the driver hadn't locked it. Alex waited for a minute, listening for any sound. He could see only a brick wall through the eyehole, but he was fairly sure he was alone. Gently, he eased down the handle to open the door and slipped out, staying close to the back of the vehicle. Nobody saw him. He took a quick look around.

He was in a large, rectangular area—it reminded him an aircraft hangar with a high ceiling and a concrete floor. It was lit by industrial-sized neon bulbs hanging on silver chains. The white van was parked next to another vehicle, a London ambulance. What was that doing here? At the far end, he could make out a glass-fronted office with four men sitting on plastic chairs, grouped around a desk, watching a television set. One of them was the Sayle guard who had brought him here. Two of them were smoking cigarettes. They were talking among themselves.

Alex looked back. There was an open door set in the wall, partly concealed by the ambulance. A large area, about a quarter of the available space, had been separated off by a cinder block wall. There was a light on inside.

Alex decided to start with the men. Their eyes were fixed on the TV, so they didn't notice as he sneaked down the side of the building, keeping low, staying in the shadows. It was obvious that this building had once been part of the market. There were still rusty meat hooks dangling from the ceiling, and although it was now disused, the smell of so much blood and death had never quite left it. It was very run-down. There were pools of dirty water on the floor and many of the glass windows had been smashed. The office itself was cold, even on this warm spring day. There was an electric heater glowing on the floor. The men had been drinking coffee out of plastic cups.

He already knew the driver. The other three men were all in their thirties. The black man seemed to be in charge. He was huge, with wrestler's arms and shoulders, thick lips, and very white, broken teeth. The top of his head was completely bald and polished, but he had a pigtail that sprouted out of the back and fell all the way to his shoulders. One of the men had untidy gray hair and glasses that had broken in half and then been taped back together again. They dangled awkwardly off his face. The other was Asian, heavily pock-marked, with creases running down the side of his face and a tattoo of a snake on the side of his neck. All three of them were dressed as paramedics, which tied in with the ambulance Alex had seen. The fourth was already pulling off his jacket and pants, getting changed.

The man with the tattoo was speaking as Alex arrived and peered around the corner, through the glass. "How long will it take?"

"That depends how long our customers can resist their free cara-mel cakes," the gray-haired man answered. "But if we leave in an hour, it should have started by then."

"Relax, Raymond." Pigtail exhaled a lengthy jet of smoke. "We'll see it on TV."

"Will people die?"

"Johann?" Pigtail didn't seem to care.

The gray-haired man—Johann—shook his head. Alex thought he might have been a medical student or a scientist. Certainly he seemed to know what he was talking about. "Bufotenine is a hallucinogen rather than a poison. I've already told you. It's actually extracted from frogs or toads . . . in Peru."

"Croak! Croak!" Pigtail muttered, then laughed.

"People will get sick very suddenly. They might think they're having a heart attack. There'll be a lot of panic. But the symptoms will disappear as quickly as they came. No one's going to die."

"Panic is what we want," Pigtail said. "An hour from now, London will be ours. Now be quiet! I'm watching the news."

The television was tuned to Sky Channel and there was a report about the banker, Frank Curtis. Alex saw a security van driving into the Old Bailey in London with the usual scrum of journalists and photographers firing off their cameras into the blacked-out windows.

"Mr. Millions!" the driver who had brought him here muttered. He was pulling on a new pair of pants. Like the others, he was now disguised as a paramedic.

It was time for Alex to make his move. If they were going to wait here for an hour, that was plenty of time for the police to find them. Alex was annoyed that he didn't have his phone with him. Cell phones weren't allowed at Brookland School, so, as usual, he'd left it beside his bed. He dipped away from the office, heading for the main door. But almost at once he saw he had a problem. The door opened and closed electronically. How could he leave the storage facility without alerting Pigtail and the others? They would hear the noise and come after him at once. It was true that he had a head start on them, but the roads were wide and empty around the meat market. He didn't like the idea of giving them the chance.

There was still the door leading into the cinder block room. Alex decided he might as well have a quick look inside. It was always possible that he might find another way out. Glancing back at the office and at the men still gathered around the TV, he made his way behind the white van and the waiting ambulance and crept inside. He saw at once that the room had no windows and no second door. There was no other way out.

The room had been turned into a miniature factory. It occurred to Alex that the four men must have spent a great deal of money on this entire operation—and he still had no idea exactly what they were planning or why they had gone to so much trouble. There was machinery everywhere, a production line, even a commercial coffee machine complete with water reservoir and plastic cup dispenser so that they could stop for a drink while they worked.

This was where the cakes had been manufactured. There were two huge ovens that would have baked several hundred of them at a time, and the floor, as well as many of the surfaces, had a thin coating of flour. A wrapping machine stood at one end. Alex saw a sheath of silver paper printed with the fake CADBURY'S legend, including the spelling mistake that Jack had noticed. There were cake crumbs everywhere, and the smell of sugar and cocoa still hung heavy in the air.

A whole section of the room was spotless. Alex walked past the coffee machine and into an area that he could only think of as a laboratory. Here, there was a gleaming sink, a sanitized work surface, and an array of glass flasks and test tubes. He noticed two large plastic containers filled with a colorless liquid. Each one carried a little sticker. It showed a crouching frog.

Bufotenine. A poison—or a hallucinogen—that made you think you were having a heart attack. Pigtail and his three friends were setting out to poison half of London with food samples that they had given out at tube stations. That much was obvious. But he still didn't know why.

That wasn't Alex's biggest problem right now. He had to find a way out of the building, and this miniature factory wasn't going to provide one. He moved back toward the door, but even as he approached it, a man suddenly appeared in front of him, carrying a tray. At first, Alex didn't recognize him. The man was dressed as a paramedic, complete with cap. He was wearing tinted glasses, and what little of his face was showing was partly hidden by a mustache. It took Alex a second or two to realize that this was actually the driver who had brought him here. He had changed his clothes—and he had also disguised himself. That made sense. Wherever he was going, whatever he was planning, he wouldn't want to be identified once it was over.

Alex was already moving. He ran forward, twisted around, and lashed out with his foot, driving the heel and the sole into the man's solar plexus. It was the fastest, easiest way to make sure that his opponent went down and stayed there, but just to be sure, Alex struck out with an elbow to the side of the head. Even as the man's eyes went white and he crumpled, it occurred to Alex that this was exactly the same move that had taken him out the last time they had met at Sayle Enterprises. Hopefully, there wouldn't be a third time.

The tray clattered to the floor and Alex froze. Would the other men hear? Would one of them come and see what had happened? He peered out the door. They were on the other side of the hangar, still watching TV in the glass-fronted office. He glanced back at the unconscious man, annoyed with himself. One way or another, he had just given himself away. When the driver failed to return, the others would know that they'd been rumbled. They might not be able to continue with their plan, but they would all get away, and Alex was determined that wasn't going to happen. If he was right, these people had just poisoned half of London. For that alone, they needed to pay.

What to do? Alex looked around him, his eyes taking in silver foil, a coil of rope, a large cupboard, a roll of parcel tape. Everything he needed was right here. Already a plan was taking shape in his head. The driver had disguised himself. He quickly examined the unconscious man. The mustache was fake, glued into place. The glasses were deliberately shaded to hide his eyes. The cap did the rest. He was only a few inches taller than Alex and about the same build.

Yes. Why not . . . ?

Five minutes later, a figure carrying four coffees walked back across the hangar and went into the office. By now, the driver was stripped to his undershorts, tied up, and locked in the cupboard.

Alex was dressed as a paramedic. The glasses and the mustache were in place. Behind the disguise, he hoped that nobody would look at him too closely. He also hoped he was right about the coffee. The tray had been the clue. Why else would the driver have come into the production facility at that moment? Keeping his head down, and without saying anything, he placed the tray on the desk and then found himself a place at the very back of the office.

"What kept you, Colin?" Johann asked.

Alex didn't reply. At least he knew what his name was supposed to be.

Johann didn't seem to notice his silence and the other two men ignored him. They were all watching the television, and as luck would have it, the story they'd been waiting for was breaking at that very minute.

"Reports are coming in of a virus that seems to have broken out in the heart of London," the newscaster was saying. "Police say their lines have been inundated by calls from people complaining of dizziness and nausea. So far, there has been no statement from the Department of Health, but food poisoning is suspected. Doctors are saying that if you are feeling unwell, you should lie down and drink plenty of water."

"It's beginning," Raymond, the man with the tattoo, muttered. He smiled and Alex saw teeth that even Dr. Sweetman would have considered beyond hope.

"This is just the start." Johann sipped his coffee and nodded at the screen. "An hour from now, the whole city will be at a standstill."

Pigtail also drank some of his coffee, then turned to Alex. "You pillock, Colin." He scowled. "I asked you for sugar."

Alex grunted his apology but said nothing.

The four of them remained in the office, watching the news: the sickness that was spreading around London, the trial of the banker, more problems in Europe. The sickness had already become the lead story.

Pigtail crumpled his coffee cup. "Time to go," he said.

The four of them went.

# Chapter Three

## Emergency Services

THE CITY DIDN'T KNOW what had hit it.

The free cake samples had been distributed all around the West End, the City, and King's Cross, and hundreds of people hadn't even waited to get to work before they had eaten theirs. Others had sat down at their desks and enjoyed the snack with their first coffee or tea of the day. The sickness, when it came, was sudden and violent. It was like being punched in the stomach. One after another, secretaries, clerks, accountants, office managers, shop assistants, security guards, and maintenance men had found themselves doubling up in pain, then staggering to the toilet, only to find long queues stretching down the corridors.

But the onslaught wasn't confined to offices and shops. Taxi drivers, bus drivers, delivery men, and police officers had all been offered the free samples, and all too many of them had succumbed. Taken ill, they had pulled over wherever they could, and the streets were jammed with vehicles parked at odd angles, many of them with figures hunched over the steering wheels, white-faced and twisted with pain. There had been crashes. At the Aldwych, five cars had collided as the drivers lost control. A truck had jackknifed on Waterloo Bridge and broken through the barrier. It remained there, jamming the traffic, the front cabin dangling over the Thames.

Tube trains had come to a halt as the drivers crawled out onto the platform and waited for help to arrive. But many of the paramedics were themselves out of action. In the hospitals, nurses and doctors staggered into each other, helpless and frightened, aware more than anyone that what was happening was impossible, that so many of them couldn't fall ill at the same time.

The rumor spread around faster than even the news channels could pick it up. London had been the victim of a terrorist attack. Someone had fired off a dirty bomb or released a deadly virus into the water system. If anyone remembered the little cube of sponge cake that they'd eaten only an hour before, they failed to put two and two together and didn't see it as the cause. Parliament was sitting, but fifty members had reeled out of the chamber, ignoring the debate. The prime minister hadn't been affected. He, of course, seldom went out on the public street. He was already on his way back to Downing Street to call an immediate meeting of COBRA, the crisis council used by the government for emergencies just like this—if only he could find enough members to attend. Inside Downing Street, half the civil servants and the undersecretaries sat, curled up in pain, gripping their stomachs, while the other half stared at them in horror, wondering what they had and whether it was contagious.

London had come to a full stop, just as Johann had predicted. Although the traffic lights changed from red to green and back again, the traffic didn't move. Horns were blasting everywhere. The sound of sirens echoed through the air. In some of the shops, alarms had gone off as if they could somehow summon help that refused to come. People who were healthy, who were unaffected, stood on the sidewalks, gazing around them, wondering when they would be hit. The worst of it was that the enemy was invisible. People were doubling up and collapsing, but nobody understood why. Scotland Yard, MI5, MI6—even Special Operations—were crippled. How could anyone take action when so many of the computer operators had abandoned their keyboards and half the managers were barely able to speak, let alone give orders as to what to do?

Alex Rider saw some of this, sitting in the back of the ambulance as it pulled away from the meat market and made its way through the city. He could hear the din of the car horns and saw all the different vehicles scattered in front of him. Outside a Starbucks, a woman knelt beside her pram, holding on to it with one hand—perhaps to support herself, perhaps to protect her child. A chef in a white hat and apron lay sprawled outside his restaurant. A newspaper seller hung out of his kiosk, crumpled pages all around him. A policeman threw up behind a lamppost. Many of the roads were blocked. A fire engine, with its complete crew, had come to a halt at one crossroads. A bus had managed to crash into the stop sign and stood there, its hood crumpled and steaming, half on the road, half on the sidewalk.

"It's brilliant," Raymond muttered. "Look at it! London down . . ."

"Just keep driving," Pigtail replied. "We're not there yet."

Alex was shocked at the scale of the destruction. It was like some modern plague. How could these men have done such a thing? What prize could be so great as to make it all worthwhile?

At the same time, he was relieved that they hadn't asked him to take the wheel. It would have been difficult, to say the least, to explain that he couldn't actually drive, and before he had spoken half a dozen words, they would have been able to see that he wasn't Colin. Raymond was driving with Pigtail next to him. Alex and Johann were behind them, watching as the ambulance slowly made its way through London, away from the meat market.

But where were they going? Alex still had no idea what this was all about. He understood that Pigtail and the others had created the perfect conditions for a crime. London had come to a halt. The police were going to be too sick or too busy to do anything. They could choose any bank or a museum and just walk in. There were millions of dollars' worth of paintings waiting to be taken in the National Gallery. Or how about the gold reserves, if there were any, in the Bank of England? Alex knew that he was close to the area known as Hatton Garden, where thousands of diamonds were on display in the shops. Whatever the target was, it had to be close. Getting across London, even in an emergency vehicle, was going to be next to impossible. At the same time, the ambulance—and the paramedic outfits—were a perfect cover. They would be welcomed wherever they went.

Alex was right. They weren't traveling far. They passed St. Bartholomew's Hospital and Alex could only imagine the chaos inside as the working doctors tried to deal with the flood of frightened patients. Next, they turned onto Newgate Street with St. Paul's Cathedral just behind them. And it was then that Alex understood. It should have been obvious from the start.

They were approaching a handsome domed building made out of gray stone with, high up, a golden statue of a woman carrying a sword and scales.

The Central Criminal Court.

Also known as the Old Bailey.

Frank Curtis, the millionaire banker. That was what this was all about.

It was quite simple, really. Curtis had stolen a fortune and hidden it away in a series of foreign bank accounts, all of them presumably with false names and code numbers. Even after he had been arrested, he had refused to tell the authorities where they could be found. He wouldn't be able to enjoy the wealth for a very long time, of course. Once he had been found guilty, he would be sent to prison for so long that by the time he came out, he would only be able to spend the money on gold-plated walkers, soft food, and slippers.

Suppose, though, that he managed to escape! He would have millions of dollars at his disposal! Suddenly Alex saw it all. There had to be a good reason for an operation this size, knocking out an entire city. Curtis must have hired Pigtail, Raymond, Johann, and Colin to free him. With everyone fighting the mystery sickness, nobody would have a moment to think about him, and by the time they noticed he was gone, he would be out of London and on his way to the other side of the planet. Maybe he would end up in South America. Maybe it would be China or Africa. Somebody would be glad to have him, and then he would be able to access his secret accounts with a computer, and all the wealth in the world would be his.

Alex was just taking this all in when the ambulance swung around a corner and stopped outside a thick, modern wall made of reinforced concrete. Vaguely he remembered that although the bulk of the Old Bailey was about a hundred years old, parts of it had been added more recently. That was where they were now.

In the front seat, Pigtail twisted around. He had folded his pigtail under his cap, and although he hadn't bothered with a fake beard or mustache, he was wearing dark glasses like everyone else.

"All right," he said. "You all know what to do. Ten minutes maximum and we're out."

Alex stared. Pigtail had taken out a gun, black and short-barreled and somehow ugly in his hand. It was a Mauser M2, self-loading and semiautomatic. He watched as the man tucked it away in his belt. He had to stop this! If there was going to be a shoot-out inside the Old Bailey, he couldn't simply stand by and do nothing. But he himself was unarmed. Colin, the man he had knocked out, hadn't been carrying a weapon when he came to get the coffees. Presumably, his gun had been left behind in the office.

Three of them stepped out onto the sidewalk. The fourth, Raymond, stayed behind the wheel, ready to drive them away the moment they emerged. Of course, this was a high-security area. On a normal day, no vehicle—not even an ambulance—would have been permitted to park here for even a minute. But there was nothing normal about this day, and right now a working ambulance would have been the most welcome sight on earth.

Certainly the security men behind the door ushered them in fast enough. There were two of them: one elderly, perhaps a retired policeman, the other plump and round-faced. The older of the two had clearly not passed a tube station on his way to work. He was healthy.

"What's going on?" he demanded. The name TRAVIS was written on a badge on his jacket. "It's pandemonium in here. We've got juries, judges, half the legal profession dying on their feet." He gestured at the other guard. "Cyril here has been throwing up for the past hour."

"It's an epidemic," Johann explained. He was the one who looked most like a doctor. That was why he had been chosen to do the talking. "It's all over London. We still don't know the cause. We need to go in."

"Of course." Travis had been trained never to allow anyone through the doors, no matter what the circumstances. Certainly he should have demanded to see the paramedics' IDs. But he had never encountered anything like this. Everyone around him seemed to be dying. Even Cyril, the man he spent hours with, chatting and doing the crossword, had been brought down. Help had arrived. Travis was in no mood to question it or hold it up.

He used his electronic key card to open a solid door with a small glass window. Ignoring the metal detectors, they all piled through, and Alex found himself following a long, brightly lit corridor with white-tiled walls and a wooden floor. They went down a flight of stairs to another locked door with a second guard outside, clutching his stomach, drool coming out of his mouth.

"I've brought help," Travis shouted. "Open the door!"

The second guard was as unquestioning as Travis had been. This door had a keypad and needed a six-figure combination before it would unlock, but the guard managed to do it, fighting his pain to reach the right numbers. Ahead of them, a second corridor stretched out, this one with cell doors placed at regular intervals. A third guard sat in a chair. He was a West Indian man with silvery hair, in his sixties. Alex saw at once that he hadn't eaten any of the free cakes either. He had been reading a newspaper as they came in, but now he folded it away.

"What's up?" he demanded. He looked past Johann and the other supposed paramedics. "What are you doing, Travis? You can't bring these people here."

"They've come to help!" Travis explained. From the tone of his voice, it couldn't have been more obvious. "Everyone's falling sick!"

"They're not authorized. You know the procedure." The guard turned to Johann. "Look, I'm afraid—"

That was as far as he got. Pigtail had taken out his Mauser, and before Alex could do anything, he swung it through the air, bringing the butt cracking down on the man's skull. At the same time, Johann produced another gun and turned it on Travis, who stared at him with terrified eyes.

"Okay, Colin. Find him . . ." Pigtail was kneeling beside the unconscious guard. He found a bunch of keys and tossed them to Alex.

Alex caught them, unsure what to do. He was horribly aware that the two men would see through his disguise if they looked at him for even a few seconds. The secret was not to hesitate, to try to keep his face turned away. Keeping his head down, he hurried forward, examining the cells. Each one had a peephole, allowing the guards to look in. The first two cells were empty. The third contained a blond-haired woman, reading a magazine. In the fourth, he found what he was looking for.

Frank Curtis was wearing an expensive charcoal suit, a white shirt, and a dark red tie. His shoes were brightly polished. He was sitting on a bunk with his hands resting on his knees. Alex saw the glint of a signet ring on his finger—one of six fingers, in fact. It was strange but absolutely true. There were five fingers next to the thumb on his left hand. The newspaper photograph that Alex had seen that morning hadn't quite done him justice. He was much smaller and neater than Alex had imagined, with a perfectly round head and a neat mustache that could almost have been drawn on with a pencil. His eyes, blinking in alarm, were a pale gray.

Alex found the right key and used it to open the door. The banker looked up curiously.

"Yes?" he asked.

Alex wasn't sure what to say—and the less said, the better. He had, after all, the voice of a fourteen-year-old boy. "Mr. Curtis?" he asked.

"That's right."

"This way . . ."

The banker got up. He pushed past Alex and emerged into the corridor, where Pigtail and Johann were waiting. It took him only a few seconds to assess the situation. One guard unconscious, the other being held at gunpoint. He nodded briefly. "You've come for me?" he asked.

"That's right," Pigtail said.

"Then we'd better go."

Pigtail dragged the unconscious man into the cell that Curtis had just left. Raymond followed, pushing Travis ahead of him. Once the two security men were inside, Alex closed the door and locked it, still doing his best to keep his face hidden beneath his cap. He was finding it hard to take all this in. A few hours ago he had been on the way to the dentist with Jack. But then a chance encounter at Oxford Circus had propelled him—for the third time—into a world that had nothing to do with him. He was in disguise. He was in the center of a massive, perfectly planned operation. How could he have let this happen to him? If he'd just kept walking, he'd have been lying on a leather chair right now with a bright light in his eyes, being told he had perfect teeth.

They made their way back through the doors and up to street level. Nobody stopped them. As they reached the entrance hall, a policeman rushed toward them, and for a brief moment Alex thought they were going to be stopped. But the policeman hadn't even seen them. He was making for a toilet. Alex heard the door slam and the sound of retching from the other side.

The ambulance was still outside in the street with its engine running. Once again, Alex climbed in the back with Johann. Curtis sat in the front between Pigtail and Raymond.

"How did it go, Sarko?" Raymond asked.

"How do you think?" Alex had finally heard the leader's name. Pigtail was Sarko. "Now let's go!"

They set off. At the same time, Raymond reached down and

turned on the siren. Although Sarko and Curtis were talking to each other, Alex couldn't hear a word they said.

The roads of London were still jammed. If anything, they had gotten even worse in the last ten or twenty minutes. Ahead of them, Holborn Viaduct was an unmoving wall of traffic. There were still sirens going off everywhere. But once again, they didn't have far to go. Raymond maneuvered the ambulance through a series of back streets, heading toward St. Paul's. At the same time, they were dipping down, and looking ahead of him, Alex saw the buildings part to reveal the wide expanse of the River Thames. They had been driving for less than five minutes, but he realized they had arrived. Across the river, the Tate Gallery, once a power station, loomed up in a clear blue sky. The Millennium Bridge, silver and slender, stretched across the water. Raymond stopped the ambulance and they all piled out, Alex feeling more exposed than ever in the bright, open air. Surely someone would see through his disguise and realize that the real Colin had been left behind.

"This way, Mr. Curtis," Sarko said.

He led the banker down to the water's edge. There was a boat moored there, a sixty-foot white motor cruiser with a single, huge living and dining area opening onto a back deck with an open cockpit and further cabins below. The boat was called *White Phantom,* and Alex saw at a glance that it was equipped with radar and radio. Every part of the plan had been thought through. The roads might be snarled up, but the river wasn't. They could take the banker through Greenwich and out to sea. Before the sun set, he would be abroad, in Holland or France. And the next day, presumably with a false passport, he would be on his way to anywhere in the world.

There was a fifth man, dressed in the white uniform and cap of a ship's captain, waiting for them. They climbed up the gangplank: Sarko and Curtis, then Alex, Raymond, and Johann. For a brief moment, Alex thought of trying to make a break for it. This was madness. Once he was on board, he would be helpless, with nowhere to run. They would be certain to discover that he wasn't Colin. They could fill him with bullets and drop him overboard. Poor Jack! What would she say when he turned up, floating facedown at Thamesmead?

But he wasn't given the chance. It was almost as if Raymond

and Johann had seen what he was thinking. As the group climbed the gangplank, they were right behind him, giving him no room to move. The captain untied the *White Phantom* and suddenly they were away, traveling down the river, being carried by the rapid tide. The captain pressed down the throttle. The sound of the engine rose. They headed east, past the Globe Theatre, passing almost immediately under Southwark Bridge.

Alex didn't like this. Sarko and the others had already taken off their caps and dark glasses, and he would be expected to do the same. He was weighing his options when he realized that, actually, he didn't have any.

"What's the matter, Colin?" Sarko was leering at him, inches away from his face. "You've been very quiet . . ."

Alex Rider waited, knowing what was coming. Sarko lashed out, the back of his hand slamming into the side of Alex's face. Alex managed to ride the blow, lessening the pain. But it was still enough to force him to his knees. He knelt there with his hands on the deck, his head spinning. Sarko took out his gun.

"You're not Colin," he snarled. "Who are you and what are you doing here? You've got three seconds before I blow out your brains."

# Chapter Four

# Down River

THE *WHITE PHANTOM* CONTINUED its journey down the Thames, its twin 1050 horsepower diesel engines carrying it effortlessly forward while the bow and stern retractable thrusters made sure that it followed a perfectly straight line. Frank Curtis was standing in front of the main cabin, watching with interest as the scene unfolded in front of him. Three men with guns. One on his knees. The London landmarks flashed past on both sides, one after another, but he didn't even glance their way. His entire attention was focused on the deck.

"Take off the cap," Sarko said. "And the glasses."

Alex hesitated, then reached up and did as he was told. He had no choice. He took off the dark glasses, then the cap. Finally he tore off the mustache. He had felt ridiculous wearing it anyway.

The three men gaped.

Johann was the first to react, adjusting his own glasses as if he couldn't believe the evidence of his eyes. He let out a brief, obvious swearword.

"He's a kid!" Raymond muttered. "He's just a boy . . ."

Sarko was equally shocked. After months of planning, the operation had been a complete success. But now, at the final moment, something inexplicable had happened. The group had been infiltrated . . . not by a policeman or an undercover agent, but by a schoolboy! "Who are you?" he demanded again.

"My name is Alex Rider," Alex said. Things were bad, and with every second they were getting worse. Southwark Bridge was already far behind him. London was slipping away. It felt as if his life was going with it.

"How did you get here? What happened to Colin? What do you think you're doing, sticking your nose in our business?" Sarko's hand tightened on the Mauser. He was aiming it directly between Alex's eyes.

Alex didn't know how to answer the questions. Where was he even supposed to begin? Looking back at the events that had taken place since he got off the train that morning, he saw that any explanation would be too complicated, too unbelievable. It was easier just to remain silent.

Slowly, Sarko came to a decision. The boy had appeared from nowhere. He had broken into the meat storage facility and had somehow gotten the better of one of his men. At the end of the day, it didn't matter where he had come from. He knew who they were and what they had done. They had to get rid of him, even if he was only a teenager. They had no other choice.

"Do it, Sarko!" Johann said. "Kill him!" He was furious. Months of planning, thousands of dollars spent. And at the end of the day, a schoolboy was making a fool of them. "We've got what we want. We've got Curtis. Just get it over with."

"Right."

Sarko took aim. There was nothing Alex could do. He was surrounded, outnumbered. But the shot never came. Sarko's arm had fallen and the gun was pointing at the deck, not at Alex. Beads of sweat had suddenly appeared on his forehead, and his eyes, wider than ever, seemed to be out of focus.

"What is it?" Raymond demanded.

Sarko jerked forward, his arms convulsing, his elbows burying themselves in his stomach. He was having difficulty breathing. "I . . ." He managed the one word, then ran to the side of the boat and threw up.

The other two men stared at him.

"What . . . ?" Johann began.

"Wait!" Raymond stared.

And then it was his turn. One moment he was standing there, utterly confident, the breeze in his hair. The next he was twisting on his feet, reaching out for support. All the color had drained out of his face. A pulse was throbbing on his forehead in time with his heart. Even the snake tattooed on his neck seemed to have come alive, writhing in pain.

The coffee.

When Alex had made coffee for the three men back at the meat market, he had come to a rapid decision. He had no gun, no gadgets, nothing he could defend himself with. Somehow he had to turn the situation to his advantage, and he had come up with the one option that was open to him. *He would attack them with their own weapon.* Even as the automatic coffee machine was filling the first of the three cups, he had been moving across to the laboratory shelves and to the plastic container marked with the crouching frog. Quickly he unscrewed it and examined the contents. The liquid inside was transparent. It had no smell. Alex had dragged the container over to the coffee machine and poured three doses of bufotenine into the hot drinks. He had no idea what sort of quantity was appropriate. He didn't particularly want to kill the men. But he wouldn't be sorry if they woke up in the critical care unit of St. Bartholemew's. After all, it was exactly what they deserved: a taste of their own medicine.

They had drunk the coffee about thirty minutes ago, before they left the meat market, and this was the result. Raymond and Sarko had been hit at almost exactly the same moment, the frog poison attacking their nervous system, their stomach, maybe even their brain. They had completely forgotten Alex. Even if they still wanted to kill him, they would be unable to shoot straight.

And Alex was already moving. He might have stolen the advantage, but he was still alone on a fast-moving boat with five men, and two of them—Curtis and the captain—hadn't drunk anything. As soon as they realized what was happening, they would be onto him, and even the reduced odds of two against one wouldn't be enough to save him.

Before Sarko could recover, he made his move, rushing across the deck and using his own momentum to cannon into the larger man, both fists acting like pistons, barreling into his chest. Sarko was taken by surprise. He cried out, fell backward, and tumbled over the side. But even as he went, he managed to fire a single shot. The .45 bullet went nowhere near Alex, disappearing over his shoulder, but right behind him, the captain cried out and slumped to the floor, blood pouring from a wound in his shoulder. At once, the *White Phantom* spun out of control, veering first one way then another, thrown about by the tide. Sarko hit the water. Then he was gone, left far behind, the great bald head bobbing up and down like an unwanted buoy.

Alex had to steady himself as the boat pitched sideways. The captain must have had his hand on the throttle when he was hit and had dragged it down as he fell. The boat was rocketing forward, doubling its speed with every second that passed. Tower Bridge with its two mighty towers and two-hundred-foot span was straight ahead. Would the boat go under it or crash into one of its massive concrete piers? Right now, that was down to luck. The *White Phantom* would make the decision for itself.

There were still three men to deal with. Alex had lost sight of the banker, but one glance told him that he didn't need to worry about Raymond. The Asian man was doubled up in pain, retching and clutching his stomach. On the other hand, it looked as if Johann hadn't drunk his coffee. The last member of the team was scrabbling for his own gun, tucked in his waistband, and as he pulled it free, Alex grabbed hold of him, his hand locking on to the man's wrist. The boat jerked to the right, and for a moment the two of them were like dance partners, twisting together as they struggled for balance. Johann was trying to bring the gun around . . . and he was succeeding. Millimeter by millimeter it was swinging toward Alex's head. Johann was taller and stronger than he was, and Alex knew that he had to play dirty if he was going to survive. He made the one play available to him, suddenly dragging the gun down, leaning forward and sinking his teeth into Johann's wrist.

Johann howled and dropped the gun. Alex tasted blood. At the same time he brought his knee up into the man's groin. The *White Phantom* was zigzagging crazily along the Thames. Surely someone would see it and realize it was out of control. The water was rushing past. Tower Bridge was looming over them. Alex had to reach the wheel before they smashed into it! And where was the banker? All these thoughts were tiny fragments spinning through his head as the boat surged on.

Raymond was straightening up. Johann was holding his injured wrist, searching for his gun. Alex threw himself forward. There was a leather seat bolted to the deck and he grabbed it with both hands, swinging his legs into the air. His two feet smashed into Johann's face, breaking his glasses and hurling him backward. Johann collapsed, unconscious.

But then Raymond was onto him, ignoring his own sickness, determined to bring this to an end. As Alex reeled back, Raymond's hands closed around his throat and suddenly the two of them were so close that Alex could smell his rancid breath. He tried to suck in air, but the man was too strong. Nothing was reaching his lungs. The world seemed to shudder and twist all around him . . . no, that was what was really happening. The *White Phantom* had gone mad. The steering wheel, with no one to hold it, was spinning so fast, it had become a blur. The bridge was looming up. Alex knew that he was about to black out. Raymond was strangling him. The brightly colored snake filled his vision. He tried to fight back, but he no longer had the strength.

There was the sound of a gunshot. Raymond's face was inches from his and he saw the look of shock and pain in his eyes. His hands loosened and he fell to his knees. Alex looked past him and saw Frank Curtis standing there, holding Johann's gun in both his hands, the second of his eleven fingers around the trigger. Smoke was rising from the nozzle. The banker looked shocked.

There was no time to talk. Alex leaped for the steering wheel and grabbed it just as the huge bulk of Tower Bridge rose up right in front of him. He wrenched the wheel down with less than a second to spare. The *White Phantom* spun sideways with water jetting out. Even so, the starboard side hit concrete, and there was the terrible sound of splintering wood as the entire length of the luxury cruiser was torn apart. Alex was sure they were going to capsize. The engines were screaming. He reached for the throttle and pulled it back, reducing their speed. And then they were out the other side, slowing down, part of the cabin crushed and the gleaming handrail a piece of twisted metal. At the same time, far behind him, Alex heard sirens. The river police had finally arrived.

Frank Curtis hadn't moved. He was staring at Alex as if he couldn't quite work out what had just happened but disapproved nonetheless. Alex was equally puzzled. The banker had just shot one of his own men and saved his life. Why?

"Are you all right?" Curtis asked.

"Yes," Alex said. "Thank you."

Curtis lowered the gun. "Well, that's that," he said. He didn't sound too happy, but then he had no reason to be. The police boats were drawing closer. In just a few minutes he would be under arrest once again.

"Why did you do it?" Alex asked.

"I'm sorry?"

"You saved me."

"That man was going to strangle you."

"Yes. But didn't you want him to? He was helping you get away."

"Is that what you think?" The banker smiled. Alex got the impression that it was something he didn't do very often. "You think these men were working for me?"

"Weren't they?"

"They kidnapped me. I had never seen them before in my life. At first I thought they were genuine paramedics. That's why I went with them. But they told me in the ambulance. They were going to force me to give them my money. They would have tortured me to find out where it was. So, actually, I was quite glad to shoot him."

Alex looked around him—at the captain, sitting by the wheel, clutching his wound. Raymond wasn't moving. He might be dead. Johann was unconscious. Two police launches had reached the boat, and he saw Sarko sitting in one of them, soaking wet and handcuffed. And finally, there was Mr. Millions in his neat suit, blinking behind his glasses, still holding the gun.

"What will you do with it?" Alex couldn't resist asking. "The money?"

"Oh—I'll hang on to it," Curtis replied. "They can't lock me up forever. And it won't be so bad, being in prison. I was at boarding school for ten years, so I know what it's like. And at least I won't be overdrawn."

The first of the policemen climbed on board, immediately followed by several others. Alex watched as the gang was arrested and Curtis was led away. One of the officers came over to him.

"You're Alex Rider?"

"Yes."

The policeman shook his head in disbelief. "We were told you might be on board. We're to escort you across London. You have an urgent meeting."

"With MI6?"

"No, sir. With the dentist."

So there was to be no escape after all. Alex climbed down into the police launch, and a moment later they were skimming across the water, heading back the way they had come.

# ACKNOWLEDGMENTS

I HAD A GREAT DEAL of help with the Russian sections of this book. Olga Smirnova reluctantly took me through some of her childhood memories and translated the chapter headings. Simon Johnson and Anne Cleminson introduced me to their friends and family, including Olga Cleminson, who cooked me a Russian lunch and helped create the village of Estrov. In Moscow, Konstantin Chernozatonsky showed me the building where Yassen might have lived and first drew my attention to the *fortochniks*. Sian Valvis took me round the city and told me of her experiences working for an oligarch. Ilia Tchelikidi also shared his school memories with me at his home in London.

A great many of the details in this book are therefore based on fact, but it's fair to say that the overall picture may not be entirely accurate. So much changed between 1995 and 2000—the approximate setting for the story— that I've been forced to use a certain amount of dramatic license.

My assistant, Olivia Zampi, organized everything right up to the photocopying and binding. I owe a very special debt of thanks to my son, Cassian, who was the first to read the manuscript and who made some enormously helpful criticisms, and to Sarah Handley at Walker Books, who suggested the title. I am as ever grateful to my generous and talented editors at Philomel Books— Michael Green and Kiffin Steurer. Finally, my wife—Jill Green—lived through the writing of this without hiring a contract killer to have me eliminated. She must have been tempted.

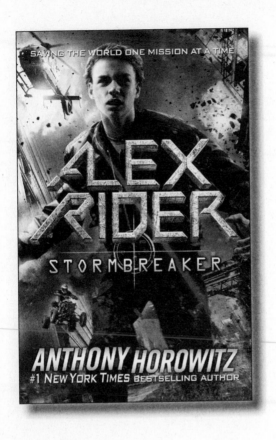

They said his uncle Ian died in a car accident. But Alex Rider knows that's a lie, and the bullet holes in the windshield prove it. Yet he never suspected the truth: his uncle was really a spy for Britain's top secret intelligence agency. And now Alex has been recruited to find his uncle's killer. . . .

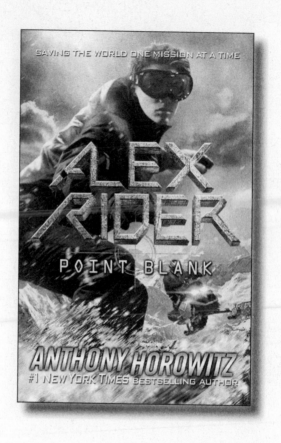

Kids are dying mysteriously at a Swiss boarding school, and Alex Rider, reluctant teen superspy, is going under-cover to find out why. But the mystery he uncovers is more nefarious than he'd ever expected, and now the clock is ticking on Alex's mission. Is his luck about to run out?

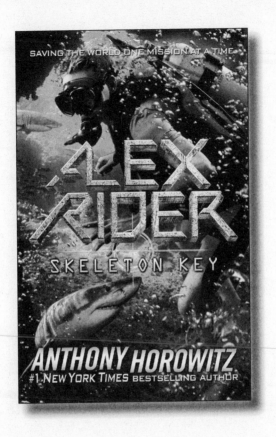

Working as a secret agent, teen superspy Alex Rider has seen it all. But Alex is about to face something more dangerous than he can imagine: a man who has lost everything he cared for, a man with a nuclear weapon who will stop at nothing to get his world back. Unless Alex can stop him first.

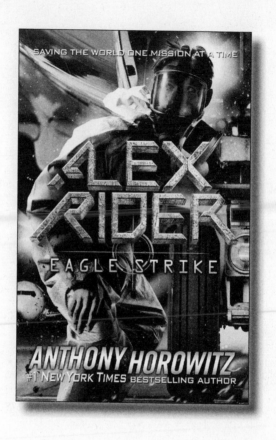

Teen superspy Alex Rider has seen his share of criminal masterminds. But none like Sir Damian Cray, the most popular man on earth, who also happens to be a madman bent on destruction. Only Alex can stop his evil plan . . . but this time, Alex Rider is on his own.

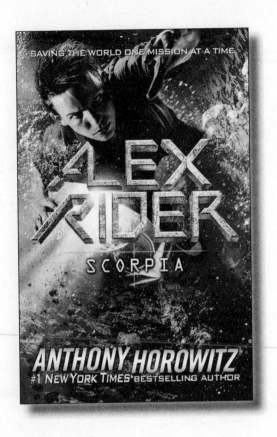

SAVING THE WORLD ONE MISSION AT A TIME

# ALEX RIDER

## SCORPIA

## ANTHONY HOROWITZ

#1 *NEW YORK TIMES* BESTSELLING AUTHOR

Teen superspy Alex Rider's world shatters when he discovers that the father he never knew may have been an assassin for Scorpia, the deadliest terrorist organization in the world. And now Scorpia wants Alex on their side, and will stop at nothing to get him.

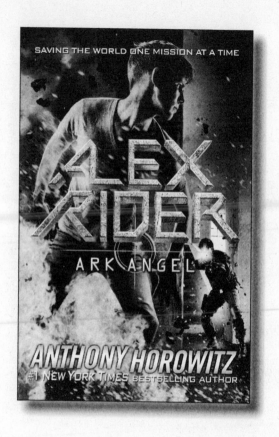

The sniper's bullet nearly killed him. But Alex Rider, teen superspy, survived—just in time to intercept a kidnapping of billionaire Nikolai Drevin's son. Drevin's been targeted by a group of deadly eco-terrorists who think nothing of killing millions to achieve their goals. Unless Alex can stop them in time . . .

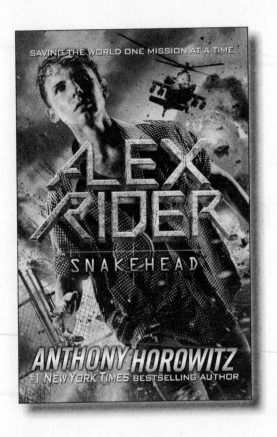

SAVING THE WORLD ONE MISSION AT A TIME

# ALEX RIDER
## SNAKEHEAD

**ANTHONY HOROWITZ**
#1 *NEW YORK TIMES* BESTSELLING AUTHOR

They murdered his parents. They shot him and left him for dead. And yet Alex Rider, teen superspy, thought he was finished with nefarious terrorist organization Scorpia. He was wrong. But even Alex can't turn down the prospect of learning more about his parents—even if it means venturing on his most dangerous mission to date.

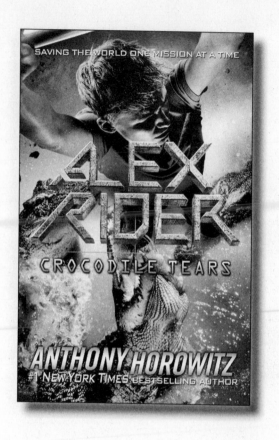

Realizing that there's big money in charity—the bigger the disaster, the bigger the money—a con artist is poised to create the biggest catastrophe known to man and release an airborne strain of virus so powerful it can destroy an entire country on a single gust of wind. The antidote? Teen superspy, Alex Rider.

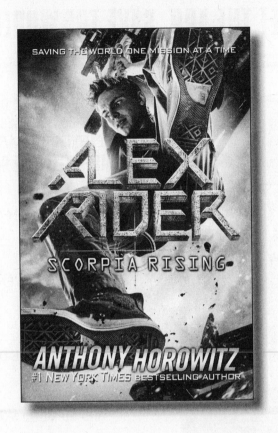

ALEX RIDER

SCORPIA RISING

ANTHONY HOROWITZ

#1 *NEW YORK TIMES* BESTSELLING AUTHOR

Scorpia has dogged Alex Rider for most of his life. They killed his parents, they did their best to con Alex into turning traitor, and they just keep coming back with more power. Now the world's most dangerous terrorist organization is playing with fire in the world's most combustible land: the Middle East. No one knows Scorpia like Alex. And no one knows how best to get to Alex like Scorpia. Until now.